Books by Daniel Landes

Hang the Innocent (2022)

Bowl Off (2023)

The Amish Cookie Bandit (2024)

Lost in Tin Cup (2025)

Lost In Tin Cup

By Daniel Landes

Elemar Publishing

ACKNOWLEDGEMENTS

To my wife, Martha Kemm Landes, for her help editing, formatting and producing this book.

PREFACE

Lost in Tin Cup is a sequel to my first novel, *Hang the Innocent*. It chronicles the life of Samuel Plummer, the older brother of Henry Plummer, the infamous sheriff of the Montana Territory, and the accused leader of a notorious gang called *The Innocents*.

After working for his father-in-law in Nevada for seven years, Samuel attempts to start a new life in Wyoming Territory with his young wife, Sandra Buckland, and his adopted son, Sam Henry. Having failed at being a farmer, he suffers a devastating loss and travels to the gold and silver region of Tin Cup, Colorado, in search of his children and a new way of life.

LOST IN TIN CUP

By Daniel Landes

"I am an old man and have known a lot of troubles, most of which never happened."
Mark Twain

CHAPTER 1

Bears, Paiutes, and Marriage

1871

ON THE PLAINS of Southern Nevada, east of the Great Basin Desert and west of Lake Tahoe, California, the noonday sun tops a grove of tall olive-tinted evergreens. The trees open to a serene meadow bordered by several rows of pungent sagebrush and sweet-smelling buffalograss. The only movement in the area is an occasional black-tailed jackrabbit or a scurry of ground squirrels making their way to a nearby stream.

The stillness ends when a 250-pound female black bear ambles out of the trees, followed closely by her three-month-old male cub. The youngster slides to a stop and playfully swats at two clouded sulfur butterflies, momentarily distracting him from his attempt to stay close to his mother, who has patches of missing fur after her recent hibernation.

The female bellows, and seconds later, a 400-pound male bear with a scarred face emerges from the same trees. He lumbers past his mate and their cub, sniffs the air, slaps his huge paw on a nearby rotting log, and snorts. Snot emerges from the boar's nostrils as he attacks the dead bark with open claws.

A colony of bees instantly vacates their hive, covering the bear's fur coat and the top of his head. Ignoring the angry swarm, he uses both paws to scoop up a piece of honeycomb, devouring most of it in a few seconds. His female companion pushes past him and gobbles down the remnants of the sweet wax.

Not wanting to be left out, the rambunctious cub scampers past his father and circles his mother. He whines as he licks the sticky nectar from his mother's paws and face.

HEADED DOWN a rutted wagon trail on a roan- colored horse, eighteen-year-old Timothy "Buckie" Buckland steers his ride away from the main road as his nephew, Sam Henry, holds tightly onto his waist.

Seated uncomfortably on a blanket behind Buckie's buckskin mare's well-worn saddle, the eight-year-old fondles two dead gray jackrabbits tethered to a rope wrapped around his waist.

The boys are wearing dirty brown felt cowboy hats with goose feathers attached to the bands, but the eight-year-old's lid is too big; the brim resting above his eyes, hiding his short-cropped dark hair and whiskey-brown eyes, which he inherited from his Paiute father, Numaga.

Buckie, whose brown hair touches his shoulders, turns to his brown-skinned nephew and announces, "Got a few more traps to check, and then we'll head home. I'm hungry enough to eat a bear. How about you?"

Sam Henry swallows hard. "I've never eaten a bear…have you?"

"Nah, I heard the meat tastes greasy…and they're ugly as sin without fur on. Saw a butchered one in the back of a wagon when some hunter stopped by our place last summer. It looked like a dead man."

Sam Henry's eyes widen as he taps his uncle on the shoulder. "I'd still like to try me some bear meat. I can spit it out if I don't like it."

Buckie smiles, and things turn silent as the steady rhythm of hoofbeats rocks him into a daydream. He never thought of Sam Henry as just his nephew. He was more like the brother he never had. If he had his way, he would be at Buckie's side twenty-four hours a day. Like a younger brother, or in this case, his nephew, Buckie, teased Sam Henry constantly and invented stories that only a boy his age would believe. Despite all the Tomfoolery, he loved his nephew for his childlike qualities and the seed of a man that was starting to reveal itself.

Sam Henry was always a curious child, full of questions. He constantly badgered Buckie, his parents, and his grandfather with never-ending questions:

'Why do people eat cows and buffalo but not horses?'

'Why do pigs wallow in the mud?'

'Why can't animals talk?'

'Why don't you have a brother or sister?'

Buckie awakens from his daydream and steers his horse into an open meadow where he knows the last of his traps are hidden along a half-mile tree line of evergreens.

Sam Henry sits ramrod straight and glares at the open field. "Buckie, this is where you saw the Paiutes and Washoe kill each other… and where you said that big black woman and you first saw my father."

His uncle explains, "She used to be a slave, but was my friend. People called her Good Time Jane. She saved my life." Buckie's eyes narrow as he continues. "Remember now, you promised me you wouldn't tell anyone. Pa doesn't even know the whole story."

Sam Henry continues. "Numaga was the only one who survived the battle… and you watched behind that tree right over there… and he scalped you."

"Scalped isn't the right word, but Numaga did cut off most of my hair. Counting coup?"

"What's counting coup?"

"Indians do that to shame their enemies… rather than kill them. Sometimes, they beat them over the head with a coup stick, but Numaga didn't have one, so he cut my hair off instead. Anyway, two weeks after the battle, your Paiute father and his bandits killed Jane, my mother, and kidnapped my sister… your mother. Enough. What else did you promise me?"

"That I'll wait for mother and father to tell me my birth story… and that I need to look surprised."

"That's right."

Sam Henry continues. "What if they never tell me the truth? What if they want me to keep believing Samuel is my real father?"

"Then you keep your mouth shut and wait. Secrets are meant to be told. He'll get around to it someday."

"I want Samuel to be my father."

"He is your father, only he didn't plant your seed. Don't forget, he was a badass Pony Express rider when our family met him. When your mother, my sister, went up to Montana to see him, she discovered he was a wanted man… who admitted to having robbed a bank and who knows what else. He even had another name… Alex Slade. Almost got himself hanged."

"Did he kill anyone?"

"You'll have to ask him that."

Sam Henry spouts. "Now, he doesn't even wear a gun."

"That's because your mother tamed him and he's a farmer now." Buckie adds, "But you inherited none of the good or the bad from him because…"

Sam Henry's voice wavers as he interrupts. "Because I'm a Paiute."

"Half of you, yes."

"Which half?"

"What do you mean… which half?"

"The good or the bad half?"

"I don't know. All I see is your Buckland side. You ask too many questions I can't answer."

Sam Henry tries again. "Is Numaga still alive?"

"Not answering that. That's something for you and your folks to talk about. Come on. It's time we check the traps."

He dismounts and helps his nephew down from the horse. After tying the reins to a tree, Buckie heads for the desert sage near the tree line. He freezes when he sees a young bear cub exit the evergreens headed his way.

Sam Henry joins Buckie just as his uncle steps back, shakes his head, and says, "Oh shit. Where's Mama?"

The sow emerges from the woods, followed closely by the boar. Sam Henry smiles and says, "It's a whole damn family."

Buckie parts his lips and takes a shallow breath. Trying to be as quiet as possible, he releases the air from his lungs, steps back, and whispers, "Don't turn around. Head slowly back to the horse."

Before either one can move, the bear stands on his hind legs and growls, echoing through the woods. Ignoring his uncle's command to back away, Sam Henry turns and runs for the horse.

The bear growls again.

Buckie freezes momentarily, steps forward, and sticks out his chest as his nephew returns with a pistol. He grabs the revolver from his hand, cocks it, and fires. The bullet hits the bear square in the chest, but the animal doesn't flinch.

He cocks the gun again, the bear charges, and his uncle fires a second time, hitting the bear in the shoulder.

The stench of gunpowder fills the air as the bear raises his paw and swats Buckie's red flannel shirt, shredding it. Before he can cock the gun a third time, the animal knocks him to the ground with both paws like a schoolyard bully.

As the beast hovers over him, ready to strike again, an arrow whizzes through the air and buries itself in the bear's back.

The animal roars and stumbles back just as a gunshot rings out, and a bullet destroys the back of the bear's skull. In slow motion, the beast growls and drops to its knees.

As Buckie struggles to get his bearings, he sits up. Before he can stand up, the animal, in one final display of anger, reaches over and slaps Buckie's arm, knocking him back to the ground.

The bear groans, teeters forward, and falls on Buckie, covering him completely.

Frightened by the earlier gunfire, the mother and cub run into the woods as two young Paiute braves emerge from the trees. The brown-skinned hunters with braided and feathered hair look the situation over.

The Paiutes grunt, join forces with the eight-year-old, and roll the bear off Buckie. As he gasps for air and groans in pain, the Paiutes look at each other and snicker.

As Sam Henry watches, the Paiutes dressed in deerskin shirts and matching britches remove their knives and begin to butcher the bear.

Not sure what to say, Sam Henry steps forward and declares, "That's our bear!" The Paiutes ignore Sam Henry and continue to skin the animal.

Buckie finally manages to sit up, holding his left side. He spits dirt and grass and gives Sam Henry a quick look. "Listen to me. Get your ass over to our horse. We're going home."

Sam Henry frowns. "What about the bear?"

"The hell with the bear. Let them have it." The younger Paiute recognizes Sam Henry's disappointment, cuts a piece of flesh from the bear, and hands the slab of meat to him.

Buckie hobbles over to the horse, clutching his side while Sam Henry trails behind with the bear meat. He manages to mount his horse, and Sam Henry crawls up behind him, clinging to the chunk of flesh like a prized possession.

Slumped over in the saddle, Buckie steers his horse with one hand and clutches the saddle horn with the other. He stares at the meadow where he first saw the Paiutes and Washoe seven years earlier, and how it was a bad luck place, a spot he never wanted to see again. He remembered his ride home with Good Time Jane Fields and how she had rescued him from Numaga, who probably would have ended his life if she hadn't come along when she did. His mind shifted to a few weeks after that, when she saved him from the family's burning cabin by covering his body with her own. Kind of like the bear had done, only to save his life, not destroy it.

Buckie reaches under his hat and scratches the back of his head. He hated the Paiutes for killing his mother, burning Good Time Jane alive, and stealing his sister. For years, he had hated Paiutes. The confusing thing was that Sam Henry was half Paiute, and the men who saved him from the bear were Paiutes.

Sitting quietly behind his uncle, Sam Henry feels no shame as he tightens his grip on the bear meat wedged against the saddle. The enormous bear had certainly frightened him, but the Indians hadn't scared him at all. All he could think about was the bear meat and how it would taste. He breaks the silence. "Buckie, were those Indians Paiutes?"

His uncle turns back and studies his nephew's face. "Yeah, they were. Hate to say it, but you look like them. Might be you're related."

Samuel Henry objects. "I don't wanna be a Paiute."

"They shared the bear with us, didn't they?"

"You shot it first. We should have gotten half."

"I'd be dead now if they hadn't shown up when they did."

"If the bear had killed you, what would have happened to me?"

"I don't know. They might have taken you with them. You'd be living in a teepee and meeting all your relatives."

Sam Henry swallows hard. "I don't want to live with any Indians. I want to live with you and Grandpa."

"What about your mother and Samuel?" Buckie offers.

"Yeah, them too."

As the boys trudge along, the light of day begins to withdraw. Buckie leans over his saddle, removes the goose feather from his hat, and tosses it on the ground. Sam Henry notices, slaps the rear of their horse, and the animal vaults forward. Buckie grabs the saddle horn, holds his side, and scolds his nephew. "What are you trying to do, kill me? A bear just fell on me."

The horse slows. "Sorry, I was wanting to get home so Mom can cook up this bear."

AS THE BOYS APPROACH Buckland Station, they spot Pete Buckland, Buck's father, and Sam Henry's grandfather. Next to him are Samuel Plummer, Sam Henry's father, and coach driver Rut "Stubborn" Long. The three men are leading fresh horses to Rut's stagecoach while four passengers watch from a safe distance.

Pete, who is starting to show his age, continues to provide fresh horses to supply and stagecoach companies, but there is talk about the railroad ending both enterprises.

Buckie, holding his ribcage, stares at the cabin in the distance and remembers. The new Buckland cabin is six years old now and was built after Paiutes killed his mother, Maria. The original home burned down with Good Time Jane and Buckie still inside. Jane had saved him by putting him in a hole in the floor and covering the opening with her body. She had saved his life by sacrificing her own.

When they arrive at Buckland Station, Buckie sees his father's corral filled with horses, a dozen chickens and geese outside the large barn, and another smaller cabin with a side garden where Samuel, Pete's daughter, Sandra, and Sam Henry live.

Five years ago, the family had started calling their son Sam Henry to avoid confusion. His namesake, Samuel's brother, Henry Plummer, who was a sheriff in Montana territory, had saved Samuel from being strung up by local vigilantes. Fortunately for Samuel, but unfortunately for his younger brother, they hanged Henry instead of him. So, as a tribute to his brother, Samuel added his Henry to his adopted son Samuel's name. The family secret of course, was that Sam Henry was his real son.

As the three men harness the animals to the coach's crossbars, Samuel Plummer looks up and spots the boys. When the forty-one-year-old sees his son and his brother-in-law Buckie leaning over the saddle, he stops what he's doing and runs over to check on them. The handsome man with long blonde hair and a two-week-old beard nods at Buckie. "You all right?"

Buckie signals with his eyes he's okay, so Samuel lifts Sam Henry off the saddle and stares at the chunk of meat in his bloody hands.

Sam Henry grins. "Bear meat."

"Throw that shit away. It looks disgusting."

"No, it's our prize meat. We shot him, but it's all we got."

Samuel turns his attention back to Buckie as his father-in-law and Stubborn shuffle over to the boys and check out what's happening. Both men are balding with grey hair and are slightly bent over. Pete gives his son a look of concern. "You all right?"

Sam Henry answers for his uncle. "The bear died and fell on him… flattened like a pancake."

Buckie, clutching his left side, elaborates. "A black bear attacked us, but two Paiutes came to our rescue."

Stubborn, his weathered face covered in dust, chuckles. "Now, that's something you don't hear every day… rescued by Paiutes."

"He was huge!" Sam Henry says. "The Paiutes claimed him, and all we got for our trouble was one hunk of meat."

Pete helps Buckie down from the horse. "Better go inside and have your sister check you out. Might have a broken rib or two."

Sam Henry pipes up again. "I thought he was a goner until the Paiutes rolled the bear off him."

Samuel pats his son on the head. "Go with Buckie and have your mother check you out, too."

"Can we keep the meat, Pa?"

"I don't know. See what she has to say about it."

Sam Henry grins. "She'll cook it up for us, I'm sure."

Pete shakes his head. The boys walk away, and Pete turns to Stubborn. "We'd best finish getting the horses changed over. Your passengers are ready to move on."

The driver frowns, embellishing his attitude by removing his hat. He rubs his hand over his bald head and face and grumbles, "They're lucky they're gettin' time for their stomachs to settle. The road up ahead ain't no picnic."

Samuel slaps the old driver on the back. "Are you ever gonna slow down? Always in a rush. I don't know why. You got nothing to do when you get where you're going anyway."

Hating being told things he already knows, Stubborn snarls, "Yeah, well, they're lucky I ain't the old me. I used ta could drive even faster. What I say is why waste the little time I got left perched behind six smelly hay burners going slow." He smirks. "Truth is, if I'd known I was gonna bust my ass all these years doin' what I've been doin', I'd have got myself a softer job. I'm all used up now. Hanging it up at the end of the month… heading out to pasture."

Pete sees a story coming, raises his shoulders, dries his mustache with his sleeve, and asks, "What? You saying you're giving up driving?"

Flanked by two horses, Stubborn spits. "Gonna miss going nowhere fast, but these bones can't take it anymore. Things that are supposed to tingle don't tingle anymore. And parts of me tingle that have never tingled before."

Pete laughs. "That's a whole lot of tingling."

"Don't matter none. They're getting ready to fire me anyway. Owners all over are shutting down the coach business. Trains are taking over. Central Pacific comes through every major town in the area once a week now… California to Kansas and back. People are getting spoiled. They don't like being jostled around and getting dirt on their clothes. Anyway, I've had the biscuit."

Samuel nods. "What ya gonna do with all your time?"

"Got me some money saved up, but I'll be spending it all at that boarding house in Carson City where I sleep. I did get myself hired part-time at the livery stable, tending horses. Be coming here to visit more than you want… that is, if you'll have me?"

Pete spits. "You're welcome anytime, and you know it. Damn, I hate change." Perspiration runs down his forehead, temporarily blinding him. "Okay, enough talk. Better finish hooking up them horses. Don't want you being' late."

Stubborn and Pete head over to the coach and start helping Samuel attach the fresh horses to harnesses and the wagon's swingle tree hooks.

THAT EVENING, Samuel, Pete, Buckie, and Sam Henry sit at a rough-cut slab table waiting for twenty-seven-year-old Sandra Plummer to join them. Sandra balances an iron skillet filled with fried chicken in one hand and a pot of boiled potatoes in the other. Sandra blows a blond strand of hair away from her face, eyes her husband, and he hops up from the table and grabs the pot out of her hand. "Sorry, dear. Let me help you with that."

Sandra lays the skillet on the table and wipes the sweat from her brow as Samuel sits at the head of the table. "Looks great, honey."

"Hold on a minute." Sandra returns to the kitchen stove, removes a slab of bear meat from a roasting pan, places it on a platter, carries it over to the table, and holds it out to her son. "You want the whole thing?"

Sam Henry smiles, and Sandra plops the huge piece of broiled bear meat on his plate. He quickly uses his knife to slide his peas to the other side of his plate. The rest of the family stares as the boy cuts off a piece, looks at it briefly, and slowly puts it in his mouth. As everyone watches, he chews heartily.

Sandra takes a seat and waits as Pete, Samuel, and Buckie begin to fill their plates. Suddenly, Sam Henry grimaces and coughs. He spits the meat out on his plate. "Bear meat tastes like shit!"

Sandra hops out of her chair, hurries over to her son, and wags her finger at him. "Young man, you apologize for using that kind of language… and for spitting food out of your mouth for everyone to see."

His mother takes his plate as Sam Henry lowers his head. The room turns silent, and he mumbles, "Sorry, everybody." Sandra hands him a clean plate as everyone at the table laughs. Sam Henry pouts for a few seconds and points. "Please pass the fried chicken."

IN A SMALL TWO-BEDROOM CABIN next door to the Buckland main cabin, Samuel and Sandra lay in a feather bed, staring at the ceiling and each other.

Their tiny bedroom is lit by a kerosene lamp, and the room has a chest of drawers, a coat rack, and a small table that Sandra's father built after the young couple moved into the place seven years earlier.

Samuel begins to laugh. Sandra tries to cover his mouth as he mumbles, "Did you see the look on his face when he put that meat in his mouth?"

"Sush, he might hear you." Sandra giggles. "He was so proud of that bear meat."

"Gurr!"

Sandra slaps Samuel on the arm. "Stop."

The couple turns silent until Samuel finally says, "Have you thought any more about us moving north? We've been living at Buckland Station for seven years. It's time to go."

"I know you're getting restless, but I'm not sure Wyoming is the place to go?"

"I told you the government is giving out free land, a hundred-sixty acres… and they're finding gold up north… Colorado, Utah, Wyoming."

Samuel knew immediately that mentioning gold to Sandra was a bad idea. Gold fever had cost his brother Henry his life and almost cost him his. Whether it was true or not, the Montana vigilantes had accused his brother of being the leader of a band of robbers called The Innocents, a gang of men who made a name for themselves robbing stagecoaches, stealing miners' gold, and murdering anyone who got in their way.

He and Henry had taken turns protecting each other from the Bannack citizens who wanted to see them both at the end of a rope. After Henry saved him from being hanged, his younger brother took his place under the hanging tree, allowing Samuel the chance to escape. Sitting on the hill looking down at the vigilantes as they lynched his brother was a sight he would never forget as long as he lived.

Sandra sits up, notices the glazed-over look in Samuel's eyes, and says, "You didn't mention anything about gold before. Hasn't gold caused enough problems in your life?"

Samuel takes a deep breath. "You're right, but gold or no gold, we need our own place. Pete has been good to us, but it's been too long, and I can't see myself tending horses the rest of my life. Sides, your father doesn't need me anymore. Stubborn says they're about to shut down all the stagecoach lines. People are all about riding trains… and they're taking over the freight business too. Pete won't miss me; he has Buckie."

Sandra lies back. "Okay, I'll go, but I want a wedding before we leave."

"A wedding? We're already married."

"I never got a wedding. Just a marriage certificate."

"How can we get married if we're already married?"

"You know what I'm talking about… a real wedding with a fancy dress, a cake, and maybe even some music."

"Where's this gonna happen?" Samuel wonders. "Do we have to go to Carson City? Find us a church and a preacher?"

"No, we'll get married right here. Father can perform the ceremony."

"He ain't no preacher."

"It doesn't matter. Like you said, we already have the license."

Samuel adds, "And then we can go to Wyoming?"

"I'll start making my dress first thing… after you ask Father for permission to marry me and after you tell him we're moving."

"Permission? What if he says no?"

THE NEXT DAY, east of the Buckland property, Samuel and Pete are repairing a wooden fence. There is a moment of silence, and Pete looks at Samuel. "You're quiet this morning. What's on your mind, son?"

"Got something to tell you."

Pete smiles. "I'm not gonna be a grandpa again, am I?"

"Nothing like that."

"What is it then?"

"Pete, you've been good to let us stay here all this time, but I'm itching to move. I want to go to Wyoming and get us a place of our own."

"Sandra got the itch, too?"

"No, but she's willing to share my dream if I wanna go."

"I was thinking this place would be yours someday."

"No, Pete. It belongs to Buckie. He knows more about this operation than I ever will."

"Well, this operation is about to change with no more stagecoaches and freight wagons coming through."

"So, what are you going to do then?"

"Guess I'll get me some cows, raise a few crops, and try not to starve to death."

"Sounds like a reasonable plan to me."

 Pete's lips tighten. "So, when are you planning on leaving?"

"Here's the thing. Sandra wants to get married first."

"Married? You're already married."

"That's what I said, but she wants a proper wedding, not just some marriage certificate."

"I guess that's all right. Does she wanna get married in a church?"

"No church. She wants it to be right here with just us. She even wants you to perform the ceremony."

"I ain't got no right to marry anybody."

"You don't need a license. We're already official. You just need you to say a few words."

Samuel laughs. "Which reminds me. She wants me to ask you for permission to marry her."

"If I say no, does that mean Sandra and Sam Henry will stay here while you go to Wyoming?"

"Please don't say no."

STANDING IN FRONT of the Buckland house, not far from the barn and the horse corral, Samuel and Sandra face Pete, dressed in a too-tight deerskin jacket with a yellow daisy pinned to the lapel. Behind the couple stand Buckie, Stubborn, and Sam Henry, dressed in their cleanest clothes and holding their hats.

Sandra is wearing a calico yellow dress with a large blue bow around her waist and is holding a bouquet of evening primroses. Samuel looks uncomfortable in his brown high-waisted trousers and a long-sleeved button-down white shirt.

Pete smiles at Sandra, and she smiles back. He looks out at the small gathering and says, "My girl here wanted a real wedding, so we're giving it to her."

Stubborn yells. "That a girl!" Buckie and Sam Henry turn and stare at him. Embarrassed, he lowers his head and mumbles, "Sorry."

Pete continues. "Like I was saying, she wanted this here wedding, so this is what I got to say. My girl picked herself a good man, who wants to move her off to Wyoming somewhere, but I ain't got much to say about it cuz it appears she's willing to go with him." Pete checks with Sandra. "You're willing to go, right?"

Sandra nods her head. "Yes, Papa."

Sam Henry's face turns red as he turns to Buckie and whispers, "Where's Wyoming?"

Buckie whispers back. "North. A few hundred miles from here."

"I'm not going."

"Sounds like you are. Shh now. We're missing the wedding." Sam Henry's eyes widen and narrow as he stares straight ahead, trying to process what his uncle just told him.

Pete continues. "I guess now is the time I ask the two of you if you want to be married to each other… even though you already are." Samuel nods approvingly, and Pete raises his chin. "So, do you, Samuel Plummer, wish to be… wish to stay married to my daughter Sandra Plummer… alias Sandra Buckland?"

Samuel smiles. "I do."

"And Sandra, do you want to be married to Samuel Plummer here, a former Pony Express rider?"

Samuel's mind flashes back eight years, remembering how he met the Buckland family. He had left Idaho territory to avoid being hanged, had ridden to Sacramento, California, and joined the Pony Express. As fate would have it, he broke his arm falling off a horse and ended up staying with the Bucklands long enough to fall in love with Sandra.

Sandra notices Samuel's glazed-over eyes and says, "Are you all right, Samuel?"

Samuel shakes his head, refocuses, and stammers, "I said I do, didn't I?"

Sandra grins. "Okay, then I do as well."

Pete looks around. "Does anyone have anything to say?"

No one says a word, so Pete shrugs and adds, "Kinda short. Anyone else wanna say something or sing?" No one responds, so Stubborn removes a harmonica from his pocket and starts playing *Jimmy Crack Corn.* Everyone claps in rhythm until he finishes playing, and then they clap softly.

Pete looks at the married couple and nods at Samuel. "Better kiss her, son. Can't end a wedding without a kiss." Samuel smiles and gives Sandra a big kiss, followed by a hug. Pete looks out at his small audience and raises his voice. "I now present to you, Mr. and Mrs. Samuel Plummer!"

Sandra turns to everyone and yells, "I baked a cake!"

INSIDE BUCKLAND CABIN, everyone is eating cake and talking, except for Sam Henry, who is in a corner on the other side of the room, opening and closing his jackknife. Sandra notices and whispers to Samuel, "You told Sam Henry we were going to Wyoming, didn't you?"

Samuel tightens his lips. "I thought you were going to tell him. I told your father."

She grabs a small plate with a large piece of cake on it and walks it over to her son. "Are you doing okay?"

"You didn't tell me we were moving to Wyoming."

"I'm sorry, I thought your father was going to tell you."

"What about Grandpa and Buckie?"

"This is their home. They are staying right here. We'll come back and visit them."

"No, we won't." Sam Henry scoffs. "Wyoming is too far away."

"Yes, we will." Sandra insists. "Buckie can come and stay with us sometime."

"Can he live with us?"

"No, he has to help Grandpa."

"I wanna live with Grandpa and Buckie."

"Not now. Maybe when you get older."

"How old?"

"Listen, I know you're gonna miss them, but we are a family, and families stay together."

Sam Henry sniffles, wiping his sleeve across his face. "Why can't Samuel go by himself?"

"No… and when did you start calling your father by his first name?"

"Today."

"Well, we're going with him, and that's all there is to it."

"I know he's not my real father."

Sandra whispers, "What did you say?"

"My father's name is Numaga."

"Who told you that?"

"I'm not going to tell you."

"It was Buckie, wasn't it?"

Sam Henry's voice wavers. "He made me promise I would wait for you to tell me."

"Samuel is the only father you have ever had. He has raised you like you're his own son. Listen to me. Don't you ever tell Samuel that he isn't your real father? You hear me?" Sam Henry doesn't respond, so his mother persists. "Did you hear what I said?"

"Yes."

"All right. Now come and join the rest of the family. This is supposed to be a happy occasion."

Sandra leads the way, and they join everyone at the table, who are laughing and still eating cake.

Sam Henry steps up to Buckie and whispers, "They're making me go to Wyoming."

"I know. Pa told me. I'm gonna miss you around here."

"I'm running away the first chance I get."

"No, you're not. You'd get lost, eaten by a bear, or killed by Indians."

"Do Indians kill other Indians?"

"Of course they do. I already told you. The Washoe tried to kill your father. If they had massacred him, you wouldn't be here right now."

"I told Mother I know Samuel isn't my real father."

"Damn it. Then she knows it was me who told?" Sam Henry's eyes reveal the truth. "Shit. Why'd you do that?"

"I don't wanna go to Wyoming."

"You're eight years old. You need to go where your folks tell you to go. Don't be so damn stubborn."

The driver hears his name and walks over to the boys. "You talking about me?"

Buckie grins. "Pa says you're moving into Sandra and Samuel's cabin when they leave."

"Yeah, he feels sorry for me. I'm here so much anyway. Figured I might as well save myself a day's ride."

"Are you gonna help out around here or just sit around and get old?"

The coach driver fakes a punch at Buckie, but the young man steps back. The old timer grins. "I ain't so old that I can't give your ass a good wuppin'."

"Come on. I'm just funnin' with you."

Stubborn curls his lip, turns to Sam Henry, and winks. "Wyoming Territory. Bet you're gonna miss this here place."

Sam Henry's face turns red. "Bet I don't."

The old timer fishes a quarter out of his pocket and lays it on the table. "Bet you this quarter you do."

Sam Henry puts his cake on the table and runs out of the cabin. Stubborn turns to Buckie. "Guess that wasn't the right thing to do."

"Yeah, not that smart."

The old timer rubs the back of his left hand with his right hand and mumbles, "Never said I was any good with kids."

SEATED IN A FREIGHT WAGON, Samuel, Sandra, and Sam Henry are packed and ready for their trip to Wyoming.

The wagon is filled with furniture, wooden boxes of clothes, and assorted bags of food and personal items. Two of Pete's strong horses are hooked to the front of the wagon, and a four-year-old sorrel colored quarter horse and a brown-skinned mule are tethered to the rear.

Pete and his son look at Sam Henry as he stares hard at them as if he is being kidnapped. Sandra notices the exchange, catches her husband's eye, and nods. "I forgot something. I'll just be a minute."

Sandra hops out of the wagon and starts for the cabin. When she nears Buckie, she says, "Come with me, little brother. You can help me find what I'm looking for."

Buckie knows something is up, but he follows his sister into the cabin anyway. Once inside, she corners her brother. "You little shit. You told Sam Henry that Samuel wasn't his real father?"

"I didn't mean to. It just kinda slipped out."

"Telling him his father was Numaga is none of your business. That's Samuel and my decision to make. Now he's a mess."

"I know. I'm sorry. Just, so you know, I didn't tell him about you being raped and or that Samuel killed Numaga."

"My God, Buckie."

"Sorry."

"You tell Samuel that Sam Henry knows he's not his rightful father, and I'll disown you as a brother."

"Sis, I won't be telling anyone anything."

"You'd better believe you won't. We're gonna be hundreds of miles from your blabbing mouth."

Buckie tries to explain. "Okay, I messed up. I can't unsay what I already said."

"All right then." She hugs her brother briefly, steps back, and grabs his shoulders. "You're my brother… my big-mouthed brother… but I still love you." She waits a moment for Buckie to respond. "Well?"

Buckie takes the hint and says, "I love you, too. Okay, what are we looking for?"

"Nothing. I found what I was looking for…. But…"

She looks around, sees an odd-shaped cowboy hat, and puts it on her head. It's too big, so she bends the front rim up and tilts it up enough so she can see.

When Buckie and Sandra exit the cabin, she gives her father one last hug. He takes her by the shoulders and looks straight into her eyes. "You come and see us now. Nothin' sadder than only talking by postage stamps. Samuel's a good man. You help him find his way."

She hugs her father again and hops into the wagon. Samuel stares at her dirty cowboy hat, and she says, "I got everything." Samuel rolls his eyes and slaps the horse with the reins. As they drive off, Buckie and Pete wave while Sam Henry lowers his head.

Samuel notices his demeanor and taps him on the shoulder. "Go give your grandfather and Buckie a proper goodbye. We're in no hurry."

Sam Henry hesitates, hops out of the wagon, scampers over to Pete and Buckie, and takes his time hugging them. Pete wipes a tear from his eye as his grandson walks back to the wagon.

When Samuel and family are almost out of sight, Pete laces his fingers behind his head, leans back, and turns to his son. "Your sister stole my favorite hat."

Five Years Later

CHAPTER 2

Birth, Death, and Caring for a Baby

TWENTY MILES SOUTHWEST of Cheyenne in Wyoming territory, a small cabin constructed from logs harvested from a nearby grove of pine trees contrasts with an otherwise flat 160-acre plot of prairie homestead land.

In the field nearby, Samuel, twenty pounds heavier, walks behind a hillside plow and an old mule as he loosens the loamy soil on a warm spring day.

He pulls up on the reins, the mule stops, and he removes his dirt-stained hat.

His long blonde hair falls to his shoulders and glistens in the sunlight as he wipes his brow and looks to his left at a corral containing two Yorkshire pigs, two buckskin horses, and one Jersey milk cow.

When he turns to his right, he sees his wife Sandra in the family garden leaning over as she finishes planting a row of Irish potatoes. He waves as he yells, "About time to eat? I need a break."

Sandra slowly straightens up, leans on her spade, and wipes her soil-covered hands on her tattered smock, revealing she's seven months pregnant. "Give me a few minutes. I'll call you when it's ready!" She looks over and admires the rows of spring vegetables: carrots, beets, peas, turnips, string beans, and kale. They are all in neat, tight rows. On the edge of the garden, she removes a bed sheet and nods at a set of tomatoes. "One more frost and it's your turn."

Samuel waves and slaps the reins to the mule. The plow moves forward, and the blade cuts deep into the barren dirt. Just as Sandra enters the sod-roofed cabin, the wind picks up, and a dust devil swirls past him, obscuring his vision.

Samuel halts the mule again, rubs his eyes, and spits dirt. As he waits for the wind to subside, he thinks about coming North and whether it was such a good idea. Sure, he was a landowner now and had built his own home, but the Wyoming winters were harsh, and for five years, he hadn't sold enough grain and corn to make ends meet.

There were times when he had been forced to leave Sandra and Sam Henry and go to Cheyenne to earn extra money at the local livery stable so they didn't starve to death. He was constantly tempted to run off to the South Pass in the Atlantic City district, where prospectors are searching for gold and silver in the hill country and creeks.

He dreamt of staking a claim, striking it rich, and bringing bags of cash home to Sandra, who would forget all the tough times they had gone through and welcome him home with open arms.

Maybe he would have been better off staying in Nevada, working with Pete and Buckie. But he was too mule-headed to mention something like that to Sandra, so he went on day after day, thinking maybe God would change his luck, especially with another mouth to feed in two months.

Despite it all, Sandra seemed happy…their son, not so much. During their first two years on the farm, Sam Henry constantly reminded his mother that she had said he could go back to Nevada to visit his grandfather and Buckie.

His complaining eased up when he found himself a few friends at his country school three miles from the cabin. Even with all the drama leading up to him becoming a teenager, Sam Henry was turning out to be a fine young man who wasn't afraid to work. He could be willful at times, but Samuel liked that.

MR. AND MRS. PLUMMER sit at a small pine-top table in their sparsely furnished home, eating a lunch of leftover rabbit, mixed vegetables from the garden, and boiled potatoes. Samuel looks at his wife and smiles. "He been kicking you today?"

Sandra gives him a defiant look. "She's… in a hurry to get out… that's for sure. I don't know if I'm gonna outlast her. Samuel, if it's a girl, I want to name her Maria, after my mother."

"I like that. What about if it's a boy?"

Sandra grins. "We'll talk about that when it happens."

"Male or female, it'll be nice having another addition to the family."

Sandra releases a short breath of air. "Our first child together."

Suddenly irritated, Samuel forks a boiled potato. "Why are you bringing that up?"

"Because…I've been thinking. Maybe we should tell Sam Henry who his real father was?"

"I'm his real father."

"Of course you are, and you've been wonderful, but some of the boys at school have been teasing him."

Samuel stiffens. "Why? He ain't dumb. His teacher says he's top-notch, the head of the class. Why are they teasing him?"

"Cuz of his skin color and his long black hair. Last week, two boys called him a half-breed. Samuel, we at least need to tell him he's half-Indian."

"School's almost over, and it's his last year."

"You know he can keep going. There's a high school in Cheyenne."

"Why? He can read, write, and do arithmetic better than both of us. He's set for life. Now he needs to help me out full-time."

"You're missing the point."

"What point? You want me to tell him some Indian forced himself on you, and I blew his brains out?"

"Samuel already knows he's half Paiute… and Numaga was his father."

"You told him?"

"No, Buckie did before we left Nevada."

"You've been holding that secret all this time?"

"I've been waiting for you to tell him. I wanted it to be your idea."

Samuel scoots back from the table. "Everyone knows what's going on except me. You sure that's my baby you got in you?"

Sandra grabs her plate and threatens to throw it at him. "Don't be an ass!"

Suddenly, she feels a sharp pain and clutches her abdomen.

"What's wrong?" Samuel hops to his feet, cradles his wife, and helps her back into her chair.

Sandra sighs, "I'm all right. It went away."

"Sorry. I didn't mean to upset you. Talking about that Indian makes me angry."

"Why?"

"Cuz it makes me remember I'm not Sam Henry's father. Then I find out he already knows."

"I'm sorry. I was wrong not to tell you. Anyway, he doesn't know you killed Numaga or that he… forced himself on me."

"Does he know that he and his renegade friends killed your mother and burned your cabin down? Maybe he thinks you fell in love with Numaga and ran off and joined the Paiutes."

"I don't know everything Sam Henry knows or what he thinks. That's why I think we need to clear the air. Are you going to talk to him, or should I?"

"Let me think on it."

"Samuel, it's been too long. He deserves to know."

"Don't push me. I'll tell him before the baby is born. And we should probably get you to town so you're near a doctor before that baby decides it's time to vacate his room."

"You mean her room. I've been counting, and she's not supposed to be here for another month."

THE LATE AFTERNOON SUN reflects off the steel blade of the plow as Samuel looks up. He sees Sam Henry approaching the cabin, clutching two books. The dark-complected thirteen-year-old with long black hair is almost as tall as Samuel, but Sam Henry has a thin frame and a gaunt face that make him look malnourished.

As he's about to enter the cabin, his father waves. Sam Henry lays his books on the steps, strolls over to Samuel, and says, "You need me to take over?"

"No… no. I'm good. How was school today?"

"All right… I guess."

"You guess? Your mom said some of the fellas have been picking on you."

"It's okay. I can take it. Only got a few more weeks left."

"Wanna tell me what they're teasing you about?

"The way I look."

"What's wrong with the way you look?"

"My hair. They think it's too long… and my skin… is too brown."

"They're just jealous." Samuel removes his hat, revealing his long blond hair. "Did you tell them that Plummer men like wearing their hair long? I can cut yours off if you want. And you can tell them your skin would be brown too if they worked outside as much as you do."

Sam Henry stares at his father momentarily, but he doesn't say anything. He grabs the mule's reins from Samuel's hands, steadies the plow, and whistles.

Samuel smiles. "Make sure your rows are straight."

THE FOLLOWING DAY, Samuel splits logs in half with a long-handled axe as Sam Henry stacks the half pieces in a neat pile. All at once, Samuel lifts his blade and holds it in mid-air. He slowly lowers it to the ground and grumbles, "Let me get this straight. You want to go where to look for gold?"

"Tin Cup. In Colorado. It's a state now, you know. Colorado, not Tin Cup."

"That's a long way from here. You're thirteen years old. What do you know about finding gold?"

"I can figure it out. I've got as much chance of finding gold as you did when you started looking for it in Montana."

"I was in my twenties, and all the gold I found belonged to someone else."

"Wait? You stole other people's gold?"

"Yes and no. That's a dark part of my life. I'll tell you about it someday… but this isn't the right time."

"I'll bet that's some story."

"Look, panning for gold isn't as easy as you might think. You can go weeks without so much as a sniff. Winter comes along, and rivers and creeks freeze up. Then you've got nothing to do but wait till spring. And if you find a little color, you gotta hope some lowlife doesn't steal all you got saved up."

"I got as much chance of being lucky as anyone else. And I'm not doing any panning. I'm gonna get me some of them sluice boxes they're using."

"You'll need a lot of savings before you can buy something like that."

"I know. I've been thinking about going to Cheyenne to find me a job."

"You have been thinking. But don't get ahead of yourself. You're only thirteen. Besides, you need to stick around awhile to help with your new brother."

Sam Henry snickers. "You mean Maria?"

The cabin door flies open, and Sandra screams, "Samuel! I need you… now!"

Samuel drops his axe and runs for the cabin with Sam Henry a few steps behind him.

Sandra stands in the doorway, holding her stomach as her husband and son look at her, waiting to be told what to do. "The baby… It's on its way."

Samuel panics, "No, you said you had a month left."

She groans. "Tell that to the baby."

He turns to Sam Henry and says, "Hitch up the wagon. We gotta get your mother to town."

Sandra moans, "I'm not gonna make it that far."

Samuel points at Sam Henry and yells, "Saddle a horse and head to the Culbertsons. Lila has had five kids. She'll know what to do."

Sam Henry runs for the barn as Samuel helps his wife inside and onto a bed. He kneels at her side. "I don't know what to do."

"I'll try to walk you through it," Sandra groans. "Go get a pan of water and some towels."

MOMENTS LATER, as Sam Henry bridles a horse, he hears his mother's screams coming from the cabin. He throws a saddle on the horse but panics when he hears her scream again, even louder. He tosses the saddle aside and jumps on the bareback of the animal.

Struggling to stay on the horse, he heads north at breakneck speed. Three miles down the road, he spots the Culbertson homestead in the distance.

A jackrabbit runs across the road and spooks his horse. It rears up and throws him to the ground. The filly snorts once and runs off into the open prairie. Shaken by the sudden fall and confused by his circumstances, Sam Henry runs for the Culbertson farmhouse.

Chickens and ducks scatter as he arrives at the Culbertsons' farmstead, dripping with sweat and covered with dirt. He hurries up the steps of the house and yells, "I need help!"

No one comes out, so he knocks hard on the door. Finally, a pig-tailed twelve-year-old girl opens the front door. She stares too long, and Sam Henry hollers, "Where's your Ma and Pa?"

The girl, holding her two young brothers away from the door, explains. "They went to Cheyenne to get supplies."

Desperate, he turns and looks back at the family barn. "You got any horses in there?"

The girl shakes her head. "They took the extra horses to town to get them shoed."

Sam Henry's face pales as he finally recognizes the girl as a classmate, Natalie Culbertson. "Listen, my mother's having a baby. Do you know how to birth one?"

She gives Sam Henry a curious look. "I'm only twelve years old."

"No, I mean help birth one."

She continues to stare, so he turns and runs for home.

As Sam Henry weaves his way down a dirt road, ashamed of his failure to find someone to help his mother, he worries about how she might be doing.

Did his father know how to deliver a baby? He was a fast runner, but what good was that if he returned home with no one to help her? Maybe he should run the twenty miles to Cheyenne for help? No, it would take him two hours to get there.

He stops, looks back, and takes a deep breath. He realizes it's too late to change directions, so he continues his journey.

When he arrives home, he staggers to the front of the house, cracks open the door, afraid of what he might see, and peeks inside.

Instantly, he hears a baby crying, and his spirit picks up. He walks inside and stands quietly until Samuel exits the bedroom, crying and cradling a newborn.

Sam Henry immediately sees the desperate look on his father's face and the blood on his hands and clothes.

"What's wrong?"

Samuel stares at Sam Henry and scowls. "Why did it take you so long?"

"The horse got spooked by a rabbit, threw me off… and the Culbertsons weren't home. I ran back here as fast as I could. Is Mother okay?"

Samuel carefully hands the baby to Samuel and plops down into a chair. "Son, your mother's dead. I couldn't stop the bleeding."

"She can't be dead. Maybe she's sleeping." Sam Henry lowers his head and begins to cry, so Samuel puts his hand on his son's shoulder. "I'm sorry. It's not your fault. It's my fault. I couldn't stop the bleeding. I don't know what we're going to do without her."

FATHER AND SON stand solemnly over a freshly dug grave, staring at a wooden cross. Sam Henry, his sister Maria cradled in his arms, watches as his father leans down and grabs a handful of dirt. A breeze picks up, and he lets the dirt filter through his fingers. He steps over to Sam Henry and uses his index finger to smudge some of the remaining residue on his day-old daughter's forehead.

TWO DAYS LATER, Lila Culbertson and her daughter Natalie, dressed in matching white sun bonnets and handmade black woolen shawls, ride up to the Plummer cabin in a buggy pulled by two workhorses. Tied to the back of the rig is Sam Henry's runaway horse.

Thirty-five-year-old Lila, her hair tied in a tight bun, grabs a wicker basket and leads the way to the front step. She hesitates when she hears a baby crying inside, steps forward, and knocks on the door with authority.

It opens wide, and Lila smiles at Samuel, who looks distraught. "I'm Lila Culbertson, and this is my oldest daughter, Natalie." They notice Sam Henry in a chair in the corner of the room, holding baby Maria, trying not to stare.

She hands Samuel her basket, and in a not-so-welcoming voice, Samuel says, "I know who you are. What can I do for you?"

Offended by the tone of his voice, Lila tightens her lips. "We brought a welcoming meal to celebrate the birth of your child… and my sons found your runaway horse. Sorry, we weren't home when your son came looking for us. Cletus and I were in town buying supplies and tending to our horses. How is your wife doing?"

Samuel grits his teeth. "She didn't make it."

Taken back, Lila's eyes dim. "Oh dear. I had no idea. When… what happened?"

"What happened was I didn't know what I was doing. When the baby finally came out, she started bleeding, and I couldn't stop it."

"Did she deliver the placenta?"

Samuel looks up. "I don't know what a placenta is."

"It develops in the uterus during pregnancy, and if it doesn't come out, a mother can hemorrhage and bleed to death."

"How is the baby?"

She's a little small, but she managed to survive."

"Then it's a girl?"

"Her name is Maria."

Lila takes a nervous breath and lifts her chin. "What are you feeding her?"

Samuel mumbles. "Cow's milk, but she can't keep it down."

Lila frowns. "That's not going to work."

"Why not?"

"She needs mother's milk. You need to find her a wet nurse."

"Where do I find one of those?"

"The truth is they are hard to find,… but maybe I can help. I took the nipple away from my youngest last week. I can start up again if you need me to."

"You'd do that?"

"Of course."

"What would your husband think about that?"

"Cletus won't care. He's too busy worrying about the farm."

"Ain't got no pay for something like that."

Lila looks over at Sam Henry. "Cletus could use your boy's help around the farm. He can live with us for a while. That would be a fair trade, I think. That way, he can keep an eye on his little sister."

"How long will she need… your milk?"

"Three months."

Samuel turns to Sam Henry. "You hear all that?" His son doesn't respond, so he continues. "We gotta do this or your sister is gonna starve to death."

Sam Henry stands up and adjusts Maria in his arms. "Whatever I need to do."

Samuel walks over, pats him on the back, and looks at his neighbor. "You got a good place where he can sleep?"

"We'll put an extra bed in our boys' room."

"And I can come and see her whenever I want?" Samuel asks.

"Of course, you can… and your son too."

"Three months, you say?"

Lila glances at him. "Three months. And don't you worry, we have plenty of clothes to fit her. Don't we, Natalie?"

Her daughter nods and shyly lowers her head.

Sam Henry heads for the door, still holding his sister carefully. Unable to contain his curiosity, Samuel asks, "Why are you in such a hurry?"

"Cuz she needs to eat," Sam Henry explains.

"All right, let me have her while you get your belongings."

Sam Henry carefully hands his sister to his father and heads to the back room.

Maria starts to cry, so Samuel begins to rock her in his arms. "I guess I ain't got the touch."

He rocks her a little harder until Sam Henry returns with a leather satchel, drops the bag on the floor, and removes Maria from his father's arms. "You're holding her too tight."

Samuel shrugs, picks up the family satchel, and opens the cabin door. He helps his son, cradling his sister into the buggy, while Lila and Natalie join them. Squeezed tight in the box of the wagon, they ride in the direction of the Culbertson farm.

Samuel begins to cry again, wipes his eyes, and walks back into his empty house.

THE AUGUST HEAT is stifling as Sam Henry scoops manure into a wheelbarrow while standing inside a pig pen with a dozen Yorkshire swine.

He opens the gate and closes it behind him as he wheels his way to the Culbertson family garden. When he arrives, he empties the contents and spreads the muck around the tall corn and sprouting potato plants.

The house door opens, and he watches as Natalie approaches him with a glass in one hand and his little sister cradled in her other arm.

After wiping his hands on his pants, Sam Henry smiles at Maria and takes the glass out of Natalie's hand. "What we got here?"

"Lemonade. I made it myself. Store-bought lemons."

He takes a big gulp and puckers his lips. "Woah!"

"Sorry, we're kind of low on sugar."

Sam Henry takes a closer look at Maria. "She doing all right?"

"Yes, she wanted to see you."

"Oh, she said that, did she?"

"No, silly. She's only six weeks old. She giggled, and I knew what she wanted."

"Won't be long, and we'll be out of your hair."

Natalie looks down at the baby. "I… we don't mind having you here… especially Maria."

"You saying you'd rather have her around and not me?"

She touches her brown hair and takes a shallow breath. "No, you're okay. I like babies, is all. I'm going to have lots of them someday."

"By yourself?"

"No, silly, I'll have a husband."

"Better get yourself one that knows how to deliver babies."

Natalie frowns. "I'll be living in a town."

"You got your life all planned out, don't you? You got a fella picked out already?"

"No. You wanna be on my list?"

"List? How old are you?"

"Twelve, but I'll be thirteen next month."

"All right, put me down as a maybe. You can scratch my name off later if I marry someone else. I'm half Indian, you know."

"I don't mind… I like your hair." Natalie smiles and starts to walk off.

"Where you going?"

"In the house to put your name on my list."

As Natalie nears the house, Sam Henry yells, "I'm not promising anything. I don't even know if I like you!"

AT THE END of three months, Samuel steers his wagon and his team of buckskin horses into the Culbertson yard. He knocks on the front door, and Sam Henry opens it. He stands frozen, looking at his father's dirty clothes and unshaven face.

Samuel steps back. "Where's your sister?"

"Inside. Mrs. Culbertson is feeding her one last time." He studies his father's face. "You've been drinking?"

"What's it to you?"

"Don't let Mrs. Culbertson smell you, or she won't let you have Maria."

Lila Culbertson appears at the door with Maria in her arms. Samuel covers his mouth and steps back.

As Samuel stands silent, she gives him a speedy explanation of things he needs to do. "She's been fed, but you'll need to feed her every three hours. And don't forget to burp her. Cow's milk should be okay now. If she won't take it, you'll have to bring her back here. Bedtime is 8 o'clock, and she sleeps through the night but wakes up early."

She reaches down and removes two bottles with nipples from a large bag. "Use these. You'll need to fill them with warm milk, not too hot. And give her porridge, soft fruit, and mashed vegetables if she'll take them. There's enough food in this bag to last a month. You may have to chew some of the food in your mouth first to make it easy to swallow. I taught your son the entire routine. Also, there are cotton diapers and some clothes in that bag. Come back when she grows out of them, and I'll give you some bigger outfits. I won't be having any more babies." She smirks. "Cletus will be pleasuring his self from now on. It's best to change her diaper right away when she's wet, or she'll develop a rash."

Sam Henry gets in the wagon. Natalie takes Maria from her mother and carries her to Sam Henry as Samuel tightens his lips and slurs his words. "Thanks for all you've done for me and my family. I owe you a lot."

She gives him a half smile. "You're welcome. Have you been drinking, Mr. Plummer?"

Samuel stares at Lila, trying to think of something else to say that won't make him sound like he can't be trusted to care for his own daughter. The truth is, he'd been drinking a lot lately. Being all alone in the cabin for three months, all he could think about was Sandra and how she had died in his arms, begging him to please stop the bleeding. It had happened so fast. One minute she was alive, and the next day he was putting her in the ground.

Lila studies Samuel's droopy eyes and asks, "Mr. Plummer, is that child going to be safe with you?"

"Oh yes, ma'am. I drank a little something before I left the cabin, cuz I was nervous about bringing her home. But I'm okay now."

"If you say so. Remember, the good book says, 'Wine is a mocker, strong drink is raging, and whosoever is deceived thereby is not wise.'"

"I'll try to remember that." Samuel tips his hat, gets in the wagon, and takes the reins from Sam Henry.

As they drive off, Samuel looks at his son and says, "You know how to burp a baby?"

CHAPTER 3

Guns, Buckland Station, and Carson City

ON A COOL FALL AFTERNOON, Tim "Buckie" Buckland, now twenty-three, aims his pistol and fires six shots at a rusty bucket fifty yards in the distance. While six small streams of water leak out of the bucket, he removes one .38 caliber bullet at a time from his gun belt and reloads his Smith and Wesson Schofield revolver.

Limping from a nearby field of corn ready to be harvested, Rut "Stubborn" Long balances himself on a hickory walking stick and cranks his head sideways. The retired stagecoach driver's back is bent, revealing his age. "You're getting kind of good at shootin' nothing. What ya firing at anyway?"

"What do you mean? That pail over there."

"No, what you shootin' in your mind?"

"I don't know. Maybe some low-down skunk like you trying to steal my gold or a dozen Paiutes coming my way."

"Don't forget they'll be aimin' back at ya." The old-timer studies Buckie's face. "What else is goin' on in that head of yours?"

"A man can't have his private thoughts without you wanting to know?"

Stubborn insists. "Come on, Buckwheat. Why so sad?"

Buckie sneaks a peek at the cabin and turns back. "I still can't believe Sandra is dead. I didn't even know she was gonna have a baby."

Deep in thought, Stubborn finally says, "Yeah, I can't believe it's been five years since they left. Always figured they'd come back with their tails between their legs."

"You don't know Samuel. He was pig-headed about making it on his own when he left here."

"He could be that way."

Buckie takes a breath. "I knew something was wrong when I opened the letter from Wyoming that was in his handwriting instead of Sandra's. I should have gone there to be with him and Sam Henry, but I didn't think I could handle not seeing my sister with them."

"And the little girl lived?"

"Yeah, Maria. They named her after my mother. I ain't much of an uncle, but I can't go there right now."

"Well, go somewhere. Pete and I can manage this place, especially since we ain't supplying horses to stagecoaches and freight companies anymore. Damn railroad took all our business."

Buckie turns serious. "Think Pa will be upset if I leave?"

"He'll be all right. Where ya thinking?"

"I don't know. Somewhere close for now, Carson City. All I know is I'm not happy just being here."

"You're only as happy as you let yourself be."

"Come on. You were young once. You know how it is."

Stubborn grins. "You're wantin' to find yourself a woman ain't ya?"

"What would be wrong with that? Not gonna find one here."

"Well, if you wanna good one, ya better get you a job and get you some money. My old man used to say, 'You need to work for it, steal it, or marry it because a pretty face will only take you so far. Women wanna a man who's going somewhere in life.'"

"Well, I ain't getting nowhere staying here."

"You saying your pa and me are holding you back?" Stubborn rethinks, tightens his lips, and agrees. "No, I hear ya. You're right. This ain't a place to waste your youth. Have you told your old man how you feel?"

"I'm trying to work my way up to it."

"Just break it to him easy, is all. He still thinks you'll be taking over this place when he kicks the bucket."

With a sardonic tone, Buckie asks, "What's there to take over?"

"We're doing okay. He replaced all the horses with cattle. Gotta give him credit for that. Growing alfalfa for hay and selling a hell of a lot of corn the last couple of years. He's finally making some money."

"There is that, but I don't like fretting about whether it's going to rain or not." Buck studies Stubborn's leather face and remembers what his father once said about the old coach driver.

One night, when his father had a little too much to drink, Pete told him that when "Stubborn" Rut Long was a younger man, he was destined for greatness and had a bright future. It all changed when the woman he was about to marry ran off with a rancher, who had a considerable amount of money and a lot more land. Said Stubborn was never the same. He lost his spunk and retreated to the life of a loner.

Then one day, Rut sold his farm and hired on as a Wells Fargo stagecoach driver. He quickly developed a reputation for being reckless and for refusing to slow down. Always in a hurry, he terrified his passengers by driving way too fast and by speeding up at a place called Dead Man's Curve.

People complained, but the company didn't fire him because he was always on time. Sometime along the way, he picked up the nickname Stubborn after he tipped over his coach a third time.

As Pete exits the barn and heads their way, Stubborn says, "Go to Carson City; kick up your heels. Get you a drink that will knock you on your ass… but don't have more than one… unless you like being knocked on your ass."

Pete stops a few feet from them, lights a cigar, and stares at the field of corn. The little bit of hair under his hat is steel grey and thinning, and his scraggly beard is snow white. He grins. "Who wants to kick up his heels?"

Stubborn grunts. "Not me. I was supposing for your boy here."

"Supposing what?"

"Supposing he should go to Carson City so he can see something more exciting than two buzzards like us sitting around waiting for the sun to go down."

"Been thinking that myself for some time." Pete reaches inside his bib overalls, pulls out a fistful of bills from a secret pocket, and holds them out to Buckie. "Take it. You earned it. Way I figure it, if I don't start paying, you'll run off… join the circus or rob some bank."

Buckie grins, takes the money, and stares at it. "What do I do with all this?"

"You'll figure out something. If you don't, I'm gonna start worrying about you. Just don't tell me what you spent it on. Stay a couple of days. Shake some of that dust off your britches. I heard the Carson City Saloon has a new piano player. "

Buckie wags his head. "You sure it's all right?"

Pete lifts his chin and tightens his jaw. "Go right now, but leave your gun behind. A man with a gun gets shot more often than a man without one."

Pete's son turns and walks towards the barn as Stubborn smiles and slaps his old friend on the back. "I'd give worlds to see what he does when he gets to town."

Pete grins. "Yeah, sometimes a fella needs a good shove in the ass to make him do something he should be doing on his own."

ON A BEAUTIFUL DAY TO RIDE, Buckie enters Carson City, a town of 3,000, surrounded by the Sierra Nevada Mountains. He slows his three-year-old quarter horse and stares straight ahead. The locals don't notice him as the smooth-faced, unarmed stranger with a red kerchief looks the town over.

As he rides down Main Street, past wooden buildings in all stages of respectability, he tilts his felt hat lower on his head, afraid of what might be in store for him.

Buckie senses something sad about the town, but he can't put his finger on it… kind of like he's seeing a mysterious stranger for the first time. Will Carson City be a friendly town or a place he can hardly wait to leave? The truth was, he still didn't know why he had come here in the first place. Maybe it was like his father always said, 'A change is as good as a rest."' At least it was close, and he could go home whenever he wanted. Or maybe like Stubborn said, he might find a woman he liked. Woman or not, at least he had a few days to kick up his heels.

He was painfully shy around females. He had never known a woman in the Biblical sense, but he had spent some time in the neighbor's hayloft kissing and groping Jenny Wagner. They both kept their knickers on, and he never tried to change her mind about that. Of course, that ended when she ran off with some young private she met at a dance at Fort Churchill.

As for strong drink, he knew he didn't like the taste of liquor or beer. His father and Stubborn were always trying to get him to share a bottle of whiskey with them, but he hated the taste. He understood how it made them feel relaxed and happy-go-lucky, but from what he saw, the pain they suffered after getting pickled wasn't worth the bother.

Curious to see another part of town, Buckie turns his horse and starts down a garbage-littered side street, riding past several white placard houses with yards flourishing with every green plant imaginable. He plugs his nose when he smells the odor of manure, finally noticing that most of the homes' front yards have mud baths with adjoining pigsties filled with pigs of all sizes and breeds.

In the distance, he hears a harmonica, a Jew's harp, and a man with a banjo singing a plaintive song addressed to Mary Ann.

As he reigns in his horse and continues his way through the run-down neighborhood, he spots a junk shop where two older men and two young boys are seated on benches in front of the store, now playing *Camptown Races*. Buckie brings his horse to a stop, raises in his saddle, and listens to the lively music.

The sadness he's feeling leaves as he thinks about the prospect of living in Carson City, finding a job, buying a house, and raising a family.

Reality sets in when he sees two filthy and half-naked children exit a dilapidated house down the street. Seconds later, the door flies open, and their wild-eyed mother, equipped with a willow branch, screams, "You little bastards! I was saving that bread for your father!!" As she chases them down the road, Buckie slaps his bridle to his horse and steers it back to Main Street.

Despite his lack of interest in alcohol, Buckie knew that the Carson City Saloon was still a place he wanted to visit. He had never been in a bar before, but he had heard stories told by his father and Stubborn about gun fights, drunken brawls, prostitution, and gambling… all vices he had managed to avoid until now.

He makes up his mind to go inside so he can watch people carry on… kind of like when he watched the battle between the Washoe and Paiutes he told Sam Henry about years earlier. Of course, he wasn't counting on someone getting stabbed, shot, or mutilated. But maybe he would get lucky and see a good old-fashioned bar fight.

When Buckie reaches the Carson City Saloon, he watches from his horse as two drunken railroad workers stumble out of the bar, laughing. He drops down from his horse and starts to tether it to a hitching post when he sees an attractive young woman coming his way.

As she nears him, he notices the slender female is wearing a white, long-sleeved, high-necked blouse covered by a brown leather vest. On her head sits a brown bowler hat that highlights her shoulder-length black hair. Her tan gingham skirt covers the rest of her body, except for the black leather cowboy boots peeking out from under her dress.

Even more curious to him is the gun belt wrapped around her waist, containing a .38 caliber pistol like the one he left at home. He tries not to stare, but she shifts her lively blue eyes his way and asks, "Do we know each other?"

Buckie tightens his lips. "I'm pretty sure we don't."

"Then you shouldn't be staring at me. That's rude."

As she walks away, he speaks up. "My given name's Timothy, but a lot of people call me… Buck. Is that gun loaded?" The young woman doesn't say anything as she continues her way across the street.

What the hell? Why did he ask her if her gun was loaded? What a lame thing to say. Why didn't he keep his thoughts to himself? Then again, if a beautiful deer crosses your path, you'd look, right… Maybe even say something?

Buck waits for her to disappear around the corner, straightens his kerchief, and walks through the saloon's swinging doors. The first thing he notices is the acrid smell of stale beer, cheap whiskey, perfume, and the strong aroma of cigar and cigarette smoke. As he inhales the odor of the bar, he gets a whiff of two nearby spittoons in need of emptying.

He coughs, surveys the room, and spots the fifty-year-old owner, Wharton Brown. The bald man with a pot belly and a brown leather apron is sweeping the floor while his wife, Fanny Brown, a big-nosed woman in her late forties with enormous bosoms protruding from her low-cut blue dress, minds the bar.

The bar stools are filled with miners, railroad men, cowboys, farmers, and businessmen in black and brown suits who talk loudly over the sound of piano music coming from the back of the room.

Three drunk vagabonds at the far end of the bar hoot and holler as they sidle up to a young barmaid. The twenty-something, who seems to be enjoying the attention, is dressed in all red with a corseted, low-cut bodice and boots decorated with sparkling white tassels.

There's no room at the bar, but he spots a small table vacated by two cowboys and sits down. He looks the bar over, trying to get his bearings as a tall, thin man with red suspenders and a black derby hat bangs out *"Oh! Susanna"* on the piano.

In the far corner, he notices five men at a table playing cards. Circling them is another young barmaid, also dressed in red, handing out shots of whiskey. As she heads back to the bar, she notices Buck sitting alone and shimmies over. "What can I get you, Sweet Pea?"

"I don't know. I don't drink… I mean, I don't drink whiskey or beer."

The redhead, her hair piled high and her shoulders exposed, laughs. "Then what are you doing here, Hon?"

"I'm here to watch?"

The barmaid shrugs. "Sure, go ahead and watch. See something you want, just let me know."

A cowboy at the next table overhears her and guffaws, "How about me, Sugar? I know what I want."

The barmaid ignores the cross-eyed man as Buck says, "You know what?" He points to men at the poker table. "Give me some of what they're having."

The young girl smiles. "My name is Linda. Ya wanna buy me a drink too?"

"Is that what I'm supposed to do?"

She smiles. "Only if you want to."

"Okay, make it two… of whatever they're having."

BUCK LEANS over the table, holding his head up with both hands. Next to him are five empty shot glasses. He looks at Linda and slurs, "Am I drunk? I think I'm drunk."

She grins. "I think you are."

"Now what happens?"

"Got any money left?"

He pulls the remaining cash from his pocket and lays it on the table. "That's all I got."

Linda smiles. "Okay, why don't we go upstairs so you can spend it?"

"I don't know. Think I should? I wouldn't know what to do."

"Come on. I'll help you figure it out. It'll be fun." Linda helps Buck out of his chair, takes his arm, and heads for the stairs. He leans heavily on her until they reach the top of the stairs.

He turns to her and says, "Whew, we made it."

MINUTES LATER, in a small upstairs room filled with cases of whiskey, barrels of beer, and other supplies, Buck is passed out on a small feather mattress with his long johns pulled down around his waist. His pants, shirt, and socks are neatly folded at the foot of the bed. His boots and hat are in a nearby corner.

Buck opens his eyes and sits up. He looks the room over, notices his bare chest and stomach, and stammers, "What happened to my clothes?"

The door swings open, and Linda enters the room wearing a white linen robe. She smiles. "There you are. I didn't think you'd ever wake up. I started to light your fire, but you passed out. You were dead to the world. Maybe this will help." Linda opens her robe, revealing her naked body.

Buck's face turns red as he looks away. "What are you doing?"

"Your time is almost up. You want some bread and butter or not?"

"Bread and butter?" He panics, jumps out of bed, and discovers his belongings at the foot of the bed. He gathers them in his arms and starts for the door. Linda covers herself as Buck opens the door and looks down the hallway. Linda protests, "You already paid me."

He hurries down the hallway, clutching his clothes. When he reaches the top of the stairs, still in his long johns, he looks down and sees several men at the bar looking up at him.

They start to laugh, so he puts on his shirt and hat and tries to climb into his pants. He manages to fit one leg in but stumbles as he tries to fit his other leg.

He tumbles down the stairs like a drunken sailor and hits his head hard on the wooden floor. Linda arrives in a linen robe, stares at her half-clothed client from the top of the stairs, and gawks.

She hurries down the steps and kneels next to Buck. She lifts his head carefully and puts it on her lap. As some of the patrons and barmaids gather around, Linda groans, "I think he might be dead."

CHAPTER 4

Recovery, Kate, and Finding Love

ON A NARROW WOODEN TABLE in a well-lit room warmed by a coal-burning stove, Buck lies perfectly still, his eyes shut. The facility is filled with bottles containing pills, liquid remedies, and jars of cotton. In addition, there are medical books, boxes of instruments, bowls of cotton, and stacked linen sheets on metal shelves.

Dr. Arnold Watson is standing over Buck, wearing his wire-rimmed spectacles halfway down his nose. The physician has wild, untamed hair, scattered in every direction, and is dressed in a white lab coat with a stethoscope draped from his neck.

Next to him is his daughter, Kate Watson, the woman Buck had introduced himself to outside the bar earlier in the day.

Arnold turns his back, removes a small metal canister from his coat, and takes a drink. He shudders involuntarily, pivots to Buck's bed, and grabs a small candle from the table.

Kate doesn't say anything, but she recognizes the sweet floral fragrance of the laudanum on her father's breath. Suddenly, her father erupts with a familiar sound of a staccato series of three dry coughs.

Kate reacts. "Father, are you all right?"

The doctor doesn't respond. He wipes his mouth with his sleeve, strikes a match, and lights the candle. Kate turns away, trying to avoid the rotten egg odor of the sulfured match and the disagreeable smell of the tallow candle.

Her father watches closely as she uses her index fingers to lift Buck's eyelids. He waits for the flame to grow and then holds the candle close to his patient's eyes. He adjusts his glasses and squints. "No one home yet." He blows out the candle and informs his daughter. "They say he hit the back of his head pretty hard."

Introspective, Kate steps back. "Most likely a concussion… maybe a brain bleed."

"I think you're right. Need to give him some time."

The office door opens, and Carson City Sheriff Garfield Simpson enters with the barmaid, Linda Sherman, a step behind him. The sheriff, a handsome, clean-shaven man of thirty-five, is dressed in denim jeans, a green flannel shirt, and well-worn leather boots.

When Garfield sees Kate, he removes his dirt-stained cowboy hat and smiles. He turns to Dr. Watson and says, "How's the kid doing?"

Before he can respond, the doctor coughs, buries his face in his hands, and turns away. The sheriff gives him a look of concern. "You okay?"

"I'm fine. My allergies are acting up, is all. Anyway, he's unconscious. Not sure he's gonna make it. You know how this happened exactly?"

Linda, dressed in her bawdy red dress again, tries to explain. "We was just getting comfortable when he got excited and ran half-naked for the stairs. I didn't see it all cuz I was busy getting my clothes on. Anyway, some of the fellas at the bar said he tripped over his pants, rolled down the stairs, and landed smack dab on his head."

The doctor nods. "Anything else?"

Linda hands Kate Buckie's boots and hat and says, "Those are his. He left them behind."

Sheriff Simpson steps up. "Linda, you know what you are doing is against the law?"

"Well, if it is, you'll need to arrest half this town. I gotta get back. I hope he pulls through. He seems like a real nice fella… at least the parts I saw." Linda chuckles and scampers for the door.

She turns back and says, "Just so you all know, we didn't get around to playing hide the sausage. He was too drunk. And when or if he wakes up, tell him I ain't giving back his money."

Kate stands frozen, holding Buck's belongings. Finally, she places them carefully on a table near her. The sheriff flirts with his eyes, but Kate doesn't return the favor, so he slaps his pistol and turns to the doctor. "Nobody seems to know his name, but they found a horse tied up in front of the saloon early this morning. I'm assuming it's his."

Kate clears her throat. "I think it's Timothy or maybe Buck."

Her father gives her a suspicious look, and she continues, "He introduced himself outside of the saloon. I assumed he was just a drifter."

Preparing to leave, Garfield puts on his hat. "If he doesn't pull through, the horse is yours. My office gets his saddle for our trouble."

The sheriff leaves, and Kate looks at her father. "I'll sit with him for a while. Go do what you need to do."

BACK AT BUCKLAND STATION, Pete and Stubborn sit in front of the main cabin fireplace, drinking coffee. Pete narrows his eyes and turns to his old friend. "I figured he'd be home by now. It's been four days."

Stubborn "Yeah, you'd think if he was having that much fun, he'd be out of money by now."

"If he doesn't show up tonight, I'm riding to Carson City in the morning."

Stubborn snorts and spits coffee in the fireplace. "Yeah, I can't blame you for that."

PETE'S WAGON MOVES at a slow pace as he shades his eyes, blocking the noonday sun. A horse and buggy approach from the other direction, and Pete pulls up on the reins. The elderly man in the buggy glides to a stop. He tilts his hat and smiles. "Good morning to you, sir. Beautiful day, don't you think?"

"Can't complain. Say, you coming from Carson City?"

"I am. Left early before dawn. Bringing home a month's supply of groceries… store-bought canned goods mostly. Got a garden. Doing well too, peas, corn, potatoes…

Pete interrupts. "Yeah, you didn't see a young man in his twenties wandering the streets of Carson City or riding a black horse this way? He'd be wearing a red kerchief."

The old man scratches his head. "Can't say I did. Plenty of people in that town I saw, but no one I remember like that."

"All right." Pete slaps his horse and rides off as the old man turns to him and says, "Got the biggest pumpkins and squash you'd ever wanna see… cucumbers too."

LYING ON A FEATHER BED in a side room next to the doctor's office, Buck breathes quietly, his eyes closed. Kate, dressed in a long-sleeved white blouse and a long black skirt, sits by him, writing in her journal.

Mother, I haven't shared my thoughts with you for a while, so I thought I had better do that while I have some time. I think of you every day and find it hard to believe it has been ten years since you left us. Father distracts himself with work and by taking long walks alone or occasionally with Aunt Margaret.

As I've mentioned before, she continues to be a godsend by helping us around the house and by relating to Father in a way I can't. They laugh, reminisce about you, and are constant companions. Their friendship helps

Margaret as well, especially after she lost Uncle Charles to cancer five years ago.

On the contrary, I know Father would be upset if he knew I was sharing this with you, but he continues to battle his addiction to laudanum. I try to turn the other way when he partakes, but it grieves me to see him continue to yield to the pain of losing you. We all have our crosses to bear, but laudanum has a firm grasp on him that won't let go. It's slowing him down too. Buttons, shoelaces, and putting his clothes on the right way now give him trouble.

At this moment, I am sitting next to an unconscious man I happened to meet on the street a few days ago. He seemed like a nice enough man with a clever sense of humor, but we hardly spoke. The story is that he hit his head on a barroom floor after falling down a flight of stairs. Father and I get a lot of barroom business, mostly gunshot wounds, broken bones and noses, and of course venereal cases... or as our clients like to call it, the French disease or the pox.

I don't have a man in my life right now, because I ended my short relationship with Sheriff Simpson. To put it bluntly, I found him to be a bore with no sense of humor, with no interest in what I have to say or what I want to do.

The young man lying next to me showed me more personality in thirty seconds than Garfield did in two months. The sheriff has been more interested in how I look than in anything I have to say. Plus, he is full of himself, always wanting me to adore him for being a lawman. He never asked me about my day or how I felt about anything. He did his best to win me over by trying to say the right things, but the more he talked, the more I knew I didn't want to spend my life with him.

I know this is indecent for me to say, but from the very beginning, I never had any desire to see the man naked. Whereas, with this young man lying next to me, I am tempted to sneak a peek under his sheet. I'm only telling you this because I know you won't be sharing it with anyone else.

Garfield, always one to have the last word, has had a hard time accepting the fact that I no longer have an interest in him, but I'm sure eventually he'll move on and find some woman who thinks he's God's gift to womankind. Heaven help me if anyone ever reads this journal other than me.

Kate lays her notebook down as Buck breaks the silence by snorting and fluttering his eyes. She sees him move his hand, and she runs out of the room, returning with her father. She gives him a hopeful look and says, "He cleared his throat and moved his hand."

"That's good news. Keep an eye out for any more movement. Talk or sing to him. It helps. Gotta get over to the Montgomery house; Thelma's about to give birth to another child. I sure hope it's a boy. They've had five girls in a row, and they're starting to blame me."

Kate sits down again as her father leaves the room. She stares at Buck and begins to hum *The Yellow Rose of Texas*. His eyes begin to flutter again, so she hums even louder. Slowly, he opens his eyes and stares at the ceiling. She whispers, "Timothy… Buck. You're back."

He looks the room over, confused. He closes his eyes again, but not before he reaches out his hand. Kate takes it, and his eyes flutter a third time. She starts humming *The Yellow Rose of Texas* again, and Buck opens his eyes a second time, turns to her, and stutters, "I hate… that… song."

She quickly removes her hand. "Good to know."

"Where am I?"

"You're in a doctor's office. You hit your head."

"How… long… have I… been asleep?"

"Four days."

"Damn. Pa… must think… I'm dead." He tries to sit up, but he grimaces, grabs his head, and sinks back onto his pillow.

Kate scolds him. "Don't do that. You have a concussion."

He lifts his head from the pillow, and Kate gently pushes it down again. "What… What's… ah… a con… cuss shun? And why can't…I… talk str… straight?"

"You hit your head hard. You most likely bruised your brain."

"Will… I ever… get back… to talk… to talking… normal again?"

"The brain takes time to heal. You need to be patient."

"Does… everything… else still work?"

"I don't know. Try moving your arms and legs."

Buck lifts both his legs and circles his arms. "Yeah, I'm… I'm ready… to fly." He starts to sit up, but Kate gently pushes him down again.

She wags her finger. "I said, don't do that!"

He relaxes and says, "Okay… okay. Don't yell. It hurts… my head and… now I'm …uh… seeing stars."

"It's normal for you to be sensitive to sound and light. And I'm sorry. I'll keep my voice down." She hops to her feet and closes a curtain to the only window in the room. "It will take a while for your sensitivity to light to fade."

"May I hold… your hand… again? It's a comfort. I'm…uh… I'm starting… to feel… faint." Buck closes his eyes, and she takes his hand. He takes a moment, opens his eyes, and says, "Much better."

Kate removes her hand. "You're kind of a smart ass!"

"Sush. You're… making… my… head hurt… again."

"No more frivolity. Lay still. Tell me your name."

"I already… told… you. Buck… Buckland, but you… can call me… what…ever you want."

"It's obvious that the fall hasn't affected your sense of humor. Do you remember what happened?"

He hesitates. "Do I… have to… tell you?"

"No, I already know. Just checking to see what you remember."

"I... re... member...uh... I didn't... do it... with..."

"You mean Linda? Are you sure?"

"Believe me... I'd... remember. I've never... done...it... before."

"All right. Enough talk. You rest for a while. I'll be back to check on you and bring you something to eat. You must be hungry. We forced water into your mouth while you were unconscious, but no food."

His mood immediately lightens. "I'm fond... of scram... bled eggs and... cris... crispy bacon."

"I'm bringing you a bowl of potato soup."

LATER THAT AFTERNOON, Dr. Watson hears a knock on the door. When he opens it, Pete Buckland and Sheriff Simpson remove their hats and step inside. Pete nods at the doctor and clears his throat. "I understand my son is here."

"Yes, Timothy. Come in. He's doing much better. He hit his head hard on a barroom floor. I'm sure he'll be happy to see you. He's in the next room. My daughter is keeping an eye on him."

The doctor leads Pete into the adjoining room. The sheriff stands quietly for a moment, puts on his hat, and yells into the other room as he walks out the door. "Guess I'm not needed here."

When the doctor and Pete enter the room, Buck looks up. "Pa, ...I'm sure... happy to... see you."

"Buckie, I wanted you to have a good time, not kill yourself. People at the bar said you were drunk and upstairs with some paid-for woman."

Buck looks at Kate, who avoids eye contact with him. "They're... right, ... but I still hate... the... taste of... liquor, and I never... touched... that woman."

56

Pete studies his son. "You still sound drunk. What kind of medicine are they giving you?"

Kate postulates. "He suffered a concussion, but his speech should improve with time."

"Yeah, so what happens now?" He turns to the doctor and says, "Can I take him home? It's a day's ride."

"He can't be riding a horse. Are you traveling by wagon?"

"No. Got one at home though."

Buck sits up. "That would… be two… more… days… laying here. I wanna…uh… go home, Pa."

Kate stands up and addresses her father. "We have a wagon. Why don't I accompany them home and bring the wagon back?"

Buck grins. "I'm for that."

Dr. Watson gives his daughter an affirmative nod.

She turns back to Buck and smiles. "You're father calls you Buckie."

He frowns, "I go by Buck now."

HEADED BACK to Buckland Station, Buck lies on a mattress in the back of the Watson freight wagon. Kate, wearing denim jeans and a brown, long-sleeved wool jacket, is seated next to him, trying to keep him steady as Pete steers his two work horses for home.

Tied to the back of the wagon are the two Buckland horses. Pete looks back at the young couple and says, "Am I driving even enough?"

Kate grins. "You're doing just fine… Mr. Buckland."

Buck looks up at Kate, smiles, and takes her hand. She avoids eye contact but lets him continue to hold it.

THE SUN IS SETTING as Pete pulls the wagon into the entryway to Buckland Station. Stubborn exits the small cabin barefoot, wearing red long johns and a filthy cowboy hat. He approaches, sees a strange woman in the back of the wagon next to Buck, and hurries back inside to get dressed.

After securing the wagon and horses, Pete hurries over to help Kate with his son. They take their time as they start to help him out of the wagon.

Fully dressed, Stubborn stumbles out of his cabin again and limps over to the wagon to help. "What's going on? Is there some kinda problem?"

Pete tightens his lips. "Buckie fell on his damn head. This young lady was kind enough to help me get him home. Kate, this is Rut Long. We call him Stubborn… well, cuz he's stubborn."

The old timer starts to offer his hand but thinks better of it and says, "Pleased to make your acquaintance, ma'am."

"Likewise, Mr. Long."

Pete interrupts their moment. "Let's get him inside."

"How do we go about that?" Stubborn asks.

Buck sits up. "I'm… pretty sure… uh… I can… walk as far… as the cabin."

"That's not a good idea," Kate says as she studies the situation. "We can help."

He scoots to the back of the wagon. "I'm gonna try."

Pete lowers the end gate, and Stubborn grins. "Now, who's being a mule?"

Buck sits on the gate as Pete and Kate each take an arm and lower him to the ground. As they slowly walk towards the cabin, Stubborn hobbles behind in case he's needed.

HER HEAD RESTING on the corner of the bed, Kate hears her patient stir, sits up, and scoots back into her wicker chair.

The morning sun peeks through a bedroom window, and Buck sighs, "My head… it doesn't… ache… so much… anymore."

"That's wonderful. I can tell you're getting stronger."

"What about…uh… my talking?"

"I think that's getting better, too."

"Are you… saying that… to make me… feel better?"

"Of course not. You're talking clearer now and with much more expression."

"Let me… uh, try to say something… without… stopping."

Kate smiles. "Okay, go ahead."

Buck grins. "I think you're the prettiest woman… I've ever met."

Kate blushes. "That was perfect. I mean the way you said it, not what you said."

Buck takes her hand. "Only one pause that time… but did you hear what I said?"

She removes her hand and smiles. "You're my patient, Mr. Buckland. Patient are prone to grow fond of their caretakers. It's only normal."

"You think… I'm just…uh… some normal patient then?"

"Well, I guess… but I have to admit you have… some … charming qualities."

"Now who's stuttering?"

"I was simply measuring my words."

Buck sits up, reaches out, takes both of Kate's arms, and pulls her close to him. She yields to his touch as he gently kisses her fully on the lips."

She slowly pushes him away and puts her hand below the curve of her slender neck. "That was highly unusual."

"I liked it."

She stands up, gently pushes him onto his back, and starts for the door. "It's getting late, so if you'll excuse me, I'm going to make arrangements for my trip home tomorrow." With a hint of sarcasm, she adds, "You appear to be recovering just fine."

"When I'm a hundred percent… may I come to Carson City… to see you?"

"As a follow-up visit for your head injury, yes."

"Not as a follow-up for my heart condition?"

"You think you might have a heart condition?"

"I do now."

She gets his drift and raises her eyebrows. "Very clever, Mr. Buckland, but I'm afraid you'll have to make an appointment. I'm a busy woman.

Kate leaves the room. Buck lies back, closes his eyes, and drifts into a dreamless sleep.

KATE IS SEATED in the driver's box of a freight wagon outside the Buckland cabin. The back of it is filled with ears of corn, and a cow is tethered to the back.

Pete and Stubborn are standing together, watching the young woman while Buck holds onto the side of the wagon next to her.

After a moment of awkward silence, she adjusts her hat, smiles, and manages to say, "Thank you, gentlemen, for your hospitality and the night's lodging. And I'm sure we'll find a use for your unusual medical care payment."

Before walking away, Stubborn offers, "Daisy's been a good cow, but she'll be even better on your dinner table."

Buck takes Kate's hand. "I'm going to miss you… caring for me." Pete notices his son's unusual display of affection and stares at the young couple.

Embarrassed, Kate gently removes his hand from hers. "I'm glad to be of service. I hope you make a full recovery." She slaps the reins to the horses, and the wagon rolls away.

Western States and Territories

1881

Four Years Later

CHAPTER 5

Alcohol, Neglect, and a New Start

THE SNOW-CAPPED Laramie Mountains, lit by the noonday sun, highlight the otherwise bleak Wyoming open prairie. Four-year-old Maria Plummer, seated in the driver's box of a freight wagon. With a smile as infectious as smallpox, she watches while her brother, Sam Henry, pries a large rock from the dirt field with a long crowbar and rolls it towards the wagon.

The seventeen-year-old is three inches taller, his long black hair is pulled back in a ponytail, and he has gained thirty pounds of muscle.

His blond sister giggles as he struggles to hoist another boulder up onto the back of the wagon. When he releases the rock, the wagon lurches forward. Maria throws up her hands and yells, "You did it!"

Sam Henry squats down, wipes his brow with his sleeves, and mutters, "That was a real ballbuster. Those rocks grow like weeds."

Maria smiles and says, "A real ballbuster."

Sam Henry straightens up. "Don't let Pa hear you say that." He looks at his sister. "One of these days, I'm gonna find me a gold nugget bigger than that rock."

"A real ballbuster."

Sam Henry shakes his head as he walks over to the brown-skinned plow horse grazing on dry grass and tethered to a small tree. He leads the animal to the wagon, attaches it to its harness, and signals Maria. "Move your fanny, Sis." She slides over, and Sam Henry releases the hand brake and climbs aboard. "Day's almost over. You hungry?"

"Chicken?"

"Afraid not. We ate the last frier last night. Need the rest of the chickens for their eggs. I shot a rabbit last night. It's still fresh."

"Why don't rabbits lay eggs?"

"I don't know. Maybe you should ask Pa that when he comes home.... if he comes home."

"He's in Shi… ann?"

"Yeah, Cheyenne. Come on. I'll empty these rocks and then I'll fry up the rabbit."

"I'd rather have chicken."

"You don't let up, do you?"

"Sammy, I've been thinking."

"Oh, boy. Now what?"

"Will the things I have to say become more important when I get older and become a woman?"

Sam Henry smirks. "I don't know. You think too much. Seems to me the closer I get to being a man, the sadder I get. Be happy with the way you are."

"Were you sad when mother died?"

"Of course, I was sad. What kind of question is that?" Maria grins. "Okay, I don't have any more questions."

Sam Herny shakes his head, slaps leather to the horse, and the wagon moves forward.

INSIDE THE PLUMMER CABIN, the fireplace lights and warms the room. The small living room is crowded with handmade furniture, piles of dirty clothes, animal hides, two wicker baskets full of potatoes, and an assortment of green vegetables in small burlap bags.

Sam Henry and Maria are seated at a simple table, eating boiled potatoes, carrots, and scraps of bread. Maria stares at Sam Henry and says, "I like drumsticks."

Sam Henry fumes. "Damn it! Why you always wantin' what we ain't got?"

Maria starts to cry, and Sam Henry softens. "Listen, I'll see if I can shoot us a rabbit for tomorrow's supper. How would that be? They taste like chicken."

Maria dries her eyes with her sleeve and pouts. "That would be good for us… but not the rabbit."

Sam Henry snickers as the cabin door flies open. Samuel stumbles inside and flops down in a chair.

Sam Henry and Maria take turns staring at their father, who has a three-day beard, an untucked dirty shirt, and filthy denim jeans. He squints. "What you two looking at?"

They turn away and focus on their plates as Samuel growls, "Get them rocks out of the north 40?"

Sam Henry lifts his head. "All I could find."

"Good boy. I'm gonna get me some sleep." Samuel heads for a corner bedroom and drops hard on the bed."

Sam Henry yells out. "We're almost out of food!"

"I'll deal with that in the morning!"

SAMUEL STRETCHES HIS ARMS and shields his eyes from the morning sun as he vacates the cabin. He fastens his suspenders and walks over to Sam Henry, who is chopping wood. "You're ambitious for so early in the morning."

Sam Henry says, "You always tell me the early bird gets the worm."

Samuel grunts. "Yeah, Stubborn used to say, 'The second mouse gets the cheese.'"

"That don't make sense. What's that have to do with getting something done early?"

"I don't know. A lot of things that man said didn't make sense, but I miss that old coyote."

Sam Henry takes a swing at a pine log, splitting it in two. He tosses the axe, wipes his brow, and looks at his father. "You got any of our money left?"

"Our money?"

"I do my share... and take care of Maria while you're off drinking what little bit of scratch we've got."

"I suggest you watch your mouth, young man. No son of mine is gonna talk to me like that."

Sam Henry hesitates and scoffs, "We both know I'm not your real son."

Samuel snarls. "Why you bringing that up now?"

"Cuz all these years you've been lying to me... too big a coward to tell me I'm a Paiute."

"Half-Paiute."

"I've kept the secret too long. I should have spoken up before you let Mother die. She was the best part of me."

"Hold it right there. Your mother died giving birth. I did my best."

"You let her bleed to death."

"And you've been holding that against me all this time? What else are you bottling up? Spit it out."

"You treat Maria and me like shit. Always going to town and coming home drunk. You don't care what happens to us."

"You ungrateful little bastard... after all I've done for you. Raising and protecting you like my own. You want the truth. I killed your father... Numaga. Splattered his head like a ripe pumpkin. Why? Cuz he killed your grandma, burned Goodtime Jane alive, and raped your mother. Is that what you've been waiting to hear?"

"None of that is my fault."

"You're right. And there's nothing we can do about it now. You're mother's dead, and you're stuck living with me."

Sam Henry adjusts his hat and raises his eyebrows. "I wanna leave… get a new start… go to Tin Cup and look for gold. Only I don't trust you with Maria."

"Don't let that stop you. We'll do just fine without you."

"What you gonna do, take her in the bar with you?"

He doesn't respond, so Sam Henry hurries to the barn while Samuel paces the ground, watching him.

He finishes saddling a black stallion, and Samuel calls out. "Stay here! Let's talk things out. You got no money, and Tin Cup's a long way off."

Sam Henry doesn't respond, mounts his horse, and rides off. In the distance, he yells back, "Tell Maria not to worry! I'll be back in a couple of hours!"

OUTSIDE THE CULBERTSON HOUSE, Sam Henry is holding the bridle of his horse and talking to sixteen-year-old Natalie. Her hair is longer now, and she has blossomed into an attractive young woman who has lost the shyness that defined who she was four years earlier. Natalie lowers her head. "Why Tin Cup? Will I ever see you again?"

Sam Henry rests his hand on her shoulder. "Of course you will. You're my gal."

"Then don't go."

"No, I need to break away for good. Samuel Plummer is not my father."

"What about your sister?"

"If things don't change, I'm taking her with me."

"She could come and live with us again. I'm sure my folks would be willing to take her in."

"I can't do that. He'll just come and get her."

"How are you going to look for gold and take care of her?"

"I haven't worked that out yet, but she'll be safer with me than… with her father."

"You're sure about that?"

"I'm sure."

"So, what happens next?"

"I'm gonna wait for the right time to leave. Then ride off and stake me a claim. When I find enough gold to start a good life, I'll be back."

Natalie protests. "No, you won't. You'll find someone else… someone prettier and smarter than me."

"Who will I find that's more beautiful than you?"

Natalie persists. "What about smarter?"

Sam Henry kisses her on the cheek. "Or smarter… I'd better head back." He pulls Natalie into his arms and kisses her passionately.

When they end their embrace, she gives him an adoring smile and says, "That better not be a goodbye forever kiss."

Sam Henry mounts his horse and smiles. "If we want to find a rainbow, we might have to put up with a little rain."

"Did you just make that up?"

"No, I read it somewhere."

AS SAM HENRY RIDES AWAY, he wonders when he'll make his actual move and head for Gold Country… and how he'll deal with his little sister. He's happy he has some money hidden away from when he lived with Natalie's family. Lila Culbertson didn't know about it, but her husband, Cletus, had slipped him some cash here and there for the work he had done. Was he being too hard on Samuel? Should he still call him father? Sure, losing their mother was hard on him, but it had been hard on all of them. And what about Maria? She never even got to meet her mother. There's no excuse for him going off and getting drunk all the time, spending what little money he had on booze and God knows what else.

When he arrives home, his father is waiting on the porch in front of the house with his saddled horse nearby. As Sam Henry unbridles his horse, Samuel mounts up and says, "Your sister… she's been fed and is asleep. I'll be home late tonight with some groceries. Pick some more rocks if you have a mind to… Sorry about all that was said."

Sam Henry watches as his prodigal father gallops off like he's in a hurry to get away. The way he figured it, his so-called father hadn't learned a thing and was still trying to escape the emptiness of not having their mother. And despite what he just said, he knew he wouldn't be home tonight or tomorrow, for that matter.

ON THE OUTSKIRTS of Cheyenne, population 10,000, Samuel Plummer aims his horse down Main Street. Originally called 'Shey' an' nah' by the Algonquian tribe, both sides of the street are lined with hotels, boarding houses, and wooden and tin ramshackle shanties.

In the distance, he sees the Bob-Tail Red Light District, home to two of the town's houses of ill repute. He'd heard you could purchase all-night tokens at both places, entitling a man to a bath with all the trimmings for three dollars. He hadn't gone so far as to pay a woman for sex after Sandra's death, but that area of town had always been a curiosity.

As Samuel rides along, several women walk past and smile at him while cowboys, farmers, and businessmen tip their hats. Nearing his old stomping grounds, he sits up straight in his saddle, and his heart begins to beat faster.

When he reaches the town's most popular bar, *The Silver Palace,* he takes a deep breath and slows his horse. The saloon-theater-dance hall, filled with gaming tables and professional gamblers, was the most popular bar in town and his favorite place to hang out.

The story he heard was that Wild Bill Hickok had ridden into Cheyenne in 1876 and spent a considerable amount of time in the saloon, gambling and raising hell.

That winter, he was said to have renewed his acquaintance with an old friend, Mrs. Agnes Lake, owner of a circus that took up residency in Cheyenne. The couple got married before Hickok moved to Dakota Territory, where he was killed in a poker game in Deadwood.

Samuel tethers his horse to a hitching post outside the bar as a wave of guilt sweeps over him. He considers getting back on his horse and riding home as he thinks about his little girl and the son he hadn't been able to get along with after Sandra died.

He knew he had been an awful father lately. Whiskey and bad luck had done that to him. The guilt and pain of Sandra's death were too much for him to handle. It was always the same. He'd get drunk and begin to feel the shame of leaving his children to fend for themselves. Then, after spending the little money he had, he'd go back home with his tail between his legs, vowing never to set foot in a bar again.

Looking at the saloon, he considers his options, yields to temptation, and untethers his horse. Suddenly, a thirty-something barmaid grabs his arm and pushes him into the bar. Barbara Sparks, dressed in a short ruffled pink skirt, a frilly low-cut bodice, and dazzling silver boots, hollers, "Are you excited, Samson? I'm about ready to dance."

Barbara takes his arm, leads him inside to an empty chair near the edge of the stage, and gently pushes him down. "Stay right there where you can keep an eye on me."

She hurries off, and Samuel signals another barmaid who knows his drink of choice. As he waits patiently for the dancing to begin, in the corner, he sees men playing a game of Faro while six others watch a roulette wheel spin around.

The room slowly fills with smoke and laughter as a man seated at an out-of-tune piano plays a series of loud, unrecognizable songs. The barmaid shows up with his drink, and he hands her a dollar. She starts to leave, but he grabs her arm. "Bring me two more whiskeys… please."

She grins. "I just delivered you one, Hun. You'll have to wait your turn."

She walks off, and Samuel downs his drink. All at once, the piano man shifts his style of play and begins to bang out a ragtime tune. Men hoot and holler as Barbara and three more scantily dressed women sashay onto the stage. They wait for their cue and start dancing their version of the Can-Can to the fast-paced song.

Several men try to rush the stage, but two hefty bouncers block their way. A fight breaks out, and the drunken men are quickly escorted out the front door.

The barmaid arrives with two more glasses of whiskey and a bottle, and Samuel's eyes light up. "I didn't ask for that."

She smiles. "No, but you might as well save yourself some money. It's cheaper by the bottle."

"How much?"

"Three dollars for everything."

Samuel reaches into his pocket and removes the rest of his money. "I only got two fifty."

The barmaid removes one of the glasses of whiskey and grins, "There. Now we're even."

Samuel shakes his head and gulps down the second glass of whiskey. He takes a moment, grabs the bottle, and fills his glass again. Feeling the effects of the locally brewed coffin varnish, he turns his attention to the girls on stage and cheers.

The girls finish their dance with a flurry as several men throw money onto the stage. The women gather the coins and exit to the main floor as some of the wealthier men meet up with Barbara and her girls with more coins in their hands.

The piano starts up again as Samuel reaches into his boot. He makes sure no one is looking and removes a silver dollar. He waits for the song to end and staggers over to Barbara. He holds out his dollar, but the burly man she has been dancing with hands her another one before Samuel can cut in.

Disappointed, he heads back to his table. Two miners are seated there. The older one empties the remaining contents of Samuel's bottle into his glass and drinks it like water. Samuel glares at him. "Mister, that's my whiskey."

The large, red-headed man sporting a scraggly beard grins, revealing a missing front tooth. "Lucky finder, unlucky loser."

Samuel squints. "What the hell does that mean?"

"It means you left this here liquor for us to claim, asshole."

"I don't want any trouble. Pay me a dollar, and I'll be on my way."

The troublemaker turns to his partner. "Hank, you hear something squeaking, like maybe a mouse?"

Samuel tries again. "Pay up, I don't want any trouble."

An off-duty deputy sheriff at the end of the bar hears the commotion and saunters over. "What we got going on, gentlemen?"

"This bastard stole my whiskey… and my table."

The deputy glares at the two rabble-rousers and says, "Is that true?"

The large man grumbles, "The table was empty… and I bought this here bottle myself."

"You lying son of a bitch!" Samuel tosses the table aside and wrestles the bearded man to the floor. He fists the large man in the face while his partner grabs Samuel by the shoulders.

He shoves him away, grabs the bottle, and slams it down on the big man's head. Suddenly, Samuel falls limp to the floor after the deputy slams the butt of his pistol down on his head.

LYING ON A COT in a Cheyenne jail cell, Samuel moans, touches the egg-sized bump on his head, and slowly sits up. The deputy sheriff who whacked him stands outside the bars looking at him. "You're awake."

Samuel stretches his neck and gently rubs the top of his head. "Why am I here?"

"Cuz, ya clobbered a fella's head over a bottle of whiskey."

"He stole it. Why ain't he in here?"

"He's in the doctor's office getting his head stitched up."

"He's lucky I didn't kill him."

"No, you're lucky you didn't kill him." The deputy nods. "I checked your story, and that was your whiskey, but you don't have the right to damage someone's skull on account of something like that."

Samuel rubs the top of his head again. "You the one who thumped my noggin?"

"I did."

"What gives you the right?"

The deputy touches his badge. "This does."

"Means nothing to me. I didn't give you that badge."

"Enough talk. I'll bring you something to eat in an hour, maybe two."

"When do I get out of here?"

"Sheriff Wilkins says four, maybe five days. Might be more if that miner happens to die or has permanent damage."

"I'm a widower. I have children at home who need me."

"Your choice was to leave them. Ours is to keep you here. Guess they'll have to fend for themselves."

HAVING WAITED three days for their father to return, Sam Henry loads the back of the freight wagon with a small quantity of food, blankets, clothing, two lanterns, and firewood.

Waiting not so patiently in the coach box, Maria is dressed in a warm wool coat and an oversized fur hat. The family plow horse and Sam Henry's stallion are attached to the front of the wagon and are anxious to move. Having tied down their possessions with leather straps, Sam Henry climbs into the seat box next to Maria, grabs the reins, and slaps the horses. Maria looks up at her brother and asks, "Aren't we gonna wait for Papa?"

Sam Henry tightens his lips. "I already explained it to you. Not anymore." As the wagon rolls forward, Maria looks back at the small homestead and wraps her arms around her brother's waist. "Will it take us long to find your gold nugget?"

Sam Henry takes a moment and says, "I don't know. We're going to see your Grandpa Pete and Uncle Buckie first."

SAMUEL LEAVES CHEYENNE, headed for home. Worried about his children, he kicks his horse in the flanks, and the animal breaks into a gallop.

A few minutes later, Samuel realizes he's about to run his horse to death, so he slows the white-lathered animal to a walk. His flanks steaming, the stallion snorts and bows his head.

In his mind, Samuel starts to make promises to himself and his children about how he's going to start a new life, a life where he swears off liquor and grows an abundance of crops that will allow him to buy more cows and horses.

He thinks about how he'll make it up to them, how he'll love Sam Henry like his own son again, and how he'll provide Maria the home she deserves. And if Sam Henry wants to strike out on his own, that will be fine. That's what young men his age are meant to do.

That afternoon, after he arrives home, Samuel scans the yard. He sees that his wagon's gone, along with his other horses. He climbs down from his horse, walks inside the cabin, and looks around. Several items, like blankets, a lamp, and most of Maria and Sam Henry's clothes, are missing. He hurries out the front door and screams, "Sam Henry!… Maria!… Where are you? I'm home!" He waits a moment and then climbs back on his horse.

AS HE NEARS the Culbertson farm, Samuel spots Lila and Natalie hanging clothes on a clothesline. In the barn, he sees Cletus and two of his sons attaching a repaired wheel to a wagon. He hops down from his horse, leads it over to a fence, and ties it to the gate. Cletus leaves the job for his sons to finish, walks over, and joins his wife and daughter.

Samuel surveys the courtyard and asks the farmer, "You haven't seen Sam Henry and Maria, have you?"

Cletus, a thin man of few words with a bulbous nose, smirks. "He was here a few days ago to see Natalie, but he ain't been back since. You know how it is."

Natalie blushes, and Samuel turns her way. "You know where he is, Natalie?" She doesn't speak, so he tries again. "I'm his father. I need to know what's going on."

She speaks softly. "He claims you're not his real father."

Samuel grits his teeth. "I'm the only father he's got."

Cletus points at his daughter, and she says, "I don't think he wants you to know."

"He can go his own way if he wants, but he's got Maria with him."

Lila turns to Natalie. "Young lady! If you know where Sam Henry and Maria are, tell Mr. Plummer right now."

"No. Sam Henry says he's a no-good drunk. He leaves them alone all the time."

Samuel stares at the Culbertsons, not sure what to say. Finally, he lifts his chin and declares, "I haven't had a drink in five days. I've changed my ways. I want my little girl back."

Natalie bristles. "What about Sam Henry?"

"Him too."

Cletus puts his arm around his daughter's shoulder and whispers. "Tell the man what he needs to know, Sweetheart."

She starts to cry and reluctantly says, "Tin Cup. He's going there to look for gold."

Samuel shakes Cletus's hand and mouths a thank you to Lila and Natalie. Without another word, he mounts his horse and rides for home.

FIFTY MILES SOUTH OF THE PLUMMER CABIN on a dirt road, Sam Henry and Maria roll along in the Plummer freight wagon, shielding their eyes from the setting sun. Maria tugs on her brother's shirt sleeve. "I'm tired. When are we going to get there?"

"I told you. It's going to take us two or three weeks."

"That's a long time."

"It is a long time, but we can do it."

Maria snuggles up to Sam Henry. "I miss our home."

"I'm going to find you a new one."

"Maybe this wagon is our home."

"Maybe. No more talk."

"I miss Pa. Do you miss him?"

"My pa was a Paiute. I'm half Paiute."

"What's a Paiute?"

"An Indian. My father was an Indian who pregnated our mother before you came along."

"I thought Pa was Pa."

"Samuel is your father, just not mine."

"I wanna be half a Paiute too."

"No, you don't. Climb in the back and take a nap?"

"It's too bumpy back there."

"All right. Just be patient. We'll stop in a minute and have something to eat."

"More chicken and beans?" Maria asks.

"No more chicken, just beans."

"Pa's gonna be mad you killed all his chickens."

"He'll get over it."

She stares at her brother. "Will he get over us, too?"

"Don't you ever stop talking?"

Maria pouts as she says, "I'm not talking now."

CHAPTER 6

Marriage, a New Home, and a Job

IN THE LIVING ROOM of Dr. Arnold Watson's Victorian-style home, a block from Carson City's Main Street, twenty-seven-year-old Timothy "Buck" Buckland stands facing Methodist pastor Charles Caulkins. The black-suited man, wearing matching trousers, has a large open Bible in his hands, and his reading glasses are low on his nose.

Dozens of candles light the room.

Two large vases of white orchids highlight the room as the groom, dressed in a white no-collar shirt, gray suspenders, a string tie he borrowed from his future father-in-law, and a new pair of blue jeans, waits nervously.

Seated in Victorian leather chairs in the front row of an eight-row configuration, Pete and Stubborn look uncomfortable in their starched white shirts and contrasting tan trousers. Behind them, two dozen people, including Sheriff Garfield Simpson, are seated in smaller wooden chairs. As the wedding attendees talk to one another, an older gentleman at the back of the room plays the violin softly.

The side door opens, and Kate enters, followed closely by her father and his sister Margaret, Kate's attractive aunt. The Watson siblings are dressed in black, contrasting with the bride's fashionable parchment-colored silk wedding gown. The bride smiles as she cradles a bouquet of red and yellow roses.

Timothy's eyes sparkle when he sees Kate. Immediately, he thinks back to when he first met his bride-to-be four years earlier, and how, after being her patient for a year, he had convinced her to let him take her out on a date. It hadn't been easy riding back and forth from Buckland Station to Carson City for another three years, especially in the winter.

Early on, they had to redefine their relationship because, as her patient, she was used to telling him what to do. Even though she was smarter than he was, he had nothing to complain about. Most of the time, he liked how Kate would ask him direct questions, like a courtroom lawyer would. 'When was the last time you ate at this restaurant? That shirt you are wearing. Did you purchase it recently? You look nervous. Are you nervous?"

Even after Kate beat him three times in a row at chess, a game he'd always considered a man's game, he noticed she never gloated. Never made him feel inferior, especially around other people.

Finally, he landed a job in town working at the Richardson Lumber Mill, found a room at a local boarding house, and began seeing Kate every day except Sundays. It took three years to convince her to marry him, and he finally stopped stuttering the day she said yes. They celebrated with a bottle of wine and a late-night check-in at The Carson City Hotel. Her father didn't look too happy when they arrived at the family home early the next morning, with no explanation, but he never said anything.

The violinist sees the wedding party, shifts his choice of music, and begins to play Mendelssohn's *Wedding March*. With her father and aunt at her side, Kate slowly walks to the front of the room with a big smile.

When she reaches her husband-to-be, the music ends, and her father and aunt step back. Buck motions to his father, and Pete stands up. Tim turns back, looks at Kate's profile, stares into her eyes, and whispers, "Yee-haw."

The minister spreads his arms theatrically and sways slightly, signaling Buck to take Kate's hand. He does, and Reverend Caulkins stoically says, "Mr. Buckland, I believe you have something you wish to say to Kate."

Timothy's face reddens as he looks at Kate and then the minister. "Is this when I make my promises?"

The reverend grins and announces loud enough for everyone to hear. "Yes, this is the time." Several people chuckle as the minister points at Timothy, and he takes Kate's hand.

"Okay, I… Timothy… Buck Buckland, take you, Kate Watson… almost Buckland… to be my wife and best friend." Several guests laugh as he continues, "And I promise to love you and cherish you for the rest of my life… or until one or both of us dies."

The preacher sighs. "Anything else you wish to add?"

Buck grins. "Oh, yeah. For richer or poorer and in sickness and in health."

The minister smiles. "Very good, then." He turns to Kate and lifts his prominent chin. "And you, Kate. What vows do you wish to make to Timothy?"

Kate squeezes Timothy's hand and gazes into his eyes. "As for me, I promise to share my life and thoughts with you, both good and bad times. And I also pledge to remain by your side in sickness and health until death do us part."

The reverend agrees with his eyes. "Very good. Now it's time for you to exchange rings." Buck reaches back and waits for his father to pull his mother Maria's ring out of his pocket, while Margaret hands Kate her deceased mother's wedding ring. The minister shakes his head, and Buck and Kate fit the rings on each other's fingers at the same time.

Reverend Caulkins looks at the wedding guests and announces, "Okay, folks, they wanted this to be a short ceremony, so I'm now pronouncing them husband and wife. Timothy, you may now kiss your bride."

Buck wraps his arms around Kate and kisses her passionately as several guests clap and cheer.

Over the noise, the minister raises his voice. "I now present to you, Timothy and Kate Buckland!

The violinist plays a light-hearted tune, and people hurry to the front of the room and congratulate the married couple with handshakes and hugs.

INSIDE THE CARSON CITY COMMUNITY HALL, near Main Street, Buck and Kate are seated at a large rectangular oak table with immediate family members and close friends.

On the main floor, other guests help themselves to a meal of breaded veal cutlets, mixed vegetables from Margaret Watson's garden, mashed sweet potatoes, and hard rolls from a local bakery.

As the happy couple ignores their food and eyes each other, the violinist, accompanied by a young female accordion player, plays an upbeat Boston waltz. Several couples dance, while others at smaller tables enjoy their meals and talk nonstop.

Buck looks at his new father-in-law, Arnold Watson, and addresses his bride. "Do you think your father is pleased we got married?"

"Well, I don't think he's displeased, but it might be a stretch to say he's pleased. Father is never pleased by much of anything."

"Oh well, it's too late now." He takes her hand, leads her to the dance floor, and they kick up their heels like everyone else.

Pete and Stubborn, seated at the other end of the head table, are drinking red wine and staring at the three-layer wedding cake. Slightly drunk, Stubborn holds up his glass and says, "Here's to living forever… so far, so good." He gulps down the wine as he continues to glare at the cake. "I feel like taking a nap, but I want some of that cake."

Pete grins. "You got all night to sleep. We're not going home 'til morning."

"What about the corn? It ain't gonna pick itself."

"It's not ready yet… and it ain't gonna stop growin' cuz we're not there. Sides, it'll be slim pickings this year. Might have to feed what we got to the cattle and pigs."

"Well, like I always say, if everything's goin' your way, you're facing the wrong direction."

"I've never heard you say that in my life."

Buck and Kate finish their dance and are heading back to the table when Sheriff Simpson cuts the newlyweds off. He circles the couple and asks, "Mind if I dance with your lovely bride, Mr. Buckland?"

Caught off guard, Buck looks at him and says, "I don't know. I guess it's all right. If Kate doesn't mind."

Before she can respond, Garfield takes her by the arm and whisks her onto the dance floor. The music starts again, and Buck walks over to the head table, sits down, and begins to pick at his food.

Kate's aunt walks past him with a large knife and moves to the cake. Stubborn catches the woman's eye and says, "Big piece for me, lots of icing." He quickly vacates his chair, walks over, and offers to shake her hand. She hesitates but finally holds it out. He shakes it like he's pumping water from a well.

"Good grief!" Margaret pulls her hand away and frowns.

Stubborn grins. "Now, how about that cake?"

"You'll have to wait. It's traditional for the bride and groom to have the first piece."

"Sorry, thought maybe you needed someone to try it out… make sure the cook didn't poison it or somethin'."

Margaret glares at him. "For your information, I made this cake myself."

Stubborn scratches his backside like a hound dog and plops in his chair. "But I bet you weren't in the kitchen the whole time."

Pete walks over and tries to ease the tension. "Ignore him. He's always joking around."

Margaret's face brightens as she smiles at Pete. "Good to know. Now, if you'll excuse me, I need to relocate the plates. Will this cake be safe while I'm gone?"

Pete gazes at Margaret for a little too long. "It most certainly will. I will guard it with my life… every crumb… from any would-be cake rustlers."

Stubborn overhears and guffaws, "That would be me."

Margaret offers her hand to Pete. "Margaret Watson. I am the bride's aunt."

As they shake hands, Pete mutters, "Pete Buckland. I'm Buckie's father."

"Buckie?"

"Yeah, he goes by Buck now."

"I see."

Margaret walks away as Stubborn rolls his eyes. "You were flirting with that woman."

"I was not."

"Were, too. She sure didn't shake my hand like that. You should be ashamed. She's your new daughter's aunt… you're hitting on your aunt-in-law."

"My conscience is clear."

Stubborn smirks. "In your case, a clear conscience is a sign of a bad memory."

Buck moves to the end of the table and joins his father and Stubborn. When the music stops, Garfield escorts Kate over to Buck. He bows his head and says, "Thanks, Kate. It was a pleasure."

Buck notices the sullen look on his bride's face and says, "You okay?"

"It was awkward, is all. I dated him for a while."

"Huh, I didn't know."

Pete rises from his chair and walks over to Margaret, seated next to her brother, Arnold. He waits for the doctor to take a bite and says, "My son just told me you're a widowed woman. Would you like to dance?"

Arnold, who has been listening, coughs and laughs simultaneously. "Go on, Margaret, dance with the man."

"Why? Because he feels sorry for me… for not having a man?"

Pete softens his voice. "No, that's not what I meant. Listen, I'm nervous. I haven't danced with a woman since my wife died… and that was in the kitchen of our cabin."

"She died dancing with you in the kitchen?"

"No, no, no."

"I'm sorry. I don't know why I said that."

"You were joking. I have to say, making light of a man's wife dying…."

"You're right. That was rude." Margaret hurries to her feet, surveys the room, takes Pete's arm comfortably, and they walk out onto the dance floor.

As they silently dance to a slow waltz, Kate's aunt takes the initiative and says, "Have you been a bachelor long?"

"I don't know. Ten, maybe twelve years. I don't keep track of time very well. I need to think hard to remember how old I am."

"I know what you mean. I can't believe Charles has been gone seven years already."

"Am I dancing all right?"

"Yes, but your hands are rough. Do you work outdoors?"

Pete's voice lightens as he tries to explain. "I raise cattle, horses, chickens, corn, and alfalfa. I guess that toughens up my hands considerably."

She smiles. "A man of the earth. I like that."

The music shifts to a polka. Pete grins, picks up the pace, and whirls Margaret around the dance floor with no hint of a limp.

THE MORNING SUN lights the Sierra Nevada Mountains as Pete and Stubborn leave Carson City in a freight wagon headed back to Buckland Station. Pete stares at the road, his hat raised above his forehead and his neck pushed slightly forward.

The old friends are silent for a while until Stubborn rubs his chest and says, "I think I got heartburn. Best cake I ever ate."

"Yeah, you had three pieces."

"Four… Didn't think you noticed with you busy charming the cake maker."

Pete doesn't respond, so Stubborn continues, "Buckie was in high spirits. I think he's landed himself a good woman."

Pete shrugs. "Just hope she's not too smart for him."

"Why would you say that?"

"Her being almost a doctor and all. She seems mighty ambitious. My son is… well, just kind of average."

Stubborn adjusts his hat. "Ambition is just a bad excuse for being lazy… someone who thinks for a living. And Buckie's not lazy. And don't give me that average shit. Half the people we know ain't average."

Pete wags his head. "The things you come up with. Back to the cakemaker. I asked Margaret to come to the ranch for a visit."

"You did? You sly dog. What'd she say?"

"She didn't say no."

"Well, that's something."

Pete sighs. "She most likely won't come."

"Yeah, we're not her type." Stubborn rubs his chest again, yawns, and says, "You all right to drive? I'm feelin' a little sluggish, like a snake that ate one too many mice. Think I'm gonna take me a nap and sleep off that cake."

"Go ahead… then it's my turn." Stubborn crawls in the back of the wagon. He rests his head between two bags of barley seed they bought before they left Carson City and pulls a tattered horse blanket over his shoulders.

Two hours later, Pete hits a rut in the road, and the wagon rocks from side to side. He looks back and yells, "You all right back there?" There's no response, so he hollers louder. "Stubborn! Your turn to drive!"

There's still no reply, so Pete stops the wagon, turns back, and slaps Stubborn on the shoulder. His friend doesn't move, so he crawls into the bed of the wagon and shakes Rut Long's lifeless body. Pete lowers his head, sits quietly for a moment, and climbs back into the driver's box.

WHEN PETE ARRIVES HOME, he climbs down from his wagon and heads for the barn. When he returns, he's gripping a shovel, a hammer, some nails, and two small pieces of wood. He shuffles over to his wife Maria's grave and begins to dig a hole, leaving a space next to her for his body when the time comes.

It's almost dark when he finishes covering his friend's grave. He leans on his shovel, stares at both wooden crosses, and orders, "Stubborn, you take good care of Maria now… until I get there."

SAM HENRY AND MARIA are huddled together in front of a campfire, eating the last of the rabbit that Sam Henry shot an hour earlier. Maria chews hard and says, "I like chicken. This rabbit's too chewy to eat."

"That's all we got," Sam Henry snaps, "Until we get to your grandpa's place."

"Isn't he your grandpa, too?"

"Yes, he's my grandpa too."

"Does he have a bed for us?"

"He'll have something softer than this ground." Sam Henry pauses and says, "Listen, I need to tell you something." Maria waits for her brother to continue. "When we get to Buckland Station, I'm gonna leave you there… while I go off and find me some gold."

Maria's face droops. "I want to find some gold, too."

"Where I'm going is no place for little girls."

"What's going to happen to me?"

"That's why we've come all this way. I'm counting on Grandpa Pete to watch over you until I come back."

"I don't like Grandpa Pete."

Sam Henry shakes his head. "You haven't even met him yet. He's a good man. He has horses, cows, geese, and chickens… maybe a few cats. You've always wanted a cat."

"I don't wanna a cat. I want you."

"I know, but I already told you. I need to look for gold."

"You like gold more than me."

"No, I don't. Enough talk. We need to get some sleep."

THE SUN SHINES through the bedroom window of a small white rental house on a side street on the east end of Carson City. Sitting on a chair at the foot of the bed, Buck is polishing his boots. Asleep on a feather-filled mattress, Kate hears him fitting his first boot on and sits up. "Buck, what are you doing?"

"Sorry, I didn't mean to wake you."

Kate sits up and shades her eyes from the morning sun. "It's barely morning."

"I've been meaning to tell you. Garfield Simpson wants to talk about me working with him."

"Doing what?"

"I'd be his assistant… a deputy sheriff."

"No. You haven't even talked to me about this."

"I'm talking to you now."

"Buckie, we've only been married a month. I'm not ready to be a widow. Law enforcement is dangerous work. You could get beat up, shot, or even killed."

"I know. I've considered all of that. But you know how much I hate the lumber business. I don't have any future there."

"Have you considered that you won't be in a safe environment?"

He snickers. "I had a board fall on my head last week."

Not amused, Kate moves to the side and puts on her slippers. "That's not funny. Garfield has been shot twice. I helped Father remove a bullet from one of his arms and two weeks later another one from his leg."

"Bet he wishes you took care of him like you did me?"

"Why would you say that?"

"I see how he looks at you… kind of like he's trying to undress you with his eyes."

"And yet you want to work with the man?"

"The thing about me is, I can dislike a man and work with him at the same time. Besides, I want the job. I want people to respect what I do."

"I respect what you do."

"You're a doctor. I cut logs for a living."
"I'm not a doctor. My father is a doctor. I'm his assistant. And there is nothing wrong with you working at a lumber mill."

"You save lives and help people. That's what I want to do… protect people and save lives."

"It sounds like you've already made up your mind."

Buck pleads with his eyes. "Come on. Don't be mad."

Kate turns away. "You do what you need to do."

Buck hops over and sits on the side of the bed. "Look at us, our first fight as a married couple."

"The first of many if you don't stop making major decisions without talking to me."

"Point well taken. No more big decisions without talking to you."

Kate continues. "One more thing. Garfield has had a hard time letting go of me. I don't trust the man."

"Do you think he's only offering me the job so he can keep an eye on you?"

"God, I hope not, but I wouldn't put it past him."

He slips on his second boot. "Well, we're only talking. He might not even offer me the job."

"And if he does?"

He grins. "That's when I beg you to let me take it."

"You're a difficult man, Timothy Buckland."

"It's Buck."

"You're still a difficult man, Buck."

"As are you, Kate Buckland… One more thing."

"What's that?"

"When we're out and about, would you mind referring to me as Buck? Buckie is kind of a kid's name."

"I guess I can do that, but I like Buckie."

SAM HENRY AND MARIA ARRIVE at Buckland Station in the middle of the night. The main cabin is dark as Maria watches Sam Henry detach his stallion from the wagon, leaving the plow horse attached. She sniffles as she watches her brother reach into the back of the wagon, remove a saddle, and fit it on his horse.

Holding Maria's hand with his right hand and carrying her bag of possessions with his left, Sam Henry leads his sister to the front door of Pete's cabin. When they reach the steps, he whispers, "This is it. I'm going to knock on this door and you wait for it to open. The man inside will be your grandpa."

"Don't you want to see him?"

He continues to whisper. "No, it would be too hard for me to leave."

Maria raises her chin. "I'm going to run away."

"No, you're not. Where would you go anyway?"

"With you."

"We've already been over this."

"You're gonna come back and get me, right?"

"Yes, I promise. I'll be back…"

"When?"

"I don't know." He lays Maria's belongings down on the porch and hugs her. "Behave yourself now. Don't give your grandpa any trouble."

"He'd better not give me any trouble."

"Okay, here we go." Sam Henry kisses the top of Maria's head, slams his fist on the door, and runs off as Maria watches him.

She begins to cry as a light in the cabin window comes on. In the darkness, Sam Henry mounts his horse and rides away as the front door slowly opens. Pete braces himself in the doorway as he holds a lit candle. His brown skin is wrinkled now, his eyes are dull, and he has lost a spring in his step. Dressed in a tattered nightshirt, he favors his left leg from the time a horse fell on it 20 years earlier. He looks down at Maria. "What do we have here?"

Maria gives Pete a reluctant curtsy and asks, "You're old. Are you my grandpa?"

"What? I don't know. What's your name? Is it Maria?"

"My brother says you're supposed to take care of me."

"Your brother? Sam Henry? Where is he? Pete peers into the dark of the night and hollers, "Sam Henry... you out there?!"

Maria wrinkles her nose. "He's going to look for gold."

Pete walks into his courtyard, raises the candle above his head, and peers into the distance. Seeing nothing, he returns to his front doorstep, picks up Maria's bag, and says, "We'd better get you inside; it's cold out here. What about Samuel... your father? Where is he?"

Maria wrinkles her nose and says, "He never came home."

Inside the cabin, the candle reveals a 9x11 black and white photo of Pete and his deceased wife, Maria. He notices Maria staring at it and says, "That's me and your Grandma, your namesake, just after we got married. Pretty huh? Looks a lot like you."

"She looks sad."

"Oh, no. We were being serious for the photographer. I hate to bring up a hurt, but I miss her a lot."

"Where is she now?"

"She died. Buried out back. We'll visit her one of these days."

"How did she die?"

"Paiutes put an arrow in her."

"Why did they do that?"

"She was in the wrong place at the wrong time."

"Sam Henry said his father was a Paiute."

"He told you that?"

"Yep, but I'm not because Samuel is my father."

"That's right, and now there's another Maria in my cabin. What do you think about that?"

"You sure ask a lot of questions, Grandpa."

Pete grins. "I do, don't I."

Maria chuckles. "Did Grandma Maria like chicken?"

"She did. We had chicken almost every night. Fried chicken, baked chicken, chicken pie, chicken and dumplings, and chicken biscuits and gravy."

Maria takes a moment, stares at Pete, and whispers, "You're old Grandpa."

"You're right about that."

"I'm four, but my birthday is in May." Maria's eyes widen. "How old are you?"

Pete scoots his chair back. "I don't know. I've kind of lost track. Still in my 60s, I guess. Let me think." He uses his fingers to check his math. "Sixty-six… yeah." Pete takes a breath, realizes he is getting old, and likes it. Despite losing some of his memory, somehow he felt wiser.

Maria raises her chin. "Sam Henry says I act like I'm sixteen."

"Huh."

IN THE DARK OF NIGHT, a hundred yards to the west of the cabin, hidden behind a Joshua tree, Sam Henry watches the cabin until the light goes out. Satisfied his sister is safe, he wipes a tear from his eye and rides off.

THE FOLLOWING MORNING, the Sun brightens against the window as Pete takes a seat across the table from Maria, wearing the same clothes he had on when his granddaughter arrived. As she slowly picks at a bowl of porridge, her grandfather watches from the corner of his eye. In front of her is a cup of milk, a piece of side pork, and a slice of dry bread.

Feeling like his house is finally alive again, Pete still grumbles. "What's the matter? You don't like your porridge?"

"Tastes like the stuff we give our horses and chickens."

"It's oatmeal. It's good for you. Go on, eat it."

She tries another mouthful, gently spits it back into her bowl, lifts a tin cup, and takes a drink.

Pete narrows his eyes. "What do you like to eat?"

"Chicken."

"Pick out a chicken, and I'll fry it up for dinner tonight."

"Can I have the feathers?"

"What are you going to do with them?"

"Put them in my pocket. They feel soft."

"Well, there you go. I'll save the feathers for you."

"Grandpa, do you have any cats?"

"Three or four in the barn."

"Can I have one?"

"You can have all of them as far as I'm concerned. Take the rest of your milk out there, and they'll come running."

Maria grabs her cup of milk and hurries to the door. Pete yells, "In this house, we thank the person who made us a meal… even if we didn't like it."

As Maria shuts the door behind her, she hollers back, "Sorry, Grandpa, it was delicious… even though I didn't like it."

THE NOONDAY SUN casts shadows on a dozen twenty-foot-high Palo Verde trees to his right as Sam Henry rides northwest, shading his eyes. Heading for Colorado, he starts to think about Maria. Did he do the right thing? Was he being selfish, greedy… foolish? All he knew was that Maria needed a safe place to live, where someone would take good care of her. He felt guilty for riding off without so much as a word, but he didn't want to explain to his grandfather why he didn't feel good about leaving her with Samuel, her father.

His thoughts are suddenly interrupted when he spots a band of Pawnees topping a small hill ahead. He reaches for his rifle but thinks better of it. Not sure if he should keep riding forward or turn and ride in the opposite direction, he pulls up on his horse and waits.

He counts nine braves wearing breechcloths made from sagebrush brush and ponchos comprised of rabbit furs and buckskin. As they ride closer on barefooted horses, he notices their shirts are decorated with feathers, their jewelry is made of colorful beads and shells, and their deerskin moccasins extend to their knees. Trailing behind are four more horses with dead antelopes draped over their backs.

Still unsure what to do, he sits frozen in his saddle, trying to decide if he should speak or remain silent. When the Indians arrive, they circle him and look closely at his horse. The band's leader slides off his painted buckskin, takes two steps forward, and checks Sam Henry's mount even closer.

He turns to Sam Henry and grunts, "Puku... mine."

Having no idea what the barrel-chested Indian said, Sam Henry offers, "His name is Midnight."

While the other braves put pinons in their mouths and spit out the shells, their leader signals Sam Henry to get off his horse. As he complies, he calmly asks, "Are you Paiutes?"

The leader lifts his chin, squeezes his Bowie knife, but doesn't speak. Afraid he's about to be killed, Sam Henry stammers, "Numaga was my father. Maybe you knew him?"

The Paiute snorts, "Uh me naa Numaga?"

Sam Henry raises his chin. "Yes... Father."

The leader turns to the others and says, "Saamu... Numaga." He turns back to Sam Henry and asks in English, "Numaga... son of Chief Winnemucca?"

They lock eyes, and Sam Henry reaffirms his claim, "Yes."

The Paiute points at Sam Henry. "You come." Sam Henry thinks about his options and remounts his horse.

THAT EVENING, the Paiute hunting party enters a village near the Truckee River. Riding next to Sam Henry, Wovoka looks straight ahead and rolls back his shoulders as village dogs and young children welcome them home.

As he rides along, Sam Henry's senses are overloaded by the smell of burning cedar and sage and a view of dome-shaped homes covered with cattails and tule mats held up by a framework of willow poles. There are also traditional teepees and temporary shelters covered with willow brush and buffalo hides.

Halfway through the village, the Paiutes stop at a lodge covered in animal hides and birchbark. Chief Winnemucca, an elderly man in his early 70s, emerges from his home. His braided hair, accented by an eagle feather, hangs below his shoulders, and he is wrapped in a large buffalo robe. He scans the hunting party. When he sees Sam Henry, he nods at the Paiute hunters as if to say, "Who is this white boy you bring to my village?"

The lead warrior points at his captive and, in his Paiute language, explains, "He claims to be the son of Numaga."

Winnemucca steps forward, circles Sam Henry, avoids eye contact, and mutters in broken English. "Wovaka claims you to be the seed of Numaga. Was your mother a pale-skinned white woman?"

Sam Henry bristles. "He forced himself on her, and I am the result."

"My son never had to force himself on any woman. You go home now."

Sam Henry stares at his Paiute grandfather. "I no longer have a family. I want to learn more about my father."

CHAPTER 7

Tin Cup, Finding Gold, and More Trouble

SAMUEL RIDES INTO TIN CUP, where people either get stuck in the mud or choke on the dust. The small mining community in Gunnison County is located approximately 110 miles south of Cheyenne in the newly formed state of Colorado.

The newcomer rides past a miner shaving himself in a mirror hanging from a tree, while his two associates relieve themselves in nearby bushes. Further into town, he sees three dirt-covered placer workers trudging down the boomtown's muddy main street, singing an unrecognizable tune and carrying shovels and pickaxes over their shoulders.

The men pick up the pace when they see the boomtown's only bar with a simple sign in the window reading *Frenchy's Saloon*. Several other miners arrive, prop their tools against the outside wall, and hurry inside.

Exhausted after four days in the saddle with little to eat, Samuel stares at rough-shod buildings, makeshift tents, and other local businesses.

On the far edge of town, he spots four men sitting on their haunches on the side of the road playing a five-card draw. He slows his horse and watches as a small man with an uneven mustache and a beard filled with dirt, grease, and bits of debris throws his cards down, revealing three queens. "Check out my ladies, three of them!"

Curious, Samuel stops his horse, circles back, and watches as Clyde Morgan removes his hat and scoops all his winnings inside it. As he prepares to leave, Rupert Weed, a large man with thin hair and hard eyes, jumps to his feet and growls, "You can't quit now, asshole. You gotta give us a chance to win our money back."

The winner nervously chews the end of his mustache and spouts, "I'm quitting while I'm ahead. I gotta get back to my claim."

"You ain't goin' nowhere!" Rupert wipes his mouth with the back of his hand, grips his peacemaker with his other hand, and sneers.

Clyde notices, looks away, and picks at a coat button with his index finger. "You planning to shoot me for takin' my winnings?"

"Watch yourself, Clyde. You don't wanna know what I'm thinking. Sit your ass down."

Still watching astride his horse a few feet away, Samuel fondles the handle of his pistol as the smaller man stares at the larger man and growls, "You ain't tellin' me what to do." The winner reaches for his gun, but Rupert clears leather first and shoots him in the chest twice.

The unlucky man looks down in disbelief as two holes expand to large circles of blood on his shirt. His eyes roll back, and he sags to the ground, as Rupert stomps over and removes the man's earnings from his hat.

Rupert turns to the two remaining card players and grumbles, "You saw that. He drew on me first. Didn't have no choice." The killer tosses the dead man's money in the middle and grins. "Big pot to start this hand, boys." He looks up, sees that Samuel is still watching, and mumbles, "What you lookin' at? You wantin' to take Clyde's place?"

Samuel sits up in his saddle. "No, I'm afraid I might win." Rupert's two remaining friends chuckle as Samuel continues, "You just gonna let that man lie dead over there?"

Rupert muses. "Why not? He ain't in a hurry to go someplace now. We'll dig him a hole when we're done here."

"Maybe you should notify the sheriff."

"Tin Cup ain't got no sheriff. He got himself shot last month. What's it to ya anyway?"

Samuel remains calm as he changes the subject. "I'm looking for a long-haired seventeen-year-old boy and his blond four-year-old sister. They might have come this way in the last week or so."

Together, the men wag their heads "no" as Rupert grumbles, "People come and go. We spend our time north of here, but there are mining camps in all directions. If they are here, they could be anywhere."

Samuel turns his horse. "Guess I'll check with the locals at the bar; maybe someone in there saw them."

Rupert laughs. "Good luck. With the kind of rotgut they serve, you'll be lucky to find anyone who knows his name."

Samuel nods and rides in the direction of *Frenchy's Saloon*. When he arrives, he jumps down and looks for a spot to tether his horse, but the two hitching posts are full. To his right, he sees a legless man resting his stumps over the edge of the wooden sidewalk. The tattered man holds out his filthy red stocking cap and asks, "Spare change, mister?" Samuel fishes in his pocket, removes a quarter, and drops it in the man's cap. The beggar grins and explains his dilemma, "God bless. Dynamite done this to me. Lit a short fuse and tripped over a rock." He pockets the coins, puts on his cap, and scoots into the bar using his hands as crutches.

Still not finding a place to tie his horse, Samuel leads it to the front of a nearby general store and ties his animal's reins to the post. As he walks away, a woman emerges from the store's front door and shouts, "You can't leave your horse here!" She points at a sign that reads, "Customers Only."

Samuel pivots and looks at the pretty thirty-something addressing him. She's wearing a grey cotton high-collared bodice and a matching long skirt covered by a white apron. Samuel stares at her as if he didn't hear what she said. He doesn't respond, so she reaffirms, "This is private property."

"How do you know I'm not a customer?"

"Because I saw you studying the bar and looking for a place to park your horse."

"I'm new in town, I'm checking out my options."

"This town doesn't have many options."

Samuel untethers his horse and apologizes. "Sorry, ma'am. Do you have any suggestions where I might leave my horse?"

"Some men tie them to trees south of town, but you might not have a horse when you return. The more civilized patrons leave them at the livery stable across the street… Barney charges locals one price and out-of-towners and saddle tramps more."

"I'll be paying more… but I'm no saddle tramp."

She starts to walk back inside, but turns back. "You said you are new in town?"

"That's right. I just arrived."

"Hoping to strike it rich like everyone else, I suppose?"

"No, I'm here looking for my son and daughter. Long story, but they ran off."

"I see. I hope you find them. I'm sure you and your wife are worried sick."

She starts to turn away again just as Samuel tells her, "My son is seventeen, and my girl is four."

"Forgive me for asking, but why did they run away?"

"Like I said, it's a long story."

"I'm sorry. I didn't mean to pry."

"It's okay… I guess I'd better head over to that livery stable." Samuel starts to mount his horse but takes a beat. "By the way, I'm Samuel Plummer."

She finally smiles. "Ruth Baxter."

Samuel looks up at the storefront sign. "Oh yeah, that makes sense… *Baxter's General Merchandise and Mining Supplies.* I'd offer to shake your hand, but it's road dirty."

Ruth grins. "That's all right. It's dangerous for a woman to shake hands with a man around here."

"That makes sense, this being a mining town with lots of saddle tramps… and all."

She raises her eyebrows. "Yes… and all."

Samuel mounts his horse. Ruth watches him ride off. and walks back into her store.

When he arrives at *Barney's Livery Stable,* shaped like a barn, he gets off his horse, tethers his horse's reins under a large rock, and looks for the owner. Not seeing anyone, he enters the dilapidated building and yells, "Anybody home?"

Once inside, he sees a wood-burning stove made of loose-fitting bricks, piles of rusty nails and barbed wire, empty whiskey bottles, and refuse iron of all shapes and sizes.

He exits the barn and circles to the back. Still not seeing anyone, he's about to leave when he sees the door of a pine-planked privy near him open. A small man in his late fifties exits and fastens the strap to his bib overalls. When he sees Samuel, he grumbles, "Was that you hollering?"

"Yeah, the woman from the mercantile said you might let me board my horse here for a couple of hours."

Barney bites down on the pipe in his mouth like it's a permanent fixture, slowly removes it, and spits a few bits of tobacco out of his mouth. "That'd be the widow Baxter."

"Widow?"

"Her husband got destroyed by a runaway freight wagon crossing the street in front of his store. Horses knocked him down, and a wheel crushed his skull like it was a ripe watermelon. Didn't see it myself, but that's what I was told."

"That's some bad luck." Samuel turns and looks back. "She runs that place by herself?"

"Had a couple of hired men come and go. Both tried to put the move on her and she fired their asses." Barney grins. "Tell you what, I'd be sniffing around her myself if I weren't so used up."

With that, Samuel changes the subject and holds out his hand. "Name's Samuel Plummer."

Barney wipes his right hand on his pants and offers it to Samuel. "Barney Luther."

"How much to board my horse?"

"Twenty-five cents. Thirty-five if he eats."

"Yeah, he needs to eat."

"All right. If you ain't back by morning, it's another quarter."

"I'll just be a couple of hours."

"Yeah, I've heard that before. An hour costs the same as a day."

As Samuel heads for the side entrance of the barn, Barney stops him. "Shorter going this way."

Samuel follows the little man, who has a noticeable limp. The stable owner turns back, sees Samuel staring at his leg, and says, "Mule kicked me ten years ago. Leg ain't been the same since."

Back inside, Samuel sees eight horses in two separate pens. Barney explains. "Studs and geldings in that pen and mares in the other."

"I got a stallion."

"He ornery?"

"No, he's good."

"All right, then put him in there." Barney points to a pen with four other male horses.

"I'll do that. I'd better be on my way."

"If you're headed to the bar, don't let them give you none of that Tangle Leg shit. They make it themselves. A big dose will kill ya."

"No, I'm not looking to drink. I need some information."

"You're not going to find a lot of truth in that godforsaken place."

"Well, I need to give it a try anyway."

"Need you to pay now while you still got money."

Samuel removes thirty-five cents from his pocket, hands it to Barney, and says, "Will you be here when I get back?"

"I sleep right over there… in the corner."

Samuel looks and sees an old mattress and a couple of tattered blankets. "Ever let anyone stay the night?"

"Boarding house down the street… comes with breakfast and a bath once a week."

Samuel tightens his lips. "I can't afford that, and I'm not looking to stay that long."

"This ain't no hotel."

"I understand."

"Who asked you to understand?" Barney looks him over again and says, "Another twenty-five cents, but there ain't no bed."

"That's fine. Some hay will do." He reaches into his pocket, removes another quarter, and hands it over.

Barney looks at it, bites the coin with his teeth, and shoves it in his pocket. He nods at Samuel. "What ya need to know?"

"Excuse me?"

"Ya said you was wantin' information."

"I'm looking for my seventeen-year-old son and four-year-old daughter. They ran off."

"Been beating the hell out of them, have ya?"

"No, but truth be told, I haven't been much of a father. I spent all my time drinking and not taking care of them the way I should have."

"What makes you think they might be around here?"

"Cuz my son Sam Henry was always talking about looking for gold here… in Tin Cup."

"Sam? Your boy goes by your name too?"

"My wife's idea."

"Must be confusin'."

"Sometimes. That's why we added the name Henry."

"Why ain't she with you lookin'?"

"She passed four years ago."

"Sorry to hear that. I lost my woman…" Barney counts three fingers on his right hand. "Three years. Maggie ran off with a plow salesman name of Clarence Smithers. Was uglier than me and missing three teeth, front ones too. After they got together, she started thinking she was better than me. Always threatening to run off with Clarence."

"I'm sorry. That must have hurt."

"Shit." Barney scratches his head like he's trying to think of something else to say. "Look at this place. I know it ain't no palace. I knew she was on the prowl with Clarence, so I started drinking hard. I'd start my morning all hopeful like she might change her mind about me, but it all backfired. Whenever I'd see her, I'd start acting like a grizzly bear backed in a corner and call her all kinds of names."

"Whiskey will do that to you."

"One night, I came home from Frenchy's, and Maggie's horse was gone. Swore the bottle off the next day, but it was too late. Never saw her again."

Samuel nods. "I had to give up drinking myself."

"Then why you going to a damn bar? That's like a fox visiting a chicken coop."

Samuel tightens his lips. "I'll be fine. I'd best be going now."

"If you don't come back, I'll be keeping your horse."

"Does that happen very often?"

Barney chortles. "About once a month. How do you think I stay in business?"

Samuel raises his eyebrows. "One more question. Why do they call this place Tin Cup?"

"It's had lots of names. Early on, it was Tin Cup cuz some prospector named Jim Taylor panned some gold out of Willow Creek and carried it back to camp in a tin cup. He and his friends named the valley *Tin Cup Gulch*. People changed it to Virginia City for a while, but that didn't stick cuz there's a Virginia City somewhere in Nevada and one in Montana. So, it's back to Tin Cup."

"You been here long?"

"Landed here about the time they started finding silver and gold in the late 50s. Built my livery stable and made a hell of a lot of money feeding and boarding horses. Had to lower my prices a few years back after most of the luck ran out."

"Good to know. Okay, I'd better go."

NESTLED UP TO THE BAR and resting his feet on a never-polished brass rail in Frenchy's Saloon, Samuel sips a glass of water. He watches dozens of miners, railroad workers, businessmen, and cowboys drinking beer and whiskey, and playing poker and other games of chance in the sawdust-smelling room.

Most of the men take turns flirting with the scantily clothed barmaids and hookers who are trying to get the already intoxicated men to buy them another drink or two… or take them upstairs for a paid-for good time.

In the far corner, Samuel spots the beggar he donated money to sitting alone on the floor next to a half-filled brass spittoon. The panhandler sees a man vacate the table near him, so he pulls himself up and into the empty chair. When he turns to the bar, he notices Samuel looking his way. He salutes his benefactor with his shot of whiskey and joins the conversation with the other men.

Hump-backed bartender Herman Lawson, sporting brown side-whiskers and a black leather apron, approaches Samuel. He leans over and barks over the loud noise, "Can't be sitting there if you're only drinking water."

Samuel notices the barman's revolver stashed in a tall beer mug as he chugs the water out of his glass. "Okay, how much for a shot of whiskey?"

"Ten cents."

He hands the owner a dime. "I'll have ten cents worth of water."

The owner shrugs, walks over to a female bartender, and whispers in her ear. The hefty redhead with enormous bosoms, dressed in a low-cut solid green dress, grabs a pitcher of water, slides over to Samuel, and begins to fill his glass.

As she pours, he notices a large scar from her right eye to her chin, enhancing her pretty face. She catches him staring at her and explains, "Long ago, bar fire. Almost died."

"Sorry to be looking so long." Samuel changes the subject with his eyes, looks at his glass, and explains, "I gave up drinking a few weeks ago. Are you Frenchy?"

"No, Frenchy's is just a name we made up."

"You own this place?"

"Me and humpback Herman over there." She grins. "Just so ya know, he don't mind me being with other men."

"Good to know." Samuel takes a sip of water.

Belle looks the non-drinker over from head to toe. "Kinda strange you hanging out here drinking water, don't ya think?"

"Was hoping someone in here might have seen my son and little girl. They're missing, and I'm desperate to find them."

"How old?"

"Seventeen and four."

"Someone steal them?"

"No, they ran off."

"What makes you think they might in Tin Cup?"

"My oldest used to talk about coming here to look for gold."

"Were you abusin' them?"

"Never laid a finger on them, even when they deserved it."

"What's your name, honey?"

"Samuel Plummer."

"Belle Pearson." She offers her hand, and Samuel shakes it. Then she turns to her husband and holds up her finger. "Hold on a minute." Belle walks to the front of the bar, leans over it, and whispers something in Herman's ear. He nods, and she puts her fingers to her lips and whistles loudly.

Everyone in the bar turns silent.

"Listen up, everyone! Samuel Plummer here is looking for his two kids, who wandered off. He thinks they might be hiding out somewhere around here. The boy is most likely looking for gold, like all you fools. She turns to Samuel. "What are their names?"

Samuel whispers. "Sam Henry... My daughter's name is Maria."

Belle yells, "Names are Sam Henry and Maria... seventeen and four. He's desperate to find them. Any of you boys seen one or both?"

Men grumble amongst themselves, but no one speaks. Finally, an old miner in the back of the room yells, "Is there a reward?"

Samuel addresses the man. "No reward, but my son, Sam Henry, has long black hair and is half Paiute! Maria has long blond hair."

There's a moment of silence, and then the men go back to drinking and flirting with the barmaids. Samuel turns back to Belle and gives her half a smile. "Thanks for trying."

She pats him on the back. "Don't give up. There are a lot of mining camps, but if those youngsters are around here, someone is bound to see them."

Samuel holds up his glass, salutes Belle, and gulps down the rest of his water. He scans the room again, waves goodbye to Belle, and starts for the swinging door.

Two half-drunk miners meet him there, and the oldest one takes him by the arm. The leather-faced man has scraggly hair and filthy clothes, and his grey fedora is with a huge stain on it. "Listen, we heard your plea for them kids of yours. Boy has long black hair ya say?"

Samuel lifts his head. "That's right. You fellas think you've seen them?"

The youngest miner, a wiry twenty-something with two broken front teeth and a tattered wool coat, stutters, "They ain't… too far… from here… are they, Carl… I mean, Bill?"

Carl stares daggers at his companion and gives him a solid push. Then he turns back to Samuel. "I think your son might have sold us his horse."

Samuel lowers his voice and asks, "Why would he do that?"

"I don't know. Maybe he's like all of us, desperate for money."

"Did he have a little girl with him?"

The young miner starts to say something, but Carl interrupts him before he can speak. "I don't think so, but it was kinda dark."

The young miner points outside. "His horse is behind the bar if ya wanna check him out."

Samuel takes the lead and heads for the back of the saloon as the miners trail close behind. When paving stones turn to grass, he turns back. "What color is the horse?"

Carl waffles, "I don't know, dark brown, maybe black."

When Samuel reaches the vacant lot behind the building, he surveys the area and grumbles, "I don't see any horse." Before he can turn around, he feels a blow to his head. Everything turns black as he crumbles to the ground.

Both thieves quickly empty Samuel's pockets of what money he has left, while the youngest one pulls off Samuel's hat and boots. Then he rolls Samuel over so he can remove his gun and holster.

Carl unfolds the money in his fist and spouts, "Not a lot of money, but enough to get us out of Colorado. Maybe we can sell his pistol too."

Samuel, lying on the ground moaning, starts to move, so the young miner raps him on the head again, and he goes limp. He puts on his victim's hat, sits on the ground, and removes his old kickers. He quickly fits Samuel's boots and crows, "Little too big, but I can make them work."

Carl growls, "All right. Gotta get out of here, for he wakes up again. Take all your old shit with you."

The youngster grabs his old boots and hat, and the thieves hustle back to the street. They look both ways, check to see if anyone is looking, unbridle their horses, and ride out of town.

SAMUEL OPENS HIS EYES and stares at the dark sky lit by hundreds of bright stars and a crescent moon. He puts his weight on one elbow and massages the back of his head. He immediately feels a mass of blood and two egg-sized lumps.

Trying to remember what happened, he looks around for something to cover his wound. Finding nothing, he tears the sleeve of his shirt off and wraps it around his head. After regaining his senses, his thoughts turn to Sam Henry and Maria.

How could he be so stupid as to let those two brutes convince him that they might have seen his children? And why had he been so gullible as to believe Sam Henry would sell his horse, no matter how much he needed the money? A man's most important resource is his horse, especially in a God-forsaken place like this.

He sits up, looks down at his bootless feet, reaches for his gun belt, and puts his hand in his empty pocket. The rest of the money he got from selling all his livestock to the Culbertsons before he left was gone. He sits quietly for a moment and then stumbles to his feet.

As he struggles to the front of the saloon, he thinks about going inside to report what happened, but changes his mind when he realizes the bar is closed.

He looks down the street at the livery stable, remembers his horse is there, and that he had paid the stable man enough so he could spend the night. As he crosses the street, a young couple in a one-horse buggy passes him, and the woman with a blue bonnet looks at his naked feet. She turns to her husband and giggles as Samuel wanders into a livery stable.

THE MORNING SUN bleeds through a small broken window and shines in Samuel's eyes. He groans as he shields his eyes with one hand and massages his head with the other.

He hears a hammer banging on metal, so he stands up, brushes the hay off his clothes, and walks to the corner of the livery stable. There, he finds Barney in front of the fireplace shaping a horseshoe with a ball-peen hammer.

The old-timer lays the hammer down and takes a swig from a whiskey jug. When he looks up, he sees a barefooted Samuel watching him. "Never heard you come in last night. Best be careful walking around here with no boots on. There are a lot of nails and shit."

"Someone stole my boots."

Barney finally notices the bloody handkerchief on his head and his blood-stained shirt and mumbles, "Must have been some poker game for you to lose your boots."

"I got bushwacked behind the saloon. Stole my money, my gun, my hat, and my boots."

"What were you doing behind *Frenchy's*? Nothing back there but trouble."

"It's a long story."

"Fella, you got yourself a lot of long stories. I'd offer you my worn-out boots, but they'd never fit ya. Got an extra shirt, but I'm not giving you one of my guns."

"I heard there's no law around here."

Barney clears his throat. "You heard right. Had us a sheriff, but someone bushwacked him right in front of his house… from a distance like he was some deer."

"Listen, I'm flat-ass broke, but I need to check out the mining camps. Can I leave my horse here a few more hours?"

"This ain't no church. I can't make a living handing out charity."

"If I don't find them or get some money, I'll be out of your hair by the end of the day."

Barney sighs, "You got until the sun goes down."

STILL IN HIS BARE FEET and wearing Barney's much too small flannel shirt and black stocking cap, Samuel walks across the street. En route to the saloon, he looks at *Baxter's General Merchandise and Mining Supplies* building. He makes up his mind and walks into the store.

Behind the cash register is Ruth Baxter. Her hair is up, and she's dressed in a full-length blue gingham dress. She finishes ringing up a local miner's order, and the rough-hewn type turns and walks past Samuel, carrying a pick and shovel.

The store owner overlooks Samuel, turns her back, and opens the door of a 60-pound cast-iron safe. She puts a bag of money inside and shuts it tight.

At the door, the miner shuffles past Samuel, stops suddenly, and stares at the stranger's feet. He grins, shakes his head, and heads out the door.

When Ruth turns back, looks Samuel up and down, bites her lip, tilts her head to the side. "Why don't you have anything on your feet?"

Samuel grimaces. "I got robbed last night. They took everything I had, even my boots."

"Did they hurt you?"

Samuel removes his stocking cap, revealing a blood-soaked handkerchief.

"Bloodied my head pretty good."

"Oh dear, I'll be right back."

Ruth runs into the back room, and when she returns, she's holding a box of gauze pads and a roll of tape.

She motions for him to sit in a chair, and he obliges.

After carefully removing his makeshift bandage and replacing it with a new one, she asks, "Does that feel any better?"

"Much better. Thank you."

He stands up, and she looks at his feet again. "I'm afraid I don't sell boots."

Samuel smirks. "That's okay. I don't have the money to buy them anyway."

"I'm sorry, but if you're looking for a handout, I'm afraid I stopped doing that long ago. Too many repeat customers."

Samuel saddens his face. "How about a job… temporarily… until I get back on my feet, so to speak?"

Ruth narrows her eyes. "Very funny. Why would I waste my time hiring someone leaving in a few days?"

"I don't know… pity. I'm at the end of my tether." Samuel stares at her, but she remains silent. He starts for the door. "I understand. You're right. I wouldn't hire me either."

"What about your wife? Don't you need to get back to her?"

"She died giving birth four years ago."

"I'm sorry." Ruth closes her eyes briefly and lowers her shoulders as Samuel reaches for the doorknob. "Okay, hold on a second. You seem like a nice enough man. The store owner sighs, "All right. I can pay you a dollar a day. Can you start tomorrow?"

"You mean it?"

"Yes, I have supplies that need to be shelved."

Samuel grimaces. "One more thing. You think in a couple of days you can give me some time off to look for my son and daughter?"

"I just hired you, and you already need time off?"

"Yeah, I know. I'm a mess."

"All right, but you'll be here tomorrow, right?"

Samuel smiles. "First thing in the morning."

"Seven am."

"Seven it is." He reaches for the door handle again and turns back. "I hate to ask, but do you think I could have a two-dollar advance? I need my horse fed… and for Barney to let me sleep in his stable another night."

Ruth opens the cash register, removes two dollars, and walks the money to Samuel. "I hope I'm not going to regret this." She looks down at his feet. "What size are your feet?"

"I don't know. Big."

"Stay right there." Ruth walks into the back room. Not sure what to do, Samuel picks up a nearby broom and begins to sweep the floor. When she returns, she is carrying a large pair of brown leather boots, black socks, and a white Stetson cowboy hat. She holds them out and explains, "These are my late husband Robert's. Maybe they'll fit."

He smiles, sets the broom aside, and tries on the hat. It is so big that it hides his eyes. He laughs, hands it back, and says, "Nope. Too nice anyway."

Then he sits down, pulls on the socks, and studies the fancy boots. Two miners walk through the front door and watch as he slides one of the boots onto his foot. Satisfied they fit, he hops up and takes a few steps. "They'll do just fine."

One of the miners looks at Samuel's new footwear and nods at Ruth. "Ma'am, you selling boots now?"

She scoffs, "No, Tom. Now, what can I get you?"

CHAPTER 8

New Job, Going Home, and Instant Family

BUCK WALKS INTO THE KITCHEN as he attaches a badge to his brown leather vest. He pours himself a cup of coffee and sits at a small table. Dressed for the day, Kate enters the room, and his heart races. As she pours herself some coffee, he thinks about how happy he is to have her as his wife. Sure, they had had a few arguments about his decision to take the deputy sheriff job Garfield offered him, but overall, things were good.

Kate had even gotten used to seeing him strap on a gun every morning and hearing his stories at dinnertime about him arresting the town's habitual drunks and wife abusers. Some of the stories he would be amusing if they weren't so sad, like the intoxicated man who left the bar one night, and they found him under his horse the next morning, face down in a pile of horse excrement, not breathing.

When they prayed at night, they always thanked God that he hadn't had to use his gun yet and that no one had shot at him.

Sometimes, Buck even got to see Kate professionally when some drunken brawler got beaten up so bad he needed medical attention. What he didn't tell her was that last week, a man had come at him with a knife when he was trying to arrest him.

Kate takes a seat across from Buck and smiles. "I've been thinking. How would you feel if I started calling you Buckie again?"

"No, I don't think so. I told you I'm not that kid anymore."

"Well, you don't like it when I call you Sweetie Pie or Honey. I need to call you something."

"All right. Call me Buckie, but only at home… when we're alone. Now, what are you up to today?"

"Father and I are going to the Evans' farm this morning to check on them. They were thrown out of their wagon yesterday when they hit a big pothole just outside of town. They have matching broken legs. What about you?"

"You know, the usual… arresting drunks, petty thieves, and derelicts who don't pay their bills."

"And I bet most of them are camped in the Carson City Saloon."

Buck grins. "You got it."

"Has Garfield been treating you all right?"

"Yeah, he asks about you sometimes. All this time, I think he still has a thing for you."

"I hope that's not why he hired you… because he has feelings for me."

"Maybe I should come right out and ask him, Do you still have feelings for my wife?"

Kate slaps her husband's arm. "Buckie, you will do no such thing."

Buck shakes his head from side to side and mutters, "Buckie."

"Well, I had better get to the office. Father will be waiting."

"Before you leave, I have something to ask." Kate nods, and Buck continues, "I haven't seen my father since the wedding, and after Stubborn died, I think he might be lonely. If Garfield will give me a few days off… and if you don't mind, I'd like to go home and spend a few days with him. You can come along if you'd like."

"No, but I know who might want to go with you."

"Who's that?"

"Aunt Margaret. She's been talking about a trip to see your father since they met at our wedding."

"You sure it was my father?"

"Yes, it appears they struck up a friendship."

"How did I miss that?"

"You were too busy looking at me."

"You're right about that. You sure you don't want to go now?"

Kate stands and kisses Buck on the forehead. "No, you go ahead. Besides, I don't know what my father would do without me."

"He's doing all right, isn't he?"

"He's starting to show his age. His hands aren't as steady as they used to be. His thinking is slow… and there's always the laudanum."

Buck hesitates and says, "Still hitting it pretty hard, is he?"

"Afraid so."

THE CARSON CITY SHERIFF'S OFFICE is quiet as Garfield Simpson sits behind his desk strewn with papers, sifting through a stack of wanted posters.

On the other side of the small room, Buck sweeps the floor. The crowded space is filled with the sheriff's desk, two wooden chairs, a pot-bellied stove, and a gun rack to the right of a metal door leading to two jail cells.

On the wall behind the desk is a gun rack with four rifles and a set of jailhouse keys. Buck puts the broom in a corner and waits for the sheriff to look up. When he does, Buck says, "I know I've only been on the job for six weeks, but do you think I could take a few days to see my father?"

"He sick?"

"No, but he's getting older, and it's been a while."

"How long are you thinking?"

"A day getting there, a two-day stay, and a day back… four days."

"Yeah, go ahead. When ya planning on leavin'?"

"Tomorrow too soon?"

"Be takin' Kate with ya I suppose?"

"No, she needs to stay here and help her father."

"Ya got yourself a fine woman. You know that, right?"

"Yeah, I know that."

The sheriff stares at Buck momentarily and picks up another wanted poster.

BUCKLAND STATION IS QUIET as Maria sits atop a corral with a black and white kitten in her lap. She watches as her grandfather breaks apart hay bales and feeds them to a dozen Hereford cows and two Longhorn bulls. Her eyes widen when she sees a bull mount one of the cows. "Grandpa, why is that cow with horns climbing on that other cow?"

Pete takes a breath. "They're being friendly, is all."

"Do they do that instead of shaking hands?"

"Yeah, something like that."

Maria hears a horse whinny in the distance and turns back. She spots Buck's wagon coming their way and almost falls off the top rail. "Grandpa, someone's coming."

Pete squints but can't identify the two people in the wagon. "Let them come."

As the wagon nears the station, Buck and Margaret wave. Pete waves back, narrows his eyes, and finally realizes it's his son with what he assumes is Kate. He yells, "Buckie? Kate? Is that you?"

Pete's son slows his two horses, stops in front of his father and Maria, and hops down while Margaret remains in the wagon. After they hug, Pete realizes the other person in the wagon is Margaret, not Kate. He smiles. "And look who you brought with you."

Pete helps Margaret out of the wagon and flirts with his eyes. "What a pleasant surprise."

"Buck suggested I come along… and since you did invite me for a visit… I thought…"

Pete interrupts, "You thought right."

Maria hops down from the fence, marches to Buck, and studies his face. "Are you my Uncle Buckie?"

"It's Buck." He smiles and looks at his father. "But yes, I think I might be your uncle. Is your name Maria?"

She grins. "Maria Plummer."

Buck looks at his father. "Sandra's girl? Are Samuel and Sam Henry here?"

Before Pete can answer, Maria lifts her chin and says, "Grandpa says I look like my mother."

Pete clarifies. "Sam Henry left her on my doorstep without a word and rode off. It's a mystery where Samuel is."

"How long has she been here?"

"I don't know. A month or more."

"What do you know about taking care of a little girl?"

"Not a whole hell of a lot, but she's teaching me."

Margaret takes Pete's right arm, and he helps her out of the wagon. Then he removes her large travel bag with his left. "How wonderful that you get to spend time with your granddaughter."

"Yeah, but I'm not sure how wonderful it is for her."

Buck grabs his bag, and they all start for the Buckland cabin. Maria tugs on Buck's sleeve. "I'm gonna be five."

A step behind them, Margaret asks Pete, "What do you do with her while you're working?"

"She follows me around. We make do."

Buck overhears his father and turns back. "Pa, she might need some indoor learning… someone to teach her proper manners and the right way of doing things."

"Don't be a smart ass. I know that. I'm teaching her how to read, write, and do her numbers."

Maria points at Buck and chimes, "Don't be a smart ass."

Pete stiffens. "Maria, what'd I tell you about using adult words?"

"That I shouldn't say hell, damn, ass, or shit."

Pete apologizes to Margaret with his eyes and says, "That's right. Now, let your uncle tell us what he has been up to."

Buck removes his badge from his pocket and flashes it at his father. "Got me a new job… Carson City deputy sheriff."

"You gotta be shitting me." Realizing his mistake, he turns to his granddaughter and Margaret and puckers his lips. "Sorry."

Maria smiles. "That's all right, Grandpa. You're an adult."

Buck continues, "Anyway, I got tired of the lumber business. I was going nowhere fast."

"What does Kate think about you being a lawman?"

"She wasn't happy at first, but she's kinda getting used to it."

"Kinda?"

"As long as I don't shoot anyone or someone doesn't shoot me, she'll be fine. So far, so good." Buckie looks over and sees another cross near his mother's grave. "Sorry to hear about Stubborn. I'd have come earlier, but by the time I heard what happened, he'd already been dead a couple of weeks."

Pete softens. "He's right over there, not far from your mother." He turns to Margaret. "Excuse us a minute."

"Not a problem. Maria and I will have a little talk."

Maria smiles. "I like to talk. Do you like to listen?"

"I like to do both."

Pete and his son stroll over to Stubborn's gravesite and remove their sweat-stained hats. Buck looks down at the raised dirt and cross and asks, "How you doin', Stubborn? Wherever you're at, I'm sure you're raising hell by now."

Pete gives his son a curious look as Buck continues. "I'm not suggesting you're in hell or anything, but I gotta admit, you being in heaven stretches my imagination quite a bit. Sorry, I wasn't here when Pa put you to rest. I guess you're all together now… you, Mother, Sandra, even Good Time Jane. Can't say I'm in a hurry to join you, but I miss you. You were never famous, but anyone who knew you will never forget you. Rest easy, my friend."

SEATED AT THE DINNER TABLE, Pete, Margaret, Maria, and Buck help themselves to several slices of boiled beef, mashed potatoes, and raw carrots. Buck holds up his fork. "Good meal, Pa."

Maria interjects. "I peeled the potatoes and Grandpa mashed them."

Margaret taps her on the shoulder. "Good job. They're so white… no black spots at all."

"Grandpa taught me… Uncle Buckie… Buck, did Grandpa teach you anything?"

"Let's see now. What did he teach me? He taught me to work hard, love hard, how to treat a woman like an equal… and oh… how to hook horses up to a wagon."

Margaret reaches over and pats Pete on the hand. Embarrassed, Pete changes the subject. "So, Buckie, how's married life? Got a young'un in the hopper yet?"

Margaret smirks at Pete, and Buck responds, "It's only been a few months, Pa. Not sure that's gonna happen anytime soon. We kind of like things being quiet."

Pete tightens his jaw. "You know what the good book says, 'Be fruitful and multiply'… but you're right. If your offspring are anything like you and your sister, there will be a lot of noise."

Buck grins again. "I'll keep that in mind."

THE EVENING MOON'S LIGHT shines through a small window in the living room as Kate, dressed for bed in a white cotton nightgown, starts to turn out the kerosene lamp when she hears a knock. She slips into a robe, walks to the front door, and slowly opens it. Standing front and center is Sheriff Simpson. "Garfield? What are you doing here?"

The sheriff removes his hat and pushes the door open further so he can see Kate's full profile. "Figured I'd check on you since Buck's out of town."

Kate grips the top of her robe and steps back as Garfield fills the doorway. "Did he ask you to check on me?"

"No, just a professional courtesy…. You being alone and all."

"I'm doing fine. I was about to go to bed."

The sheriff tries to move forward. Kate doesn't move, so he rocks back. "I see. I won't keep you then." He pivots to leave but turns back. "Kate, I'd be remiss if I didn't say you're looking mighty fine this evening."

"That's nice of you to say, but I need to go to bed now. I have an early morning appointment."

"I see… One last thing I've been meaning to ask you for a while now."

"What might that be?"

"You remember our first kiss, right?"

Kate raises her eyebrows. "I'm not sure I like the direction this is going."

He frowns. "Just humor me."

"Okay, I do remember. It was our only kiss. You forced yourself on me, and I was too afraid to push you away."

"Huh, I don't picture it that way at all. Felt to me like you was more than willing."

"Perhaps you suffer from memory loss… or maybe you need some kind of therapy."

Garfield chuckles. "Always got you a clever comeback, don't you? Kate, that's one of the things I like about you. But now that you're a married woman, I'm sure you're spoiled… getting all the compliments and affection you need from Buck."

"I don't think that's any of your business. I'm going to close the door now. And please don't check on me again."

The sheriff backs away, and the door shuts. Outside, he looks at the moon, fits his hat, and shuffles away.

ALONG A SMALL UNNAMED CREEK, not far from Buckland Station, Pete and Margaret stroll alongside each other, enjoying the colorful sights and fragrant smells of a cool fall morning. As butterflies flutter above their heads, Pete reaches down and pinches off a wild sunflower. He sniffs it and hands it to Margaret. She smiles, takes his hand, and leads him to the edge of the creek.

They find a quiet spot on the Indian rice grass near the creek and sit. Finally, Pete says, "My wife and I used to come here a lot, especially at this time of year."

"I'll bet you miss her a lot."

"I do, but do you know what bothers me most about her being gone?

"What's that?"

"She didn't get to live a full life. Why do some people get to live longer than others?"

"That's a good question. Remind me to ask God. Forgive me for asking, but how did she die?"

"While I was in town picking up supplies, I found out the Paiutes were on the warpath not far from our place. By the time I got home, they had killed Maria, kidnapped my daughter, and left my son and a good friend for dead… not to mention they burned down our cabin. Buckie survived, but our friend, Jane, didn't."

"I had no idea."

"Yeah, this place has a lot of memories… some of them not so good. What about you? How did you lose your husband?"

"Nothing as dramatic as your story. I lost Charles six years ago. He died of cancer."

Pete tightens his lips. "That goes back to what I was saying earlier… good people dying young, while a considerable number of evil people go on living."

"Not trying to quote scripture at you, but Jesus said this about God the Father: *He makes his sun rise on the evil and on the good, and sends rain on the just and on the unjust.*'"

Pete nods. "Yep, that about sums it up." He smiles at Margaret as his cheeks start to redden. "Think maybe I could have me a kiss? It's been a long time."

Margaret grins. "I don't know. What are my eyes telling you?"

"I think they're saying, go ahead and help yourself." Pete leans over and kisses Margaret full on the mouth. He pulls away and considers what he just did. "Wow, that was worth the ask."

They hold each other briefly, stand up, and take turns gawking at one another as they stroll back to the cabin.

When they reach the Buckland homestead, Pete takes Margaret by the arm and says, "I need your thoughts on something."

"I'm listening."

"Maria and I have been getting along real well, but I think she needs more than I can give her. Do you think my son and his new bride would take her in… at least until her father or brother comes to claim her?"

"Well, I can't speak for them. That would be their decision. But, if you and your son decide it would be better for Maria to live in Carson City, I'd be willing to help them out."

FATHER AND SON are replacing a fence post. Buck drops a pine pole in a two-foot hole, clears his throat, and wipes his brow. "Good to have you home, son… and it's sure nice having a woman in the house again."

"It's good to be home." Buck looks at the cabin. "So, I guess Margaret and Maria are still taking a nap?"

"Yep, that girl sleeps two hours every afternoon. Gives me some alone time."

"You and Margaret seem like a good match."

Pete grins. "Ya think so? We're getting to know each other… a little at a time."

"It's okay for you to love someone else, Pa. Mom's been gone a long time."

"Yeah, after you left and Stubborn died, I was fighting off bein' lonely. Then Maria showed up."

Buck nods. "You gonna keep raising her as your own?"

"I don't think that's a good idea. Here's the thing. She's a sweet thing, but she needs a real family… and a woman's touch."

"Maybe her father or Sam Henry will show up soon."

"I think if they ever do, it won't be for a while. You don't suppose you and Kate…"

Buck interrupts his father. "No. You can't ask that. Kate and I just got married. We have jobs. Neither one of us is at home during the day."

"Margaret said she'd help out. Maria would be in school most of the day. She needs to be around other kids her age, not some old dirt farmer like me. She's all alone here, nobody to talk to but me."

"Sandra and I were raised alone."

Pete smirks. "Yeah, and look how you turned out." Pete laughs. "I'm joking, but you had your mother teaching you to be smart and how to behave."

"She's your granddaughter."

"And you're her only uncle. She deserves the best."

He lowers his head. "Let me think on it a while."

THE EARLY MORNING SUN PEEKS over the Sierra Nevada Mountains as Buck, Margaret, and Maria ride towards Carson City. Seated in the back of the wagon on a blanket, Margaret shows Maria how to crochet while up front, Buck thinks about what's in store for him when he gets home.

What has he gotten himself into, and what will Kate say when he shows up with Maria, someone she's never met? He figured Kate wasn't ready for a family yet. They hadn't even gotten around to talking about having children. Maybe Maria would only be with them for a week or two. Surely, Samuel will come around soon looking for his daughter. And what about Sam Henry? Why did he drop his sister off at his grandpa's doorstep like she was some orphan child? There's got to be a story there.

Maria breaks the silence when she says, "My butt is sore. When are we gonna get to Carson City?"

Margaret tries to help. "It's only another five miles. We're almost there."

"Are the people there nice?"

Buck guffaws, "Most are, some not so much."

"I'm not going to live with Grandpa anymore?"

Buck reminds her of what he told her earlier. "That's because he thinks you'd be happier in a town with Kate and me… and Aunt Margaret. Your grandpa doesn't think he's good at taking care of little girls."

"He was doing a good job taking care of me," Maria argues.

"I know, but Carson City has a school where there will be a lot of kids your age."

Maria starts to cry. "Pa didn't want me, Sam Henry didn't want me, and now Grandpa doesn't want me."

Buck brings the horse to a stop, pulls Maria close to him, and hugs her. She wrinkles her face, pushes him away, and says, "I can't breathe."

ON THE OUTSKIRTS of Carson City, Maria's eyes sparkle. Her voice rises when she sees chimney smoke in the distance. Uncle Buckie, "I've never lived in a town before."

He looks at her and says, "I told you, no more Buckie. People around here call me Buck."

Maria grins. "But I like Buckie."

"I know, but you can only call me that when we're alone or with Kate and me… or Aunt Margaret. I'm Buck the rest of the time, okay?"

"Okay, Buckie."

When they reach Carson City, Buck parks the wagon in front of the house and helps Margaret down from the wagon like she's an old lady. Buck hands Kate's aunt her bag, and Margaret reaches down and hugs Maria goodbye. "I'll be seeing you later, young lady." As she walks away, she pivots back and says, "Tell Kate hello for me. I need to get home before I fall over."

Margaret walks off as Buck lifts his niece out of the wagon. He takes her by the hand, grabs both bags from the wagon with his other hand, and they walk to the front door.

He drops their bags on the porch and is about to open the front door when Kate walks around the corner of the house and smiles. She immediately notices Maria and smiles. "And who do we have here?"

The four-year-old raises her chin and says, "Are you Kate?"

"Why yes, I am."

Maria wrinkles her nose. "You're pretty."

"Well, thank you. You're also pretty, and I like your hair."

"Grandpa lets me comb it by myself."

Kate stares at her husband until he explains, "Kate, this is Maria, my sister's daughter, and my mother's namesake."

"And you brought her here for a visit?"

"Yeah, we need to talk." He takes his wife aside and begins to whisper. "I brought her to live with us… until either her father or brother comes back for her."

"And when will that be?"

"Honestly, I have no idea."

Maria, who has been listening in, bites her lower lip. "You don't want me either?"

Kate turns her way. "Oh no, darling. Your Uncle Buck's announcement took me by surprise, is all."

Maria points at her uncle. "He says we can only call him Buckie, but no one else can."

Kate smiles. "Yes. We will have to figure this whole name thing out. It's confusing."

Maria tugs on Kate's arm. "Do you have any cats?

"No, we don't."

"I had to leave my cat behind… Sally. Grandpa said it would have been too hard on her… and he needs her to eat the mice."

"You're grandpa is probably right."

BUCK AND KATE are lying in bed. They both stare at the ceiling until Buck finally breaks the ice. "You think she'll be all right sleeping on those blankets until we find another bed?"

Kate takes her time. "She'll be fine for now, but what are we going to do with her when we both go to work?"

"Like I told you, Margaret is willing to help out. She can watch her most every day… at least for now." He continues, "We can send her to school, right?"

"How old is she?"

"She told Pa she was four when she showed up at the cabin, but she says she's almost five."

"That's not old enough," Kate tells him. "She needs to be at least six before she can go to school."

"She already knows how to read. We can claim she's six. No one will know."

"We can't do that. She barely looks to be four. The teacher will know she's too young."

"I don't know. She's awfully smart. We could always say she's small for her age. And if Margaret can't watch her, I can always take her to work with me. Make her a deputy or lock her in a cell… I don't know."

Kate slaps his arm. "Stop. You're not funny. Put her in a cell. I guess I can take her to the office with me sometimes."

"There you go. We'll figure it out." Buck reaches over and takes Kate's hand. "Are you upset with me?"

"No, Maria's a sweet girl who needs a home. I just wasn't prepared for motherhood yet."

"You can't blame me. I've been trying to change that. Besides, this will be good practice to see if we want kids or not."

Kate slaps his arm again. "Come on. We need to make her some breakfast."

CHAPTER 9

Shilah, Evil White Men, and Lake Tahoe

INSIDE A CONE-SHAPED PAIUTE LODGE, Sam Henry, with a new Indian name, Shilah, meaning *Brother*, is seated cross-legged next to his grandfather, Chief Winnemucca.

The Paiute tribal leader and his grandson are dressed in traditional rabbit fur robes that cover their sagebrush bark aprons and deerskin breechcloths. Their knee-high leather leggings are decorated with colorful glass beads and porcupine quills, and Shilah's long hair is pulled back and braided like his grandfather's.

Winnemucca hands Shilah a feather-decorated clay pipe, and he takes a long meditative drag. When he releases the smoke from his mouth, it filters into his nostrils, and he coughs.

Seated in the corner of the lodge, a few feet away, Tuboitonie, Winnemucca's newest wife, and Pamahas, their youngest daughter, giggle. Winnemucca glares at them, and they go back to making baskets from the fibers of willow and sagebrush.

The chief takes the pipe from Shilah, sucks on it, blows smoke in the air, and it hovers above his head. He offers it to his grandson again, but Shilah waves it away and apologizes, "Sorry, it's making me sick."

In broken English, Winnemucca says, "Your father, Numaga… he no smoke pipe either." There's a moment of silence, and then Winnemucca whispers to Shilah. "I see you look at Pamahas. You wish her to be your woman?"

"No, thank you. She is old enough to be my mother… and if she's your granddaughter, that would make her my aunt."

Winnemucca cackles. "Pamahas is not Numaga's sister. She is my daughter by… what you say… another woman."

"Still, we're kind of related."

Shilah climbs to his feet and starts for the lodge's exit. "I must leave now, Grandfather. I am going with the other hunters to look for food for our people."

WOVAKA, THE HUGE PAIUTE who took Sam Henry hostage and introduced him to his grandfather, is mounted on a brown and white pinto. Next to him are five other red and white face-painted Paiute hunters. As they prepare to leave the village, Shilah rides up to the hunting party and nods.

The deer and antelope hunting leader, Wovaka, grunts in broken English. "You are late, Washo. That is not the Paiute way. You will ride behind us and watch our riderless horses."

Shilah responds by slowing his horse and tucking in behind the other hunters. He takes the reins of the two pack horses designated to bring their bounty home and thinks back over the last two months and all the changes that have taken place in his life.

Wovaka had proven himself to be a good friend. He could speak English and French, and he taught him to shoot an arrow straight, dress like a hunter, and behave like a Paiute. He even gave him one of his knives and taught him how to use it.

His desire to leave the village and his new Paiute family had diminished with each passing day. He stopped thinking about looking for his fortune in Tin Cup after only a few days and started to feel comfortable living the life of an Indian with his father's people.

He missed his sister, and though he would never admit it, he missed Samuel. And, of course, there was Natalie. Sometimes at night, he would pleasure himself thinking about her… imagining her naked body that he had never seen. He had promised he would return to her, but he didn't know how he would do that because, for now, he was living the life of a Paiute.

Armed with rifles, knives, bows and arrows, axes, rabbit sticks, harpoons, and fishing nets, the seven hunters ride off. The early fall morning is cool as several children and dogs run behind them. Out of breath, they give up when they reach the edge of the village.

The older boys continue the chase until the warriors' horses break into a full gallop.

Minutes later, the Paiutes slow their horses to a walk, and Shilah again contemplates his decision to become a Paiute.

They had made him feel special. Even held a ceremony for him and put him in the center of a circle of costumed men and women who danced and sang songs he did not understand. They lifted his arms in the air like some tribal hero.

When evening came, two elderly women offered him a young girl named Chenoa to spend the night with. He was tempted by her golden skin, appealing shape, and long black hair, but all he could think of was Natalie, who was waiting for him at home.

He understood why he was being welcomed in such a manner by the tribe. It was because he was Winnemucca's grandson and Numaga's son, the man who had stolen his mother and was responsible for the deaths of his grandmother, and Buckie's friend, Good Time Jane Fields, a runaway slave.

His deep thoughts end when a large jackrabbit spooks his horse. He rides forward with the two pack horses in tow and joins Wovaka. "Where are we going?"

The leather-faced leader looks at the mountains to his west and points in the direction they are riding. "We go to the lake they call Tahoe. Washoe come each year to hunt, fish, and trade with the white man… before winter comes."

"You mean a rendezvous? Shilah asks."

"Yes, rendezvous. You speak like the French?"

"No. That's the only word I know."

Wovaka continues. "Traders come from all directions… speak many languages."

"Yeah, that's a rendezvous… but we are not Washoe."

"Not all Washoe look the same. We will… What is the English word?

Shilah offers, "Blend, mix, mingle, merge?"

"Yes, all of those words."

"But they are our enemies. What will happen if they find out we are Paiutes?"

"The white man in you asks too many questions."

"I just want to know if you have a plan."

"We will not speak to anyone. We will fish their waters, hunt their game, gather their sacred pinons, and leave like a silent breeze."

As Shilah falls to the back of the shapeless formation, he wonders what Natalie would think of him now. Would his looks frighten her, or would she understand he was the same person who had ridden away months earlier? How much longer will he stay with his father's people? Will he slip away in the middle of the night when he gets the chance, or will he remain an Indian, marry an Indian maiden, and live the rest of his life as a Paiute?

WHEN THE BAND OF HUNTERS reaches the California border and the high-altitude Tahoe Basin, Wovaka scans the area and shifts his eyes to his comrades. In his native Paiute language, he spouts, "They are removing the sacred trees."

Shilah nods in agreement as he looks to his far right and sees a dozen men using axes and cross-cut saws to bring down evergreen trees in the patch-patterned forest circling Lake Tahoe.

West of them and not far from the lake, men in freight wagons wait as lumberjacks roll clean-shaven logs in their direction. In the distance, the men and women working at a sash sawmill on the west side of the lake stand waiting for the next delivery wagon to arrive.

On the east side of the lake are several makeshift dwellings and tents occupied by regional Washoe and white traders from California, Nevada, Washington Territory, and Western Canada. Milling about not far from the lake shore, Washoe men and women exchange furs, handmade blankets, and clothing for metal knives, rifles, and other man-made merchandise.

Keeping their distance, Wovaka takes the lead, and the Paiutes disappear into the Jeffrey pine trees a quarter mile from the south end of the lake.

They find a small grassy meadow hidden in the trees and quickly construct two shelters from deadfall logs, fallen limbs, and low-lying pine tree branches.

Before the sun stops peeking through the nearby trees, two Paiutes pile dry twigs and branches together and manage to start a fire by slapping two pieces of flint stone together.

THE NEXT MORNING, armed with bows and arrows, the hunters break into pairs. Wovaka points at the youngest Paiute, who lowers his head, realizing he has been chosen to watch the horses and rifles.

The others quickly disappear into the trees, headed in three directions. Shilah, teamed with Wovaka, follows him into the forest, dodging branches and hopping over deadfall trees.

Deep in the woods, Wovaka stops suddenly and holds up his right hand. Fifty feet away, frozen behind a giant Ponderosa Pine, a large bull elk lifts his head, revealing a large rack of ashen white antlers. He raises his bow, and both men wait patiently as the bearded elk grazes on a shrub and the dry grass below it. He slowly turns his head to Shilah, and the first-time elk hunter quietly fits an arrow into his bow.

The eight-hundred-pound animal moves forward, exposing himself, and the hunters draw back their arrows.

Wovaka takes a shallow breath and nods at Shilah.

Two arrows fly as the elk looks up, sensing something's wrong.

Before the massive animal can move, an arrow hits him in the neck while another one buries itself in his rear flank. The tan and white-rumped beast takes a few steps, grunts, drops to his knees, and emits a long, high-pitched bugle.

In a nearby cold stream stands Rupert Weed, the killer Samuel Henry's father had met on the streets of Tin Cup a few weeks earlier. The Tin Cup miner raises his metal pan, turns in the direction where the elk blared, swivels back to his two card-playing friends, and whispers loudly, "Hear that? That's dinner calling." The three men grab their rifles from the creek bank and head for the trees.

A quarter mile away, the Paiute hunters stand admiring the dead elk. Blood seeps from the animal's nostrils as they decide what to do next. Finally, Wovaka says, "Go back and get the pack horses. We can't move this beast without them."

Shilah looks down at the huge, glassy-eyed elk and brags, "My first kill with a bow and arrow. Shot a deer with a rifle once, but he wasn't half this size."

"I will make him ready to be carried."

Shilah trots off and quietly disappears into the trees. Wovaka doesn't waste any time as he draws his knife and prepares to gut the animal. Before he can make his first cut, he hears twigs breaking and the sound of three miners approaching.

He picks up his bow, fits an arrow, and waits. When Rupert and his men emerge from a grove of trees, their rifles drawn, the miners are surprised to see the Paiute brave standing with his bow and arrow aimed directly at them. Rupert chuckles, "What we got here? Appears you're providing dinner for me and my boys."

The Indian tightens his grip on his bow and pulls back the string.

The three intruders step back.

Rupert tightens his teeth and snarls, "What ya gonna do, chief, stick all three of us with one arrow?"

Wovaka points. "Only you… big talker."

Rupert grins. "Well, now. An Indian who speaks English."

"When I need to."

"Most of the time I can tell a tribe by looking at a face," Rupert says. "You ain't no Washoe."

Wovaka doesn't respond, so Rupert tightens his grip on his rifle. "You willing to die on account of some piece of meat?"

"It's my meat."

"You're one mulish Indian."

Milton Young, a young miner with a lazy eye and pot-marked skin, voices his opinion. "Rupert, we don't wanna kill him. Washoe or not, the Indians outnumber us around here. They hear shots, they'll come runnin'."

Rupert growls, "Shut up, Milton! If I want your belief, I'll ask for it." The gangly third miner starts to say something, but changes his mind.

Before Rupert can say anything else, Shilah approaches from the trees, aiming his rifle at the intruders.

Rupert shifts his rifle, aims it at Shilah, and sputters, "Now what do we have here? Another damn Indian?" The horses neigh in the trees where Shilah exited, and Ruppert adds, "Don't suppose there are more of you in there?"

Shilah lies. "A dozen… all aiming at your chests."

"You talk awful white to be an Indian."

"We don't want any trouble, mister." Shilah reasons. "Leave before someone gets hurt."

Rupert growls, "Guess it all comes down to how many of us are willing to take a chance on dying for a good meal. How about sharing? Ya got plenty to go around."

Shilah adjusts his rifle. "This elk is gonna feed our people."

"Huh. Guess we got ourselves a situation." Rupert stares at the trees. "All right, you win, but if I ever see you again, your living is over." Rupert lowers his rifle and steps back. "Not gonna shoot us in the back now, are ya?"

"No, go!" Shilah says.

"Just in case." Rupert and his friends back away, but keep their rifles aimed at Shilah and Wovaka. After they disappear into the trees, Rupert yells, "You haven't seen the last of us, ya heathens!"

Wovaka lowers his bow and turns to Shilah. "Where are the horses?"

Shilah grins. "Tied them to a tree so I could come save you."

"I didn't need to be saved."

"Three-to-one odds. It didn't look good to me."

"The white man always outnumbers the Indian. Enough talk. We need to get our kill back to camp."

SHILAH AND WOVAKA vacate the pine trees and enter their campsite with the pieces of the butchered elk draped over the two pack horses. Shilah and Wovaka snicker when they see the small game lying on the ground, including pheasants, grouse, turkeys, and rabbits.

Shilah proudly points at the butchered elk and raises his clenched fist. His feathered companions grunt and turn away.

In the Paiute language, Wovaka says, "We can't go home with so little meat. One elk, six birds, and small fur animals. They are not worthy of our journey. We need deer and antelope, but we must hurry, or what we have will be unfit to eat."

Shilah thinks he knows what Wovaka just said and speaks his mind. "We brought rifles. Why don't we use them? Traps and arrows are only good for smaller animals. We were lucky to kill the elk. We cannot get close enough with bows and arrows to kill deer and antelope."

Wovaka argues in English. "If we fire our rifles, white men and Washoe will come. They will steal what little meat we have, take our weapons, and end our lives."

Shilah counters. "When we left our village, you said we might have to blend in with the locals. There are many kinds of Washoe gathered here, so let's be Washoe. If we are forced to talk, we can speak English… you and me… the others can remain silent."

Wavaka sniffs the air. "Lots of words. You talk like a white man."

"Coming here was your idea. We need to make the best of it."

THE SEVEN PAIUTES ride along the shore of Lake Tahoe with their bounty covered with wool blankets on trailing pack horses.

With their heads lowered, they pass lumberjacks, mill workers, vendors selling food and drink, and groups of Washoe and white traders bartering over animal hides, guns, knives, and jugs of corn whiskey.

They approach an even larger group of traders, including several drunk white fur traders, Tin Cup miners, and Washoe. Shilah spots Rupert Weed and his two colleagues and looks away. They don't notice him because the miners are arguing with several Washoe men over the value of their shovels and pick axes.

The Washoe speak loudly, hold up their hides and handmade jewelry, and tout their value. Meanwhile, several white fur traders use the distraction to flirt with the Washoe men's wives and teenage daughters.

Rupert finally notices the band of Paiutes as they ride away. He spots Wavaka and Shilah and sneers, "Paiute trash."

Shilah avoids eye contact by turning his head and staring at the lake while Wavaka glowers at Rupert until the reprobate growls, "You still got my elk, asshole?"

Wavaka turns and looks straight ahead as Rupert tries again. "Gonna get my revenge. Wait and see." Rupert watches the silent hunters ride off, loses interest, and turns back to his drunken friends.

On the east end of Lake Tahoe, Wavaka and three other Paiutes ride off to hunt for deer while Shilah and the other two ride in another direction.

SHILAH AND HIS COMPANIONS busy themselves harvesting pinion nuts from small pine trees lining the side of a steep hill overlooking Lake Tahoe as two bald eagles overhead head for their high mountain nests.

Shilah stuffs his mouth full and spits out the shells as he fills his small basket with the edible seeds. The other two Paiutes finish filling their baskets, empty the nuts into canvas bags, and strap them to their horses.

Shilah is about to mount his horse when two twenty-something Washoe women wearing deerskin dresses emerge from the nearby white firs. Surprised to see the strangers in their private pinion gathering place, they step back and defiantly squeeze their arms across their chests.

The women glare at him as Shilah walks toward them. He raises his chin, and the oldest girl raises her eyebrows and in her native Washoe language, says, "Our pinion trees."

Shilah hears the word pinion and says in English, "We didn't mean to interfere. We'll be on our way."

As the three Paiutes mount their horses, the young women stare at the pack horses with the partially uncovered elk meat strapped to them. Shilah hops down from his horse and covers the meat.

The Washoe women whisper to each other as Wovaka and the other three hunters arrive with two deer secured to the other pack horse.

Wovaka sees the women, turns to Shilah, and asks, "Do they know we are Paiutes?"

"I don't know, but they know we don't belong here. I spoke to them in English, but they didn't answer back. One thing for sure: they're not happy about us taking their pine nuts."

Wovaka signals with his hands for the women to remain calm, but they panic and run for the white fir trees. He raises his rifle as if to shoot, but Shilah reaches over and pushes his gun aside. "You can't kill them because they caught us stealing some damn pinions."

"They know we're Paiutes. They will tell all the Washoe they know."

Shilah raises his chin. "Then it's time to go home."

A SUDDEN DROP in temperature envelops the area, and a thick fog covers the ground five miles east of Lake Tahoe as the Paiutes make their way home. The ghostlike conditions worsen as a cold wind picks up, causing the hunters to lower their heads and cover their shoulders with wool blankets and buffalo hides.

Large snowflakes begin to fall, blinding both the men and the horses. As they pass through a narrow valley cutting through the Sierra Nevada Mountains, Shilah looks up and sees two bighorn sheep on a cliff looking his way. Suddenly, they turn, look the other way, and bound off.

Shilah hears faint voices and whinnying on the ridge ahead but sees nothing unusual. Before he can react, a volley of gunshots echoes through the canyon. Shilah looks to his left and watches as three of his companions are pelted with bullets.

As if in slow motion, they fall from their horses and hit the ground, already dead. Two have mortal wounds to their chests, and the other one has a large bullet hole above the bridge of his nose.

When Shilah looks in the direction the shots came from, his fellow Paiutes, including Wovaka, grab their rifles, slide off their horses, and look for cover. Before they can find a place to hide, two more hunters are riddled with bullets from a bluff behind them.

As Shilah unfastens his rifle, two more bullets hit his horse in the chest, and it drops to its knees. He rolls off the groaning stead and hops to his feet, avoiding three more bullets that strike the ground behind him.

He sees Wovaka and rushes over to him. They drop to their knees and crawl towards the tall pine trees a hundred feet away. Bullets fly past, splatting the wet ground around them until the desperate men reach the tall evergreens.

Safe behind the trees, the two remaining Paiutes stagger to their feet. Shilah looks through the tree branches and into the fog, where he sees Rupert Weed, Milton Young, and four other Colorado miners celebrating their victory.

Wovaka and Shilah glare at the miners as the killers examine the Paiute horses and look under the blankets of the pack horses at the meat meant to feed the Paiute village.

Enraged by the death of his Indian brothers, Wovaka aims his rifle at Rupert and fires, grazing the Tin Cup miner in the arm. Rupert drops to the ground, grabs his arm, and screams, "God damn it! Kill them fuckin' Indians! There are two more in the trees!"

Before they can fire again, the miners rattle the trees with a barrage of bullets, one hitting Wovaka in his right thigh.

Realizing they are outnumbered and have limited firepower, Shilah shoulders Wovaka, and they stumble deeper into the woods.

As the snow continues to fall and the tendrils of fog wrap around them, Shilah helps his friend move at a moderate pace. Behind them, they hear the miners grumbling as they close in on the slow-moving Paiutes.

His leg bleeding badly, Wovaka sinks to the ground, and Shilah pulls him back up. In the distance, they hear Rupert yell, "Over here. At least one of them is a bleeder!"

Unable to walk anymore, the Paiute leader points at a tree and says, "Put me against the tree. You go."

Shilah insists, "I am not leaving you."

"Why should you die? Stay alive and seek revenge for me and our brothers."

The voices are growing louder as Shilah helps his friend sit down at the base of a large pine tree. He takes his friend's weapon and says, "I will try my best to fend them off."

"No, they will kill us both. Hide yourself."

Shilah looks around as the voices grow louder. Finally, he starts to climb the tall tree where Wovaka is resting.

Struggling to balance the rifle as he climbs, he manages to reach the top of the tree, where he finds a thick branch behind a cluster of branches. As he secures his position, he hears the miners below hooting and hollering, having found the wounded Paiute under the tree.

Shilah peeks through the needled branches and sees his friend thrusting his Bowie knife at the six jeering miners. Milton laughs. "I'm real scared! Watch out, boys. Chief here has got himself a big knife."

Rupert hisses, "What ya gonna do, stab all of us to death?" Rupert touches the wound on his arm and adds, "See what you did? Now, I'm gonna kill you like you was nothin'."

Milton steps forward again and grins. "Make you a deal chief, tell us what direction your chicken shit partner ran off to and I'll give you five more minutes to live."

Without hesitating, Wovaka throws his knife and hits Milton square in the chest. Milton lowers his head and stares in disbelief as his shirt turns bloody. The other men watch as he removes the knife. Instantly, spurts of blood like a small fountain squirt from the deep wound in his chest with every beat of his heart.

Confused, Milton leans over and makes a deep guttural noise like someone with consumption and coughs up blood. He looks at Ruppert, pleads with his eyes for help, drops to his knees, and falls face down on the forest floor.

All the miners except for Rupert pull their pistols and pepper the Indian's torso with bullets. Rupert rolls the young miner over and pulls the knife from Milton's chest. Then he walks over to Wovaka. He lifts his chin and with one swipe of the knife removes his scalp. He stares at it and tosses it aside.

Perched directly above them, looking down, Shilah aims his rifle at Rupert and prepares to fire. He skips a beat, thinks better of it, and lowers his weapon.

Now kneeling at Milton's side, Ruppert makes sure he is dead by lifting his eyelids. Satisfied, he stands, points at the surrounding trees, and commands, "Let's find that other Paiute bastard and cut his balls off! We'll bury Milton when we get back."

The other four miners follow Rupert into the pine trees and start to look for any sign of the second Indian. Ruppert commands, "We'll split up." He points left. "Frank and Dusty, you go lookin' in them willow trees over yonder. Me, Leonard, and George will head the other way. We'll meet back here in a few minutes."

As the five men hurry off to look for the surviving Paiute, Shilah slides down from his hiding tree and quietly walks over to

Wovaka. His face darkens when he sees the bloody top of his friend's head.

Angry, he lays Wovaka's rifle on the ground, removes his knife from its sheath, and walks over to Milton.

SHILAH EMERGES from the grove of trees and sheaths his knife. Still equipped with Wovaka's rifle, he looks at the freshly fallen snow and starts to follow the tracks of the men who are pursuing him.

When he hears voices in the distance, he trails the sound, finds a large tree, and hides behind it.

His head spins as he waits for a chance to avenge Wovaka's death. If he gets the chance, should he fire at the two men and risk that the other miners will hear the shots and come running… or should he wait?

Before he can make up his mind, the youngest of the two miners, Dusty Mills, dressed in a blue flannel shirt with a red kerchief, informs his partner, Frank Keller, "I gotta take a whiz… be right back."

The slim twenty-five-year-old heads in Shilah's direction, so he slides over and hides behind another tree a few feet away. When Dusty lowers his pants, Shilah removes his knife and quietly circles the tree.

Having never killed a man before, he freezes for a second. When the young man turns back, Shilah grabs his head and slits his throat from ear to ear. As the blood flows freely, Dusty starts to groan, so Shilah covers his mouth until he sinks to the ground.

Growing impatient, Frank yells out, "What the hell, Dusty? We ain't got all day!" The older miner waits a little longer and then starts in the direction he saw his partner go. When he reaches the spot where he thinks Dusty might have gone, he sees a pair of legs sticking out from behind the tree. His face tightens as he smells the odor of blood and piss.

Before Frank can react, Shilah swings around the tree and buries his knife in the older miner's stomach. Frank staggers back with his arms flailing, stumbles forward, and reaches out like he expects his attacker to help him.

Shilah steps back and watches as Frank leans over, brushes some snow away from the forest floor, and sits down like he's preparing to eat a picnic lunch. The miner's breathing turns raspy, his eyes close, and he topples over.

Thinking the second miner is dead, Shilah turns his back. Behind him, the mortally wounded man opens his eyes again and grips his pistol. Too weak to clear it from his holster, Frank still manages to pull the trigger. The shot echoes through the trees, warning the other miners a quarter mile away.

Shilah spins around, grips his knife in one hand and his rifle in the other, ready to either stab the miner a second time or shoot him. Before he can respond, the miner takes a final breath and dies.

Distraught over having killed another man, Shilah tries to make some sense of what just happened. Did the men he killed have wives? Did they have children? Would anyone miss them?

A crow caws in the distance, and his thoughts shift to his survival. He quickly climbs the tree where he killed Dusty. When he reaches the top, clutching Wovaka's rifle in his off-hand, he manages to find a secure branch to sit on.

As he looks down, the three remaining miners enter the clearing with their rifles at the ready. The men approach the tree where Shilah is hidden and stare at their friends' dead bodies. Rupert spews, "That coward can't be too far. I can smell him."

Leonard Sparks, a pale-faced Californian with buck teeth, snarls, "Rupert, he's already killed three of us. I say we leave. He ain't worth dying over."

Rupert growls and aims his rifle at him. "We ain't goin' nowhere. That fuckin' Indian's not gettin' away with this."

For some reason, Leonard looks to the top of the tree where he sees Shilah aiming his rifle at him. Before he can open his mouth, Shilah squeezes the trigger, sending a bullet into Leonard's forehead. He crumbles to the ground while Rupert and George Murphy, a fat-faced Irishman, fire away at the top of the tree.

Shilah shoots again and hits the oversized miner in the stomach. Rupert blasts away while gut-shot George, now clutching his stomach, gasps for air.

George reaches out and grabs Rupert's arm for support, but the renegade pushes him away. The big man stumbles to the ground and takes his last breath as Ruppert empties his rifle at the top of the tree.

By chance, Rupert's final bullet hits the branch that Shilah is sitting on. It cracks, and he falls through the tree limbs to the ground. Dazed by the sudden impact, Shilah manages to sit up and remove his knife.

Ruppert smiles and aims his rifle at him. "Time to meet your maker, red man." Shilah stares straight ahead as the villain squeezes the trigger… click… empty. The rogue reaches for his pistol, but his holster is empty. "Damn, my luck!" He checks the ground and sees it lying next to George's dead body.

Before Rupert can retrieve it, Wovaka's rifle falls out of the tree and lands at Shilah's feet. He scoots over and picks it up before Rupert can retrieve his pistol. The last miner standing panics and runs off into the trees.

When the coward reaches the clearing, he sees Wovaka still propped up against the tree. He looks down, sees a bloody scalp in the Indian's hand, and hollers, "What the hell!"

When he pivots around, he spots Milton lying face up with the top of his head cut off.

Ruppert runs off again. A quarter mile later, out of breath, he slows to a walk. As he struggles to push his way through the thick brush, he looks back and begins to whimper, thinking Shilah might be right behind him.

He hurries off again, emerges from the trees, and sees a dozen horses milling around and four dead Paiutes lying on the ground. He spots his horse, mounts up, and rides away.

THE FOG RISES from the ground as Shilah mounts Wovaka's horse. Exhausted from loading his dead friends on their horses, he leans down and holds his ribcage, damaged by his fall from the tree. Behind him, tethered to one another with leather straps and ropes, are the remaining miners' horses and meat-carrying pack horses.

As he rides away, he passes stubbled cornfields and thin cattle grazing in snow-covered fenced pastures. Colored leaves swirl in the wake of his horse's hooves as he thinks about Wovaka and how he buried his friend in a shallow grave rather than try to carry him out of the trees and take him home like the others.

He felt guilty that Wovaka would not be with his friends in the Paiute burial grounds, but he also knew he would spare his wife and children the shame of seeing him with the top of his head cut off.

The snow begins to fall again as he considers his options. Should he remain with the Paiutes or keep his promises to Maria and Natalie and go back home and be a white man again? And what about his dream of striking it rich in Tin Cup? Then there was Rupert. He needed to find the miner who was responsible for all these deaths and exact revenge for the lives he took.

CHAPTER 10

Canned Goods, Mining Camps, and Dynamite

1882

FIFTY-ONE-YEAR-OLD SAMUEL PLUMMER, his wife dead, his children missing, and without a penny to his name, opens a case of pork and beans and starts to stack the cans on the top shelf in the middle aisle of Baxter's Mercantile.

Ruth Baxter, dressed in denim jeans and a blue wool sweater, is wearing lipstick and perfume for the first time in six months. The forty-eight-year-old owner watches her new hire with interest as Samuel finishes his task.

She walks across the room and lowers the window shade, welcoming in the early morning sun. She makes her way to the aisle where Samuel is admiring his handiwork.

Still wearing the stocking cap gifted to him by Barney, Samuel sniffs the air, straightens up, and grins. "What do you think? Straight enough for you?"

Embarrassed that Samuel noticed the smell of her perfume, she turns one of the cans so the label faces forward. "There… Have you worked in a store before?"

He hesitates and glibly remarks, "No, but I kidnapped a store owner's wife once… in Montana… a mining town called Bannack, where my brother was sheriff."

"Wait. You kidnapped someone?"

"Yeah, I went in to rob the place and one thing led to another."

"So, you took her instead?"

"Yeah, a gal named Lucy Vedder. Her husband was abusing her, so she didn't mind me stealing her. I let her go the next morning."

"I'm sure there's a lot more to that story."

"Oh, yeah. I can tell it to you if you want."

"No, that's okay." Ruth squares her shoulders. "You're not going to kidnap me, are you?"

Samuel snickers. "No, you're safe. I've been good for eighteen years… at least most of the time."

"I hate to ask, but did you ever spend time behind bars?"

"Jail… not prison. Wait? You're not one of those people who think if you've been to jail, you're guaranteed a place in hell?"

"No, but I need to be able to trust you if you're going to work for me."

"I told you I've changed. Taking a wife, having two children, and giving up drinking will do that to you."

"How did you manage taking care of two children after your wife died?"

"Not very well, I'm afraid. I blamed myself for letting her bleed to death, started drinking, and leaving my kids alone while I went to Cheyenne and got myself plastered."

Ruth sympathizes. "And now you don't know where they are? Is that why your children ran off… because you…?"

"Because I was an idiot and left them to fend for themselves. My oldest, Samuel Henry, watched my daughter while I was off in a bar, numbing my feelings. It wasn't right of me, I know. It was my job. I'm a changed man now. Haven't had a drink in six weeks."

"Then why did you go into the bar?"

"I went in looking for someone who might have seen my children."

As Ruth wipes down the counter, she nods. "Let me guess. Someone said they had seen them."

"Yeah, two numbskulls claimed my son sold them his horse, took me out behind the bar, beat me over the head, and took everything I had."

She pulls her hair back and fans her neck. "I'm sorry."

Samuel shakes his head. "Yeah, not so smart, huh? I've gotten soft trusting people. Being a farmer, you change your ways. Enough about me. What's your story? You ever kill someone, rob a bank, or spend time in prison?"

Ruth smirks. "No, I managed to avoid that. My only crime was marrying a man I didn't love."

"Why would you do something like that?"

"Because I was penniless and afraid to say no, and he was wealthy. I was desperate to find a better life."

"Well, I hope he treated you well."

"He did, and just when we began to talk about starting a family, he walked out on the street one Friday morning, and got himself killed by a runaway wagon. Never had a chance to say goodbye."

"Barney told me all about it."

"Now it's just me and this store."

"Nice looking… smart woman like you must have had a few suiters."

"I have, but they were either looking to spend my money, too full of themselves, or dumber than a pile of bricks. Besides, I enjoy living free from some man's plan for me."

"You used the word desperate earlier."

"Yes, I was young and living in Chicago. I attended college just long enough to become a teacher. I managed to get a job teaching first grade and was living in a rental house. The pay was so poor my folks had to help me out by paying half my rent. They died within six months of each other and left me with nothing. I taught a while longer, but Chicago wasn't very kind to me. It's hard to survive on a teacher's salary if you're a single woman with no husband.

Then Robert, ten years older than me, came along, liked how I looked, and offered me the moon. I fell in love with his promises, and we moved to Tin Cup. I helped him manage the store until he died, and I just kept going. Business is good."

"I gotta say, ma'am, you've done pretty well for yourself."

"Thank you. Call me Ruth. And where are you from?"

"Addison, Maine. I'm the son of a poor fisherman. When I was twelve, I got kidnapped by two ruffians. The oldest lout, a skunk named Warren Spivey, introduced me to a life of crime, and I ended up stealing gold in Montana Territory."

"Oh dear, another chapter."

"Yeah, there's more. My brother Henry came west looking for me. He ended up becoming a Montana sheriff and saved me from being hanged.

After I escaped Montana, I got married and settled down. Got bored with Nevada, moved to Wyoming Territory, and tried my hand at farming. The problem was I couldn't grow a damn thing."

Ruth shakes her head. "My word, you make my life seem like a walk in the park."

"That's my fast version of what happened. I'll slow it down if ya ever wanna hear the whole thing."

"Yeah, maybe small doses would be better. I already know about you being a kidnapper, a gold thief, and serving time in jail… and did you say you almost got hanged?"

"Yeah, twice."

"How does something like that happen?"

"Big misunderstanding. The locals claimed my brother and I were part of a gang called *The Innocents*."

Ruth grins. "Good grief. Every time your mouth opens, there's another storm in your story."

"Yeah, I've lived a few lives, but like I said, I did settle down for ten years… and then my wife died, and my kids ran off. Now I'm unsettled again."

"I know you said when I hired you that you'd like some time off to look for them. Would you like to do that now?"

"I would if you think you can keep these cans straight."

Ruth smiles. "I'm pretty sure I can do that."

"Can you give me the rest of today and tomorrow off?"

"Of course." She holds up her hand. "Hold on a minute."

Ruth walks into the back room of the store. When she returns, she's holding a black wool coat and a beaver fur trapper hat. She hands them to Samuel and assures him, "You're gonna freeze to death dressed like that. It's cold outside."

Samuel removes Barney's stocking cap and puts on the fur cap instead. Like the Stetson she offered him earlier, it falls over his eyes. He snickers, "At least my ears won't get cold."

Ruth takes a handkerchief from her pocket, removes the hat from his head, and stuffs the kerchief in the lining. She puts it back on his head, looks into his eyes, and insists, "It looks fine to me."

"You keep dressing me in your late husband's clothes, I'm gonna start lookin' like a well-kept man."

Ruth's face tightens. "It's only temporary… until you get back on your feet… and I really would like to hear the rest of your story sometime."

"I don't know. It's a doozy. I'd kind of like to keep this job for a while." He fits one last can on the shelf and looks at the front door. "Well, I'd better get myself going."

SAMUEL ENTERS THE LIVERY STABLE on the lookout for Barney. Not seeing him anywhere, he walks out the back door. From the privy, he hears someone talking. The outhouse door swings open, and Barney shuffles towards the stable, adjusting his suspenders.

He doesn't see his lodger until Samuel says, "I thought maybe you had someone in there with you."

"Damn it! Don't be sneaking up on me like that."

"Sorry, I didn't know I was sneaking.

Barney loads his pipe in his mouth and enlightens Samuel. "Just me talking. I do most of my praying in there."

"I didn't take you for a praying man."

"A lot you don't know about me. Probably best to keep it that way."

Samuel agrees. "Not a problem." He starts to leave and turns back. "Wanna let you know I'm riding off for a few days to look for my young ones. Be back tomorrow night."

"Fine by me. You can do whatever you wanna do as long as you keep paying."

"I appreciate that."

Barney studies Samuel's new look. "That coat and hat belong to Robert Baxter."

"Yep, Ruth felt sorry for me and gave them to me to wear."

"Boots, shirt, now this. What else is she providing you?"

"Enough money so I can pay you… That's all."

"That's a shame. Woman's got a lot she could give."

"Well, I need to get going. Like I said, I'll be back." Samuel starts to leave, but turns around. "Barney, I'm not forgetting what you've done for me… shirt, hat, place to stay."

Embarrassed, Barney's face reddens and his voice wavers, "Nothin' that anyone else wouldn't do… for some scratch."

"Still, I appreciate it."

"Go on. Get. I got work to do."

Samuel leaves, and Barney continues to smoke his pipe.

WINTER REFUSING to let go of its grip, Samuel hunkers down in his saddle dressed in Robert Baxter's hand-me-down coat and fur hat. Five miles north of Tin Cup, he rides past several open pit mines and abandoned tunnels with tattered no-trespassing signs.

The six inches of snow on the ground make for slow going as he passes several miners carrying pickaxes, shovels, and buckets. Further down the road, he spots a young family of five Utes in a freight wagon parked next to two young Shoshone men dressed like white male prospectors.

Ahead, he spots a small, tattered canvas tent, where twenty men and two women are talking loudly. Curious, he brings his horse to a stop. He watches as an Old Testament bearded salesman with a prominent chin and excrescence on the end of his nose carefully places bars of soap on a wooden display case.

Dressed in a dark blue jacket covering a white lacy shirt, Jefferson "Soapy" Johnson raps his knuckles on the case and waits for everyone to quiet down.

Samuel slides out of his saddle and leads his horse to the rear of the gathering. The fast-talking barker suddenly delivers his opening pitch. "Ladies and gentlemen, what you see here is my homemade soap… not ordinary soap, mind you; it's prize-winning. My name's Jefferson Randolf Johnson, and my special formula is guaranteed to clean the dirt off your grimy hands and bodies, even your nether regions."

Several men laugh, and Jefferson continues, "Not only will it cleanse your filthy hide, but one in every five bars has guaranteed prize money inside with winnings up to twenty dollars." Jefferson picks up two bars wrapped in plain brown paper and waves them at his audience. Who will be the first to purchase one of these blue-ribbon winners for a mere dollar?"

A silver-haired man with a bowler hat twirls his mustache until it looks like a corkscrew and jeers, "Who do you think we are mister… a bunch of country bumpkins? A dollar for a bar of soap? You're full of shit."

People laugh until a stout, curly-blond-haired man moves through the crowd and hands Soapy a silver dollar. Soapy, his mouth working as if he's having a hard time breathing, grabs the coin and hands him a bar. The curly-blond wearing a tattered gray Confederate jacket tears off the wrapper. Inside, he finds a five-dollar bill. He holds it up, waves it at the crowd, and yells, "Five dollars! Damn! I got myself five dollars!

Three men and a woman squeeze past the other spectators and hold out their hard-earned cash. Soapy grabs their money, stuffs it in his pocket, and hands each of them a bar.

Another man, wearing a wide-brimmed slouch hat, unwraps his bar and screams, "Ten dollars!"

The salesman holds up another bar and yells, "Still got a chance at twenty dollars, folks!" A handful of bystanders make a beeline for the front, and Soapy sells them his remaining inventory.

While people unwrap their bars of soap, Soapy grabs his wooden display case and slips away. People grumble as they open their purchases and find nothing but chunks of misshapen soap made of cheap oil, water, and lye. Several people toss their bars aside and begin to look for Soapy, but he is nowhere to be found.

Immediately, a drunk miner screams, "Anybody find a hundred dollars?"

Several people yell out as one. "We want our money back!"

Samuel steps up to two pissed-off miners blocking their way. "Sorry to bother you fellas, but have you seen a long-haired eighteen-year-old boy and a blond four-year-old girl in the area? They're my children, and I'm trying to find them."

The oldest miner pulverizes the bar of soap in his hand and growls, "Nobody I've seen."

The young, red-faced miner next to him wags his head and adds, "Me neither."

As they walk away, Samuel tries again. "If ya see them, I'm at Baxter's Mercantile in town."

The younger man turns back. "Sell you this bar of soap for fifty cents."

Samuel frowns. "No thanks, I think I'll pass." He mounts his horse, watches briefly as the crowd disperses, and tries again. "Anyone seen a long-haired teen and a four-year-old sister around here?" Most people don't bother to look his way, while others shake their heads no and go their own way.

Samuel rides off, studying the landscape and the ramshackle buildings he passes, looking for any sign of Sam Henry and Maria.

After a few minutes, he sees a small stream and ties his horse to a tree. Then he grabs a canteen from his saddle and a chunk of bread and dried beef from his saddlebag. He sits down, removes his new boots, and soaks his feet in the water while he eats his lunch.

BACK IN THE SADDLE, having seen no sign of civilization for a couple of miles, he notices a crudely built wooden shanty to his far right beyond a grove of yellow aspens.

He instantly veers off the beaten path where he sees smoke curling out of a small chimney pipe in the center of the building's tin roof. Unsure of his surroundings, he hides his stallion in a small clearing beyond the trees.

As he walks towards the shanty, he surveys the surrounding area. He notices a small corral with two horses and a small freight wagon parked beside it. Suddenly, he hears a dull sound coming from the back of the shack, so he circles behind it.

He sees two men with their backs to him standing over a hole. The man with a shovel turns around, and Samuel immediately recognizes the blond curly-haired man as the first lucky prize winner at the soap sale he witnessed earlier. Still wearing a gray Confederate jacket, too big for him, the hefty man spits and tosses a shovelful of dirt into the hole.

The second accomplice and money winner, still wearing a wide-brimmed hat, raises his shotgun and emits a predatory snarl. "What you doin' here?"

Samuel has a moment of blank astonishment as he stares into the man's dead eyes and the dull-witted expression on his face. He reaffirms that the two men in front of him are shills planted in the crowd by the salesman to bait people into buying one-dollar soap that's not worth a nickel. Should he call them out on their deception or play dumb and keep his mouth closed?

He bites his lip when he realizes there is a dead man in the hole. "I don't want any trouble. I'm just lookin' to find my children… a young man and his little sister."

The man with the wide-brimmed hat snarls, "No young'uns here."

Samuel nods at the body. "Sorry for your loss. "I'll be goin' now."

The hatted man grins. "You ain't sorry. You're nosey."

Jefferson "Soapy" Johnson exits the cabin's back door and eyes Samuel. "What we got here, boys?"

"Says he's looking for his kids," the blond-haired man says.

The con artist's voice thickens, and the folds of his neck wiggle like the gills of a turkey. "You didn't buy any of my soap."

Samuel stiffens. "I don't have a dollar."

"Where's your horse?"

"I'm on foot."

"The hell you are. Where is he?"

Samuel points in the opposite direction from where he left his horse. "Back in the trees."

Jefferson stares into the distance and says, "You carrying a gun?"

Samuel nods. "No, it got stolen a few days ago when some fellas bushwacked me behind the Tin Cup saloon.

"Is that a lie, too?"

Samuel grins. "No, that was the truth. Like I said, I'd better be going."

Jefferson nods at the man with the wide-brimmed hat and points his shotgun at Samuel. "Suppose you're gonna tell about this man in the hole and seeing me and my prize-winning boys bein' here… like we're killers or thieves or something?"

"Like I told your friends, I don't want no trouble."

"Don't act like I don't know your kind," Jefferson grumbles. "You think we killed that man in that there hole, don't ya?"

"It did cross my mind."

"We happened along after he killed himself. Must have gone crazy living all alone."

Samuel lifts his chin. "Yeah, I noticed the bullet hole in his back. Must have been some stretch." Samuel nods. "Listen, I'm not interested in telling anyone anything. I'm only trying to find my children."

"What about us being soap tricksters?"

"If those people you duped were ignorant enough to fall for something like that, they deserve what they got… a cheap bar of soap. I'm sure as hell not gonna go back there and rub their noses in their stupidity. People believe and unbelieve all kinds of shit."

Jefferson wipes his nose. "I don't believe you. Boys, take this liar inside and show him some hospitality."

Jefferson points the way, and the wide-brim-hatted man opens the door and pushes him inside.

TIED TO A COWHIDE CHAIR with heavy ropes, Samuel surveys the interior of the crude building made of rough wood, sheet metal, and thick black tar paper, looking for anything that might help him escape.

Seated near a wood-burning fireplace, he twists his body and spits. Then he coughs as he tries to avoid the flames that are dangerously close to him. The pungent odor of animal fat and alkali fills his nostrils, emanating from two cast-iron pots filled with a waxy substance that will soon be passed off as "prize" soap.

Jefferson and his two assistants enter the hut armed with soup ladles, stirring sticks, and a large wooden mold with small squares. They shuffle over to the pots, stir the contents, and ladle the molten liquid into the mold.

The liquid hardens quickly, and Jefferson slams the mold on the floor. His assistants grab the bars and wrap them in small pieces of cheap waxed paper.

While the pots cool, the three men carry the bars of soap outside, load them into a wagon, and walk back into the shanty. While his men take the pots and their possessions to the freight wagon, Jefferson moves to the corner of the room, picks up a bundle of six sticks of dynamite, and attaches a long fuse to it.

Confused, Samuel asks, "What's with all the dynamite?"

As Jefferson places the package in the center of the room not far from Samuel, he grumbles, "Gonna blow this place to smithereens."

"With me in it?"

Jefferson doesn't look at him as he sneers. "I can't have you claiming we killed someone and blabbing our soap secret now, can I? Put an extra-long fuse on so you can pray a little longer."

"Isn't this place worth anything to you?"

"Not my place. We showed the owner the door a few weeks ago."

"Does that mean you killed him?"

"Let's just say he was reluctant to leave."

The door opens, and the stout, curly-haired thug pokes his head inside. "Loaded and ready to go, boss."

Jefferson nods. "All right. Once I light the dynamite, we don't wanna be lollygagging. This shack is gonna blow sky high."

The wide-brimmed hat man walks into the shack in time to hear the word dynamite. He grins. "Let me light the fuse, boss. I ain't blowed up a building with a man in it before."

"Go on if it'll give ya pleasure."

Samuel watches as the dim-witted man locates the dynamite and lights the fuse. The brutes watch for a second and then hurry out of the shanty. Outside, Jefferson climbs in his freight wagon while his partners mount their horses. As they ride off, Jefferson looks back. "I guess he won't be finding those kids of his after all."

Alone in the shanty, Samuel hears the sizzle of the fuse as he frantically tries to free himself from the ropes. In what he believes are his final thoughts, he closes his eyes and visualizes Sandra, Sam Henry, Maria, and his brother Henry. Will he see them again? Is there a heaven or hell? Where will he end up?

He opens his eyes. As the fuse leading to the dynamite sizzles, he lifts his chair a few inches off the ground and scoots to the front of the cabin, one foot at a time. When he reaches the door, he leans back in the chair and furiously kicks it with his feet until it finally gives way. Still attached to the chair, he hops out of the shanty and past the porch.

He hops two more times and then hears a deafening explosion that sends him soaring through the air, his arms flailing like he is trying to fly. He lands face down in the dirt fifty feet from the shanty, broken pieces of the chair and parts of the rope still attached to his body.

Jefferson and his men turn back when they hear the explosion. They wait for the smoke to clear and chuckle when they see the flattened shanty and debris scattered everywhere. The blond-haired man turns to his boss and says, "I'm tempted to go back and see what's left of that fella."

"There's not enough left of him to find."

As the three hombres ride off, Samuel lies motionless on the ground until he parts his dry lips, releases the air from his lungs, and slowly inhales. He coughs and tries to shift positions, but his legs are cramped, and his ears are ringing.

He finally manages to free himself from the bindings and sits up. His only thought was that even though his shoulder is aching, his chin throbbing, and his ears ringing, he is still alive.

With the air gray with smoke, Samuel makes it to his knees and struggles to his feet. He scans the area and limps over to the shanty to see what's left.

Curious, he makes his way to the remnants of the fireplace and finds a four-foot divot where Jefferson put the dynamite. He looks down, sees a giant rock layered with silver and gold nuggets, and steps into the hole. He kneels and works feverishly to remove the dirt around the ten-pound chunk of bejeweled quartz.

AS SAMUEL RIDES BACK through the mining camps, he spots several people he saw at Jefferson Johnson's soap sale. A long-armed man with short legs standing in front of a tent looks at the coat covering Samuel's treasure and says, "Must be something special under that coat for you not wanting to wear it. It's colder than a witch's tits."

Samuel doesn't respond, so the man totters off, cradling himself.

When Samuel reaches the edge of Tin Cup, a weathered-looking Rupert Weed passes him riding in the opposite direction.

Samuel realizes it's the wrongdoer he saw three weeks earlier in Tin Cup who killed a man for wanting to keep his winnings, but he doesn't say anything.

AS THE SUN DROPS below the mountains west of Tin Cup, Samuel climbs down from his horse, tethers him to a post, and heads into the local assay office.

Harrison Baltimore, wearing a black tweed jacket and white shirt with red suspenders, looks up when he hears the door open. He watches as Samuel struggles to carry his coat-covered rock to the counter.

The proprietor, sporting a thick British accent, leans forward, lowers his spectacles, and squints. "Lucky you caught me, lad. Feeling rather gutted and headed for home. What you got here?"

Samuel grins as he takes in the man's accent. "I take it you're not from around here?"

"West London. Been stateside ten years now. I'm knackered, so go on, show me what you're so proud of so I can close up for the weekend."

Samuel clears his throat and removes his coat, covering the rock. Harrison's eyes light up. "I'll be gobsmacked!" Harrison lowers his glasses and stares at the gold and silver-clad rock. "I've never seen anything like this. It's a big one, innit?"

Samuel beams. "Am I rich?"

The sixty-year-old gold and silversmith picks up a magnifying glass and carefully looks the rock over. "This is the bloody motherlode of all rocks. Where'd you find it?"

Samuel takes a deep breath through his nose. "Think I'll keep that to myself. I will tell you this much. There was a lot of dynamite involved." He nods, "So, how do I get paid for something like this?"

Harrison removes his glasses and puts them on the counter. "Lad, this rock is full of silver and gold, but it needs to be broken down and picked clean. It's gonna take a hell of a lot of work."

"Who can I get to do something like that?"

"I can do it, but I charge ten cents on the dollar."

"How do I know if you're gonna give me my fair share... ninety percent?"

"You can come back and watch if you wish, but I've never been accused of being a dodgy man. A bloke like me doesn't keep a job like this being a liar and a cheat."

"And you won't tell who you got this from?"

"Mum's the word."

"How long until I get paid?"

"Three, maybe four days."

"Can you give me an advance? I'm broke."

"I can give you fifty dollars until we settle up."

"That works for me."

A few minutes later, Samuel walks out of a Tin Cup clothing store wearing a different set of clothes than when he left town a day earlier. He has on store-bought jeans, a new blue flannel shirt, a brown felt cowboy hat, and a pair of boots that fit him.

As he starts down the street with the clothes that Ruth loaned him earlier, he greets passersby with a newfound confidence.

He enters Baxter's Mercantile, where he finds Ruth behind the counter looking at her inventory list. She looks up, sees Samuel standing proudly in the doorway in his new clothes, and stares. "You're back early... and you look like a different man."

Samuel smirks. "I didn't find my children, but I am a different man."

CHAPTER 11

Thanksgiving, New Love, and Stealing Money

DR. ARNOLD WATSON'S DINING ROOM TABLE, decorated with considerable charm, is covered with the usual Thanksgiving Day delectables: an oven-baked twenty-pound turkey stuffed with cornbread dressing and giblets, two bowls of mashed potatoes and sweet potatoes, and three side dishes filled with green beans, buttered corn, and mixed vegetables. At the far end of the linen cloth-covered table is an Italian Terracotta bowl filled with cranberries and a silver platter stacked high with Arnold's sister Margaret's crescent dinner rolls.

The aging doctor, dressed in a dark blue pin-striped suit with a white shirt and a black ribbon tie, is seated at the head of the table. On his right are his son-in-law, Timothy "Buck" Buckland, and his daughter, Kate Buckland. Next to Kate is Maria Plummer, wearing a white pinafore and a blue ribbon in her hair.

Across the table and to Arnold's left is his sister, Margaret Watson, who sits quietly in a green flowered dress. Next to her is Pete Buckland, decked out in new denim jeans and a white shirt with a bolo tie.

Arnold lowers his head and says, "Let us give thanks." Everyone bows their heads, and the doctor prays, "Bless us, oh Lord, and the food you have provided us. And a special thank you to my sister Margaret, who prepared most of this food…. And last of all, may we continue to be grateful for any future gifts you provide us in the coming year. Amen."

Pete echoes the end of Arnold's prayer with a hearty "Amen!" and grabs the bowl of mashed potatoes and scoops some onto his plate.

Margaret reaches under the table, places her hand on his knee, pats it softly, and whispers, "I'm so thankful we found each other."

Pete squeezes her hand as he pours gravy from a silver gravy boat onto his potatoes and picks up a fork with his other hand. "Likewise, my dear."

Margaret quietly asks, "Don't you think we should wait for my brother to carve the turkey?"

Embarrassed, Pete lays his fork down and says, "Sorry."

The doctor walks to the center of the table, picks up a large-bladed knife, and slices the turkey.

Pete removes his dinner napkin from his shirt collar and whispers to Margaret. "I'm gonna tell them."

He stands up, winks at Margaret, and looks at everyone around the table. He clears his throat and says, "Before we go to eating, I have something to say. The way I figure it, this is as good a time as ever to make this kind of announcement… the whole family being together and everything. Anyway, I asked Margaret here to marry me last night, and she has agreed to be my wife."

Arnold drops the knife and forces the words from his mouth like he's afraid of what he might say. "I didn't see that coming. First, let me say congratulations to the happy couple. Sister, you are full of secrets. Not that it's any of my business, but where are you two planning to live?"

Pete sits up straight, checks with Margaret, and says, "My place… at least until I give up raising cattle and growing crops."

Margaret adds, "I'm keeping my house, and when Pete is ready to retire, we'll come back here."

Buck turns to Kate and whispers, "Who's gonna take care of Maria?"

Kate adjusts the squared-off neckline of her full-length blue dress and speaks through tight lips. "Don't worry. We'll figure it out."

Arnold finishes carving the turkey, takes his seat, and everyone begins to fill their plates with food. In between bites, Pete aims his fork at his son and asks, "How ya like bein' a sheriff?"

Buck touches the badge pinned to his brown leather vest and corrects his father. "I'm a deputy sheriff, and you know it."

Pete winks. "Well, you'll work your way up to it." Then he turns to Margaret and says, "I ain't worried… He's got what it takes."

Across the table, Maria takes a bite of turkey, swallows, and tugs on Buck's shirt sleeve. "Why do they call it a turkey? It looks like a big chicken to me."

Buck grins. "I don't know, Maria. Horses and cows kinda look the same."

"Do they taste the same?"

"No, I don't think so."

Maria's eyes widen. "Chickens and turkeys taste the same, and they both lay eggs, right?"

"That's right."

"And they have feathers?"

"Yes."

"Then, a turkey is a big chicken."

Buck laughs. "Kind of… now eat your dinner."

KATE AND MARIA walk hand in hand up the stairs leading to her father's medical office. Kate opens the door and watches as her father turns his back, wipes off his mouth, and puts a small brown bottle in a nearby drawer. Maria tugs on Kate's sleeve and asks, "What was Grandpa drinking?"

Kate whispers, "It's kind of a cough syrup."

Maria whispers back, "Does he have a cold?"

"Something like that."

Kate's father walks over and nods. "Better get ready. Hank Dressler will be here in a few minutes to get that goiter removed." Kate gives her father a look of disdain, turns back to Maria, and leads her over to a chair. As she lifts her up and into it, she says, "You need to sit there while I help your grandfather."

"Then am I gonna go to Aunt Margaret's house?"

After Kate puts on a white apron, she explains, "Not today. She's busy packing and getting ready to marry Grandpa Buckland."

ON THE OTHER SIDE OF TOWN, in the Carson City sheriff's office, Garfield and Buck are seated on pine wood stools, polishing their boots. Suddenly, the door flies open, and Tyler O'Neill, a local bank manager with high cheekbones and a bald head, rushes inside. "Sheriff! Two men just robbed my bank! Stole two thousand dollars, maybe more!"

The lawmen grab their boots and start putting them on as Garfield asks, "What did they look like?"

The banker makes a curious gesture and presses his back against the door frame as if to keep from falling. Then he says, "Big but not too big. Sounded young. Faces were covered with white towels, but dressed the same… looked kinda odd … brown sack coats and white cabbage tree hats… too clean to be miners."

"Any idea which way they were headed?"

Tyler kicks the floor and says, "I waited a while and ran out on the street in time to see them headed east riding bay and gray horses."

"Any other witnesses?"

"No, just me. They followed me inside when I unlocked the door this morning."

"All right. I'll get some men together and see what I can find."

GARFIELD, BUCK, AND THREE OTHER MEN ride west out of town towards the Carson Range, a branch of the Sierra Nevada mountains. Like the sheriff and deputy, the red-haired Irishman, Conner Reilly, and former Mississippi slave, Sanford Jefferson, are equipped with Springfield model rifles and Colt .45 revolvers.

The final posse member, Thomas Berry Eater, a Shoshone Indian in his late twenties, slides down from his horse and studies the tracks in the freshly fallen snow while the other men shade their eyes from the sun topping the mountains in the distance.

Armed with only a knife, the short-haired and scar-faced Shoshone looks up at the sheriff, finds his voice, and suggests, "Two horses... riding faster than we are."

Garfield lifts his shoulders, relaxes them slowly, and orders, "Okay, let's pick up the pace. Maybe they think no one is coming after them and they'll slow down." Thomas mounts up, and the five men slap leather to their horses and race off at a fast gallop.

Four miles down the road parallel to Carson River, the sheriff raises his arm, signaling the men to stop. "We can't ride like this all day, or we'll kill our horses. We'll stop here, give them a breather, and some water. If we don't see any sign of them, we'll head back."

Garfield, Conner, and Sanford climb off their horses and lead them to the bank of the Carson River while Buck rides over to Thomas, who hops off his horse and kneels on the ground. The deputy watches momentarily and says, "I don't know how you can tell one horse's tracks from another."

Thomas doesn't look up. "Earlier, I noticed one of the robbers' horses had a broken shoe."

"Huh, good catch." Buck grins, and his thoughts turn inward. He liked Thomas the first time they met at the lumber mill where they worked together. Garfield, however, only saw him as a typical Indian with a reputation for being a good tracker. But Thomas was more than that. He had a secret sense of humor that most people never got a chance to see. Men at the mill thought of him as the strong, silent type, but Buck quickly found out that under all that silence was a clever man with a tone of voice that suggested his emotions were always under control. He wasn't one of those back-slapper kinda guys who can't talk when he thinks or can't think when he talks.

One time, Thomas told him he had attended a Catholic boarding school like most Indians in the area, but then he ran off and returned to his old Indian way of living. He even went back to dressing the way his ancestors dressed years ago. People always teased him about wearing deerskin clothes, but he didn't care.

He asked him once if he was married. The Indian grinned and stared into the distance. Finally, he said, "Marriage is like living between heaven and hell… maybe purgatory." But then he smiled and said, "I married because I love the warmth of a Keya's body on a cold winter night and the taste of her flesh on a hot summer evening."

When he heard him use the word purgatory, he asked if he was still Catholic. Thomas laughed and said, "When he was forced to go to school, he pretended to be one to make the nuns happy, but after he ran off, he gave up being Catholic because he hated being told what was right and what was wrong."

A flock of honking Canadian geese flies overhead, waking Buck from his thoughts. Thomas climbs to his feet and walks his horse over to the water, and Buck follows suit.

Thomas sidles up to Garfield and assesses the situation. "They were here. Probably watered their horses like we're doing now."

"How long ago do you figure they were here?"

"About as long as it would take you to swim across that river."

"What the hell? Are you saying they rode their horses across the river?"

"No, their tracks suggest they're still headed west."

"Then why didn't you just say that?" The sheriff turns to Buck. "Did any of that make sense to you?"

"Yeah, it kind of does."

Garfield snarls, "All right, men. Thomas says the men we're chasing are about as far ahead of us as it would take us to swim across the river. His idea of time and mine aren't the same. The way I figure it, they're ten minutes ahead of us."

Back on the road headed west, Sheriff Simpson and company scan the countryside, looking for any sign of the bank robbers. Up ahead to their right, they see a grove of flowerless dogwood trees, so they slow their horses and turn quiet.

Suddenly, they hear two gunshots. Conner grabs his left arm and hollers, "Shite! I'm hit!" The horses kick their hind legs in the air, pin their ears back, and spin in circles.

All the men except Thomas grab their rifles and start shooting into the stand of trees. Two more shots ring out from the trees, and Garfield hollers, "We're sitting ducks! Find cover!"

It starts to rain as the five men jump off their horses and drop down into a nearby drainage ditch on the side of the road. They struggle to control their panicked horses, who rear up and pull away. Another volley of bullets from the grove comes their way, forcing them to let go of their reins.

The horses run off into a nearby field as Buck crawls through the mud to the Conner and looks at his arm. He winces when Buck lifts it. The Irishman questions Buck's medical skill with his eyes as he speaks calmly with a lilting Irish brogue. "Careful there, lad. It might be briste, yeah."

Buck stares at him. "Briste?"

Conner explains. "My arm... for sure is broken... I felt it shatter."

After removing his shirttail from his pants, Buck cuts off a piece and carefully applies a tourniquet above the wound. "Try not to move it."

"I won't have to try very hard."

Buck crawls to Garfield's side and stares at Sanford, who looks shaken. "You all right?"

A bullet hits the dirt a few feet away from him, and Sanford hunkers down and takes a deep breath. When he raises his head, he tugs his hat down like he's trying to hide inside it. He grumbles, "Been beaten, whipped, tarred, and feathered, but I ain't never been shot at before."

The sheriff shakes his head. "I don't like this any more than you do."

Buck turns to his boss and says, "What now?"

The sheriff grits his teeth. "Don't like being pinned down like this. When you get a chance, you and Thomas circle to the back of the trees and see if you can get a clear shot at them. I'll lay down cover for you."

Buck tries to reason with him. "Thomas only has a knife, and he's never fired a gun."

Garfield looks at the Irishman. "Well, Conner ain't no use to anyone... and Sanford here has lost his gumption." The sheriff looks at the embarrassed man and asks, "You doin' any better?"

Sanford lowers his head. "I ain't goin' out there. I got a wife and two sons to worry about."

"Then why in the hell did you come with us in the first place?"

"I don't know, but I lost my desire to be brave."

Buck presents his suggestion. "Why don't we take the lead together? We're the law."

The sheriff avoids eye contact. "I'm going to stay here with Conner and Sanford… protect them."

The Shoshone crawls forward and joins Buck. "Let's go."

Buck argues, "Maybe, I should just go. You don't have yourself a gun."

Thomas removes his knife from his sheath and holds it up. "All I need. Not interested in hiding in a hole like a white feather."

Garfield scoffs. "What's a white feather?"

The Indian gives Garfield an icy stare. "You're a white feather."

"White feather, my ass! Go! Both of you go! I'll fire away."

Buck nods. "We'll go around the back way." Thomas and the deputy move to the back of the muddy drainage ditch, where Conner is shivering and waiting for someone to do something."

Up front, Garfield waits as Buck and Thomas prepare to leave. He fires once and holsters his gun as the pair crawl out of the ditch, hop to their feet, and run for the backside of the trees. Conner grits his teeth and growls, "Why ain't you still firing, you son of a bitch? You trying to get them boys killed?"

"Saving my bullets to protect you and Sanford's asses."

"Hell, if you are, you lying son of a bitch!"

Suddenly, the men in the ditch hear a series of gunshots in the distance, followed by return fire. The sheriff looks back at Conner and brags, "See that? They're doing just fine."

The Irishman snarls, "You're nothing but a lily-white coward."

HAVING REACHED a grove of dogwood trees, Thomas stands tall as Buck yells, "Give yourselves up! You have no chance at all!"

Hidden fifty yards away, one of the thieves hollers back, "There are only two of you!"

"Well, we're coming for you just the same!" Buck pulls his pistol from his holster and offers it to Thomas. "Nothing to it. Just aim and pull the trigger."

He waves the deputy off and holds up his knife. "I can aim better with this."

Buck eyes the Shoshone. "How we gonna get these fellas to surrender without killing them? Any ideas?"

Thomas cuts two branches off the dogwood tree they're hiding behind. He hands Buck one and motions for the deputy to follow him.

As they circle to the other side of the grove, they hear the same thief again. "Where'd ya go? Don't be sneaking up on us now. We've never been killers, but we'll shoot you if we have to. No money is worth dying for. Come nightfall, we're riding out of here, and you'll never see us again. What ya think of that?"

Two crows fly overhead, squawking. Then Buck and Thomas hear a second voice coming from the trees like a loud whisper. "Don't be telling them our plan, ya mooncalf."

The Shoshone leads the way as they move closer to the other side of the trees where the voices are coming from. They find a large growth of sagebrush and hide behind it. They wait patiently as Buck tightens his grip on his rifle. The Indian disagrees with his eyes and then shakes his head from side to side.

Buck lowers his weapon.

The robbers begin to whisper as Thomas pushes a branch to the side. Still wearing their brown sack coats and white cabbage tree hats, the young men turn their way. Buck quickly realizes it's Walter and Sol Pickett, two young brothers he and Thomas had worked with at the sawmill. They had quit the mill shortly before Buck had. He'd never had a conversation with either one of them, but he knew their father owned a farm mile north of Carson City.

Thomas interrupts Buck's train of thought as he shakes the limb in his hand. He whispers, "We'll wait for the right moment and go for their legs."

Buck whispers back. "If they don't shoot us first."

When the Pickett brothers turn and aim their rifles at the ditch, preparing to fire again, Thomas and Buck creep out of their hiding place.

When they reach the thieves, they spring to their feet and swing the tree branches at the brothers' legs. Walter and Sol scream in pain, fall to the ground, and drop their rifles. Before they can react, Thomas and Buck grab their weapons and step back.

The brothers sit up and start rubbing their knees. Buck leans forward, studies their profiles, aims his rifle, and issues a warning. "Don't move or I'll shoot you."

Sixteen-year-old Walter Pickett slaps his eighteen-year-old brother Sol Pickett's arm. I knew we wouldn't get away with this."

"Shut the hell up, Walter. What did I tell you? We needed to keep riding."

Sol pleads with his eyes, "We ain't never done nothin' like this before. You can have the money back. Just let us go our own way."

Buck studies Sol's face again and says, "You robbed a bank and shot Conner Reilly. You could have killed any one of us… and you want us to let you go?"

Sol resumes his apology. "We weren't trying to hit anyone, honest. We know Conner. He's our neighbor. He gonna be all right?"

"You winged him in the arm, but he'll be all right. Do you know who we are?"

Walter makes an assessment. "I don't know… sheriff and… Indian."

Thomas speaks. "We worked with you at the lumber mill."

Sol turns to his brother. "I knew I'd seen these two before." He turns back. "Listen, fellas. What we did was wrong, but that bank was trying to steal our farm."

"How do you figure that?" Buck asks.

Sol narrows his eyes and says, "Our pa got kicked in the head last fall, and he ain't been the same since. Can't even talk. That's when we quit our jobs at the mill… so we could help Pa out full-time. The problem was nothin' we planted grew, and the bank wanted money we didn't have. Then some fella from California shows up and threatens to take our farm… said he represented the Carson City Bank. We threatened to shoot him, and he rode off saying he'd be back."

Walter explains further. "We only robbed the money to repay the bank for the money Pa borrowed last year."

Buck tries to make sense of it all. "You're telling me you robbed the Carson City Bank so you could pay back the loan with the bank's own money?"

"Sounds stupid, I know, but we thought it might work."

Buck looks at the boys' strange attire. "I'm curious. Where did you find those fancy coats and hats?"

"We ordered them from a Montgomery Ward catalog with the last of our money. Figured no one would guess who we were dressed like this."

Buck can't help himself and grins. "You're right about that."

Thomas pulls Buck aside as the deputy continues to aim his rifle at the brothers. In a soft voice, the Indian explains his thinking. "Some judge will put these two in prison for twenty years. What good will that do?"

Buck removes his hat and stares at Thomas. He whispers, "You knew it was these two boys, didn't you?"

"After I heard their voices, yes."

"And that's why you went with the tree branches? You didn't want me shooting them."

"I say we turn them loose. Prison won't do them any good."

"We can't do that."

"Why not? Prison will ruin their lives. We got the money. What more do we need?"

Buck takes a moment and turns back to the brothers. "I can't believe I'm gonna do this. You promise you won't pull a stunt like this again?"

Walter is the first to speak. "Promise, sheriff. We'll never do anything this stupid again."

"First off, I'm only a deputy. Second, if you ever tell anyone we let you go, I'll ride to your farm and arrest you for bank robbery and attempted murder."

Sol grabs Buck's hand and shakes it hard. "Thank you, thank you. If you change your mind, we'll be at the farm trying to figure out how to raise the money."

Buck snarls. "Without robbing a bank."

Sol removes the bag of stolen money from his saddle and hands it to Buck. He looks at the deputy and says, "Now what?"

"We wait here until dark while you two ride west. Find you a place and hide out for a couple of days. When you come back to Carson City, if anyone asks, tell them you went to visit a sick cousin or some other relative."

Buck reaches into the canvas bag, pulls out a twenty, and hands it to Sol.

Sol looks it over and says, "What's this for?"

"Get yourselves some new clothes and burn the God awful ones you have on."

Two hours later, in the dark of the night, Buck and Thomas emerge from the dogwood trees and walk towards the drainage ditch. Buck holds up the bag of cash and yells, "We got the money! Don't shoot!"

When they reach the ditch, it's empty, but their horses are tied to a nearby fence post. Buck surveys the area and says, "What the hell?"

BACK IN CARSON CITY, Buck and Thomas ride down Main Street and past the dark jailhouse, half-expecting the Sheriff Simpson to walk out and greet them. Neither of them says a word as they go their separate ways.

When Buck arrives home, he unsaddles his horse and leads it to the small corral behind his house. After watering and feeding it, he walks to the front door, carrying the bag of stolen money. He enters the house and finds Kate sitting at the kitchen table next to a dimly lit lantern. Dressed in a full-length cotton nightgown, she gives Buck a curious look and says, "Where have you been? It's late. I've been worried about you."

Buck kisses Kate on the forehead, puts the bag on the table, and sits beside her. He tightens his lips and explains, "Two fellas robbed our bank, and five of us tried to chase them down."

Kate's eyes open wide. "Oh dear, did anyone get hurt?"

"Conner Reilly got shot in the arm, but the rest of us are fine."

"Did you catch the bank robbers?"

"Well, we kind of did."

"Kind of?"

"Garfield sent Thomas Berry Eater and me into the trees to arrest them while he and the others hid in a ditch."

"While he hid in a ditch? Why would he do that?"

"I don't know. I think he was trying to get me shot."

"Why would he want to do that?" She takes a moment. "Oh."

"Yeah, he's still always asking about you. I think he feels like if I'm out of the way, he'll have a chance to win you over again."

"Again? I told you, there was never a first time. My God, Buckie! You need to quit that job. That man is evil."

"Well, tomorrow I'm gonna give him a chance to explain himself. Maybe he had his reasons."

"Back to the bank robbers. Did you arrest them or not?"

"We let them go."

"Why would you do that?"

"They were two young brothers who only stole the money to save their father's farm."

"What did Garfield say about that?"

"I haven't seen him. He and the two other men in the ditch rode off and left Thomas and me to fend for ourselves."

"I told you. There's something wrong with that man… what's in the bag?"

"The stolen money. Come on, let's get some sleep."

Kate looks at Buck and says, "You're not going to keep that money here, are you?"

"Nobody knows I have it except Thomas. Let's go to bed."

BEHIND HIS DESK, facing Buck, Sheriff Garfield Simpson attempts to explain his decision to abandon his deputy and Thomas Berry Eater. "Conner got to bleeding so much, and it was getting dark, so I thought it best for us to head home."

"And you left us there? What if we needed help?"

"We didn't hear any more shooting, so we didn't know who was alive and who was dead. I had no help. Conner being wounded, and Jefferson being worthless. Sanford and I gathered your horses for you if'n you did come back. I was planning to go back there this morning."

"That's some story…"

He interrupts Buck. "So, what were you and the chief doing in those trees all that time… having a picnic?"

Buck takes his time. "We came up on them all slow-like, but they got the drop on us, tied us to a tree, and rode off."

"Get a good look at them?"

"No, they still had towels over their heads."

"Why?"

"I don't know. Maybe cuz they knew we were coming and they didn't want us to see their faces… or maybe because it was getting cold. I don't know."

"Any sign of the money?"

"No, they took it with them."

"Damn. The bank was offering a five-hundred-dollar reward."

"You didn't mention that."

"Huh. I must have forgotten."

Sheriff and deputy sit quietly for a moment, stewing in their lies until Buck walks to the pot-bellied stove to get a cup of coffee.

He hadn't lied since he was sixteen when he told his father he was late coming home because his horse ran off. Truth be told, he was at Ralph Wagner's farm in a hayloft with his daughter.

Buck comes back to reality when he hears Garfield's order. "Bring me a cup." Buck pours a second cup, hands it to him, and walks to the window. He looks outside, sees Thomas ride past, and sips his coffee.

BUCK RIDES UP to the Pickett family farmstead and climbs off his horse. Sol and Walter exit the barn and walk over to the deputy sheriff. Sol stares at Buck, waiting for an explanation. Finally, he asks, "Did you come here to arrest us?"

Buck reaches back to his saddle, removes the bank bag, and hands it to Sol. "Our secret. Pay off your Pa's loan gradually. Tell the bank a rich uncle died and left you some money. Then wait a few more days, and don't let them see that bag."

CHAPTER 12

No Longer a Paiute, Looking for Gold, and Revenge

DRESSED LIKE A PAIUTE HUNTER, Shilah prepares to leave the village where he has lived for more than a year. His grandfather, Winnemucca, exits his lodge and says, "You are welcome to return if you wish." He hugs Shilah, and his grandson mounts his saddled horse. Shilah nods. "If I don't see you in this world again. I will see you in the next one."

Winnemucca waves his hand, suggesting his agreement.

As Shilah rides out of the village past several wickiups, young boys and girls chase after him, but he doesn't look back. Moments later, Shilah's mind begins to wander as he thinks about Wovaka and his other Paiute friends who died needlessly at the hands of the greedy white miners. Should he head back to Wyoming to see Natalie… or maybe to his grandfather's home in Nevada to check on his sister, Maria? He knew it was selfish, but he still wanted to go to Tin Cup to search for gold.

After a night under the stars, Shilah takes a well-traveled road and steers his horse west in the direction of Colorado. When the sun reaches the top of the sky, he reaches into the cloth bag attached to his saddled horse, removes a piece of dried venison, and chews on it. A few minutes later, he grabs his deerskin water pouch, raises it to his lips, and takes a long drink.

SIX WEEKS LATER, after a long and arduous journey through the deserts of Nevada, numerous mountain passes, and the salt flats of Utah, Shilah crosses into Colorado.

Thirty miles and a day later, he sees the town of Grand Junction in the distance and the confluence of the Grand and Gunnison Rivers.

Determined to make it to Tin Cup before the first snowfall, he digs his heels into his horse's flanks. When he slows down, he spots an Indian community and rides up to two young Ute women filling their water pots in a nearby freshwater creek.

The slender girls have braided hair, matching deerskin dresses, and knee-high moccasins. Startled by his sudden appearance, they jump to their feet. Shilah drops down from his horse and nods. "Do you know how far Tin Cup is from here?"

The girls step back and give him a confused look, so he asks another question. "Food?" They still don't react, so he cups his hand, pretends to take something out of it, and puts it in his mouth.

As he pretends to chew, the girls start to giggle. Finally, the older girl takes Shilah by the hand and leads him to a small shelter fashioned out of young willow trees, like Paiute wickiups.

As Shilah stands waiting like a prize trophy, the girls' mother exits their home and looks the visitor over. The oldest daughter grins and points at Shilah. "Tukapi."

A few minutes later, Shilah is seated between the two sisters, eating squirrel meat, while the mother smiles her approval. She hands him a small fruitcake containing dried crickets, grasshoppers, and cicadas mixed with berries. He takes a bite, looks to see what is so crunchy, smiles, but says nothing.

When the girls' mother goes back inside their house, Shilah spits the contents of the cake into his hand and buries it next to his leg. The girls notice and begin to giggle. When their mother returns, he smiles, and she offers him another cake. He quickly shakes his head left and right and tightens his lips.

Later that night, not far from the girls' lodging by the warmth of a fire, Shilah rests under a blanket, staring at the stars. He is about to fall asleep when he feels the two sisters crawl under the blanket with him, one on his right and one on his left. As the girls snuggle close to him, he starts to feel aroused, so he sits up and says, "No. I'm already spoken for."

The girls reach up and gently pull him back down. Not sure what to do, Shilah closes his eyes and doesn't move. The sisters look at him, giggle again, and close their eyes, pretending to sleep.

When the girls wake up the next morning, they toss back the red woolen blanket their mother made last winter as if they expect to see Shilah. Not seeing him, they rush over to the tree where his horse had been tied. They look in the distance and lower their heads when they realize their guest left them in the middle of the night.

THE MORNING IS SILENT as Shilah rides into Tin Cup. Not seeing anyone on the town's only street, he begins to worry. Where are all the gold and silver miners he expected to see? Then he realizes the miners wouldn't be in the town of Tin Cup itself. They would be outside on the outskirts, a mile or two away.

As he rides past *Barney's Livery Stable, Baxter's General Merchandise and Mining Supplies* store, and *Frenchy's Saloon,* he smiles, thankful he finally made it to Tin Cup, where he had always hoped he would discover more gold than he could ever imagine.

A mile north of town, Shilah slows his horse and rides past a dozen miners on the side of the road carrying pickaxes, shovels, and cases of dynamite.

An empty freight wagon with a bed layered with coal dust pulls up alongside him. The driver leans forward and signals him to stop. "You looking for a job?"

Shilah halts his horse and says, "I'm looking to find some gold."

The burly man with a salt-and-pepper-colored beard lowers his glasses and smirks. "You and every other fool that has set foot around here. What's your name?"

"Shilah."

"Got a last name?"

"Just Shilah."

"Well, Shilah. My name's Jed Horton, and I'm looking for someone to work in my coal mine a few miles from here."

"Coal? Huh. Like I said, I'm lookin' to find gold."

"The thing is, the coal around here ain't hiding like gold is. Don't pay as much, but there's plenty of it. As for me, I'd rather find a shitload of somethin' than a whole lot of nothin'. You got you a grub stake?"

"A what?"

Jed grins. "Money to buy supplies, food, and other necessities. You're gonna need all that to find gold."

"I'm gonna get me a pan, find some cold water, and remove some gold flakes. Then I'll buy what I need from there."

"You are a dreamer. Listen, I pay five dollars a day except Sundays. Plus, I can give ya a place to stay and plenty of food. Quit whenever you want. I'll even throw in a new set of clothes so you don't... well, look like an Indian."

"I look like an Indian because I am part Indian."

"I understand, but people around here won't treat you like an equal if you ain't dressed like them."

Shilah stares at the coal man. "I can leave any time I want?"

"That's right. I'll even pay you and my other men ten percent of the jackpot if you're lucky enough to uncover a motherload of gold in my coal mine."

"All right, as long as I can leave whenever I want, I'll give it a go."

"Okay then. Follow me… Shi… lah"

A QUARTER MILE inside a mineshaft at the base of the Sawatch Mountain Range, black-faced Shilah leans on his shovel, struggling to breathe as three other men covered in black dust use picks and shovels to extract chunks of coal from the solid black wall in front of them. Like the other three men, he is wearing a dirty felt hat with an attached oil headlamp. Unlike the others, he has a red bandana wrapped around his neck, and his long hair is pulled back in a ponytail.

Two men cough, reminding him he should get back to work. He scoops up a chunk of coal and struggles as he lifts it. He balances his load and drops it into a small cart resting on wooden tracks extending beyond the opening of the mine shaft.

Above them, spaced every ten feet, are wooden posts resembling railroad ties supporting the ceiling. And despite the light shining from two kerosene lamps and the men's headlamps, the long tunnel is still dark.

Dressed in denim jeans and a black cotton shirt, Shilah accidentally kicks a bird cage, and the canary inside begins to chirp. He looks at the other men, apologizes with a nod, and fills his shovel with another piece of coal. He drops it in the cart just as two twelve-year-old boys called Hurriers enter the mineshaft with an empty cart and park it next to the loaded cart.

Without saying a word, the boys reverse directions and push the low-grade anthracite out of the mine shaft.

The ten-hour day ends, and the four miners exit the underground tunnel stooped over. The sun starts to disappear behind the mountain as the men make their way up the hill to a small log cabin not far from the mine.

Leading the way is Anders Nilsson, a tall thirty-five-year-old Swede with blond hair and a loud laugh. Behind him are Bill Sanborn, a forty-eight-year-old Northern Civil War veteran, and sixty-year-old Chick Pearson, a former blacksmith and undertaker with a gimpy leg.

After dinner, Shilah lies inside the cabin, cluttered with mining equipment, in an odd-shaped bed made from mine shaft posts and willow branches. Having eaten a second portion of venison stew, Chick put together two days earlier, his stomach grumbles, and his mind drifts.

He thinks about his dream of finding gold. Would it ever happen? He hadn't come to Tin Cup to spend the day digging coal to make another person rich. The ten days he had spent shoveling had been backbreaking, but he liked the men he worked with, even though they got rowdy after emptying a jug of moonshine every night. They always offered him the jug, but after what whiskey did to his supposed father, he didn't want anything to do with it. Chick did all the cooking but wasn't very good at it. Plus, he drove everyone crazy at night, coughing.

Shilah's thoughts are interrupted when he hears Chick start to pluck his fiddle. He turns and watches as the old man begins to play his rendition of *Old Joe Clark*. The Swede bounces over to Bill, pulls him to his feet, and they dance their version of an Irish jig.

THE NEXT DAY, the four miners sit in the mine shaft with shovels and pickaxes at their sides, eating lunch. Having already devoured their meat and cheese sandwiches, Anders removes four cake doughnuts from his lunch bag and hands one to each of them. Bill grins, takes a bite, and talks with his mouth full. "Where'd ya get these, Swede?"

"Woman down the road. She was selling them by the dozen. I already ate the others."

Chick attacks his doughnut and says, "You sure like your sweets, Swede?"

"Jah, I'm a sockergris."

Bill squints. "Socker what?"

"Sockergris… a sugar pig. It's what we Swedes call someone who has the sweet tooth."

The men laugh, toss their lunch bags aside, and pick up their shovels.

An hour passes, and the miners use pickaxes to remove coal from the solid wall in front of them. The Swede takes a big swing, and suddenly, the wooden beams behind and above the miners begin to rattle, sending pieces of coal and rocks down on their heads.

Shilah hears a loud cracking noise, and the walls give way. Then he feels a powerful blast of air, so he covers his head as he falls to the ground. Rock and debris cover his body, and his only thought is I think I am about to die. What will happen to me after that? Then, he feels his chest start to swell as he takes what he thinks is his final breath.

Above ground in the dark, the Swede, buried in rubble up to his waist, frees himself and crawls over to where he thinks Shilah might be. Using his hands, he furiously tosses rocks and scrapes away the dirt covering Shilah's body. When he finally finds the young man's face, he leans down and puts his mouth on Shilah's mouth, breathing air into his lungs and sucking it out.

Shilah finally exhales deeply, painfully, and tries to move his arms, but they won't budge. With his body still partially covered with rubble, he struggles to breathe. Then, for some strange reason, he looks into the Swede's eyes and remembers their conversation the night before. Anders had been standing with him outside the cabin, smoking a cigarette, when the Scandinavian looked up at the sky and said, "Don't you just love the night?"

Shilah's mind goes blank again, and his body sags as his will to live disappears like the sun passing behind a cloud.

A few seconds later, he feels the air return to his lungs and a hand nudging his chest. When he opens his eyes again, he sees the black-faced Swede kneeling over him outside the mine shaft. He feels a cool breeze and the bitter smell of coal dust, while a few feet away, the young Hurriers stand close together, worrying that somehow they might be responsible for the mine collapsing.

Shilah loses consciousness and closes his eyes again.

SHILAH LIES flat on his back in the mining cabin on a dirty mattress filled with Spanish moss, corn husks, and shredded wood. He opens his eyes and sits up. His head is wrapped with a white bandage, and he has several cuts and lacerations on his face.

Next to him, perched on a pinewood-slatted chair, is Jed Horton. His boss removes his glasses and cleans the lenses with his handkerchief as Shilah adjusts to the light shining through the cabin's only window. "You're lucky you ain't still buried in that mine shaft. I don't know how that Swede managed to pull you out of there. He's got a broken leg, three broken ribs, and a busted skull. Had to take him to town; he was so bad."

"What about Bill and Chick?"

"They didn't make it. They'll be in that mine until Jesus comes again. No point digging them out and putting them back in the ground again."

"Damn. I'm gonna miss those fellas."

"Yeah, they were mighty fine people and good workers."

Shilah looks himself over. "How am I doing?"

Jed sighs. "You'll be fine. Bad cut on the top of your head, no broken bones… a few bruises. You've been sleeping a lot. Dentist who checked you out says you have one of them concussions."

"Dentist?" Shilah touches the back of his head and realizes he has been sheared. "What the hell?"

"Yeah, he's all we had. Anyway, he had to scalp you so he could clean and stitch up your wound. I know it was your pride and joy, but it'll grow back."

Shilah takes a moment. "I owe Anders big time."

"You sure do." Jed reaches down and picks up a tin gold pan full of money. He lays it next to Shilah. "Month's pay, plus half of what I owed Bill and Chick. The Swede gets the other half."

"Thanks. You want your pan back?"

"Keep it.

"What happens now?"

"Gonna shut the mine down for good. That pan will come in handy if you wanna look for that gold you've been talking in your sleep about finding."

WEST OF TIN CUP near Willow Creek, Shilah rides past an open pit mine where he sees a dozen men sifting through surface rocks and dirt looking for evidence of gold or silver.

As the spring day warms, the former coal miner removes his fur-lined brown leather coat. Still dressed in mining clothes, including the red kerchief around his neck, he removes his black stocking cap, revealing the bandage around his head. He wipes the sweat from his brow and looks straight ahead. In the distance, he sees four barefoot men standing in the water with their pants rolled up, panning for gold.

The prospectors don't look up as he rides slowly past them. Further upstream, he spots an abandoned campsite, evidenced by charred wood and black dirt. He climbs down from his horse, ties the reins to a nearby willow tree, and removes the tin pan strapped to his saddle.

He walks over to the water, drops to his knees, and scoops up some sand from the bottom of the stream. As he shakes the pan, looking for color, a green and brown brook trout swims past him. He waits for another fish to appear, repurposes his pan, dips it into the water, and waits patiently. Sure enough, a second fish swims his way, and he ladles it into his pan and tosses the trout onto the shore.

Finished for the day, Shilah kneels in front of a small fire, holding a fish skewered on a willow stick over the flames. Satisfied that his meal is fully cooked, he carefully removes the small trout from the stick, trying not to burn his fingers.

THE MORNING SUN filters through the nearby willow tree branches, waking Shilah. He shades his eyes, rolls up his blanket, and walks to his horse. He removes a piece of burned beef and a handful of dried berries from his saddlebag and begins to eat.

As he gnaws on his breakfast, he picks up his tin pan, fills it with sand from the creek, adds water, and gently shakes it in a circular motion. He repeats the process several times until he spots three specks of yellow metal at the bottom of his pan.

Encouraged by his discovery, Shilah pulls a small leather bag from his back pocket, squeezes one particle of gold at a time between his fingers, and drops them into his bag.

Later in the afternoon, having not found any more gold, Shilah puts his pan next to him and lies back. He's about to drift off when he hears voices in the distance. He sits up, grabs his pan, and dips it in the water.

When three saddle tramps appear, Shilah recognizes one of them as Rupert Weed, the man responsible for killing his six Paiute friends. One of Weed's traveling companions, a white-bearded Mexican named Jesús Sanchez, is riding a dapple-gray mule and wearing a sugarloaf sombrero with a braided hatband. The second man, Harold Letcher, has a stubbled face and a long, narrow nose. He clears his throat, flutters his eyes, and asks, "Finding any color?"

Shilah feels the blood rush to his face. The men look away, and he pulls his stocking cap lower on his head. Trying to avoid making eye contact with Rupert, he stands and mumbles, "A few flakes is all."

Rupert leans over his horse. "Do I know you?"

"Don't think so. I'm out of Wyoming Territory."

"You gotta name?"

Shilah feels his skin prickle as he protects his Paiute name by using his real name. "I go by Sam Plummer."

Jesús removes his sombrero and grins, revealing his tobacco-stained teeth. "Pleased to make your acquaintance, Señor Plummer." The Mexican pulls his six-gun, points it, and lowers his voice. "Éste es nuestro lugar. We were here first… Primero."

Rupert interrupts. "Put the gun away, Jesús. He ain't no threat. He'll find himself another spot, won't you, Sam?"

"I didn't know someone could claim an entire creek."

Rupert tightens his teeth and spits. "Well, now you know."

Without a word, Shilah grabs his tin pan, mounts his horse, and rides away. In the distance, he hears the three men laughing.

That evening, Shilah lies on his back looking at the full moon and the sky filled with thousands of stars. He wanted to avenge his Paiute friends' lives and ride back and shoot Rupert and his cronies in their sleep. Or maybe he could just kill Rupert and scare the other two off. But he knew that wouldn't be any good because someone would probably hunt him down, hang him, or turn him over to the authorities. What a strange way to die. Rope around your neck, trying to breathe.

His mind shifts. He didn't know what was worse, having a Paiute father who killed his grandmother and kidnapped his mother, or having some fake father who was always drunk and didn't give a damn about anybody but himself. Finally, Shilah shifts to his side, clears his mind, and drifts off.

The next morning, after riding upstream, Shilah finds another abandoned campsite and ties his horse to the branch of a lone oak tree. He grabs his pan, walks to the gurgling cold water stream, and begins to sift for gold again.

After only finding a few more flakes of gold, he removes his pan from the water and walks over to some cranberry bushes to relieve himself. As he lowers his pants, he looks through the trees lining the bushes and sees a small hill twenty-five yards to the east. He finishes his business, weaves his way through an opening in the trees, and squats down at the foot of the hill.

Using his pan as a shovel, he scoops dirt away from the surface of the hill until he finds several fist-sized rocks. He looks them over and tosses them aside. He digs again until he uncovers a large iron oxide rock the size of a watermelon. The more dirt he removes, the more he sees it's layered with gold and silver.

He puts his pan aside and starts using his hands to remove similar rocks from the hill. He finds several more gold and silver-covered rocks and places them carefully in a pile.

It's almost dark as the exhausted nineteen-year-old finishes relocating his precious metal findings on his nighttime blanket. Excited by his discovery, he ties the four corners of the blanket together and pulls his treasure away from the hill and through the trees. The heavy load is almost too much, but he takes a breather and manages to maneuver his newfound wealth back to his campsite.

Worried the rocks might be too heavy for his horse to carry, Shilah uses his tin pan to dig a hole under the oak tree where his horse is tethered.

He places most of the rocks in the hole, covers it with dirt, and smooths the ground where the bulk of his treasure is now hidden.

He looks around, makes sure no one is looking, and puts the remaining smaller rocks in his saddle bag and pants' pockets.

Just as he is about to mount his horse, Rupert, Harold, and Jesús ride up and look him over. The Mexican smiles, "So we meet again, mi amigo."

Shilah avoids eye contact and climbs on his horse. "You can have this place, too. I'm moving on."

Ruppert studies Shilah's face, draws his gun, and points it at him. "Get off your damn horse."

Shilah does as he's told as Rupert growls, "You're that Indian, ain't ya?"

"Half of me is Indian, yes."

"No, not just any Indian, you're the Paiute that killed five of my friends."

Shilah surprises himself and says, "Four. Wovaka killed the other one… after you killed all my friends… for no reason.

"I thought you said your name was Sam Plummer."

"It is."

Rupert notices Shilah's bulging pockets. "What you got in them pants, Paiute?"

"That's none of your business."

In tandem, Rupert's cohorts draw their pistols, and Jesús says, "Your negocio is our negocio, amigo. The boss, he want to know what is in your bolsillos?"

Shilah touches the handle of his pistol but thinks better of it. Instead, he removes a handful of small treasure rocks from his pockets and tosses them at the feet of the intruders' horses.

The mule brays and the horses whinny and rear up as Shilah touches his revolver again. Before he can draw, Harold slides off his horse, picks up one of the rocks, and hands it to Rupert. The rebel looks it over and smiles. "Where'd you get this?"

Shilah lies. "On a road a few miles back... before you ran me off this morning. It most likely fell out of some unlucky miner's bag."

"Got any more?"

"No, that's it."

Rupert points his gun. "I think you're lying. Drop that gun and plant your ass on the ground."

Shilah does as he's told as Rupert nods to Jesús and growls, "Check his horse for more lies."

Shilah watches as the Mexican struggles to remove the heavy leather bags from Shilah's horse.

Jesús drops the bags at Shilah's feet, kneels, and opens one of them. He removes a rock covered in gold and silver and holds it up for his boss to see. Rupert snaps, "You lying son of a bitch!" Then he turns to Jesús and shouts, "Shoot that half-breed bastard. He killed three of my friends."

Shilah corrects him again. "Four."

Jesús unholsters his pistol, but before he can fire, Shilah drops to his knees and grabs a knife hidden under his pant leg. He throws it hard, burying the full blade deep in the Mexican's chest. Jesús turns and looks at Rupert as he sinks to the ground. He sputters blood, breathes heavily for a few seconds, and takes one last breath.

Rupert panics and reaches for his rifle. Before he can aim, Shilah crawls over to Jesús, grabs the Mexican's pistol, and fires it at the feet of Rupert's horse.

The animal rears up, trying to buck Rupert off. Unsuccessful, the steed runs off as the thief hangs on to his saddle horn for dear life.

Shilah fires again.

The horse skids to a stop and bucks again. This time he vaults the Rupert high in the air, his arms flailing. The culprit lands headfirst on a rock on the edge of Willow Creek and doesn't move.

Harold arrives, and Shilah turns back and aims his gun at him. The frightened man blinks twice, clears his throat, and puts his pistol back in his holster. His voice rises as he raises his arms in the air. "Don't shoot. I ain't no threat."

Shilah stares at the man's pants as they darken around his crotch. "Your asshole buddies tried to kill me. Why didn't you try and help them?"

"I'm no killer, mister."

"Just a thief. You were willing to steal my gold, right?"

Harold stares at the ground, so Shilah says, "I don't know why, but I'm gonna let you go. First, we're gonna check on your boss over there. If he ain't dead, you're gonna shoot him."

They ride over to Rupert's horse, who is drinking out of the creek. Shilah climbs off his animal and readies Jesús's gun just in case. When he leans over the bank of the creek, he sees that most of Rupert's body is submerged in water except for his head, which rests on the huge rock.

He takes a closer look and sees a pool of blood close to the back of Rupert's skull and a smaller mass on the rock near his mouth. He turns to Harold as two buzzards begin to circle overhead. "What do you think? Bury him and the Mexican, or leave them lie?"

Harold grunts. "They wouldn't take the time to dig me a hole. I say we leave them where they are. Someone will come along."

Shilah agrees with his eyes and points the Mexican's pistol at Harold. "Drag the Mexican over here and put him in the water."

Harold hurries over to Jesús, grabs him by the arms, and drags him over to the creek bank. Harold shoves the Mexican in the water next to Rupert, and Shilah nods. "There. Now, they can go to hell together." Shilah studies Harold's face. "Listen, I don't wanna ever see you again. If I do, I'll shoot you down like the coward you are."

Harold defends himself. "Listen, I'm not as horrible as you think. I could have shot you, but I didn't."

"There's no difference between killing someone or letting someone do it for you. Go. I'm sick of your face."

The survivor grumbles, "Which way am I supposed to go?"

Shilah points. "Follow the creek 'til it ends and keep going. Like I said, I don't wanna see you again."

Harold rides away but looks back, unsure he's headed in the right direction. Shilah confirms he is with a wave of his arm and waits until the coward is out of sight.

Shilah rides back to the oak tree where his rocks are buried. He ties his horse to a bush and removes the dirt from the hole where most of his treasure is hidden.

Hands covered in black mud and grime, Shilah loads two burlap bags filled with the biggest rocks on the backs of Jesús' mule and Rupert's horse. Next, he fills his pants pockets with the smaller stones, mounts his horse, and turns for Tin Cup.

Back at the creek, three buzzards drop from the sky and land on Jesús and Rupert's backs. Two of them peck at the Mexican's neck, while the third one nibbles on Rupert's right index finger. The scoundrel moans, his hand moves, and his finger twitches.

The birds fly off, and Rupert rolls on his side, opens his eyes, and looks skyward. He takes a deep breath, struggles to his knees, crawls out of the creek, and collapses face-first on the bank.

CHAPTER 13

Budding Romance, Barney's Secret, and Going Home

INSIDE THE TIN CUP ASSAY OFFICE, as the clock on the wall ticks silently, Harrison Baltimore counts out twelve hundred dollars and places the bills carefully into Samuel's waiting hands. The precious metal appraiser smiles. "What are you going to do with all that money, chap?"

"First, I'm gonna buy myself some new protection. I haven't had a weapon since I got robbed last month. You know where I can buy a rifle and pistol?"

Harrison takes his time and looks around as if he's being watched. Then he reaches under the counter and removes a holstered pistol and a rifle. "I can sell you mine. Been thinking about retiring them for a while now. I only bought them when I came here to fit in… and in case someone tried to whack me."

"You sure you wanna give them up?"

"If I'm unarmed, I'm less likely to get shot."

Samuel exits the assay office, carrying a lever-action Winchester rifle and a holstered single-action Army revolver strapped to his waist. He fondles the handle of his new pistol, mounts his horse, and rides down Main Street headed for the mercantile.

THE NEXT AFTERNOON, Shilah enters Tin Cup and rides straight to the assay office with Rupert and Jesús's horse in tow. He ties all three horses to a hitching post and walks inside. Harrison looks up and says, "What can I do for you, young man?"

Without a word, Shilah removes six rocks from his pockets and lays them on the counter. Harrison picks one up, adjusts his glasses, and studies the specimens. "Layered with gold in silver, alright."

"How much can I get for them?"

Harrison looks at another rock and rubs his chin. "I can give you twenty dollars."

"For all of them?"

Harrison grins. "No, twenty dollars apiece, lad. All total, two hundred and twenty dollars."

Shilah offers. "I've got more outside. A lot bigger than these."

"Well, you're the second fella that's come in here with a gold and silver-covered rock. Only he had one… but it was bigger than any nugget I've ever seen."

"I've got some big ones too."

"Well, bring them on in. Let's see what you've got."

Having sold all his valuable rocks and two horses and their saddles to Harrison, Shilah exits the assay office with a smile on his face. He unties his horse, looks at the other two, leaves them tied to the hitching post, and rides away.

Down the street, Samuel stands in the doorway of *Barney's Livery Stable* with his back to the street as Barney sweeps the interior of the building with a stable broom. The stable man tosses the broom and grins. "Look at you all dressed in fancy duds. What's going on? Now, Ruth's giving you all her money, too?"

"No, I went lookin' for my kids and found a motherload instead… a one-time rock that paid me enough to get me back to being myself."

"That mean you're quitting your job at Baxter's and leaving town?"

"No, but I did find a place with a real bed."

"I knew it. You're bedding down the widow Baxter now, ain't ya?"

"Nothing like that. I'm staying at Mrs. Clark's boarding house down the street."

"Can't blame you for that. Sleeping in the hay next to shit dropping horses ain't no treat."

Samuel looks at the whiskey jug at Barney's feet and sniffs the air. "Kinda early to be drinking, don't you think?"

"It's Thursday, right?"

"Yeah, I guess so."

"I always drink on Thursdays."

"Why Thursdays?"

"That's the day of the week Maggie and Clarence disappeared." Barney looks over Samuel's shoulder at the street and watches Shilah ride past, but he doesn't say anything.

Samuel turns to see what his friend is gawking at, but doesn't see anyone. When he turns back, he scratches his nose and sighs. "I'd better get back to the store, or Ruth's gonna fire my ass."

Barney smirks, "Glad I don't have an answer to no woman anymore."

"Just a little advice, Barney. If you can't see or hear a woman, it might be best to let them go."

"Says the man poking a rich woman."

Ignoring his remark, Samuel asks, "You think I can leave my new rifle and pistol with you? Ruth doesn't want me armed while I'm in the store."

"Sure, why not? But if someone bumps you off, they're mine."

Samuel grabs his rifle from his horse, removes his gun and holster from his waist, and hands them to Barney.

The livery owner's arms are full as he holds the reins to Samuel's horse and watches his ex-boarder cross the street, headed for *Baxter's General Merchandise and Mining Supplies* store.

As he crosses the street, a freight wagon pulls up to the front of Baxter's, and the driver, Hank Foley, climbs down. Samuel walks over to the wagon and nods at the driver. "What you got today, Hank?"

"The usual, shovels, pickaxes, barbed wire, lanterns, and dynamite."

Samuel asks, "Did you say dynamite?"

"Yeah, your boss orders ten cases every month. I'm always nervous loading and unloading it, but hauling it here is worse. Every time I hit a bump in the road I almost piss my pants."

Ruth exits her store and joins the men as they each pick up a case of explosives. Hank nods at the pretty woman. "Where do you want the dynamite, ma'am? Same place?"

"Yes, in the supply room."

Samuel gives her a curious look. "There's enough explosives there to blow up this whole town."

"I know. It's a special order from Denver. It's a bit risky having it in the store, but the miners around here say they need it for their jobs. I think they like to blow things up for the fun of it."

Samuel and Ruth finish putting away the new supplies and lean against the counter. Ruth looks at Samuel a little too long, and he asks, "Is something wrong?"

"You think you might want to have dinner with me tonight?"

"Really?"

"Yes… Really."

"I don't know. Mrs. Clark is serving chili and cornbread tonight." Ruth starts to turn away, but Samuel quickly says, "I'm joking. I'd love to have dinner with you."

Ruth smiles. "Good. I'm going to close early. We can put the rest of this stuff away tomorrow. I'll go start supper. Let's say six o'clock."

"Good, that gives me time to check on Barney. He hasn't been doing so well lately."

"I'm sorry. Is he under the weather?"

"No, I think he misses his wife, Maggie."

Ruth hesitates. "You know Barney was never married to Maggie."

"Wasn't sure, but I kind of figured."

"They were never even in a relationship. He liked her a lot, but she didn't feel the same. It's sad, but I think she was using him so he wouldn't charge her to leave her horse at his stable. Anyway, she and her boyfriend Clarence just up and disappeared one day."

"Huh, that's a little different story than I heard." Samuel studies the rug at his feet. "I guess sometimes a man wants to be stupid if it lets him do a thing his intelligence forbids."

"Are we still talking about Barney?"

"Ahh, I see what you did there." Samuel starts to walk away and turns back. "I don't even know where you live."

"Oh, I'm sorry. It's a small house behind the church."

"This town has a church?"

"Yes, it's two blocks east of here."

"Okay, I'll find it. See you at six."

Ruth locks the front door while Samuel goes across the street. When he reaches the livery stable, he looks inside for Barney, but he's nowhere to be found.

He opens the rear door and peers at the outhouse. "Barney, are you in there? You meditating again?" He hears someone mumbling in the latrine and waits patiently. Barney finally staggers out, carrying his jug of whisky. Samuel looks at the little man and grins. "Hey, I just remembered, it's only Wednesday."

Barney spits. "I can God damn drink whenever I want."

"Woah, sorry. I was only correcting myself." Barney stumbles and almost falls on the ground, so Samuel helps his former landlord through the back door and into the livery stable. Barney stumbles again, so Samuel helps him take a seat on a bale of hay. "I take it you're having a rough day?"

"Three years today."

"Excuse me?"

"Since Maggie left me."

"And you were in your outhouse…meditating about that?"

"Yeah, sometimes I talk to her in there."

"But you haven't seen her… in three years?"

"Nobody's seen her."

Samuel continues. "I guess she started a new life somewhere else."

"No… she's still here."

"Here? You mean in Tin Cup?"

Barney points out back. "In the privy."

Samuel doesn't understand. "You mean you feel her spirit when you go to your outhouse?"

Barney slaps the hay. "No, she's in there… in the shit hole… her and that plow salesman."

"Wait. Maggie and Clarence are buried under the outhouse?"

"Yeah, them and all my shit."

Samuel leans over and starts to gag. After he straightens up, he spits and drops to his knees. "You killed them?"

Barney points at the large sledgehammer in the far corner by the fireplace. "Two swings… one each."

They remain quiet until Barney finally says, "Ya gonna turn me in?"

Samuel tilts his head. "She wasn't even your wife, Barney. Why did you have to kill her?"

"It was a Thursday, and I'd been drinking. They stopped by to get her horse… that I was boardin' for nothin'. Told me I was a joke and they was set to leave town… for good. When I begged her to stay, they laughed at me like I was a nobody. When they turned their backs, I whacked them both dead."

"Them wanting to leave town is no reason to end their lives."

"I never had a woman before. I felt violated."

"She wasn't your woman, Barney. Ruth told me she was using you."

"Well, in my mind we was in love."

Samuel stands up. "Now, what am I supposed to do? That's a huge secret you've unloaded on me."

"It won't do any good to tell the authorities. It won't bring them back. Hell, we ain't even got any authorities."

"Jesus, Barney. That's not the point. You can't just go around sledgehammering people whenever you want."

"They were my first and only time."

Samuel starts for the door. "I don't know what else to say, but you need to dig yourself another hole and move that outhouse. That's disgusting."

SAMUEL SPOTS A WHITE CHURCH and circles behind it, where he discovers a small cemetery with two dozen headstones and several wooden crosses. He notices a small slab that reads, *Matt Erikson, Tin Cup Sheriff, 1874-76.* Next to it, another rock reading, *Rex Rearson, Tin Cup Sheriff, 1878-80.*

Samuel walks a little further until the pine trees separate, and he sees Ruth's tiny brown stucco house. The brick chimney emits smoke, with a backdrop of orange clouds lit by a sinking sun.

He stands quietly, thinking about his upcoming dinner with Ruth. He hadn't eaten dinner with a woman since his wife died. Maybe she was only feeling sorry for him. After all, he'd had his fair share of trouble lately. Or was there more to it than that? She was a fine-looking woman, no question about that... and she was intelligent with a kind spirit. But she could also be intimidating, especially when she insisted he do things a certain way in the store. Of course, it was her store, and he did work for her.

He hears the wind blowing through a privet behind him and he starts to turn back. His attention shifts back when he sees the front door open, and Ruth steps out onto the porch. She is dressed in a white linen blouse and a matching full-length cotton skirt. Her cheeks are rose-tinted and her lips are painted ruby red. Her eyes sparkle as she says, "I saw you standing out here like you were afraid to come in."

"No. I was admiring your beautiful home. It reminds me of the house I lived in as a boy growing up in Maine."

"That's right, Maine. Your father was a fisherman."

"Good memory."

Ruth walks over and takes Samuel's arm. "Come in, dinner is almost ready."

Samuel takes a moment and stares at Ruth's face. She notices and says, "Do I look like a whore?"

He grins. "Of course not. I was only thinking your house is not the only thing worth admiring. You look beautiful."

SITTING ACROSS from each other at a small dining room table, Samuel and Ruth take turns smiling while they eat slices of roast beef, mashed potatoes, a medley of fresh vegetables, and freshly baked dinner rolls. and an apple pie just out of the oven at the end of the table.

After finishing their main course, Ruth stands up, walks to the end of the table, and cuts two pieces of apple pie. She places them on small plates, returns to Samuel, and leads him into the living room.

The room is small but neatly furnished, featuring a flower-patterned couch, a mahogany coffee table, a brown leather chair, and a pinewood-upholstered rocking chair. She sits on the sofa, pats the cushion next to her, and Samuel settles at her side.

Before he takes a bite, he stares at the rocking chair. She notices and says, "My father made that, but my mother made him put that fabric on it to match the curtains."

"It's certainly unique."

"I think the word is hideous. My father didn't like it either, but he didn't want to upset Mother, so that's that. It's the only thing I brought with me from Chicago."

Samuel pats his stomach. "Thanks so much for the wonderful meal. It's been a while since I've eaten like that."

"Better than chili and cornbread?"

"Much better… and your house makes me feel… I don't know."

"Comfortable?"

"Yes, comfortable."

Samuel looks nervous as he takes his fork and prepares to sample Ruth's apple pie. He changes his mind, places his plate carefully on the coffee table, and takes Ruth's hand. "I think I'd like to kiss you."

She smiles. "I think I'd like you to kiss me."

He puts his hand on Ruth's shoulder, pulls her close, and kisses her softly. He pulls away, looks at her, and kisses her again. Their passion mounts as they embrace one another.

He kisses her a third time, and he gently lays her down on the couch, covering her with his body. She takes a moment and whispers in his ear, "Stop." She gently pushes him up and away from her, and they both sit up.

Samuel shakes his head. "I'm sorry, I got carried away."

She smiles. "No, it's okay. Let's go into my bedroom. It's more comfortable in there."

His eyes sparkle. "Are you sure?"

"Yes, but it's been a long time. I might be out of practice. Be patient with me."

He grins. "Oh, I'm the most patient man you'll ever meet."

She stands, takes his arm, and pulls him up from the couch. "Come on, before one of us changes their mind."

SAMUEL AND RUTH STAND on the front porch lit by the moon and fireflies. Now, wearing a white robe, Ruth leans over and kisses Samuel on his cheek. "Do you still want to work for me?"

Samuel smiles. "More than ever."

"And you don't mind me telling you what to do?"

"As long as it's not in your bedroom."

Ruth grins. "I can live with that."

"I guess I'd better be going."

"Okay, I'll see you in the morning."

Samuel kisses her goodbye, turns, and heads for the church. When he reaches the cemetery, he strikes a match and looks at the headstones of the deceased sheriffs again.

Back on Main Street, headed for the boarding house, he stops at Barney's Livery stable when he sees smoke behind the barn. He hurries inside and yells, "Barney, is everything okay?" He finds a candle, lights it, and walks over to the bed of hay where the stable owner usually sleeps.

When he raises the candle, he sees Barney hanging from a rope attached to the rafter above him. He stares at his dead friend, lowers his head, and whispers, "She wasn't worth it. You deserved better."

Still smelling smoke, Samuel opens the back door of the livery stable, steps out, and sees the outhouse in flames. Instead of trying to put it out, he watches until it burns to the ground.

THE FOLLOWING MORNING, Samuel opens the store's front door and steps aside as two miners carry two cases of dynamite past him. He looks at Ruth and says, "Only two cases left."

Her face turns serious. "You and Barney were friends. Why would he take his own life?"

"All I can tell you is he'd been hitting the bottle hard lately and talking about how Maggie left him."

Before she can respond, the front door opens, and Sonja Benson, dressed in baggy jeans, a red flannel shirt, and a cowboy hat, walks inside. Samuel looks closely at her and sees a badge pinned to her shirt. She eyes him and says, "Samuel Plummer?"

"Yeah, who wants to know?"

"My brother. He needs to see you right away."

"Who is your brother?"

"Sheriff Floyd Benson. I'm his deputy, Sonja Benson."

Ruth interrupts. "I didn't know Tin Cup had a sheriff."

"They do now. Governor appointed Floyd last week."

Samuel stares at Sonja. "And you're his sister… and deputy?"

"That's right. You got a problem with that?"

"No, just curious.'

"You want me to escort you to his office, or do you wanna come on your own?"

"No, I can find it. Give me a few minutes."

Sonja nods and leaves. Samuel turns to Ruth. "No idea what that's about, unless it's against the law to sleep with a man's boss."

Ruth slaps Samuel's arm and says, "Don't say that. Go."

SAMUEL ARRIVES at the sheriff's office, opens the door like an intruder, and walks inside. Across the desk from Sheriff Floyd

Benson are Rupert Weed and Harold Letcher. "You wanted to see me?" Samuel asks.

The sheriff nods at Harold, who clears his throat and flutters his eyes. Then he turns to Rupert, who has a bruised face and a dirty white bandage around his head. The handsome lawman with a handlebar mustache explains, "These men claim a young man calling himself Sam Plummer stole their gold, killed one of their friends, Jesús Sanchez, and caused Rupert Weed here to have a bad accident. I told them it couldn't be you, you being older and all, but I thought maybe you might know someone with your same name… a son or relative."

Samuel turns to Rupert. "Was he alone?"

"Yeah. Why you askin'?"

"Just curious. How old do you think he was?"

"Like I told the sheriff here, twenty… more or less. First met him when he was a Paiute. He and his kind butchered five of my men on our way back from Lake Tahoe."

"Wait, a Paiute?"

"Yeah, killed everyone but me."

Sheriff Benson asks, "And you're sure it was this same fella?"

"No mistake. He was changed into white man's clothes and cut off his Indian hair, but that didn't fool me. I don't know why he claimed to be Sam Plummer."

Benson interjects. "Why would he give you that name if he knew you knew he was a Paiute?"

"I don't know, but I gotta say, there was something white about him." Rupert tightens his eyes, points his finger at Samuel, and grumbles, "I know you."

"Yeah, Samuel Plummer. That's why I'm here. I met you a couple of months ago when I arrived here." Samuel turns to the sheriff. "Mr. Weed was playing cards and shot a man because he wanted to leave the game while he was money ahead."

Rupert attempts to defend himself. "He drew on me first, and there was no law in this place when it happened."

The sheriff frowns. "I'll look into it, but first things first."

Benson turns to Samuel and hands him a poster. "These two described the man to my sister, and she drew his likeness for the wanted posters we're gonna put up."

Samuel grabs the poster and looks it over closely.

**MAN WANTED FOR MURDER AND GOLD THEFT
MIGHT HAVE KILLED 6 MEN, MAYBE MORE
LAST SEEN NEAR TIN CUP, COLORADO
GOES BY THE NAME OF SAM PLUMMER
LOOKS TO BE 20 YEARS OLD AND MIGHT BE A
PAIUTE INDIAN**

Samuel stares at the crude drawing of a young man with a stocking cap covering his head and a kerchief under his chin. He looks a little longer and lays it back on the desk. There was something about the eyes. Was Sam Henry capable of killing someone? Was anything this scoundrel said true? Had his adopted son become an Indian? And what about Maria? Where was she?

Sheriff Benson interrupts Samuel's train of thought. "Well, what do you think?"

"Could be anybody." He lays the poster on the sheriff's desk.

Rupert and Harold stand up and head for the door as the sheriff tells them, "I'll keep an eye out, but the chances are he's riding away from here as fast as he can. I'll be mailing them posters to Nevada, Utah, and California."

Rupert and Harold leave, but Samuel lingers behind. He takes the poster off the sheriff's desk and asks, "Mind if I take this with me? You never know."

"Help yourself. I got plenty." The sheriff nods. "I heard you were the one who found Barney Luther."

"Yeah, not something I'll forget."

"Any idea why he did it?"

"Don't know. He had a lot of secrets."

"Yeah, I guess we'll never know for sure."

"I guess we won't. Good luck with the new job. I was in the church cemetery last night, and it appears the lifespan of a Tin Cup sheriff is two years."

Floyd's face sags as he watches Samuel walk out the door. He looks down at his badge, touches it, and clears his throat.

Instead of returning to the store, Samuel heads for the assay office. When he enters the building, Harrison looks up, sees Samuel, and grins. "Another rock to sell?"

"No such luck." He lays the wanted poster on the counter and points at it. "Anyone come in here looking like this?"

Harrison studies the face on the poster. "Can't say for sure, but a young bloke wearing a cap like that stopped in two days ago. Sold me a whole lot of gold and silver-covered rocks… like the one you brought in, only a lot smaller… and not nearly as loaded." Harrison looks at the poster again. "Eyes are kind of the same, but you never know. Not much of a likeness if it is him."

Samuel continues. "He give his name?"

"He was in such a hurry, I forgot to ask."

"You pay him well?" Samuel asks.

"Four hundred and fifty dollars."

"That's a lot."

"Yes, he seemed pleased."

ON HIS WAY BACK to the store, Samuel sees Rupert and Harold crossing the street. Rupert notices him and yells, "I ain't forgettin' 'bout you blabbin' on me, you son of a bitch."

Samuel snaps back, "And I'm not forgetting about you killing an innocent man over a pocket full of money, his money."

When Samuel enters the mercantile, Ruth waits for him behind the counter. Her eyes reveal her curiosity. "I see the sheriff didn't arrest you."

He doesn't respond, so she tries again. "Everything all right?"

Samuel walks over and kisses her on the cheek. "Yes… and no. My son might have been in the area a few days ago."

"I assume that's a good thing… I mean the 'yes' part."

"Yeah, but the 'no' part is two hoodlums are claiming he's a gold thief and killer. Worse yet, he wasn't with my Maria."

NORTH OF TIN CUP near the Sawatch Range, Shilah steers his horse over a twelve-thousand-foot mountain pass, continuing his way back to Wyoming Territory.

CHAPTER 14

Burying a Father, Becoming a Sheriff, and Unexpected Forgiveness

DRESSED IN FUNERAL BLACK, Kate Buckland sits at the kitchen table lit by two candles, writing in her journal.

I can't believe Father is dead. He was only 62. I never got a chance to say goodbye. The laudanum killed him. Thursday morning, when I got to the office, he was lying on the floor, not breathing. For some reason, he was still in his bed clothes. His eyes were milky white, his mouth corners were covered with tiny bubbles, and his face looked like it was on fire. I tried to revive him, but it was no use. I was just happy Maria wasn't with me because who knows what kind of damage seeing her grandfather like that would have done to her.

I knew he was addicted to opiates, but I didn't want to believe it. Now I realize an unbelieved truth is worse than a lie. I continue to blame myself for not putting a stop to it. I didn't want to hurt his pride, so I tried hiding the bottles, but he always managed to get his hands on more.

The church was so crowded that people had to stand outside in the cold. He was everyone's doctor. Mayor Kelly says he's hoping to find another one in a week or two, so I guess I'll have to do what I can to fill in until he gets here.

Poor Aunt Margaret. She and Pete got married last week and had just arrived at Buckland Station when Buckie rode up and told them Father had died.

After unloading my aunt's belongings from the wagon, they headed back here for the funeral. They are going back in the morning, but I don't know how I would have held up without Aunt Margaret being here.

Maria was saddened by the news that Father died, but I continue to marvel at how resilient she is for her age. Having lost her mother, her father, her brother, and now the man she learned to call Grandpa, she still manages to have a cheerful disposition. Of course, sometimes she surprises me by asking me poignant questions I can't answer, like the one she asked right after the funeral: "Do you think Grandpa is in heaven or hell?"

The best I could come up with was, "That's a good question, Maria. We'll find that out when it's our time to meet the Maker."

Buck enters the room wearing a loose-fitting white nightshirt and yawns. "I know it's been a rough day, Kate, but shouldn't you get some sleep?"

Kate closes her journal, stands up, and blows out the candles. Buck takes her by the hand and leads her into the bedroom.

ON OPPOSITE SIDES of the room, Sheriff Simpson sits behind his desk, reading a gun magazine, while Buck sits in a chair, cleaning his revolver. Garfield looks over and says, "Sorry about Kate's father. He was a good man."

Buck raises his thumb. "He was an even better father-in-law."

"Yeah, I'll bet. He was almost my father-in-law, you know?"

"I hate to disagree with you, but Kate said you two weren't even close to getting married."

"She said that, did she?"

"Not in so many words, but that was my impression."

"Well, it's her loss. Look how she ended up."

Buck glances at Garfield, like someone who just woke up. "I assume you are referring to me marrying her?"

"Yeah, I never thought she'd fall for some plow boy."

"If you think so little of me, why did you hire me?"

"I'll give you one guess."

Buck slowly puts his pistol in his holster. The blood beats in his temples as he unfolds himself from his chair and walks over to Garfield's desk. "Yeah, I worked on a farm… and I'm proud of it." Then he smiles like a pirate, looks Garfield full in the face, and continues. "The truth is Kate saw the evil in you, I'm just now seeing. I could kick your ass, but I'm not gonna waste my time on some coward who hides in a hole while he sends his men out to risk their lives."

Buck removes his badge and slams it on the desk. "I'm done working with someone I don't respect…. and find your own woman so you don't have to lust after mine."

As he starts for the door, he points at the flyer on the wall and reads it out loud. "*Reelect Garfield Simpson, Sheriff.*" He puts his hand on the doorknob, looks back, and says, "Better be looking for another job. Come November, I'm taking your place."

The sheriff yells, "You? You don't have a chance in hell! This town loves me."

"I'm not so sure about that." Buck hurries out the door, slamming it behind him.

IN HER FATHER'S MEDICAL OFFICE, Kate finishes examining a middle-aged patient while Maria sits in an outer room reading a book.

He finishes buttoning his shirt, grins at Kate, and smirks. "Never had a female doctor look at my private parts before."

"I just got word that a new doctor, Addison Gardner, is coming to Carson City, fresh out of medical school. Maybe you'll be more comfortable with him." She hands Mathias a jar and says, "Apply that ointment twice a day and stay away from the women in the *Carson City Saloon* who lie on their backs for a living."

"You're not going to tell my wife are you?"

"Wait. You're married?"

"Afraid so, but we ain't familiar with each other anymore."

"Yeah, she still needs to know what's going on down there."

His face turns red as he stands up. "Nobody else needs to know, right?"

Kate tightens her lips. "No, but if you don't tell your wife, I will."

As Mathias leaves, Buck pokes his head around the corner of the open door and says, "All clear?"

"Yes, come in."

Trailing behind her uncle, carrying a book and a dictionary, is Maria. Buck kisses his wife on the cheek and looks down at his niece. "I can't believe you're reading *Little Women* already. You're only six. I didn't read that book until I was sixteen."

"I'm in first grade, you know."

Kate squints at her husband. "You read *Little Women?*"

"Yeah, I thought it was, you know, about little women."

Maria giggles. "You make me laugh, Uncle Buckie."

"Do you understand everything that's going on in that book?"

"No. That's why I carry this dictionary wherever I go."

Kate changes the subject. "Why are you here? Is something wrong?"

Her husband's face turns serious. "I quit my job as deputy sheriff today."

"You did? You seem so happy."

"Yep, it's a big relief. I couldn't handle working with Garfield any longer."

"I hate to admit it, but I'm glad."

"Well, before you get too excited. I've decided to throw my hat in the ring and run for sheriff… against Garfield in November."

"No." She turns to Maria and points. "Maria, go into the other room and read while your uncle and I talk."

Maria smiles. "Are you going to argue?"

"Maybe. Do as I say."

Maria exits the room, and Kate shuts the door behind her. She turns to her husband, who says, "I probably won't win."

"And what if you do?"

"I'll get paid more."

"I don't care about the money. I want you alive."

"I need your support, Kate. This is important to me."

She sighs. "Okay, but don't make any announcements yet. Give me some time to soak all this in."

"I'm not asking you to like it, Kate. I need your support."

"We went through all this when you decided to be a deputy. You had my hopes when you said you quit. Now you tell me you want to be a sheriff. You know how I hate violence and everything associated with it."

"I know, but my job will be to keep Carson City safe from anything or anyone that might wanna change that. Well?"

"Well, what? You've already made up your mind."

The election is in November. I've got two months to convince people to vote for me instead of Garfield. I'm going to need your support."

"I'm not even sure I'd vote for you."

Buck smiles and kisses his wife on the cheek again. "Hey, until the new doctor arrives, maybe I can help out around here."

"Don't try to change the subject."

"Come on."

She shakes her head. "Truthfully, I could use your help, especially with male patients."

"And if I'm not out campaigning, I can look after Maria when she's not in school."

"If she's not in school, you can still take her with you… campaigning."

Buck grins. "That must mean you're on board?"

"Leave. I have a female patient coming in for a breast exam in a few minutes."

"You sure you don't need an extra hand?"

Kate slaps her husband's arm. "You're not funny. Go."

KATE STANDS in front of forty women from the local suffragettes' organization, seated on benches in the local Methodist church. She adjusts her reading glasses, looks at her notes, and removes them. "As you ladies know, I am here to support my husband, Buck Buckland, and his bid to become the new sheriff of Carson City.

I have a speech prepared, filled with salacious assertions and pronouncements against our current sheriff, Garfield Simpson. However, I have decided to take the high road and only promote the virtues of my husband, a man from a rural background, where he was tasked with feeding and caring for horses and cattle and serving the needs of several freight and stagecoach companies. Furthermore, he was held accountable by his father for the way he treated his family and other people in the community. The principles of honesty and integrity instilled in him only made him stronger as he matured into a man with a firm but gentle spirit. Not to mention, he's easy on the eyes."

Several women laugh as Kate takes a sip of water. "I realize full well that the federal government and the Nevada state legislature have still not granted women the right to vote… shame on them." Several women express their opinions by booing and stomping their feet. She waits for the room to quiet down and continues. "However, we do have the power to influence the men in our lives who do have the right to vote by reasoning with them…

and if that doesn't work, there's always the dinner table and the bedroom."

Women laugh and talk amongst themselves as Kate gathers her notes and walks away from the lectern.

ACROSS TOWN in Carson City's only livery stable, filled with horses, mules, and a dozen chickens, Buck addresses a large group of farmers, ranchers, local businessmen, miners, and day workers.

Up front among the listeners are Thomas Berry Eater, his two Indian friends. Behind them are Conner Reilly and three other Irishmen. At the rear of the crowd is Sanford Jefferson, his two teenage sons, and former bank robbers, Walter and Sol Pickett.

After beginning his speech talking about the weather and the crops, Buck ends it by admitting he might not be the best fighter, but that he's a good diplomat. "As sheriff, sometimes it's best to discover a man's trigger, and talk him out of reaching for it." He scans the crowd. "So that's my story and why I wanna be sheriff. If you have any questions, come see me, and I'll try not to lie."

From the back, Conner yells out, "Buck here is too nice to shovel hell, but Simpson is an asshole and a poltroon." Several men chuckle as Conner continues. "As all you know, I've got an itchy tongue. Three months back, our current sheriff hung Thomas Berry Eater and Buck out to dry. The sly dog sent the two of them into the trees after two bank robbers while he hid in a hole waiting for the sun to go down. Then he left them to fend for themselves. I don't know about you, but I don't want a coward like that watching over my town."

The Pickett brothers are the first to leave as the remainder of the crowd disperses. Buck sees Thomas Berry Eater and his friends and waves them over. "Thomas, it's good to see you. Thanks for coming out."

Thomas explains. "We can't vote, but we have Carson City friends who can. Some of them respect our opinions, and we think you should be the next sheriff."

"Well, I appreciate your support. I guess it's up to the other men of Carson City to decide; they've got two weeks."

ON A COOL FALL AFTERNOON, twenty restless men are lined up outside the *Carson City Saloon* waiting to go inside and cast votes for the next Carson City sheriff.

The wind starts to blow hard, and several men step out of line to retrieve their hats. A broad-shouldered man, Zeke Bannister, stands in front of the doorway smoking a cigarette. He hears a bell ring and ushers one more voter into the bar.

A five-foot-tall red-faced shopkeeper, Shorty Wilson, bypasses the line and walks directly to the door. Zeke snarls, "Where ya think you're going, Shorty?"

"I already voted. I wanna beer."

"Oh, yeah. All right, go on in."

Inside the bar, the piano player pounds out a lively tune as the bar owners, Wharton and Fanny Brown, manage the two ballot boxes. One is labeled Simpson, and the other Buckland.

A local rancher enters the bar ready to vote, and Fanny stares at the man, making sure he's a Carson City resident. She nods at her husband, and Wharton hands him a paper ballot and pencil. "Circle the name and put it in the right box. If you can't read, let me know, and I'll help you out… and I want that pencil back."

The rancher marks his ballot, holds it up, and proudly yells, "Sheriff Garfield Simpson!"

Wharton points at Simpson's box as a dozen men boo. The man slips his ballot into the slot and sits down at the bar.

The saloon is full of men who have already voted and out-of-towners curious about how the election will turn out. In the rear, at a corner table, Conner Reilly and his three Irish friends are talking loudly, drinking beer, and playing Faro.

Conner spots the sheriff and three of his supporters and spews, "Hey, Simpson. Got you a new job picked out yet? I hear there's an opening at the livery stable shoveling pig shit. You have a lot of experience doing that, yeah."

Garfield doesn't respond, so Conner turns to his friends and mutters, "What a manky-assed feck, he is."

The last voter casts his ballot just as Buck and Kate walk into the saloon. The reigning sheriff notices and sits up straight. Two men at a small table make room, and the couple sit down. Kate looks uncomfortable as she looks around the room, hoping to see other women. In her mind, she counts three skimpily dressed barmaids and Fanny Brown.

The clock chimes six o'clock, so Fanny rings a bell and yells, "Voting is closed!" The piano man stops playing, and Fanny continues, "I need one person who voted for Mr. Simpson and another who voted for Mr. Buckland to join my husband and me to verify the counting of the votes."

Conner hops to his feet and yells, "I, Conner Finn Reilly, will be happy to represent the next Carson City sheriff, Buck Buckland!" His Irish friends slap him on the back and push him towards the bar.

Fanny waves at him. "Well, come on then."

One of the men at the sheriff's table stands, walks over to the bar, and introduces himself. "I'm Malcolm Holmes. I'll serve as a proxy for Sheriff Simpson."

"I know who you are, Malcolm," Fanny says. "You come in here every night."

Several nearby men laugh as Wharton unlocks the padlock on Simpson's ballot box and says, "Let's get this rolling. People have been waiting long enough."

The music starts up again as Wharton hands his wife a second key, and she opens Buck Buckland's ballot box. She explains, "Okay, first Wharton and I will count the ballots and then the two of you will count them." She hands each man a tally sheet and a pencil. "If all four of us come up with the same number, our job is done."

Wharton and Fanny begin to count the ballots as a barmaid arrives at Buck and Kate's table. Buck recognizes the woman as Linda, the barmaid who took him upstairs during his first visit to the bar.

Linda smiles at Buck like he's her long-lost friend. Then she turns, matter-of-factly looks at Kate, and asks, "What can I get you two?"

Kate politely smiles and says, "I'll have a glass of water, please."

"One water. What about you, darling?"

Buck grins. "I'll have a beer."

Linda walks away, and Kate takes Buck's hand. "That's the woman you were with when you damaged your head, isn't it?"

"Yes, but remember, nothing happened between us."

"Yes, I remember, that's what you said."

Buck squeezes his wife's hand. "You were my first, and I'm planning on you being my last."

"Thank you. That's true for me as well."

"Okay, back to the election. Who do you think is going to win?"

"You, of course. There's no doubt in my mind."

Linda arrives with a glass of water and a beer, and Buck offers her fifty cents. She grins. "Your money is no good here, sheriff."

"Not yet, but thank you, Linda."

The barmaid walks away, and Kate nods. "That's nice. You still remember her name."

As she leans back against the bar, Fanny holds up her hand and yells, "Attention, everyone! We have the results." The room immediately turns silent. "Garfield Simpson received five hundred and twenty-two votes." Men cheer and clap, while others boo and hiss. Fanny waits for the room to quiet down again and continues. "However, his deputy garnered five hundred and seventy-eight votes. Carson City's new sheriff is Buck Buckland!"

Several men whoop and holler, while others leave the bar disappointed. Conner and the men at his table hurry over to Buck and congratulate him by slapping him on the back.

THE SALOON is almost empty now as the former sheriff and his friend, Malcolm, sit at the end of the bar, drinking whiskey. Malcolm finally stands up, toasts the former sheriff, and empties his glass. "It was a good run, my friend. How many years?"

Garfield grunts. "Ten."

"A decade of public service you should be proud of."

"Go home, Malcolm. Your wife is probably wondering where you're at."

"My wife died three years ago."

Garfield slams his shot glass on the table and snarls, "Well, go home, anyway."

Malcolm lays a silver dollar on the counter and starts for the door. A thirty-something woman, dressed in all blue with a black Genevieve bonnet, passes him, and he tips his hat. He turns and follows her with his eyes as she lays her two carpet bags on the floor in front of the bar counter. Malcolm mutters to himself, "If only I were twenty years younger."

Wharton hears him as he passes him with a scrub bucket and chuckles. "Malcolm, you've never been twenty years younger."

The stranger addresses Fanny, who stands with her back to her washing beer mugs in a tub of water. "Ma'am, could you tell me where I might find a Kate Buckland?"

Before Fanny can turn around and answer her, Garfield scoots his stool back from the bar and grumbles, "What you want with her?"

The newcomer steps in his direction, removes her bonnet, and offers her hand. Garfield almost falls off his chair trying to shake it as he stares at her radiant face. "Oops, watch it there, fella." She steps back and says, "My name is Addison Gardner, and I am here to fill Carson City's vacant physician's position… left behind by Dr. Arnold Watson."

"You… a woman doctor?"

"Yes, as a matter of fact, I am. Is there something wrong with that?"

"No. Just a little unusual is all." Suddenly interested, Garfield stands to his feet and smiles. "Let me point you the way." He motions for Addison to go first, and they head for the saloon door. She stops at the end of the bar and starts to pick up her bags, but the ex-sheriff moves forward and grabs them.

He leads the way out as Addison waves goodbye to the saloon owners.

Outside, Garfield sets the bags down and points to his right. "Go down Main Street here until it ends. Take a right, and you'll see a white house with an elm tree in front of it. That's where you'll find her… Kate." He pauses. "Listen, let me show you the way. It's getting dark."

"I don't want to put you out."

He picks her bags up again as Addison puts her bonnet back on and smiles. "If all of the men here are this kind, I'm sure Carson City will make for a wonderful place to live." She takes a moment and says, "If it isn't too presumptuous of me, what is your name and line of work?"

"Garfield Simpson." He smirks. "As of tonight, I'm a retired sheriff."

"You're too young to be retired."

"Tell that to the guy who replaced me, Kate's husband."

"Oh, dear. Sometimes I ask too many questions."

When they arrive at the Buckland house, Garfield sets the doctor's bags down and says, "Forgive me for not staying long enough to introduce you, but you know…"

She interrupts. "It's okay. I understand. I'm sure I'll see you again, Mr. Simpson."

"It's a small town. I'm sure we will."

As he leaves, Addison walks to the house and knocks on the door. Kate opens it and stares at Addison. "May I help you?"

The doctor reaches out her hand and says, "I'm Addison Gardner." Kate's face shows her surprise as she shakes her hand. "The new doctor?"

Addison grins. "It's okay. I get this a lot. You thought I was going to be a man."

"No… yes. I am happy you're a woman. Come inside, and I'll introduce you to my husband and Maria."

Addison walks inside. "Thank you, but I can't stay long. I just wanted to meet you. Thank you for arranging a place at the boarding house for me to stay until I find permanent housing."

"I was happy to do it. After we chat, I'll have Buck take you there."

AT THE KITCHEN TABLE, Buck, Kate, and Maria are eating breakfast. Buck forks a piece of bacon onto his plate and asks, "So, how are you and the new doctor getting along?"

"Yes, Addison… I struggled with her methods for a while, but things are fine now. How are things going with you?"

"Kind of quiet with no one to talk to, but I guess that's what you want if you're a sheriff."

"Tomorrow's Saturday, so you'll need to take Maria to the office with you."

"Okay, but I still don't like the idea of having to lock her in a jail cell if there's an emergency and I have to leave in a hurry."

"You'd better not do something like that," Kate says. "If there is an emergency, have her walk to our office. Mrs. O'Brien will be watching her on Saturdays from here on out."

The new sheriff smiles. "Looks like you're gonna be my deputy again tomorrow, Maria."

"Do I get to wear a badge again?"

"Of course, every deputy needs a badge."

As Kate starts to clear the table, she asks, "Have you seen Garfield since he moved his things out of the office?"

"Funny thing, I saw him coming out of the Methodist Church the other day, and it wasn't even Sunday."

"That's odd. I've never known him to be a churchgoer."

"Yeah, well, Deputy Plummer and I had better get ourselves to the office so we can do our jobs."

LATER THAT AFTERNOON, Buck, seated behind his desk, sifts through some paperwork while Maria sits on a chair not far away, reading *The Adventures of Huckleberry Finn*. The door opens, Kate walks in, and Buck looks up. "What are you doing here?"

"I finished early, so I thought I'd stop by and pick up Maria."

"You wanna stay awhile?"

"No, I have things to do at home."

"All right. I shouldn't be more than an hour."

Buck ushers Maria to the door, helps her with her coat, and kisses Kate on the cheek. "See you two later."

Kate and Maria leave, and Buck returns to his desk. He starts looking through the papers again, sees a wanted poster, and reads it softly to himself.

MAN WANTED FOR MURDER AND GOLD THEFT
MIGHT HAVE KILLED 6 MEN, MAYBE MORE
LAST SEEN NEAR TIN CUP, COLORADO
GOES BY THE NAME OF SAM PLUMMER
LOOKS TO BE 20 YEARS OLD AND MIGHT BE A PAIUTE INDIAN

Buck studies the drawing, and his head begins to spin. This couldn't be his brother-in-law. Too young. What about his nephew, Sam Henry? Tin Cup, Colorado? His father had mentioned that Maria had told him her brother was all about looking for gold there.

He looks around the office as if someone is watching. He stands up, wads up the poster, moves to the wood-burning stove, and drops it inside.

He hears a knock at the door. He rolls back his shoulders, walks over, and opens it. Front and center stands the former sheriff, Garfield Simpson. Buck narrows his eyes. "You leave something behind?"

"No, can I come in?"

Buck steps aside, and Garfield walks in. Buck points at an empty chair. He sits, and Buck takes a seat behind his desk. "What can I do for you?"

Garfield cracks his knuckles. "Let me get right to it. I'm here to apologize. I've been an asshole coward and I treated you like shit the whole time you worked with me."

Buck stares in disbelief. "I have to say, this is a bit of a surprise. Why are you admitting all this?"

"I assure you. I'm genuine. I thought being a sheriff made me a cut above everyone else. When they voted you in and me out, I realized I wasn't any better than anyone else. Fact is, I discovered I was worse than everyone else… lusting after your wife and sending you into those woods like I did, hoping you'd get shot. God strike me down if I'm not a changed man.

"I saw you coming out of the church."

"Yeah, the new pastor there said me seeking forgiveness would be a step in the right direction. Never told anyone this before, but when I was a young man, I was all set to be a minister myself. My heart changed, and God and I went our separate ways." Garfield stands up. "So, that's all I've got to say. Just hope you and Kate can forgive me."

"Might take a little time getting used to the new you, but I think we can do that."

The former sheriff starts for the door, turns back, and stammers, "If ya think you might need a deputy, I'm available."

"You saying you'd be willing to lower yourself to being a deputy?"

"Like I said, things are different now… and being a lawman is all I know."

Buck rocks back and then steps forward. He shakes his head and grins. "Right now, my deputy's a six-year-old."

Garfield gives him a curious look, and Buck says, "Just a little joke. I'll explain it to you in the morning when you get here."

Garfield rocks back on his heels. "Really?"

"Why not? You know the ropes, and I ain't got nobody."

"Thanks… sheriff."

"Fair warning. It might take a while for me to trust you again."

224

"I understand. The old me would've laughed at such a request. Thank God you're not me. See you tomorrow." Garfield turns and walks off as Buck backs into the office and drops into his chair like a felled tree.

BUCK AND KATE are lying in bed, wide awake. Kate adjusts her blanket and says, "And you made him your deputy sheriff just like that?"

"I know it sounds crazy, but I think he's a different man. He apologized for treating me like shit, admitted he had been lusting after you, and even said he sent me into the woods hoping I'd get shot. Why would he admit all of that if he hasn't changed?"

"It's only been a week. That's a quick turnaround for a man who wanted you dead only a few weeks ago."

"I know, but he claims he found God. Maybe it is too soon, but I felt sorry for him. Might even do us some good to forgive him."

"Father used to say, 'A repentant man deserves a second chance, but you need to keep an eye on him.'"

"Yeah, what's the worst that can happen? If he goes back to his old ways, I'll fire his sorry ass."

"Buckie, sometimes you surprise me with your vulgar talk. Kate smiles. "I like it."

CHAPTER 15

Finding Natalie, Seeking the Truth, and Going Back to Nevada

SAM HENRY SPOTS A wooden sign that reads, *Wyoming Territory, Cheyenne-20 Miles*. He stops his horse, turns back, and then looks straight ahead at the distant cloud-covered Laramie Mountains, buffered by high prairies and forests.

A cold wind begins to blow as the sky emits a strange combination of light rain and large, intermittent snowflakes. The wanted man hunkers down in his saddle and thinks about his future.

He felt bad he'd shed his Paiute name a few days earlier, but didn't figure he'd ever use it again. And when he gets home, he isn't even sure if he will admit to Natalie that he was an Indian for a year or that he killed four men… maybe five, counting Rupert falling off his horse and crushing his skull.

As far as Natalie knew, he was still in Colorado seeking his fortune. Then again, he didn't wanna go back to her and only tell half the truth… how he found gold and silver and had a lot of money in his pocket. Oh, well. Maybe none of it mattered. She might be married by now or in love with another fella.

ON THE OUTSKIRTS of Cheyenne, Sam Henry sees three men hobbling down the road coming his way. When they get closer, he realizes they are covered in black tar and chicken feathers, except for their faces. Behind them are two local Cheyenne men on horseback, rifles at the ready. The oldest one, Sheriff Lou Wilkins, with a badge pinned to his vest, raises his rifle and yells, "If I hear about you trying to sell them soap bars anywhere near here and cheating people out of their hard-earned money, me and my boys will hunt you down, hang you from the nearest tree, and let the crows peck out your eyes."

Jefferson "Soapy" Johnson, dressed in a tar-covered jacket and what used to be a white lacy shirt, pleads his case. "Least you could have given us our horses, wagons, and firearms back."

Sheriff Wilkins sneers, "Bull shit. I'm keeping them instead of putting the three of you in my jail for three months. I don't wanna feed your ugly faces."

One of Jefferson's cohorts, his curly blond hair matted with tar, growls, "How are we supposed to get this shit off anyway?"

"Soap, use plenty of soap." The sheriff laughs. Then he turns and acknowledges Sam Henry's presence. "And who might you be?"

"I'm nobody. I'm just headed back home. My family has a farm on the other side of Cheyenne."

"What's your name?"

He lies. "Ned… Ned Anderson."

"Maybe I know your Pa. Who is he?"

Sam Henry lies again. "Amos Anderson."

"Huh, don't ring a bell. Thought I knew everyone around here." Wilkins turns to his deputy. "Let's head back. I got dinner waiting for me."

Jefferson's second crony, wearing a wide-brimmed hat, complains, "Wait a minute. We're gonna freeze to death out here. There ain't no town around here for miles."

"Not my problem." The sheriff and his deputy turn their horses and start back to town.

Sam Henry waits for the dust to settle and speaks up. "There's a small place just across the border… Wyocolo. I saw a sign."

Jefferson speaks up. "How far is that?"

"Seven… maybe eight miles."

The blond-haired accomplice complains, "I don't got eight miles left in me. I'm about to starve to death… and it's getting dark."

Jefferson looks at Sam Henry and snickers. "How much for that horse of yours?"

"Mister, you don't have anything I want."

The bossman looks at his fellow travelers again and spouts, "Too bad I don't have a gun. I could shoot Ned here, and we'd have at least one horse." He looks at his companions again and grumbles, "Or how about if we help him vacate his animal just the same?"

The men lurch forward, but before they reach him, Sam Henry digs his heels into his horse and gallops off. A safe distance away, he yells back, "Good luck. I hope you make it to Wyocolo!"

Jefferson spits. "Wyocolo my ass."

AS THE SUN SETS, Sam Henry rides down Cheyenne's main street, checking out the changes in the town since the last time he was there a few years earlier. He notices several new clapboard buildings, including a bank, a grocery store, a blacksmith shop, and a Lutheran church.

He hitches his horse to a post in front of a grocery store and walks inside. He quickly finds what he needs and lays it on the counter. An older man with a white apron moves to a cash register and calls out each item as he adds up the total. "Loaf of bread, half-dozen eggs, pound of bacon, box of matches, frying pan, and a small box of chocolates… anything else?"

Sam Henry nods. "No, that will do." As the man fits Sam Henry's purchases in a burlap bag, out of the side of his eye, he sees a long-haired woman stacking cans on a shelf. He pivots to look at her, but her back is to him, so he can't make out her face.

He turns around when the grocer announces, "Three dollars and twenty cents." Sam Henry pays him, grabs the bag, and leaves.

ON THE OTHER SIDE OF CHEYENNE, having spent the night on the ground, Sam Henry sits in front of a small fire. He holds his frying pan over the flames, watching the eggs and bacon sizzle. Having no utensils or plate, he tilts his frying pan and slides the bacon and two eggs onto a piece of bread.

As he eats his breakfast, he watches two scrawny coyotes in an open field sniffing the air. He grabs his grocery bag and quietly strolls over to where the coyotes are standing. They back away, so he reaches into his bag, removes four eggs and several strips of bacon, and places them on the ground. When he returns to his campsite, he packs up his belongings and mounts his horse. As he rides past the prairie wolves, he watches them devour his breakfast gift.

HOURS LATER, Sam Henry approaches his family's old farmstead. He immediately notices the missing and damaged tiles on the roof of the house, the weed-infested garden, and three huge tumbleweeds lodged against the front door. The barn is still intact, but the paint is peeling, and the front door is lying on the ground.

Ten minutes later, when he arrives at the Culbertson farm, he spots Lila Culbertson on the side of the house hanging shirts of all sizes on a clothesline. She doesn't see him as he quietly climbs down from his horse. He checks out the farmyard, walks over to Lila, and clears his throat. She turns back, stares at him, and gasps, "Sam Henry, oh my God! Is that you?"

"Yes, ma'am. It's me."

"I didn't know if we'd ever see you again."

"Good to see you. Is Natalie here?"

"No, Natalie is in Cheyenne. She's working at a grocery store now. She's got a little place right behind it."

"Are you joking with me?"

"Why would I joke about something like that?"

"It was in that store a few hours ago."

"Sorry you missed her. It's Friday. She comes home every weekend. Doesn't get off work until late tonight, but she'll be here in the morning."

"I hate to ask, but does she have a man-friend?"

"Of course not. She's been pining over you since the day you left."

"I didn't know I was gonna be gone so long. I had a few unexpected stops along the way."

Lila raises her eyebrows. "Do you know how to write?" She clears her throat. "Never mind, it's too late for that now. How are your father and Maria?"

"I don't know, but I hope to find out soon. I left her in Nevada with my grandfather. Right after I leave here, I'm going back there to see her. I have no idea where Samuel is."

"He sold us everything on your farm and rode off looking for the two of you. Not sure why, but he wouldn't sell Cletus his land."

"Hate to ask, but I've been in the saddle a long time. Think, maybe I could spend the night in your barn? I wanna see Natalie."

"Nonsense, you can stay in your old room with my boys. They are older and take up more space, but they'll be happy to see you again.

SAM HENRY IS LYING ON THE FLOOR on a feather mattress in the corner of a small bedroom fitted with two small beds. Joshua, 16, and Jacob, 14, share a bed, while Jude, 6, has one of his own. From across the room, Joshua looks at Sam Henry and says, "You could share Jude's bed, but he still pees in it."

"Not every night," Jude pouts.

Sam Henry taps the floor. "I'm good right here."

"Are you in love with my sister?" Jacob asks.

"That's kind of personal. I think I'm going to keep that to myself."

"She says you are."

"Well, maybe she'll change her mind about that when she sees me tomorrow."

Sam Henry turns down the lamp. One of the boys farts, and everyone laughs.

IT'S ALMOST NOON, and Sam Henry stands in the yard, clutching the store-bought candy and staring into the distance. In the barn, Joshua and Jacob are loading hay into a wagon when Joshua puts his pitchfork down. He shuffles over to the open door, turns back to his younger brother, and says, "Yep, he's still standing there."

Jacob joins his brother. "It's been two hours."

Joshua has a little grin on his face. "Yeah, he's got it bad."

All at once, Sam Henry shifts his weight and leans forward. Natalie comes into focus as she tops a small hill, riding her father's old quarter horse. He waits patiently until she sees who it is and digs her heels into the flanks of the unsuspecting horse.

When she reaches the farmyard, she slides out of the saddle, and the horse trots to the barn where her two brothers unsaddle it and lead it inside.

Natalie runs her fingers through her long brown hair and strolls shyly over to Sam Henry. She stands motionless for a moment, taking in his new look. Unable to contain herself any longer, she wraps her arms around him and embraces him with all the strength she can muster.

Sam Henry gently pushes her away, lays the candy on the ground, pulls her back into his arms, and kisses her passionately. The barn's hayloft door flies open, and Joshua and Jacob simultaneously yell, "Woo hoo!"

They separate, and Sam Henry leans down, picks up the box of candy, and hands it to her. "This is for you."

She stares at it and says, "We sell this candy at our store."

"I know. I was in there yesterday."

"You were in my store? Why didn't I see you?"

"I think I saw your backside." Sam Henry takes Natalie's shoulders, turns her around, and stares at her butt. "Yep, that was you."

She pivots back around and smirks. "You're a bad man, Sam Henry. You've been gone so long. Did you find that gold you were looking for?"

"It's a long story. Can we wait until I get my fill of you first?"

"You'd better not ever get your fill of me."

SITTING ON A HAY BALE and holding hands, Sam Henry grins at Natalie. She looks in his eyes and purrs, "I'm so happy you're back. I was worried I'd never see you again."

"Even after everything I told you?" he asks.

"Of course, but I would have liked to have seen you when you were an Indian… and I can't believe you killed all those men."

"Probably shouldn't have told you. That's not something I take lightly, but I didn't have much of a choice."

"I won't tell anyone, not even my folks."

"Especially your folks. I don't want them worrying about their daughter being with a killer. There are people in Colorado probably looking for me."

"It's kind of sad and exciting at the same time… you being a wanted man."

"Question is, do you want me?"

"You know the answer to that." Natalie puts her hand on Sam Henry's knee. "When you were a Paiute, did you poke any of those Indian girls?"

He grins. "Had my chance, but I was saving myself for you."

She lays her head on his shoulder. "I like your Indian name, Shilah. Can I call you that sometimes?"

"No, that's going to be our son's name."

Natalie sits up straight. "Our son?"

"Yeah, let's get married… right away."

"You haven't even asked me yet?"

"You're gonna make me ask you?"

"Yes."

Sam Henry drops to his knees. "Natalie Culbertson, will you marry me?"

She smirks. "I don't know. You're a wanted man." She takes a moment and nudges Sam Henry with her elbow. "Of course I will, silly."

"Right away."

"Okay, but you have to get permission from my father."

"What if he turns me down?"

"He won't do that. He thinks the world of you. Sides, I think he'll be happy to see me go."

"Why is that?"

"Cuz, I'm always siding with Mother… So, when exactly?"

"Soon as we find us a minister."

"Really? There's a retired preacher who lives a mile down the road."

"That's handy."

"Are we going to live on your old farm?"

"I'm no farmer… and that's… Samuel's place?"

"You're calling your father by his first name now?"

"Yeah, there's still a lot of bad shit between us."

"Okay, but we need to live somewhere."

"First, we need to head to Nevada to my grandpa's place. I promised Maria I'd come back and check on her. I got enough money for us to make a go of it for a while."

IN THE BACKYARD of the Culbertson house, Sam Henry and Natalie stand facing each other. The bride is wearing a white cotton dress, and the groom is dressed in his only clothes with a flower fastened to his shirt.

Facing them is a wrinkled-faced preacher turned farmer with a bald head and thick eyebrows. Directly behind the couple are Cletus and Lillie Culbertson and all their children. Lillie looks stoic while Natalie's father wipes a tear from his eye.

The newlyweds finish reciting their vows and kiss passionately while Natalie's siblings whistle and cheer. Not sure what to do next, the happy couple walks hand in hand to the front of the house and disappears inside.

SEATED IN AN OLD FREIGHT WAGON, Mr. and Mrs. Sam Henry Plummer prepare to leave. Cletus rubs his tear-stained eyes as Natalie, dressed in jeans and a heavy fur coat covering her flannel red shirt, turns to the back of the wagon. She adjusts her suitcase, bulging with clothes, and pats her new husband's leg.

Two bay-colored mares take turns pawing the dirt, anxious to leave. Tied to the back of the wagon is Sam Henry's horse. The happy couple waves as they roll off. Seconds later, Sam Henry turns to his new wife and says, "Nice of your father to gift back my father's old wagon and horses."

Natalie tightens her coat, takes a moment, and says, "We're not gonna spend our first night together on the ground, are we?"

Sam Henry grins. "No, I'm gonna rent us a hotel room in Cheyenne."

"Oh, good. I'm glad we're stopping there. I just remembered I haven't quit my job yet."

Sam Henry catches Natalie staring at him. "Why are you looking at me like that?"

"When we get to town, we need to get you some new clothes… and a bath."

AFTER LEAVING their wagon and horses at the Cheyenne Livery Stable, the newlyweds walk down Main Street carrying Natalie's suitcase and a small carpetbag. When they reach the local hotel, Sam Henry turns to his wife and asks, "Are you nervous?"

Natalie grins. "No. Should I be?"

"I don't know about you, but I'm looking forward to seeing you naked." Natalie slaps Sam Henry's arm, and they walk inside the hotel.

Standing at the front desk, they wait for the young clerk to give them a key. When he turns around, he hands Sam Henry a brass skeleton key and says, "Up the stairs, down the hallway, room twelve."

The newlyweds pick up their luggage and head up the stairs. When they reach room twelve, Sam Henry tries to put the key in the door lock, but he can't seem to make it fit. Natalie gently takes it out of his hand, slides the key in the lock, and unlocks the door.

He holds up his hand, suggesting she stay put, grabs the luggage, and carries it into the room. When he returns, he scoops her into his arms and carries her into the room. He lays her on the bed and smiles. "I'll be right back."

Later, after taking a bath, Sam Henry pulls up the sheet covering all but their shoulders and heads. The married couple looks at one another, not sure what to say. Finally, Natalie whispers, "Last night was exciting. It hurt for a while, but it was a lot of fun."

"You know that's how people end up with children."

Natalie grins. "Oh really?"

"How are we gonna be sure we don't end up with a baby right away?" Sam Henry asks. "I think we should wait for a while."

"You and me both. Mother says the only sure way to prevent children is abstinence."

"That doesn't sound like something I'd like."

"Another option is for you to leave early."

"Leave early?"

Natalie smiles. "You know… before the big explosion."

Sam Henry finally catches on. "That doesn't sound like much fun either."

"Mother also said certain times of the month are better than others."

"How will we know when that is?"

"I'll let you know. Also, some of the girls I met in Cheyenne told me about condoms."

"Condoms?"

"They're kinda like a raincoat you put on your… hooter, but you can still feel things."

"Does it hurt?"

Natalie giggles. "No, silly."

"Boy, having sex is a little more complicated than I thought it would be."

"If you'd rather not…"

"Oh, no. We'll figure it out."

236

SAM HENRY SHIELDS HIS EYES from the morning sun as he waits in the wagon while Natalie goes inside the grocery store to inform the owner that she can't work for him any longer, because she just got married and is leaving for Wyoming. When she exits the building, she gives Sam Henry a thumbs-up.

A MONTH LATER, Sam Henry, wearing a straw hat, jeans, and a blue flannel shirt he bought before leaving Cheyenne, and Natalie, wearing a yellow cotton dress and matching sun bonnet, crest a hill and see Buckland Station in the distance. Sam Henry waves both hands and hollers, "We're here!"

When the travel-weary couple reaches the front yard near the main cabin, Sam Henry halts the wagon when he sees a woman working in the garden. Margaret removes her gloves and walks over to his wagon. "Hello. May I help you?" Sam Henry politely removes his cowboy hat and introduces himself and his new wife. "I'm Sam Henry Plummer, and this is my wife, Natalie."

Margaret smiles and asks, "Pete's grandson? He's been worried about you. I'm Margaret… Margaret Buckland. Your grandfather and I got married three months ago."

"Wow. Natalie and I got married a month ago."

Margaret grins at Natalie. "Welcome to the family."

Sam Henry looks around. "Where's Grandpa Pete?"

"Inside, taking a nap. I'm surprised he didn't hear you drive up." On cue, the cabin's front door flies open, and Pete steps out. He adjusts the strap on his bib overalls, squints, and asks, "Who do we have here, Margaret?"

"It's your grandson, Sam Henry."

Pete walks over, plants his feet, and stares. "I haven't seen you for so long, I don't know if it's you or some pretender. Tell something only you would know."

Sam Henry thinks for a moment. "Me and Buckie brought home a chunk of bear, mother cooked it, and it tasted like shit."

"That's you all right. I was only kidding. You got your mother's smile. Who is this pretty lady?"

"This is my wife, Natalie."

"Wife?"

Natalie speaks. "Nice to meet you, Mr. Buckland. I've heard a lot about you."

"Some of it good, I hope." Pete turns to his grandson and says, "You've got a lot of explaining to do, young man."

"I know. Where's Maria?"

"Carson City, living with Buckie and his wife. They are raising her as their own."

"Buckie's married?"

"Her name is Kate. Buck's a sheriff, too.

"You call him Buck now?"

"Yeah, for me it's back and forth. Buck around strangers and Buckie when we're alone."

Come inside and tell me what you've been up to for who knows how long."

INSIDE THE CABIN, Sam Henry finishes telling his grandfather the story about him being abducted by Paiutes and living with them for a year. He even told him how he survived a coal mining accident in Tin Cup and discovered rocks covered with gold and silver on the side of a hill. He finishes by saying, "I left a lot out, but I can tell more if you wanna hear it sometime."

"You've lived more lives than a cat, but you left out the part about running away from home and leaving your sister with me. And what about Samuel? Where has he been hiding?"

"Here's the answer to both your questions. We ran off because after my mother died, he started drinking. He would ride off to town and not come back for days."

"That doesn't sound like the Samuel I know."

"Her dying changed him. We had our disagreements, but him abandoning us all the time was more than I could handle. I knew I couldn't take care of Maria where I was going, so that's why I left her with you."

"You could have at least explained yourself instead of riding off the way you did."

"I was afraid you'd talk me into staying."

Pete pats Sam Henry on the back. "Water under the bridge now."

"I hate to ask, but do you think maybe Natalie and I could stay with you for a few days before we go to Carson City to see Maria? We're both pretty worn out."

"Stay as long as you want. Never know, maybe one of these days this place will be yours. Buckie is a townsman now. Doubt he'll ever wanna move back here."

Sam Henry pauses, and his mind meanders as he considers what his grandfather said. Finally, he says, "I don't think I'm cut out to work the land or raise animals. I wanna find a job where I'm done at the end of the day… but I sure don't mind helping you while I'm here."

"That would be good. Allows me to get to know you again… and your wife."

"Natalie."

"Yeah, Natalie. You and Natalie are welcome to the small cabin next to ours. Can't pay you much, but I've got plenty of work to share for as long as you wanna stay."

"I don't want your money, Grandpa. "Being here is pay enough."

CHAPTER 16

Dynamite, Going Home, And a New Life

A VIOLENT BLAST OF ENERGY, followed by a blinding flash of light, sends shock waves ripping through *Baxter's General Merchandise and Mining Supplies Store*. The windows shatter, the door explodes, and all four walls collapse as the air fills with intense heat and smoke. What's left of the building burns as debris floats in the air and ashes cover the street.

People come running from nearby houses, many in nightshirts and some half-dressed. Ten minutes later, Sheriff Benson arrives and pulls his gun when he sees two looters already helping themselves. "Get the hell out of here, before I arrest your sorry asses." The men drop shovels, axes, canned goods, and other stolen treasures and walk off, grumbling.

As the building smolders, Samuel arrives with his pistol strapped to his waist. In the distance, he sees Ruth hurrying down Main Street with her left hand covering her mouth.

After Ruth joins him, they stand with a dozen other people. Many are holding torches and staring at what's left of her store.

The sheriff shuffles over to the couple and sighs. "Ma'am, I'm sorry for your loss. Any idea how something like this happened?"

Samuel puts his arm on Ruth's shoulder, and she says, "There were two boxes of dynamite inside, but someone would have had to take them out of the boxes, attach a fuse, and light it. Why would anyone want to do that?"

"Maybe to cover their tracks. One of them didn't make it out alive. We found what's left of his body in the ashes."

Samuel asks, "Any idea who he was?"

"No way of knowing. His face is gone."

The sheriff's sister, Sonja, appears and whispers something in her brother's ear. He turns to Samuel and Ruth and says, "She thinks there was a second man."

Samuel asks, "Why does she think that?"

Floyd signals his sister. Go on, Sonja. Tell them."

The deputy touches her chin. "I found boot prints suggesting someone was carrying something heavy. It led me to the back of the saloon, where I found two sets of horse tracks leading out of town east. I think one of the horses didn't have a rider."

Samuel asks, "Why do you say that?"

"Cuz the second horse's tracks weren't that deep."

The sheriff pats Sonja on the back. "Go work, Sis."

EARLIER THAT NIGHT, Rupert Weed and Harold Letcher stand in front of the door of Baxter's store as rain falls lightly on the ground. Rupert looks both ways down Main Street, making sure no one's watching, points at the door, and whispers, "Hurry it up. I haven't eaten in two days."

Harold lifts a pickaxe above his head, takes a measured swing, and destroys the panel above the door handle. Rupert reaches through the hole and unlocks the door.

Once inside, Rupert lights a candle and hurries behind the counter. He opens the cash register, finds a few bills and coins, and spits. "Not enough here to get us drunk." He looks behind him and spots the small cast-iron safe. He spins the lock, hoping the door will open, but nothing happens. Harold joins him as Rupert manages to lift the safe in his arms.

Harold chuckles and says, "What are you gonna do with that?"

Rupert puts the safe down, sees a pile of empty burlap bags, and tosses one to Harold. "Fill it up with any shit worth taking."

Rupert and Harold rush down the store aisles, pulling items off the shelves and loading their bags with knives, cigars, cheap jewelry, boxes of bullets, canned goods, and other foodstuffs.

Avoiding the mining supplies because they are too hard to carry, Rupert motions Harold to follow him into the supply room in the back of the store. Rupert holds up the candle and looks around, trying to identify anything of value.

They are just about to leave when Rupert spots two boxes of dynamite. He nods and grins at Harold, who says, "What we gonna do with that?"

"We're gonna blow this damn place up."

Harold argues. "Why you wanna do that? Let's take what we can carry and get the hell outta here."

"That tell-all Samuel Plummer works here, but he ain't gonna work here no more. Sides, I got some meanness to get out of me." He points, and Harold uses the end of his pickaxe to pry open the boxes. Rupert quickly identifies a blasting cap and attaches it to one of the sticks of dynamite. He finds a two-foot-long fuse, fastens it to the blasting cap, and warns Harold. "Once it's lit, we've got a minute or less to get out of here." He reaches into his pocket, pulls out a match, swipes it across the floor, and lights the fuse.

Rupert leads the way as they hurry out of the supply room and head for the front door with their bags of stolen goods in tow. Harold struggles as he carries a pickaxe in his left hand and drags the bag with his right.

When Harold reaches the canned goods aisle, he trips over a can, fumbles with his pickaxe, and lands headfirst.

Rupert turns back, sees him lying motionless on the floor, and grits his teeth. The thief takes a step back to help him, changes his mind, and tosses his bag of stolen goods aside. He hurries behind the counter, cradles the safe, and hurries out the front door.

Harold manages to sit up, and tries to clear his head. He remembers the situation, panics, and stumbles to his feet. He steps toward the open door, and the building explodes, catapulting him into the air against the ceiling.

He lands on the floor face down; flames engulf him and everything around him.

Rupert doesn't look back as he struggles to carry the safe down Main Street. As lampposts become trees, Rupert finds two horses tethered to the limb of a white pine in a forested area behind Barney's old Livery Stable.

Rupert drops the safe on the ground and attaches the second horse's reins to the saddle blanket of his horse. Then he picks up the safe and carefully positions it on his saddle. He mounts the animal and settles behind the saddle. As he steadies the safe with left hand, he guides his horse out of town with his right.

SAMUEL AND RUTH continue to stare at what's left of her store as three men empty buckets of water on the still-smoldering ruins. Samuel glances at Ruth. "Good thing you had insurance on this place. You can always rebuild."

"I can't think about that right now. I'm completely overwhelmed."

"I understand, but I think I know who the thieves were."

The sheriff, who has been listening, slides over. "You do?"

"Yeah, those hoodlums who were in your office… Rupert and Harold."

"Why do you think it was them?"

"I don't know. I have a feeling."

Sheriff Benson nods. "Well, do you and your feeling wanna ride with me and my deputy to look for whoever it is?"

He turns to Ruth. "Do I?"

"I'm so angry, I'm gonna say yes. Promise me you'll be careful."

"Now that I'm older, I'm all about being careful."

SAMUEL AND THE BENSON SIBLINGS ride out of Tin Cup headed east, the opposite direction of the mining camps. There's a light dusting of snow on the ground as a few flakes fall from the sky. Sheriff Benson shades his eyes from the rising sun and says, "This may be a wild goose chase."

Samuel responds. "That's all right. This goose needs chasing."

A quarter mile later, Sonja climbs off her horse, kneels, and studies fresh tracks. She looks back at her brother and says, "Same two horses."

"How do you know that?" Samuel asks.

Sonja answers, "Didn't think much of it before, but the riderless horse has a shoe a tad bigger than his other three. He drags his rear leg every three or four steps, leaving a small divot."

"Where'd you learn to spot that?"

"I had two Indian friends growing up. They worked with the Colorado Militia as scouts. They taught me everything I know."

"You were in the Colorado Militia?"

"I was a tomboy growing up, so they hired me to care for the horses at night. Sometimes I would go along with the scouts, but I got tired of being the only woman and left after six months."

The threesome continues to follow the trail until Natalie looks down and pulls her horse to stop again. Samuel and the sheriff follow suit and look at Sonja. "Now what?" Floyd asks.

Sonja points. "Fresh shit… still steamin'."

Samuel leans over his horse and responds. "I think you're right."

Sonja looks down the road. "Can't be more than a few minutes ahead of us."

The sheriff scoffs. "Okay, keep your eyes open. We don't what that asshole is capable of."

Samuel grunts. "Believe me, sheriff, he's capable of plenty."

"Yeah, if he is who you think he is."

A mile later, Sonja puts her index finger to her lips and points with her other hand. Samuel and Floyd look ahead and see smoke coming from a stand of yellow aspens off the side of the trail.

They quietly dismount and walk their horses to the grove of trees, where they tether them. Sheriff Benson pulls two branches aside and spots Rupert sitting on the unopened safe. He's dressed in a heavy coat and wearing stolen deerskin gloves. He stands up, and holds his hands over a small fire. While he waits for a can of beans to warm, he chews a piece of beef jerky.

The thief spots a nest of small rats, kicks it aside, and the pests scatter. He gingerly pulls the can from the fire, waits for it to cool, and uses his knife to open it. He sits on a log, removes his gloves, and starts eating the beans with his fingers.

Floyd turns to Samuel. "You were right. It's Weed. Listen, we outnumber him, so we're gonna step out of these trees with our pistols pointed his way. Don't be afraid to shoot if he draws on us. You ready, Sonja?"

She raises her head as she pulls her 32 from its holster. Floyd takes the lead as they quietly step out of the trees. Rupert immediately sees them, climbs to his feet, sees he's outnumbered, and raises his hands to the sky. "Don't shoot, I ain't packin'."

Samuel lowers his pistol, satisfied they have everything under control. Rupert spits a mouthful of beans and snarls, "Why you sneaking up on me like this? I ain't done nothin'."

"I'm arresting you for robbing the mercantile store and blowing it up."

"How you figure me doin' that?"

"We tracked you and your horses here… and I'm guessing that bag hanging from your extra horse is full of stolen merchandise."

"Not saying I did anything like that… cuz I might've found that bag alongside the road. But I'm curious. What kind of punishment would a fella get for something like that?"

"That'd be up to a judge to decide. Walk yourself over here nice and easy so I can cuff you. Samuel, go ahead and bring his horses this way."

Samuel holsters his gun and starts for the horses. The sheriff turns to his sister and says, "Good job, Sis."

Rupert sees his chance, reaches behind his back, and pulls his pistol from his belt. He fires once and hits Sonja in the leg. Floyd panics, grabs his sister before she can fall to the ground, and helps her into the trees.

Samuel tosses the horses' reins aside and starts to draw his weapon, but it's too late. Rupert is already aiming his gun at his chest. The liar growls, "Drop that gun and come over here, for I shoot your sorry ass."

Samuel lays his pistol on the ground and steps the culprit's way. Suddenly inspired, he sees a tree root in front of him and pretends to trip over it. On his knees, with his back to Rupert, he finds a rock, shoves it in his pocket, and stands up. The miscreant growls, "What the hell?"

"Kinda clumsy. Didn't see that root."

Rupert circles behind Samuel, waits for him to stand up, and holds his gun to his head. Hidden behind Samuel, he yells into the trees. "You still in here, sheriff?"

Floyd hollers back. "Yeah, me and my rifle are waiting for a clear shot, Weed."

"Too bad about me wounding your sister. Don't like shootin' women."

"Lay the gun down. Don't wanna kill you, but I will if I have to."

"Here's the thing. I've got the drop on this traitor here… and if you don't get your sister back to town soon, I'm thinkin' she'll more than likely bleed out. But if you're stupid enough to stay and shoot it out, you're gonna hit my shield before you get to me. So, you got no choice, sheriff. You and your sister are gonna head back to town. Once you're gone, I'll ride off with Plummer here. Come after me, and I'll plug him as soon as I see it's you."

Behind the trees, the sheriff looks down at his sister, who has a bloody tourniquet around her leg made from the sleeve of her brother's shirt. He removes his hat and yells, "My sister is bleeding pretty hard, Samuel!"

Samuel's anger simmers as he yells, "I understand! Do what you gotta do! There's no bargaining with this snake. Go!"

The sheriff yells back. "All right. "I'm going now."

Rupert watches as the sheriff helps his sister on her horse and mounts his own. When Rupert sees them ride away, he aims his gun at Samuel and demands. "Now you stay put, while I think on this." There's a long pause until Rupert finally says, "Okay, we ride together until I know I'm safe. Then I'll leave you on the side of the road for the buzzards to eat." Rupert removes his hat and scratches his ass. "You know what? I changed my mind. I ain't takin' any chances. I'm gonna end you now."

Rupert steps over to his horse and removes his rifle hidden under a blanket. Seeing his chance, Samuel reaches into his pocket and pulls out the rock. When Rupert turns back, Samuel winds up like Old Testament David, preparing to smite Goliath.

Rupert sees what's happening and starts to aim his rifle. Samuel throws the rock and hits the thug square in the forehead. The villain drops to his knees and falls to the ground as Samuel leans over and picks up his rifle.

Flat on his back with his wide mouth open, Rupert breathes heavily. As blood flows freely from the fallen man's forehead, Samuel steps back when he sees a small rat vacate his nearby nest. The varmint runs up Rupert's leg and scampers across his chest. The hungry rodent pauses on his chin, sniffs the blood, and his beef jerky breath. The vermin stands to his feet, sniffs the air again, travels to Rupert's lips and squeezes his way into his open mouth.

The wounded man chokes and coughs as the rat chews its way down his throat, through one of his lungs, and into his stomach. As Rupert struggles for air, he quivers, and blood oozes out of his mouth. He coughs twice, his hand twitches, and he stops breathing.

Samuel rides back to Tin Cup with Rupert's body straddled over the back of Harold Letcher's horse. Tethered to the second horse's saddle is a rope attached to the stolen safe. As the safe slides on the ground behind, Samuel turns back and looks at Rupert's corpse. "Why do I get the feeling no one is going to miss you?"

THE DIFFUSE LIGHT from the sun, softened by the frost-covered bedroom window, wakes Samuel. After several random thoughts, he turns to Ruth, staring at the ceiling. Samuel clears his throat and asks, "What's on your mind?"

She turns to him. "What a horrible way to die."

"I know, but don't forget that bastard was ready to end my life." Samuel yawns. "By the way, he had your safe. I brought it back."

"Huh, it didn't notice it was missing."

"Well, at least you got back what was in there."

"It was empty. I take my money home every night and hide it under the bed."

Samuel grins. "Good to know."

Ruth slaps Samuel's arm, takes a moment, and says, "I don't know why I'm asking, but where did they bury him?"

"He's buried behind the church between the two sheriff's graves. We figured that was appropriate, since the rumor is he and his men might have killed them both."

Ruth slides into Samuel's open arms and surprises him when she says, "I can't lose you. You're the only man I've ever loved."

"Now that's something I never thought I'd hear from you. You sure you're still not feeling sorry for me?"

"You did look pretty pathetic after those men beat you up and took everything you had."

"I was a mess. Listen, I have something I need to tell you."

"I'm listening."

"I found out my son might have been in the Tin Cup area... only a few days ago."

"Why didn't you say something?"

"Cuz two men claimed he killed someone and stole their gold."

"You think he's capable of doing something like that?"

"Can't be sure. The men claiming he did it were Weed and Letcher, the idiots who destroyed your business."

Ruth touches Samuel's arm. "So, what makes you think it might be your son?"

"The description they gave fit him... his age... him looking like an Indian... and the drawing on the wanted poster even looked a bit like him."

"Where do you think he might be?"

"Don't know. But here's the thing: I can't rest until I find him... and Maria."

"I understand. But where do you start?"

"I'm gonna start by going back to Wyoming. He has a girl back there, I think he might want to see again."

She sits up. "Are you leaving for good?"

"I have to...."

"Are you going to take me with you?"

Samuel stares at Ruth. "What? You'd go with me?"

"Only if you make me an honest woman."

"Are you saying you'd be willing to marry me?"

"I don't know. You haven't asked me yet."

"Not long ago, you told me you liked living free from some man's plan for you."

"Well, I've changed my mind. You're not just some man."

"What about your store? I thought you were gonna rebuild it."

"With the insurance money I'll be getting, I can build it anywhere I want."

"And you'd leave Tin Cup and this house and come with me… to who knows where?"

"I won't miss Tin Cup, but I'll miss this house." She stares at Samuel. "It kind of sounds like you're trying to come up with excuses so you don't have to take me with you."

"Not true at all. It's just that it's been such a skunk week with the store burning down and me almost getting killed. Plus, I never thought you'd even consider marrying someone like me. I have a son who is wanted for murder and robbery, a daughter who is still missing, and I don't have a job anymore. "

"I know all that, so let me be the one who decides whether I want to marry you or not."

Samuel drops to one knee. "Since this is all sudden-like and I don't have any well-thought-out words to say… here goes. Ruth Baxter, would you do me the honor of marrying me? There is no one I'd rather spend the rest of my life with than you."

Ruth reaches down, takes Samuel's hand, and pulls him up to her. She smiles, initiates a kiss, and wraps her arms around him. He whispers in her ear, "Is that a yes?"

She gently pushes him back. "That's a definite yes."

He tightens his lips. "I'm excited, but I'm a little bit worried."

Ruth leans back. "It's not too late to change your mind."

"No, I'm worried about how we're gonna make things work. If you do build another store, I don't know how something like that will pan out. Being married to you and working for you are two different things."

"It'll be our store. We'll be partners."

"The thing is, I'm an outdoor kind of guy."

"Then you'll have to find yourself an outdoor kind of job. I'm not interested in marrying a version of myself."

"You'd be all right with that?"

"Of course. Being with you twenty-four hours a day isn't my idea of a happy marriage anyway."

"We can have horses and cattle?"

"You can have all the animals you want, as long as you're willing to take care of them while I'm minding the new store."

"And don't forget I have a son and a little girl."

"I haven't forgotten. I think we can work that out, too. First, we need to find them."

"You want a short engagement or a long one?" Samuel asks."

Ruth surprises him by saying, "How about two days?"

RUTH AND SAMUEL stand in the Sheriff's office with their hands resting on a Bible held out to them by Deputy Sonja Benson, leaning on a crutch.

Next to her is her brother, who is officiating the wedding. Ruth and Samuel look at Floyd as if to say, What's next? But the sheriff interrupts the moment by scratching his head and mumbling, "Well, that's all I've got to say. Now is when you two kiss each other."

Samuel, dressed in a new pair of jeans and a blue shirt, leans into Ruth, wearing a white cotton dress with small sunflowers, and kisses her softly.

Two prisoners who have been watching through jailhouse bars, hoot and holler, and begin to clap. The miners finally lose interest and sit back on their beds.

The sheriff and his sister hug Ruth and shake Samuel's hand as they show them to the door.

Outside, a freight wagon filled with Ruth's belongings waits. Tied to the back of it is Samuel's horse. The married couple climbs aboard, and Samuel slaps the reins to the horses.

As they pass what's left of Ruth's store, she takes one last look and notices the blackened wall of Frenchy's saloon to the left of it. She kisses her new husband on the cheek and comments, "A lot of good memories here and some not so good. Truthfully, I'm happy to be leaving Tin Cup."

"Why is that?"

"Because I'm confident the remaining years of my life are about to be wonderful, with plenty of surprises… good surprises."

Samuel turns philosophical. "I'll never know all there is to know about your past, and you'll never know all there is to know about mine, but I think what we learn about each other from now on will be worth the journey."

Headed north out of town, the married couple takes turns smiling at each other until Samuel asks, "How does it feel to be married again, Mrs. Plummer?"

Ruth rests her head on his shoulder and whispers, "Do you think either one of us will get any sleep tonight?"

He whispers back, "I hope not."

CHAPTER 17

Murder, Secrets Exposed, and Betrayal

AT THE KITCHEN TABLE, sipping coffee, Kate puts her cup down, puts pen to paper, and begins to write in her journal.

Yesterday was an extraordinary day. Dr. Gardmer Addison and I delivered identical twin boys to the home of first-time parents David and Deirdre Adams. They named their sons Lincoln and Jefferson after the couple's favorite presidents.

Deirdre claimed that if they had been girls, she would have named them Addison and Kate, after the two of us. I doubt they would have followed through with that, but it was nice of her to say so. As far as I know, the twins are the first duplicates born in Carson City.

Addison and I continue to work well together and have become close friends. She is intelligent and has a wonderful bedside manner, unlike my father, who could be a real grouch. I miss him a lot, but working with her is less stressful, and she treats me like I'm an equal and not some lowly assistant.

After moving into my father's house, Buckie and I suddenly had more room to pursue our own interests. I got back to quilting, Maria still reads a lot, and Buckie has taken up carving wooden animals.

I continue to worry about him being sheriff, but he seems happy, so I keep quiet. I still find it strange that he hired Garfield as his deputy. Especially considering how he treated Buckie when he was his deputy. People change, I know, but I still don't trust his sudden about-face.

Buckie still believes Garfield is a new man, still claiming he found God. When I stopped by the office the other day, he even apologized to me in front of Buckie for trying to continue our relationship after I told him to leave me alone.

Another strange thing is that he's courting Addison. They see each other three or four times a week. Addison has nothing but good things to say about him. I did tell her we saw each other briefly, but I never let on how possessive he was with me or how he overreacted when I told him I didn't want to see him anymore. I guess I don't want to spoil her chance at happiness. I hope the relationship works out for them, especially if he has changed for the better.

Maria is still as sweet as ever and oh so smart. Last week, she made me sit down and she recited The Declaration of Independence, word for word. I asked her if her teacher made her learn it, and she said, "No, I saw it in my history book, thought it was important, so I memorized it."

Despite her age, she never avoids adult subjects. Friday, she came home from school angry because the boys were teasing her because she didn't have a penis. I tried to explain the benefits of being a girl, but she just shook her head and said she wanted to be a boy. I asked her why, and she explained that all the books she reads have heroes who are boys and men. I tried to supply her with a list of female heroes, such as Joan of Arc, Queen Elizabeth, and referenced the March sisters in Louisa May Alcott's Little Women, but she wasn't satisfied.

She said she could do anything better than any of the boys in her school. I already knew that because last week I had a meeting with her teacher, Miss Swanson, and she told me she has had to scold Maria numerous times for wrestling with some of the smaller boys, who sometimes make the mistake of thinking she is an easy mark. Miss Swanson seemed almost proud when she told me Maria could outrun all the boys (big and small) and was the best marble player on the playground. She went on to say that some of the parents have been complaining because Maria has won all of their sons' marbles. I am sure there is a side of her that she doesn't reveal at home, but quite honestly, I like that about her.

She does have a softer side. Almost every evening before bedtime, she comes over to my chair where I am quilting. She leans her head against my knee until I lay my fabric down and use my fingers to soothe her hair. When she starts to drift off, I pick her up, carry her to her room, and help her get ready for bed.

She does continue to ask when she'll see her father and brother again, and I have run out of ways to say I don't know. I have never told anyone this, but I think it would almost be better if we found out they were dead. That way, she could stop worrying about them. But that is in God's hands, not mine.

INSIDE THE SHERIFF'S OFFICE, Buck sits behind his desk reading the local newspaper, *The Morning Appeal,* while Garfield cleans his 45 caliber Spencer repeating rifle. Buck lays his newspaper down and looks at his new deputy leaning over his rifle with his eyes closed. He waits for Garfield's eyes to open again and asks, "Were you praying over your rifle?"

"No, just praying I don't have to shoot anyone today."

"I'm curious, how many times have you cleaned that rifle this month?"

"A clean rifle is a happy rifle." He looks down the chamber. "This weapon is my best friend. It doesn't speak until I want it to speak."

Buck chuckles. "Does Addison ever get jealous?"

"That's a good one. I'll have to ask her."

"Another question. Now that you're a Godly man, do you ever have problems reconciling your being a lawman?"

"No, the opposite. God has his commandments. I'm just helping enforce them." He grabs his rifle and heads for the door. "I guess I'll do a walkabout, then I'm having lunch with Pastor Miller at the church."

"You and him are getting to be good friends."

"Yeah, we see eye to eye on a lot of things. I gotta say we got ourselves a spiritual connection."

"You're taking your rifle with you to the church?"

"Yeah, I wanna show it to him. He don't own a gun, but he's curious about mine."

When Garfield opens the door, Maria walks inside and sits in a chair across from her uncle. Garfield grins and tips his hat. "Deputy Plummer, it's good to see you."

Maria smiles. "It's good to see you as well, Deputy Simpson."

When Garfield exits the office, Buck turns to his niece. "What can I do for you?"

"Uncle Buckie, I thought you could use some help around here. I need to make some money."

"What do you need money for?"

"I want to buy my very own horse... a white and brown one."

"A pinto. Maria, horses aren't cheap. They cost $50 or more. Then you need to buy a saddle, find a place for it to board it, and then make sure it gets fed and watered twice a day. Maybe you should think about saving up for another doll."

"Dolls are boring. They lay around all day like they don't have any sense."

Buck grins and looks around the office. "Let's see. I could have you empty the ashes out of the stove, sweep the floor, and take out the garbage. What do you think about that?"

"How much does that pay?"

"How about a dollar a week?"

"How about two dollars?"

"No, a dollar is all I can pay for that kind of work."

Maria kicks her copper toes against the table leg, hops out of her chair, and heads for the door. "Maybe I'll come back when you can pay more."

He snickers, stands up, and opens the door for her. "You do that."

Outside, Maria takes a step and turns back. "How much does a dog cost?"

"A dog? Huh. I can find you one of those for next to nothing."

As Maria walks off, she yells, "Okay, I'll take a dog… a brown and white one."

A MILE WEST of Carson City, Conner Reily exits a small barn and heads for his one-bedroom wood-paneled bungalow that has never been painted. When he reaches the front door, he thinks he hears something and turns back. Seeing nothing, he goes inside.

Without warning, a lit torch lands on the roof of his shanty, and the wood shingles instantly catch fire. A beat later, Conner's home fills with smoke, and he catapults out the door with a bewildered look.

The fire spreads quickly, covering the entire roof as Conner surveys his yard. Seeing no one, he hurries to the water pump by his freshwater well. He pumps furiously, filling a five-gallon pail.

He carries the bucket back to his house and stands frozen, trying to decide how to make the best use of the water. He realizes it's too late to save the roof, so he tosses the contents on the door.

The interior of the shanty is engulfed by fire and smoke as the Irishman stands clutching the empty bucket. When he hears the cracking of wood behind him, he turns and sees that his barn is also on fire. He hears his animals' frantic, high-pitched squeals, so he tosses the pail aside, takes two steps toward the barn, and a bullet hits him square in the chest.

Seconds later, the barn door opens, and two horses, a milk cow, and a dozen chickens scurry out. Conner, clutching his chest with one hand, reaches out with his other as if to shoo the animals away from the burning barn. He takes a deep breath, and he falls to his knees. His eyes roll back in his head, and he lands on the ground face-first, dead.

IT'S EARLY EVENING, and Buck and his deputy are standing next to Conner Reily's neighbor, Vincent Thompson. Buck removes the horse blanket covering Conner's upper torso and shows the body to Garfield. "Right through the chest. Not sure he even saw the man who shot him."

The three men scan the blackened remains of Conner's house and barn. Vincent explains, "Like I told you, it was about noon when I spotted the smoke. I rode over here and found him lying there dead to the world."

"Gotta assume the assassin was in the barn," Garfield says.

"Why do you think that?" Buck asks.

"I think he was facing that way when he got shot."

"I don't know how you know that. He was lying face down on the ground when I rolled him over."

"Yeah, but he pointed at the barn. Anyway, I checked for unusual tracks when we got here… nothin'."

As Buck puts the blanket back on Conner's body, he turns to Vincent. "Any idea who might have done such a thing?"

The tall man with a yellow straw cowboy hat and bib overalls snorts. "Nope, he's been living here alone since his wife left him a few years ago. Never bothered me or the other neighbors… but he was a different man when he got to town."

Garfield asks, "What do you mean different?"

"Well, when he got to drinking, he'd get all mean like. He'd pick a fight if someone looked at him too long. He hated the government and despised anyone telling him what he should believe."

"He mention anyone in particular?" Buck asks.

"You know, the President, the Governor." Vincent turns to Garfield. "He sure didn't have anything good to say about you when you were competing with Buck here to be sheriff."

Garfield snorts. "Yeah, I remember. He was still holding a grudge against me for getting shot when he was tracking down those bank robbers a few months back."

Buck shakes his head. "I don't know if we should take him back to town for a proper funeral or not. Doesn't have any relatives in Carson City that I know of."

Vincent spits. "Has a few Irish drinking buddies, is all. Depending on their mood, they won't care if he's alive or dead."

"Did he have a wife?"

"Sister. She got tired of him always being drunk and went back to Ireland." Vincent snorts and continues. "Conner comes from a high-strung family, all of them still in the home country. One night, he rode over to my house, drunk as a skunk. Unlike most men who lie when they drink, the drunker Conner got the more he told the truth. Anyway, he told me he and his sister left Ireland because the men in his community hanged their father."

Garfield raises an eyebrow. "He say why they hanged him?"

"The story Conner told was his father killed two of his neighbors for letting their cattle graze on his land. After he warned them several times, his old man snapped and took a shotgun to them. If ya ask me, Conner's strings were tuned as tight as his father's."

Garfield kicks the ground. "I say we bury him here… on his land, let people know he's dead, and anyone who wants to pay their respects to him can come by for a last goodbye."

Buck nods. "Good idea. Anybody got a shovel?"

"Got two in my wagon," Vincent volunteers.

NOT FAR FROM THE WELL, the three men finish digging a hole as the sun sets in the west. Buck and Vincent walk over, pick up Conner's body, and carry him to the hole. They gently drop him inside it, and Garfield starts to cover his body with loose dirt.

Buck asks, "Anybody got any words to say?"

Garfield scoffs. "You heard the man. Conner didn't like me, he liked you."

"All right, I'll give it a try. Buck clears his throat. "God, you know what happened here… so, I'm asking that you help Garfield and me find his killer… so justice can be served. Anyway, we are committing his body to the ground for you to do with as you please… earth to earth, ashes to ashes, dust to dust." Buck puts his hat on and nods at Vincent and Garfield. "You think that's good enough?"

Vincent steps back as Garfield mutters, "Good enough for me."

"All right, we'd better get back to town. "We'll spread the word about him being killed. Maybe someone will know something."

Garfield adds, "I have the newspaper office print up some flyers, and I'll put them around town."

"Good idea. See ya, Vincent."

GARFIELD AND ADDISON are headed north out of town in a lightweight four-wheel buggy. As the bay horses plod along at a moderate gait, Addison, wearing a white cotton dress, smiles. "What a beautiful day for a picnic. I can't think of a better way to spend a Saturday."

Garfield grins. "Thought you might enjoy leaving town for a little while. There's a place next to the river where we can eat."

"Sounds like you've been there before."

He takes a moment. "Yeah, sometimes I go fishing there."

Addison raises her eyebrows. "What kind of fish do you catch there, Mr. Simpson?"

Garfield shakes his finger at her. "I see what you're doing there."

"It's okay. I know you've been with other women."

"No one as special as you."

"Not even Kate?"

His tone of voice darkens. "Has she been talking about me?"

"No, I've tried to get her to talk about you, but she always bites her tongue."

Addison's suitor steers the horse off the main road, down a smaller dirt road, and into a small grove of trees near the water. He vaults out of the buggy, grabs the picnic basket from the back, and leads the way to the bank of the Carson River.

Addison spreads a red and white checkered blanket on the ground, and they sit. As the off-duty doctor removes sandwiches from the basket, she asks, "How are you and Pastor Miller getting along? I heard you were friends."

"We're doing all right."

"Kate told me Buck told her the two of you had lunch together a couple of days ago."

Garfield snorts, picks up a nearby rock, and throws it in the water. "Damnation. It's hard to keep a secret in this town."

"I'm sorry. I didn't know it was a secret."

"It isn't a secret. I just don't like them two knowing my business is all."

"Well, pastor Keith seems like a nice man." She giggles, "And good-looking, too."

"You know him by his first name?"

Addison hands the deputy a sandwich and says, "Yes, after I moved here, I started attending services. One Sunday, outside the church, he was greeting people, so I... well, I was last in line, and he surprised me by asking me if I would join him for dinner sometime. I didn't even know he was single. Anyway, I said no because the two of us had just started seeing each other."

"Wow, I didn't know I had competition."

"No, it wasn't like that. I haven't been back to the church since… You're not jealous, are you?"

"Should I be? You did say he was a good-looking man."

Addison chuckles. "Come on. Let's eat our lunch." She removes two glasses, pours fresh lemonade into them, and offers one to Garfield.

He waves it off as his face darkens. Instead, he takes a bite of an egg salad sandwich and turns away. Addison notices and asks, "Is everything all right?"

"I don't want you seeing him anymore."

"I told you. I haven't been back to that church."

"Don't argue with me. Do what I say."

Addison's face reddens as she tightens both of her fists. "First of all, I'm a grown woman, and you have no right to tell me what I should or shouldn't do. Second, I'll see whoever I want to see. You don't own me. Now, I want to go back to Carson City. I've lost my appetite."

Garfield lowers his head. "I'm sorry. I was out of line. Let's not ruin a beautiful day like this by talking like jealous teenagers."

"I'm not a teenager, and you're the one who's acting jealous, not me. You going to give me a ride back to town, or do I have to walk?" He reluctantly stands up as Addison grabs the blanket and picnic basket.

As Garfield aims the horse back to Carson City, he stares straight ahead, afraid to look at Addison, who is looking at the right side of the road. Finally, he breaks the ice by saying, "I was wrong, Addison. I said I'm sorry, but I'm saying it again. That wasn't me back there. That was the old me. Let's not spoil the day with anger."

Addison turns his way. "I appreciate the apology, but I'm going to need some time to think about our relationship and whether it should continue or not."

"I understand. I'll give you all the time you need." For some reason, Garfield peers quietly at Addison's ankle, and she moves it aside.

"I want to go home now."

Garfield quickly unwraps the reins from the buggy, turns the horses so sharply that the wheel screeches against the guard, whips the horses, and they head south to town at a fast trot.

FLAMES CRACKLE in the fireplace while Addison sits in a rocking chair in her rental house, reading a book. Lit by a kerosene lamp, the room is filled with stacks of books, boxes of clothes, and other miscellaneous items that haven't been unpacked yet. Other than the rocking chair, the only other furniture in the living area is a mahogany coffee table and a small leather sofa.

The silence is broken when she hears a knock at the door. She waits momentarily, moves to the front window, parts the curtain a few inches, and sees Garfield standing on her porch, his head low. She doesn't move until he knocks again.

She tiptoes over to the kerosene lamp and blows it out. From the other side of the door, she hears him plead. "I know you're in there, Addison. I just wanna talk."

Addison sits down in her chair and waits. Finally, she hears him again. "Don't be a bitch Addison! I didn't do anything wrong!"

She responds by opening one of the boxes and removing an ivory-handled two-shot Deringer. She sits back down in the rocking chair and waits.

Minutes later, she returns to the curtain, pulls it aside, and looks outside. Standing on the street in front of her house, lit by the moon, her stalker stands smoking. She watches him until he tosses his cigarette on the ground and stomps it out.

She backs away from the window, lies down on the sofa, pulls a quilt up to her shoulders, and centers her small pistol on her chest.

ON A SMALL PLOT OF LAND near Carson City, Thomas Berry Eater and his wife Keya emerge from their domed-shaped shelter, which is covered with animal hides, willows, and sod. Not far away, their recently built barn made of wood and stone stands in stark contrast to the Shoshone couple's traditional home.

As the couple walks toward the barn, Thomas reaches behind Keya and pinches her butt. She responds by grabbing his crotch and cupping it. They both laugh as they walk into the barn.

A few minutes later, Thomas exits on his favorite horse as Keya walks alongside him. The Shoshone is about to ride off when a shot rings out. He grabs his stomach, and his white cotton shirt immediately oozes with blood. The puzzled man stares at his befuddled wife and silently points at his bloody shirt.

Fearing for her life, Keya runs for their home. When she reaches the door, another shot rings out that hits her square in the back. She crumbles to the ground and doesn't move.

Having just witnessed his wife's death, Thomas groans, falls off his horse, and gasps for air. He manages to look up, sees someone he knows, and takes his final breath.

BUCK WALKS down Main Street, carrying a stack of fliers. When he reaches the Carson City Saloon, he goes inside, where he finds Fanny and Wharton Brown standing behind the bar. He hands a flyer to Wharton, and the bar owner frowns. "I heard someone greased Conner. Any idea who done it?"

Buck taps the counter. "Damned if I know."

Fanny takes the flier out of Wharton's hand, studies it, and says, "He was a pain in the ass, but why would anyone want to end him? It doesn't make any sense."

"I know. He didn't have much worth stealing… and all his animals were still in his barn."

Wharton snorts. "Revenge and jealousy."

Buck straightens his hat. "You know something I don't know?"

"No, but revenge and jealousy get you killed faster than robbing a bank. Conner was a big talker. Lived for his enemies. Always calling people cowards. Why, I don't know."

Their attention shifts when Garfield walks into the saloon and sputters, "Got some bad news. Two friends of Thomas Berry Eater stopped by the office and said they found him and his wife shot to death at their place."

Buck considers what his deputy said and slams his hand down on the counter. "What the hell is going on?"

SHERIFF AND DEPUTY ride back into town with the bodies of Thomas and Keya Berry Eater draped over two horses and under blankets they found in the couple's home. They pull up to the office as people walking down the street pass by, staring at the horses.

Buck removes his hat and wipes his brow. "Why don't you go on inside? I'll ride them over to the funeral parlor."

"You sure you don't want me to do that?"

"No, Thomas was my friend."

BACK FROM THE FUNERAL PARLOR, Buck sits in his office chair staring at a crack in the ceiling. Across the room, Garfield is cleaning his rifle again. The deputy breaks the silence. "You're right. It don't make any sense. Who would wanna kill Thomas?"

Buck takes a breath. "It could be a revenge thing."

"Revenge?"

"Yeah, that's what Wharton claims it is if there's no reason for someone dying."

"I don't think Thomas had any enemies."

Buck taps his desk. "None I know of."

"Maybe his old lady was cheating on him, her lover came along, and there was a shoot-out."

"Nah, Keya thought the world of Thomas."

Garfield puts his rifle in the gun rack and snorts. "All right then. I'm goin'. All this killing is wearing me out."

"Go ahead. I'm staying here for a while... Hey, if you know anyone wantin' to get rid of a puppy.... Maria wants one."

"Huh. I'll keep my eye open."

Garfield exits the office, crosses the street, walks a block, and finds a young birch tree by an empty building next to an alley. He looks around, makes sure no one is watching, and digs a hole near the tree with the heel of his boot. He removes three objects from his pocket, drops them in the hole, and covers them up.

He looks around again. Seeing no one, he heads for home.

Maria, watching him through the window of a local corner grocery store across the street, waits for Garfield to disappear and exits the building carrying a bag of penny candy.

She goes directly to the tree, drops to a knee, and uncovers the dirt where she saw the deputy bury his treasure.

Minutes later, Maria enters the sheriff's office. Buck lays his pencil down and grins. "Hey, Maria. How was school today?"

She smiles. "It was good."

"I'll just be a minute, and then we can go home."

"Okay." Maria sits quietly for a moment and then removes three bullet casings from her pocket. She carefully lines them up on Buck's desk like they are tin soldiers.

Buck looks up. "Maria, where did you find those?"

"Deputy Garfield buried them under a tree, but I uncovered them. I think they might be valuable."

"Under a tree?" Buck scoops the shells up and examines them closely.

Maria complains. "Hey, those are mine."

"You sure there weren't any more?"

"No, just three."

"Take me to where you found them." Buck puts the casings in his pocket, opens the door, and Maria follows him to the street.

She points, "It's that way."

Maria and Buck cross the street, walk a block, and stop at the base of a small birch tree. She kicks the dirt. "Right here. He dug a hole and buried them."

"You're sure it was right here?"

"Yes. Am I going to get in trouble for stealing his treasure?"

Buck looks around. "No, it'll be our secret."

"Can I have them back now?"

"No, I need to keep them for now."

"Are they valuable?"

He removes one of the shells from his pocket and stares at it. "I think they might be."

As Buck and Maria walk off, Garfield stands a block away, hidden behind a wagon and a team of horses, having witnessed the entire scene. Looking like someone threw snow in his face, he loosens his collar, emits a backwoods sneer, and struts off.

CHAPTER 18

Truth, Forgiveness, and a Family Dinner

THE HEAT IS STIFLING as Samuel and Ruth's wagon exits Colorado, where the newly married couple see a sign reading *Wyoming Territory*. Ruth wipes the perspiration from her face with a handkerchief, and Samuel looks concerned. "It's not much farther, dear. We should arrive at my place in two days or less if we don't get held up by Wyoming desperadoes."

"Desperadoes?"

Samuel smirks. "I'm kidding. There hasn't been any trouble around here for years."

"You know you really shouldn't joke about something like that. You never know."

"I'm sorry. Sometimes, I find myself reminiscing."

"Reminiscing?... like maybe you want to go back to being a desperado again?"

"No, nothing like that. All that ended in Montana when vigilantes hanged my brother."

"Do you miss him a lot… Henry?"

"Of course, but he didn't have much time left anyway."

"What do you mean?"

"He had consumption… what some doctors are calling tuberculosis now. He had a bad case of it. That's why he risked his life saving me. He knew he was gonna die anyway."

"Okay, maybe we should talk about something a little more pleasant. Tell me about your little girl. What is she like?"

Samuel grins. "Maria is as smart as a whip. Curious about everything and crazy about her brother. She used to follow Sam Henry around like a little puppy. That's why I can't believe they're not together."

"I'm sure it will all make sense when we find them."

"I'm counting on it."

TWO DAYS LATER, as the sun dips below the peaks of the Laramie Mountains, the couple arrives at Samuel's old house. The building is in bad shape, with pieces of wood siding on the ground, a broken front window, missing shingles, and a yard filled with tumbleweeds and other debris.

Samuel climbs out of the wagon, surveys the area, and wanders inside the house. He quickly returns, grins at Ruth, and says, "Guess we'll be sleeping under the stars again tonight. Come morning, we'll head over to the Culbertsons to see if they have seen anything of Sam Henry or Maria."

Ruth nods. "We can sleep inside your house if you want. I think I can handle it for one night."

"No, it's full of rats. I've already seen what a rat can do."

THE NEXT MORNING, Samuel and Ruth arrive at the Culbertson farm, and Samuel hops down from the wagon. The chickens scatter while Ruth remains seated in the wagon.

Samuel knocks on the door, and Lila opens it. She steps onto the porch, and Cletus follows close behind. She squints at Samuel, looks at Ruth in the wagon, and tightens her lips. "What do we have here? The prodigal father returns."

Samuel agrees. "Yeah, that's probably fair."

"You been in Colorado all this time?" Cletus asks.

"Yeah, looking for my kids. But time kind of got away from me. That's why I'm back. I was hoping you might have seen them." He turns to Ruth. "But I need to introduce you to my wife. We got married a few weeks ago. Ruth, this is Lila and Cletus. The Culbertsons were kind enough to watch my children when I was going through some rough times."

Ruth climbs down from the wagon, walks over, and shakes both of their hands. "It's a pleasure to meet both of you. Samuel has told me all about you."

Samuel interrupts. "Okay, back to my children. Have you seen them or not?"

Lila answers quickly. "Sam Henry came along two weeks ago, married Natalie, and rode off for Nevada."

"Married… to Natalie?"

"Yes, and they're extremely happy," Lila assures him.

"What about Maria? Was she with him?"

Lila continues. "No, that's why they went to Nevada. Last year, he left her with their grandfather, so now he's goin' to check on her."

"That explains a few things. He tell you he's a wanted man?"

Cletus leans back. "Yep, he didn't say anything at first, but when he asked us for Natalie's hand in marriage, he fessed up. Told us he got kidnapped by Paiutes right after he dropped off his sister… and then he changed to being an Indian. That ended when he and five other Paiutes got ambushed near Lake Tahoe, so he gave up being an Indian and went to Tin Cup to look for gold like he wanted to all along." Cletus nods. "You want me to keep going?"

"Yeah, give me the whole story."

"He ended up as a coal miner for a while, but the mine collapsed… almost buried him for good. From there, he found some gold-covered rocks, and three men tried to steal them. He killed one of them and has been on the run ever since. I left out some of the killin' parts when he was a Paiute. He can tell them to you if he wants."

"After you heard all that, you still let him marry your daughter?"

"She would have run off with him anyway. The girl's got it bad for your son."

"And you think everything he told you was true?" Samuel asks."

"I'm sure it is. I know the boy's heart. He ain't one to lie."

Samuel looks at Lila. "I hate to ask, but would you mind if we spend the night? We can stay in the barn. It's been a rough journey."

Lila tightens her lips. "Of course, but you're certainly not going to sleep in the barn. Natalie's bed and room are empty now."

Samuel turns back to Cletus. "I'd like to hear more about Sam Henry being here if you don't mind."

"Not sure I have any more to add. He wasn't here very long, and you're welcome to stay as long as you wish. Ain't that right, Lila?"

Ruth finally speaks. "Thank you, Mr. and Mrs. Culbertson. That's very kind of you."

Lila smiles. "Of course, it's the only Christian thing to do."

The next morning, after a good night's rest and a hearty breakfast, Samuel and Ruth climb back in their wagon and head west for Nevada.

SAMUEL AND RUTH spend the next thirty days traversing Utah's diverse landscape. After sleeping under the stars and taking in the beauty of the Wasatch Mountains and the northern deserts, the travel-weary couple bypasses the Great Salt Lake and crosses into Nevada.

AT BUCKLAND STATION, Sam Henry and his grandfather are repairing a barbed wire fence on the northeast corner of the property when Pete smiles. He reaches over and gently shifts the wire cutter in his grandson's hand. "It's easier if you grip it like that."

Sam Henry nods. "Sorry."

"It's okay. If you're not making mistakes, you're not learning."

Sam Henry looks in the distance and sees a wagon heading their way. "Looks like we got company, Gramps."

Pete straightens up, wipes his brow, and leans on his post-hole digger. "Let them come."

As the wagon nears Buckland Station, Sam Henry's interest mounts when he spots his father seated by an unfamiliar woman. Pete sees who it is, tosses his post-hole digger aside, and smirks. "Well, I'll be damned."

Samuel hands the reins to Ruth, hops down from the wagon, and shakes Pete's hand. "It's been a while." Then he turns to Sam Henry and asks, "Who do we have here?"

Pete breaks the ice as Father and son stare at one another uncomfortably. "This is my new hired hand. He practically runs the place now. I sorta help him out."

Sam Henry corrects his grandfather. "That's not true. I'm just trying to earn my keep while I'm here for a few days."

Pete looks at Ruth and then at Samuel. "Are you going to introduce your woman friend or not?"

Samuel rocks his head apologetically and looks at his wife. "I'm sorry. This is my used-to-be father-in-law, Pete Buckland, and Sam Henry, my son." He takes Ruth's hand. "Ruth and I tied the knot three weeks ago. We met in Tin Cup when I went there to look for Sam Henry and Maria."

Pete hurries over and shakes Ruth's hand while Sam Henry hesitates a moment and then follows suit.

Pete returns to his spot and says, "Okay, it appears to me that the whole family is married now, except Maria. My wife Margaret and Sam Henry's wife are in the house. How about I walk you there, Ruth, so these two can get reacquainted?"

Ruth grins. "That sounds like a good idea."

Pete helps her out of the wagon while Father and Son watch. As Pete and Ruth start for the cabin, Samuel eyes Sam Henry. "I've been lookin' for you and your sister a long time."

"I know. We didn't wanna be found."

Samuel's voice softens. "Natalie's father told me about you bein' a Paiute for a while. Did you meet any of your relatives?"

"I'm having a hard time talking to you right now."

"I understand. I can wait if you want."

Sam Henry takes his time as he peers into the distance. Finally, he says, "I met my grandfather."

"Winnemucca? He must be old by now."

"I asked him how old he was, and he said he didn't know. You know how old I am?"

"Twenty."

"That a guess?"

"You were born October 10th, 1863. I should have been there."

"Buckie told me you were in Montana Territory."

"Yeah, I was on the wrong trail and about to be hanged for something I didn't do."

"And they hanged your brother instead."

"Yeah. Your namesake, Uncle Henry. When we have time, I'll tell you the whole story. We've had too many secrets for too long."

"Yeah, you're pretty good at hiding things."

"I think that's the definition of a secret."

Sam Henry grumbles, "You could have told me I wasn't your own. I could have handled it."

"I guess I was afraid you would stop loving me or that you'd hold it against me for killing your father. The first time I saw you was when your mother came to my jail cell just after you were born. I was all set to hate you because you weren't my son, but then everything changed when I reached through those bars and held both you and your mother's hands. I'm sorry I never told you before, but it was right then and there that I fell in love with you. Maybe you won't believe this, but you and your mother were always the most important part of my life."

"Until she died."

"Okay, I know. Her death messed me up big time, and I abandoned you and Maria. I'm sorry for a whole lot of things, but mostly I'm sorry because I wasn't there for you and Maria. I could come up with a shitload of excuses, but none of them hold water. I was only interested in how I felt after she died when I should have been thinking about how I needed to take care of you and Maria."

"Did you ever come home?"

"I got delayed by a bar fight and got myself thrown in jail. When I got home, you were both gone. Right then and there, I gave up drinking and started looking for you. I rode to Culbertson's place, and Natalie told me you were headed for Tin Cup, so that's where I went. I looked for you and your sister for months."

"I never made it that far."

"Yeah, Cletus told me all about it. Now that I'm back, I was hoping you and your sister would find it in your hearts to forgive me. She's in the house, right?"

"No, she's living in Carson City with Buckie and his wife."

"Hard to believe he's married, too."

"Yeah, I haven't seen him yet, either."

"Then you haven't seen your sister for a while either?"

Sam Henry sighs. "Guess both of us are pretty good at leaving people behind."

"At least you came back for Natalie." Samuel smiles. "And married her…. And I'm sure you've been planning to go to Carson City to see Maria the first chance you get."

"Been thinking about it for two weeks. I've just been putting it off by helping Grandpa around the farm."

"Okay, give Ruth and me a few days to recover."

"That works for me."

"All right. Let's go inside so I can meet Pete's wife, say hello to Natalie, and you can get better acquainted with Ruth."

As they walk towards the cabin, Samuel asks, "Does it bother you that I married another woman?"

"No, Mom would have wanted you to be happy, assuming she makes you happy?"

"Oh, she makes me very happy."

As they pass the horse corral, Samuel and Sam Henry hear the loud squeal of a horse gone mad. The ten-year-old bay horse with a patch of white on his forehead rears up. He breaks the top board of the wooden fence, leaps over it, and runs off. Father and son watch as the wild animal runs off into the desert.

Pete exits the cabin and approaches the awestruck men. "What's going on?"

Samuel tries to explain. "That bay of yours went crazy, busted your fence, and ran off."

"Yeah, third time this year. Only I ain't going after him this time. Good luck to whoever finds him."

Samuel nods. "There's gotta be a story there."

I bought him from a fella who was about ready to shoot him… fifteen dollars. He was honest with me. Said he spent more time on the ground than in the saddle and the horse was so mean he'd eat a rider off his back if he could. I got willful about being able to change his disposition… the horse's, not the man's. Now the hayburner just takes up space. I don't know why I haven't shot him myself."

"Looks like you got taken, Grandpa."

"You think? Let's go see what's cookin'."

INSIDE THE BUCKLAND CABIN, Pete, Margaret, Samuel, Ruth, Natalie, and Sam Henry are finishing a dinner of fried chicken, mashed potatoes and gravy, turnip greens in bacon grease, and fluffed up buttermilk biscuits.

Pete scoots his chair back and surveys the room. Then he eyes Samuel. "It's been a long time, Samuel. A lot has happened since you arrived here twenty-odd years ago."

Samuel smiles with his eyes. "Some good, some not so good."

"Well, it looks like things are headed in the right direction. Look at us: new love, good food, and high hopes for the future."

Margaret's eyes sparkle. "Well said, dear." She offers him her pink cheek, and he kisses it.

Pete changes the mood when he pushes back from the table and belches. Everyone laughs except Margaret, who points her finger and admonishes him. "Pete Buckland, that is just rude."

Pete grins. "Come on. It's just air. What would you want me to do, hold in so long it comes out the other end?"

Margaret rolls her eyes, hurries into the kitchen, and returns with a sweet potato pie. She lays it down in the center of the table and says, "It is so nice to have all of you here under one roof. Come Saturday night, there will be three more of us at mealtime at Buckie and Kate's house."

Pete says, "I probably should warn them we're coming."

Margaret argues. "I don't know that's going to happen unless you're planning to build a fire and send smoke signals." Everyone chuckles, and Margaret continues. "Besides, let it be a surprise. That way, they don't have to fret about us coming. They have enough to worry about. Now, who wants pie?

CHAPTER 19

Mystery, Abduction, and Justice Served

SHERIFF BUCKLAND SOFTLY OPENS the front door of the Methodist Church and walks inside. He moves to the altar, where Reverend Keith Miller stands on a ladder loosening one of several bolts that attach a porcelain figure of Jesus to a large wooden cross. Buck sits on a bench a few feet away, waiting patiently.

The slender and handsome minister's wrench slips, injuring his thumb, and he shakes his hand and mutters, "Shit!"

Buck chuckles, and the minister turns back, almost falling off the ladder. "Oh, I didn't hear you come in."

As Keith climbs down, Buck stands to his feet, looks the sanctuary over, and asks, "Do you have a few minutes, pastor?"

"Of course." The minister sits on the bench, pats a spot next to him, and Buck joins him. "Now, what can I do for you?" Buck sits as Keith removes a flask from his jacket pocket, takes a sip of whiskey, and puckers as if he has just poisoned himself. He looks at Buck and apologizes. "Bad habit of mine. Now, how can I help you?"

"I know you and Garfield are friends, so I need to ask you a few questions about him."

"It's my practice not to divulge any personal information about the people who attend my church, but since your deputy has never attended my church, nor is he a personal friend of mine, what do you need to know?"

"Wait. You didn't have lunch with him last week, and he didn't come to see you about turning over a new leaf?"

"No lunch… no leaf. The only time I saw him was when I first arrived here, and he claimed your office was entitled to twenty-five percent of all the money this church takes in. We got into an argument, and I haven't seen him since. When I first saw you, I assumed you were here to try and collect the money yourself."

"My office has no interest in taking money from the church."

"Good to know." The minister raises one hand in the air, as if he is about to give a benediction, and says, "I've been planning to visit your office anyway."

"Why's that?"

"Because yesterday, I got a visit from Dr. Addison Gardner. I believe you know her."

"Yes, Addison works with my wife, Ruth."

"Well, Miss Gardner has been living in fear for the last three days. She doesn't want me to say anything, but your deputy has been harassing her because she broke things off with him."

"I thought things were good with them?"

"I'm afraid not."

"How has he been bothering her?"

"He randomly knocks on her door and demands that she talk to him, stands in front of her house for hours late at night, and yesterday he followed her home from work. She didn't want to complain because she thought you might fire him. So, instead, she came to me. But this is too big a secret to keep. Sheriff, his obsession with her is out of hand."

"I thought the man had turned his life around."

"I don't know you very well, but I don't like the fact that you have a deputy working with you who stalks women."

Buck stands to his feet and heads for the door. "Thanks for filling me in. I'll check it out and let you know what I find."

"Not to complicate matters even more, but yesterday, Addison gave me permission to court her."

Buck nods. "You know what? I'd hold off on that until I sort things out." When Buck reaches the door, he turns back and looks at the figure of Jesus hanging by one arm from the cross. "One more question. Why are you taking Jesus Christ down from the cross?"

The minister grins. "This used to be a Catholic church, my parishioners have been complaining that Jesus looking their way makes them feel awkward.

As Buck emerges from the church, Garfield exits a clothing store across the street wearing a new Stetson cowboy hat. He sees Buck and steps back inside until the young sheriff walks past.

Once Buck is out of sight, Garfield hurries to the street where he buried the shell casings earlier. When he reaches the secret tree, he begins to dig a hole with his hands, like a dog trying to uncover a bone. Not finding anything, he tries again.

A young couple walks past as he digs a second hole. They look at one another and laugh. Embarrassed, he removes his pistol from his holster, points it at the gawkers, and they hurry off. He spits in their direction, holsters his gun, and walks off.

DR. ADDISON GARDNER finishes examining a local twenty-five-year-old woman, Teresa Ames. She hands the stethoscope to Kate and smiles at their buxom patient. "You are four months along, Miss Ames. Everything seems to be fine. I know you're not married, but do you know who the father is?"

Teresa covers her mouth with her hand, removing it slowly. "I most certainly do. Do I have to tell you who he is?"

"Of course not, but he needs to help you out."

"He wants to keep it a secret. He says if anyone finds out, it will ruin his career."

"Well," Dr. Gardner says, "It's his child, too. He needs to be held accountable."

"I don't want to pressure him any more than I am now. He'll probably think I'm pressuring him to marry me."

"Well, if he's going to impregnate you, he should marry you."

Teresa squeezes her lips together and climbs down from the examination table. Kate helps her to the door, hands the woman her black wool coat, and she leaves the office.

Once their patient is beyond hearing distance, Kate whispers, "This will be her second child. I don't know if it's the same father or not."

Addison sighs. "Oh, dear."

Kate lifts her chin. "Now let's get back to what we were talking about earlier. I can't believe Garfield has reverted to his old self. I was starting to believe his transformation was real."

The doctor's face droops. "I had such high hopes for us. Now, I'm afraid to walk home at night. He's so angry. Who knows what the man might do?"

"Have you told anyone else about what's going on?"

"I told Pastor Miller yesterday, but I made him promise me he wouldn't say anything. I thought maybe Garfield would give up, but I saw him following me to the office this morning."

"You don't know him like I do. When I get home, I'll let Buck know what's going on."

Buck hears his name as he walks into the office. "Let me know about what?"

Addison looks away as Kate turns to her husband. "Your deputy won't leave Addison alone."

"I know. I just spoke with pastor Miller."

Addison neither looked at Buck nor avoided his eyes. "He wasn't supposed to say anything."

"Don't blame him. It just kinda came out. I went to the church to talk to him about his supposed friendship with Garfield, and it turns out they aren't friends at all. Garfield has been lying all along about starting a new life. His talk about finding religion is just that… talk. Are you all right?"

"I'm sleeping with my pistol."

"Yeah, the man's not only been hiding who he is, but I think he might have something to do with Conner Reilly and Keya and Thomas Berry Eater's deaths."

Kate's face tightens. "Oh, my God. Why do you think that?"

Buck explains, "Maria unearthed three empty shell casings he buried under a tree, and three people have been killed, one bullet each… same caliber rifle. We don't get a lot of coincidences around here like that. I haven't had a chance to confront him yet, but I think he's been harboring a grudge against Conner and Thomas since they shamed him for hiding in a hole when we went after those two bank robbers a few months ago. Thomas's wife was just an innocent bystander."

"Do you think he would murder them for something like that?"

Wharton Brown says revenge and jealousy are responsible for almost all murders."

Kate continues. "Do you think he knows you're on to him?"

"I don't know, but I don't want you and Addison being alone right now. Head over to the saloon and wait for me."

"Why the saloon?"

"There'll be too many people there for him to try anything."

"What about Maria? She gets out of school in a few minutes."

"I'll walk you to the saloon and head over and pick her up."

ON THE FRONT STEPS of a two-room schoolhouse, a half a mile west of Carson City's Main Street, Garfield stands on the front steps of a tall white building with tall windows. He is holding a black and white mix-breed puppy and talking to Miss Deidre Swanson, a young woman in her early twenties with black-rimmed glasses and wearing a black and white checkered store-bought dress.

The puppy whines while the deputy prepares to explain to the first-grade teacher why he is there. "Yeah, Sheriff Buckland wants me to bring Maria to our office so he can keep an eye on her. Her after-school caretaker, Mrs. O'Brien, is busy this afternoon and can't watch her."

Deidre smiles. "I see. Is that yours?"

"It's for Maria. Sheriff told me she wanted a dog, so I picked one out. If she doesn't want it, I'm keepin' it myself."

Miss Swanson smiles. "That's nice…. Well, you're a bit early. Our usual dismissal time is four o'clock."

The deputy rubs his neck and grins. "I don't think ten minutes is gonna make much of a difference, do you, Miss Swanson? I'm a busy man… so if you don't mind?"

Deidre's face turns red. "Of course. I'll just be a minute." She retreats inside and returns with Maria, who looks surprised to see Garfield. She spots the puppy, and her eyes light up.

He hands it to her. "All yours."

Maria hugs the dog and giggles, "Thank you, thank you, thank you. Is it a boy or a girl?"

"A girl." He steps back and grins at Miss Swanson. "We'll be going now."

"Yes, you being the sheriff's deputy, I'm sure Maria is in good hands."

He nods again, and Deidre waves at Maria. "Okay, Sweetie. I will see you tomorrow."

Maria waves goodbye and follows Garfield to a nearby tree. He unties his horse, lifts Maria, and positions her behind the saddle.

As she clutches the dog, she kicks two long ropes attached to the saddle away from her feet.

Miss Swanson yells, "Deputy Simpson, I assume you are taking Maria straight to Sheriff Buckland?"

He thinks about the question and shouts, "Sorry, I can't hear you. We gotta get goin'."

Not loud enough for her teacher to hear, Maria says, "I've never ridden on your horse before."

Garfield gives Miss Swanson a final wave goodbye, and the teacher notices something in his eyes that she doesn't like.

When the deputy spurs his horse and rides in the opposite direction from town, Deidre hurries into the schoolhouse. When she returns, she is wearing a light blue jacket and is accompanied by an elderly teacher, Sadie Lillard. "Would you please dismiss my students? I need to find the sheriff."

Francis whispers, "Of course. Is everything okay?"

"I don't have time to explain." Diedre exits the schoolyard, cleaning her glasses, and breaks into a run after a few steps. When she reaches the edge of town, she sees Buck fast walking her way, so she runs even faster.

Buck senses something is wrong and shouts, "Miss Swanson, is everything all right?"

Out of breath, Diedre explains. "Your deputy came to our school a few minutes ago and rode off with Maria. He said he was picking her up on your behalf, but when he turned and rode north with her, I grew suspicious. Please tell me you directed him to pick her up."

Buck stutters with revulsion. "How long... ago... did this happen?"

"Ten, maybe fifteen minutes."

"And they rode north, you said?"

"Sheriff, I didn't know."

Buck turns and runs for Main Street. As Miss Swanson hurries back to the schoolhouse, several students pass her, headed home. Two of the older ones give her a look of concern when they see the exhausted teacher, and one of them politely says, "Are you all right, Miss Swanson?"

"No, I'm not. Go home."

SEATED AT A TABLE in the Carson City Saloon, looking uncomfortable, Kate and Addison do their best to ignore the pungent smell of male body odor, the barmaids' overabundance of lilac perfume, and the aroma of whiskey and beer. The interlopers stare at each other as they sip from their glasses of water.

The place starts to fill up as men leave work and drop in for a drink. Like the three barmaids in red dresses and the owner, Fanny Brown in all yellow, the doctor and her assistant stick out like nuns in a brothel.

Two local ranchers, grinning like a pair of alligators, walk over and sit at their table. Addison grips the tops of their chairs and barks, "What do you think you're doing?"

The older rancher smiles, revealing an inch of his gum line, and says, "Just trying to be friendly. Can we buy you ladies a drink?"

Addison tightens her lips. "No, we have what we want to drink. Please leave us alone."

The men slide away as the youngest one whispers, "Bitches."

The older rancher adds, "Hags."

Addison hears them and can't resist. "Assholes!"

There is a moment of silence in the bar as Kate pats Addison on the arm and says, "It's been a rough week. Buck shouldn't be too much longer."

As the Carson City sheriff hurries down Main Street towards the saloon, he tries to decide his next step. Should he fetch his horse and ride solo north? Maybe he should form a posse. No, that would take too long. Suddenly, he knows what he wants to do. He'll tell Kate and Addison what is happening and ride after Garfield before he gets too big of a lead.

Buck bursts into the saloon, spots Kate and Allison, and hustles to their table. "Listen, Garfield kidnapped Maria from school and rode north with her! I'm going after them. I'll meet you at home."

Kate and Allison stand up, and Kate corrects her husband. "We're going with you."

"No, you need to stay here."

"Why, because we're women," Kate argues.

"No, because I'm the sheriff, and you're not."

Allison plays her hand. "Isn't it customary for a sheriff to round up a posse and take them with?"

"I don't have time for that."

Both women point at each other and simultaneously say, "We're your posse."

Buck shakes his head. "Okay, but if there is any shooting, promise me you'll take cover and hang back."

The women don't respond, so Buck leads the way out of the saloon.

ON THE EDGE OF CARSON CITY, Kate slaps the reins to the backs of the wagon horses as the posse of three heads north out of town. Next to her is Addison, who looks over at Buck, riding next to the wagon, and says, "I think I know the place where he's going."

"How do you know that?"

"He took me there for a picnic. It's next to the Carson River. It's not far."

Buck digs his heels into his horse and rides off as he yells back at the women. "I'm riding ahead. I'll meet you there."

Minutes later, Buck turns off the beaten path, climbs off his horse, and walks with it towards the river. When he gets closer, he spots his deputy and Maria sitting on the bank, watching the puppy drink from the stream. The sheriff draws his pistol just as his horse steps on a twig and snorts.

Garfield immediately hops to his feet, grabs Maria by the arm, and puts his revolver to her head. "What took you so long? Come any closer, and you can say goodbye to your little girl."

Buck lowers his gun and puts it in his holster. "Okay? What is it you want?"

"You know what I want."

"What? You want me? Why do you hate me so much?"

He spits. "Let's see, you stole my woman and my job, and you and your friends accused me of being a coward."

"So, you admit it. You killed three innocent people."

"They weren't innocent to me."

"You can't just kill people because you don't like what they say."

"I can do anything I want."

Kate and Addison arrive, climb out of the wagon, walk over, and stop a safe distance behind Buck. Garfield notices them and shakes his head. "I was counting on you comin' alone, Buck. Now we got us a situation."

The women fit their rifles and aim at Garfield. He growls, "Hey, ladies, did you bring a picnic basket?" He kneels next to Maria. "Do you even know how to shoot those rifles? Wouldn't want you hitting Maria or the sheriff here by accident."

Buck looks back and signals Kate and Addison to lower their weapons, and they do. They take another step forward, so Buck yells, "Stay back! Let me handle this!" He turns to Garfield. "So, how do I know you'll let everyone else go if I give myself up?"

"You don't, but I got all the cards in my hand."

Buck hears something behind him, turns back, and sees that Kate and Addison have moved closer. "I thought I told you two to stay back."

Garfield's left eye goes up, and he snarls, "You know you ladies oughtn't be dancing around with guns."

Kate looks the situation over. "How about a trade? Addison and I for Maria? Two for one."

"Shit. I don't trust either one of you."

Kate continues. "You don't want to be burdened with a little girl. Wouldn't you rather have the two of us as hostages… the two women who broke your heart?"

Buck takes a deep breath and releases the air in anger. "You and Addison, go back to the wagon. He wants me."

Addison plays her hand. "No, I think he wants me." She glares at Garfield. "How about it? Me for Maria? You can't kill all of us without getting killed yourself. I'll make it worth your while." She smiles at Maria. "Sweetie, cover your eyes."

Maria does as she is told and places her hands over her eyes. Garfield's face turns the color of old ashes, and he grumbles, "What the hell?"

Addison drops her rifle on the ground and removes her dress, revealing her back to Buck and Kate, who notice her ivory-handled Derringer tucked in the lining of her white petticoat. She gives the perpetrator a fake smile. "Isn't this what you want?"

"Put your dress back on, woman. You ain't the one I want."

"Come on. You might as well get something you want for all your trouble.

"I ain't interested in raping no woman."

"It's not rape if I'm willing."

"And then what?"

"Then we ride off together until you get tired of me… or shoot me… whatever you wanna do. You'd be in charge."

"Put your dress back on so I can think."

As Addison reclothes herself, Maria whispers, "Can I look now?"

Kate says, "Yes, Sweetie, you can remove your hands now."

Buck catches Addison's eye. "You don't have to do this, Addison."

She replies, "Take your family and go home, Buck. Your deputy and I want to be alone."

Garfield snarls, "Who do you think you're foolin'?" He shifts his gun from Maria's head and aims it at Buck's chest. "Nobody's going anywhere until I figure this out." He kicks some dirt, scratches his head, and reveals his decision. "Kate, you and Maria leave."

Kate persists. "What about Buck and Addison?"

"They're staying with me. You send anyone back here, and they're dead."

"Then I'm not going."

Buck takes Kate by the arm. "Take Maria and go. We don't have any choice." He whispers, "Don't listen to him. Round up some men and send them this way right away. Just don't come back here yourself."

"Is there a shorter way home?"

"The road you know is shorter than the one you don't know."

Garfield growls, "Don't be tellin' secrets. I'm standing right here." The disgraced ex-sheriff tightens the grip of his gun and thrusts it at Buck and then at Kate. "Remember, the first person I see coming our way, both Buck and Addison here get a bullet to the head… and leave one of them wagon horses behind."

She argues. "I have to tell somebody something. People are gonna know."

"You can tell anyone you want, but not until morning. Just hide out in your house."

Kate glares at him and says, "I'll give you two hours."

"The hell you will. You send a posse before dawn, and these two are both dead."

She shifts the rifle in her left hand as Buck repeats himself. "Don't argue, Kate. Go."

Garfield scowls, "And leave the rifle."'

Kate hesitates but drops the rifle in the dirt as Maria tugs on Garfield's shirt. "I'm taking this dog with me."

Garfield grits his teeth. "I don't give a shit. That mutt is more trouble than it's worth."

He pushes Maria away, and she scampers over to Kate with the puppy. She hugs her aunt with her free arm. Kate checks with Garfield one last time. "What are you going to do to them?"

"Whatever I want. Now go before I change my mind and kill all of you."

Garfield, Buck, and Addison watch as Kate and Maria ride off in the wagon pulled by one horse.

ON THE OUTSKIRTS of Carson City, Kate stops the horse and says, "I'm sorry, Maria. This is as far as I go. You need to walk to Mrs. O'Brien's house. Tell her I will stop by and pick you up later. I need to go back and check on Buckie and Addison."

"Can I take my dog?"

"Of course. Now hurry."

Maria hops out of the wagon, and Kate reaches under the seat and removes her revolver. She circles a hundred and eighty degrees and slaps the horse's rear end with the reins. The wagon lunges forward, and she yells, "Be back before you know it!"

Maria yells back. "You're not supposed to go back until tomorrow!"

UNDER A LARGE ELM TREE, seated in the saddle of his horse, Buck tries to steady his skittish animal with his knees. There's a hangman's rope around his neck, his arms are behind his back, and there are handcuffs around his wrists.

A few feet away, Addison is seated on the ground, attached by a rope to the trunk of the same tree.

Garfield walks over to his ex-lady friend and looks down at her. "After I hang Buckie boy, I'm gonna shoot you." He tightens his lips. "Or maybe I'll shoot you first and hang him… I don't know. Do you have a preference?"

Addison's cheeks turn brick red, her eyes open wide, and she takes a deep breath. "I thought you were going to take me with you?"

"I'm no fool. I wouldn't be able to sleep knowing you might try to cut my throat. Besides, you already said that if I get tired of you, I can go ahead and shoot you. Well, I'm tired of you."

He walks over and strokes the head of Buck's horse as Addison tries to reach the Derringer under her dress. As she struggles with the ropes restricting her arm movement, Garfield turns her way, and she turns perfectly still.

Buck gives his Garfield a spiteful grin, and he snarls. "I don't need any goddamn look from you. I'd be worrying whether there's a heaven or hell if I were you."

As he continues to stroke the horse's head, Garfield reveals his plan. "Okay, this is how it's gonna work. First, I'm gonna shoot Addison over there, and then I'm gonna hang you. After that, I'm ridin' west to California to start a new life. Find me some gold if there's any left."

He turns to Addison who quickly stops moving again. "God, I wish things would've turned out differently, Addison, but forcing a snake to care about somebody is a losing proposition."

"You're the snake, Garfield."

"You might be right." Garfield spits. "Guess I'll find me a California woman who ain't so full of herself and live happily ever after."

Addison narrows her eyes. "I pity the woman who believes your lies."

Garfield turns to Buck and prepares himself to slap the horse. Somehow, Addison manages to loosen the ropes around her arms and removes the Derringer from her petticoat. When she tries to shift the small gun to her right hand, she drops it on the ground in front of her. When she leans over to pick it up, Garfield hears something and turns to her. He cocks his pistol and aims it at her chest. "Bet you're wishing you'd been nicer to me now, huh?"

Addison raises her weapon, and Garfield's eyes widen. "What the hell?"

Garfield fires first, but his bullet hits the tree trunk behind Addison's head. The sound of gunfire spooks Buck's skittish horse, and it bolts away, leaving him dangling from the rope attached to the tree limb. The rope instantly tightens around his neck, and Buck gasps for air.

Before Garfield can fire another round, Addison aims her small gun, pulls the trigger, and hits him in the groin. He panics, grabs his crotch, and limps off into the trees.

Addison sees Buck struggling for air, finishes releasing herself from the rope, and hops to her feet. She hurries to him, wraps her arms around his legs, and tries to lift him to ease the tension on the rope. Too heavy to hold him up any longer, she ducks under him, and Buck kneels awkwardly on her shoulders.

As she struggles to balance Buck, Garfield limps out of the trees, clutching his manhood. He growls, "You shot off one of my balls, bitch!!"

He points his gun at Addison, changes his mind, and aims it at Buck's head. Before he can pull the trigger, a shot rings out, and the back of his head explodes, splattering blood on Buck and Addison.

Kate, pistol in hand, exits the trees and hurries to Buck and Addison. Together, the women lift Buck just enough so the rope eases from his neck. Kate manages to remove the rope, and Buck falls to the ground.

Addison removes the handcuff keys from Garfield's pocket and unlocks the cuffs around Buck's wrists. He sits up, rubs his wrists, and then his neck.

Exhausted, all three sit on the ground under the swinging rope, while Buck tries to catch his breath. Continuing to rub his neck, he looks at Kate and says, "I thought I told you not to come back here."

She smiles. "You want me to help you back on the horse so we can put the rope back around your neck?"

CHAPTER 20

Forgiveness, Family, and New Beginnings

"I'M NAMING HER ADDIE," Maria announces. She pets her two-month-old dog, removes a piece of biscuit from her pocket, and feeds it to her.

"And how'd you come up with that name?" Buck asks.

"Addison's name and your name together… because you saved my life."

The sheriff, who's been carving a miniature horse out of a piece of basswood, lays his knife on his desk and grins. "Clever. Addison and my name combined. But what about your Aunt Kate? She's the real hero."

Maria's expression changes, and she tries again. "Addieka?"

Buck shakes his head. No, that's not gonna work. How about Kaddie? That covers all three of us."

Maria grins as she pets her dog. "I like that… Kaddie."

Now, get busy and sweep out the jail cell like you said you would, deputy. I want my money's worth."

Maria grabs a broom. "Can Kaddie help me?"

"Sure, but if she pees in there again, you gotta clean it up."

"She's been doing a lot better. Only one puddle all day yesterday." Maria leads the way as Kaddie follows her into the jail cell. A moment later, Maria yells, "This place stinks! I think someone puked in here!"

Buck smiles, and his mind wanders as he looks the room over. No more Garfield. He still didn't understand how he was so naïve as to allow the evil man to dupe him. Kate was right all along. She never complained, but he knew she still had dreams about killing him almost every night. He continued to tell her she didn't have to feel guilty because he would have been hanged anyway for killing Conner, Thomas, and Keya. Officially, the district judge ruled Garfield's death to be justifiable homicide.

DONE FOR THE DAY, Buck and Maria exit the office. Riding past them are three men: Jefferson "Soapy" Johnson and his two colleagues, a curly blond-haired man, and a man wearing a wide-brimmed hat. Trailing behind, tethered to the curly-haired man's horse, is a mule loaded with pots, pans, and stuffed burlap bags.

Jefferson notices Buck's badge, tips his hat, and says, "Nice town you've got here, sheriff."

PETE GUIDES HIS WAGON down the road, headed for Carson City. Seated next to him is Margaret. Riding horses on their right are Sam Henry and Natalie.

Further back, Samuel steers a second wagon while Ruth looks at the countryside. Pete clicks his tongue to the roof of his mouth, and his horses pick up the pace. "Only two more miles, folks."

Samuel says, "This is quite the caravan. Where are we gonna stay?"

Pete answers. "Bucky and Kate are living in her father's old house. They've got plenty of room now."

Margaret speaks up. "If not, I still have my old house… I'm waiting for Pete to retire so we can move back into it."

"Well, I'm not leaving until I find someone to take over Buckland Station. I spent too much of my life there to sell it to some stranger. Buckie, he don't want it. Sam Henry's not interested." Pete looks back at Samuel and Ruth. "What about you, two?"

Samuel speaks loudly enough for everyone to hear, "Ruth has her heart set on building or buying another general store. Sorry, Pete."

Pete shakes his head. "Damn, I can't even give my place away."

MARIA CHASES HER DOG around the living room until she hears a knock at the door. She yells, "Aunt Kate, someone is here!"

From the kitchen, Kate yells back, "Well, go see who it is. I'll be right there!"

Maria tosses the small rubber ball in her hand, Kaddie runs after it, and Maria rushes to the door. The dog drops the ball at her feet as she opens the door.

Before she looks up to see who knocked, she bends down and picks up the ball. When she straightens up, Samuel and Sam Henry look down at her and together say, "Maria."

The seven-year-old gawks at her father and brother, and her eyes widen. Her attention shifts as she tries to identify the four people behind them.

Overwhelmed, Maria backs away and starts to cry. Kate arrives, sees the two strange men front and center, and asks, "Do I know you?"

Samuel removes his hat and says, "I'm Samuel Plummer, and this is my son, Sam Henry."

"Oh my God." Kate finally sees Pete and Margaret behind them, and two women she doesn't recognize, Ruth and Natalie. She sighs and says, "Aunt Margaret, Pete, what a surprise." She drops to her knees and consoles Maria, who is still crying. She whispers, "It's okay, dear. I know it's a lot to take in."

Kate stands and opens the door wide. "Come in… Buck… Buckie went to his office for a while, but he'll be right back."

As everyone enters the house, Samuel bends down and whispers to Maria. "I've missed you a lot… and you have grown so much. You look a lot like your mother now."

"My real mother died. Aunt Kate is my mother now."

"I know. It's so kind of her to take care of you all this time… and your grandfather too. You know who I am, right?"

"You're my father… You went to town and never came back."

"I know, and I'm so sorry. I'll try to explain what happened when we get some quiet time together. You think maybe I could have a hug?"

Samuel drops to one knee, and Maria hugs him long and hard. As they end their embrace, Sam Henry walks over and looks down at his sister. "Remember me?"

Maria hugs Sam Henry's leg and starts to cry again. "You said you'd come back and get me."

"I did come back. It just took longer than I expected."

Maria sputters, "I bet you didn't even find any gold."

Samuel interrupts their moment. "We both found gold, Maria, but not enough to excuse our not being with you."

Pete and Margaret stand in the corner, surveying the room while Kate talks to Ruth and Natalie.

All eyes shift to the front door as Buckie walks in with a surprised look plastered on his face. "What do we have here? Pa, Margaret… and…."

Sam Henry hugs Maria and whispers in her ear. "I need to talk to Buckie. I'll be right back. Be nice to your father. He's been looking for us for a long time."

Maria looks up at Samuel. "I'm supposed to be nice to you."

Samuel gathers her in his arms, catches Ruth's attention, and waves her over. "Maria, this is my wife, Ruth."

Maria studies Ruth's face and asks, "Are you my mother now?"

Taken aback by her question, Ruth says, "Well, yes. I suppose I am."

"What about your Uncle Buckie and Aunt Kate?"

Samuel explains, "You'll still get to see them. We'll work everything out."

Maria climbs out of her father's arms. "It's six o'clock. I need to feed Kaddie."

Ruth smiles. "May I help you?"

"Okay, but we can't feed her too much or she pukes."

Ruth and Maria walk away as Samuel tries not to laugh. He walks over and joins Natalie and Kate, who are quietly getting to know one another.

On the other side of the room, Buck and his father are talking. Pete finally walks away, and Sam Henry makes a beeline for his uncle. He holds out his hand and grins. "It's been too long… Uncle Buckie."

Buck bypasses his hand and gives his nephew a bear hug. "My God. I can't believe it's you."

Sam Henry steps back. "I don't know who else I would be." He spots the badge on Buck's vest and grins. "Look at you, the town sheriff. Your father has been telling us about all your exploits for days."

"Not all of them, I'm afraid. It's been a tough couple of weeks. But things are better now."

"Tougher than being mauled by a bear?"

"Well, let's see. My deputy turned on me, kidnapped Maria, and put a noose around my neck. He was about to hang me when my wife had to shoot him to save my ass."

"Wow, that is a tough week, but I think I can almost top it with the year I've had."

Buckie raises his hands, inviting him to share. "Go for it. I'm dying to hear what you've been up to."

Before he can respond, Samuel joins his son and nephew. "See, you two are making up for lost time."

Sam Henry grins. "Just like old times. Buckie telling me stories, and me trying to compete."

Buckie takes a deep breath and releases it slowly. "Before you top my story, I have something to ask. I ran across a wanted poster a few months ago with the name Samuel Plummer on it, but sorta looked like you, Sam Henry."

Samuel defends his son. "It was supposed to be him, but the men who accused him of murder and robbery were killers themselves. They destroyed Ruth's store with dynamite… and one of them, Rupert Weed, shot a Tin Cup female deputy sheriff in the leg. He was set to kill me when I hit him with a rock. He fell on the ground, swallowed a rat, and died."

"Wait? He swallowed a rat? How is that even possible?"

"It was a small rat… but hungry. Long story. All you need to know is the man deserved to die more than once."

Sam Henry turns his attention to Samuel. "That's not all. Before I got to Tin Cup, when I was a Paiute, Rupert and his men killed five of my Paiute friends."

Samuel adds. "Rupert claimed you killed several of his friends."

"Four, plus the one Mexican who drew on me first."

Buck narrows his eyes. "Wait. You killed five men?"

"None of them left me a choice."

"How long were you a Paiute?"

"A year… maybe longer. I told you I have my own story to tell… living with Paiutes, being attacked by a half dozen miners, almost dying in a coal mine accident, finding gold, and being robbed."

Buck shakes his head. "You win. Maybe we should turn our thoughts to pleasanter things." He scans the room. "It's great having everyone back together again. Tomorrow, I'll show you my office and walk you around town. I'm sure things are quite different from the last time you were here."

BUCK, SAMUEL, AND SAM HENRY exit the sheriff's office after an early morning tour of the office. Buck locks the door and joins his brother-in-law and nephew on the street. "So, that, gentlemen, is my humble abode. Kinda quiet now with no deputy to talk to."

As they walk down Main Street, Sam Henry asks, "You gonna get you another one?"

"Another what?"

"You know, another deputy."

"Maybe. I'm in no hurry with what just happened with Garfield."

"Why do you think he went crazy like that?"

"Because he was evil, and evil doesn't need a reason. Kate saw it first, but it took me a while."

"Yeah, he was some story," Samuel remarks.

Buckie changes the subject. "What about you and Ruth? Where ya planning on living?"

Samuel takes a deep breath. "Ruth wants to either build or buy a new store. As for me, I wanna raise cattle, a few horses, and maybe even give farming another try."

Buck smiles. "Gonna be hard pleasing both of you."

"Don't I know it… Plus, we've got Maria to consider."

Buck turns to his nephew, Sam Henry. "How about you?"

"Natalie and I are all about living in town."

"Carson City's a good place to live. Safe, too… law-abiding citizens for the most part."

Samuel quips, "Except for the sheriff's deputy who killed three people and tried to hang the sheriff here."

Buckie smirks. "Yeah, except for that."

As they continue down the street, they see a crowd of thirty people or more gathered in front of the Carson City Saloon. Samuel hears Jefferson "Soapy" Johnson's familiar voice and grits his teeth.

Buck notices the grimace on Samuel's face and says, "You know him?"

"Yeah."

"He's some kind of snake oil salesman?"

"No, but he's a con man who sells expensive soap… and might have murdered a man so he could steal his cabin. I never saw him do it, but I'm pretty sure he did."

Sam Henry speaks his mind. "I know them too. They got themselves tarred and feathered and thrown out of Cheyenne for what they're about to do here."

The three men hide at the back of the crowd and wait. Having waited long enough, Buck steps forward. "I'm gonna shut him down before he gets started."

Samuel pulls him back and whispers, "No, just let it play out. Let's catch them in the act."

The fast-talking salesman finishes stacking two dozen bars of soap on his new wooden display case and adjusts the tar-stained blue jacket he wore in Tin Cup and Cheyenne. Then Jefferson "Soapy" Johnson unholsters his pistol, raps the handle on the case, and everyone turns quiet.

Buck and his relatives remain hidden as Soapy delivers the same opening pitch he used in Tin Cup. "Ladies and gentlemen, what you see here is my homemade soap… but it's not ordinary soap; it's prize-winning soap. My name's Jefferson Randolf Johnson, and my special formula is guaranteed to clean the dirt off your grimy hands and bodies, even your nether regions." Several men laugh, and a few women gasp as the swindler continues, "Not only will it cleanse your filthy hide, but one in every five bars has prize money inside with winnings up to twenty dollars."

Jefferson picks up two squares of soap wrapped in plain brown paper and waves them at his audience. "Now, who will be the first to purchase a bar of my soap for just one dollar?"

A young woman, cradling a baby, sneers. "I can buy a bar of soap at the store for ten cents."

Jefferson grins. "You're missing the point, ma'am. You have a chance to win yourself twenty dollars."

"I've been foolish a time or two in my life, but I ain't falling for a fool trick like that." The woman pulls her baby close to her chest and walks off.

"What a shame. What a shame. That poor woman looks like she could use twenty dollars."

On cue, Jefferson's two partners, the curly-blond-haired man and the man with a wide-brimmed hat, move forward and offer him a silver dollar each. Soapy hands each of them a bar, and the rascals quickly remove the soap wrappers.

Inside his bar of soap, the curly-haired man finds a five-dollar bill. He waves it at the crowd and yells, "Five dollars! Damn! I got myself five dollars!"

The wide-brimmed hatted man unwraps his bar and screams, "Ten dollars!"

Two men and a woman push their way to the front of the crowd and hold out their cash. Soapy grabs their money, stuffs it in his pocket, and hands each of them a bar of soap.

Having seen enough, Samuel hurries to the front of the crowd as Buck and Sam Henry follow close behind. When he reaches the fraudulent salesman, he removes his gun from his holster and aims it at him. The crowd quiets as he addresses them. "Folks, this man is a fraud, a con artist." He shifts his gun and points it at the curly-haired man and then at the man with the wide-brimmed hat. "These two shills are in cahoots with him. They've been planted to make you think there's money to be made."

Buck, Sam Henry, and several other men in the crowd unholster their guns and aim them at Jefferson and his two cohorts. Outnumbered and dumbstruck by being found out, the bandits remain silent as Samuel explains the scam to individuals in the crowd.

When he finishes talking, the crowd disperses, and the three duped soap buyers walk up to Jefferson and hold out their hands. The fraudulent man reaches into his pocket, pulls out the money they gave him, and hands it back.

LATER IN THE SHERIFF'S OFFICE, Buck and company stand outside one of two jail cells, looking at Jefferson and his two goons. The soap man lashes out. "This is ridiculous. You can't keep us locked up in here for trying to make a little money selling soap."

Buck disagrees. "From what I understand, you've been cheating people out of their hard-earned money for a while now."

Jefferson argues. "I gave the money back. Besides, those people willingly bought my soap."

"You can tell that to the judge when you see him."

Samuel takes a step forward and grips the cell bars. "You don't remember me, do you?"

Jefferson stares hard at Samuel. Finally, the blond curly-haired man speaks up. "Boss, he's the fella who was looking for his kids."

The soap salesman grumbles. "Shit."

"Yeah, and you're the ones who tied me to a chair, set off a load of dynamite, and left me for dead."

The man with the wide-brimmed hat turns to his boss and glares. "I knew we should have gone back to make sure he was dead."

Jefferson barks, "Will both you idiots shut up?!"

Buck taps the bars with his fingers. "Now we have attempted murder to add to your charges."

"Nobody saw us try to blow you up."

"I just heard your partner here make a full confession. And I quote, 'I knew we should have gone back to make sure he was dead.'"

Samuel adds. "Plus, I saw them bury the owner of the cabin."

The hatted man spouts, "He had a heart attack."

"You said he killed himself."

"You're dumber than a fence post." Jefferson shoves the hatted man, and he falls back onto a small bed next to the back wall. Samuel steps forward again and announces, "I have a proposition, Sheriff. Why don't we put these soap peddlers back on the street?"

Buck grimaces. "What?"

Samuel explains. … with appropriate punishment, which I'll explain later. If they don't take us up on it, I'm sure the judge will believe my story over theirs and send them straight to prison."

SEATED IN FRONT of the Carson City Saloon on an uncovered porch, Jefferson "Soapy" Johnson and his two partners have their legs and arms tied to the backs of three wooden chairs. Each of them has a bar of soap stuck in his mouth with a hand-painted sign behind them reading:

We tried to scam the good people of Carson City. Liars and thieves get their mouths washed out with soap.

The day passes as townspeople go about their business. Just as the sun begins to disappear, a thunderhead sails across the mountains, followed by a cool April wind that settles over the town. Two men exit the bar, stop not far from Soapy and his men, and peer at the black cloud directly overhead. The older man nods. "Christ Almighty. Looks like a son-of-a-bitchin storm."

The second man agrees. "Ain't that something. Where's the rain when we need it?"

Immediately, the cloud rumbles like it's angry, and a flash of light fills the sky. The men run back into the bar as a torrential downfall turns the street into a huge mud puddle, filling the air with the sweet smell of ozone.

Stuck in their chairs, the soap salesmen lower their heads with every clap of thunder. The large drops of water instantly soak their clothes, plastering their hair to their foreheads.

When the storm finally subsides, a dozen men exit the saloon to assess the storm's impact. When they pivot to their right, they see the soapers, gawk at the scoundrels a moment, and laugh.

Trying not to gag, the rabid dog-looking culprits spit bubbles and white foam out of the sides of their mouths.

As bystanders continue to laugh, Sheriff Buckland appears, looks the three men over, and announces, "All right, that's enough. Don't wanna poison you. Then I'd have to bury you." Buck cuts the men loose and points West. "You can be on your way, now."

Soapy speaks. "What about our horses?"

"No horses. Train leaves in an hour. You'll be heading that direction."

"We ain't got no money."

"Not my problem."

The men quickly shake the ropes off and kick their chairs away. As they stumble down Main Street, they spit and curse until they are out of sight.

Buck turns to people on the street who have gathered to watch and shakes his head. "God, that must taste awful."

THAT EVENING in Buck and Kate's spare bedroom, Samuel and Ruth lay awake thinking about their future. Kate turns on her side, faces Samuel, and says, "I've been thinking."

"Am I in trouble?"

"No, just listen. I hate to tell you something you've already thought about, but I know you want a place of your own where you can raise animals and grow a few crops."

"And you want to open a store again."

"Let me finish. I'm willing to put owning a town store on hold so you can realize your dream of having your own place again. So, we should use the insurance money I got from my place burning down and buy Buckland Station. I can turn the smaller cabin into a gift shop where people can stop and buy a few things if they want."

Samuel smirks. "You know, there won't be a lot of people stopping by to shop."

"Not for a while, but word will spread. I noticed houses going up on our side of Carson City. Won't be long before people will be building as far as our new place."

Samuel grins. "You're serious about buying Pete's place?"

"Yes, I'm serious. He said he wants to keep it in the family."

"What about Maria? She needs to go to school."

"And she will. Are you forgetting I was a school teacher for two years?"

Samuel takes Ruth's hand. "You sure you want to do this?"

"Yes. And don't keep asking me, or I'll change my mind."

"I'll talk to Pete in the morning... Huh, I've always loved Buckland Station."

"Plummer Station, dear. Plummer Station."

EPILOGUE

SEATED AT THE KITCHEN TABLE, Kate opens her journal and begins to write.

Everything has quieted down after our family members went their separate ways… and *there have been a lot of changes. Most of them are good.*

After they buried Garfield, Teressa Adams, the young single woman who is five months pregnant, finally admitted that Garfield had fathered her first child and is responsible for the one she will give birth to in a few months.

I still haven't gotten over having to shoot Garfield, but I keep reminding myself that if I hadn't gone back, Garfield would have hanged Buckie and most likely would have killed Addison.

Samuel and Ruth bought Buckland Station from Buckie's father at a reasonable price. Pete's took only enough to cover the cost of his livestock and farm equipment, but his father was happy to keep the place in the family. They got all the land, buildings, and farm equipment for free, but Buckie is okay with that because he has no interest in making a living off the land.

Of course, they took Maria with them. I miss her, but she's where she belongs. Other news is that we received a visit from a man who claimed he represented an oil firm in Ohio that wants to drill on Samuel's old farm in Wyoming. Who knows, maybe Samuel's land is worth something after all.

Last week, Pete and Margaret moved to Carson City and into my aunt's old house. They seem happy, but Pete seems restless. Margaret says he's always looking west toward his old place.

We let Sam Henry and Natalie move into our old house because Buckie surprised us all by announcing that his nephew had agreed to be his new deputy. When it happened, Natalie had a lot of concerns, like I had when Buckie told me he wanted to be a deputy and then a sheriff. I told her it would take some time for her to get used to him being a law enforcement officer. What I didn't tell her is that I wake up every morning worried that Buckie might get shot.

That brings me to another important announcement. I'm going to have a baby. I haven't told Buckie yet because I'm waiting for the right time. He's still grieving over the loss of Maria, but I need to tell him soon before he sees that my stomach is growing. I want a girl, but I think Buckie would prefer a boy. He has a name picked out… Pete. I'm going to try to get him to change his mind. Another Pete would be confusing. We already have two Samuels in the family.

Work is going well, but Addison never recovered from the mayhem with Garfield and left town on the train. She moved to San Francisco. Now, I'm working with a new doctor, Maxwell Henderson. He's an older gentleman with no sense of humor, but he knows what he's doing and is kind to our patients, so I'm happy about that.

I had better stop writing now or I'll be late for work. Dr. Henderson and I are scheduled to perform a Caesarean procedure this morning on a woman whose baby refuses to come out on its own.

Later this afternoon, I have an appointment with an elderly man to help him identify the right medication he needs for his fast-beating heart. Witnessing the cycle of birth to death is an amazing part of my job that I appreciate more and more every day that I live. God is good.

ON THE STEPS of Plummer Station cabin, Ruth joins Samuel, and they watch Maria and Kaddie race around the courtyard. Maria giggles when the dog stops, barks, and she chases after her.

Ruth sits, hands Samuel a mug of coffee, lifts her cup, and takes a sip. They sit silently, looking at the snow-capped mountains in the distance. Ruth finally says, "Do the cows need milking?"

"Already done."

"How about you? Need help making that apple pie?"

"No, it's already in the oven."

Samuel reaches over, takes Ruth's hand, and squeezes it.

ABOUT THE AUTHOR

Daniel Landes is a retired Assistant Dean of Arts and Sciences and an English professor who spent the last eight years of his academic career at South Dakota State University.

Originally from Williston, North Dakota, Daniel earned a Bachelor of Science in History from Minot State University, a Master of Science in English Education from Bemidji State University, and a Ph.D. in English from the University of North Dakota.

Over the years, he has taught hundreds of writing and literature courses and coached cross country and track at numerous high schools and colleges. He and his wife Martha live in Rio Rancho, New Mexico, where Dan continues to pursue his passions for writing novels and screenplays, bicycling, and traveling the world with his wife.